Bob Olivier

Australian Phoenix

This is a work of fiction. Names, characters, and incidents are products of the author's imagination or are used fictitiously. Any resemblance to actual events, or persons, living or dead, is entirely coincidental.

First published in 2021

Copyright © Bob Olivier 2021

All rights reserved. No part of this book may be reproduced or transmitted in any form or by any means, electronic or mechanical, including photocopying, recording or by any information storage and retrieval system, without prior permission in writing from the publisher. The Australian *Copyright Act 1968* (the Act) allows a maximum of one chapter or 10 per cent of this book, whichever is the greater, to be photocopied by any educational institution for its educational purposes provided that the educational institution (or body that administers it) has given a remuneration notice to the Copyright Agency (Australia) under the Act.

Cover design: Diana TC, triumphbookcovers.com

ISBN 979-8497058147

"We warned Australia before not to join in the war in Afghanistan, and against its despicable effort to separate East Timor. But it ignored this warning until it woke up to the sounds of explosions in Bali. Its government subsequently pretended, falsely, that its citizens were not targeted."

Osama bin Laden 2002

Prologue

Iraq: 20th March 2003

The howling of the US war planes was terrifying. Like the Gods of mythology these man-made thunderbolts hurtled through the night sky over Baghdad, hurling missiles down upon the city, while helpless humans cowered in their apartment buildings. Operation Shock and Awe was unleashed.

The targets were military establishments, and the US fighters were equipped to deliver their payload with pinpoint accuracy and minimum 'collateral damage' - as civilian deaths were termed. But mistakes still happened. One such stray missile hit the apartment building in which The Iraqi and his family lived, destroying the structure and killing most of the occupants. But not all its occupants, and not immediately.

The Iraqi was trapped under a section of his apartment's ceiling which had collapsed under the weight of the falling floors above. A column had remained upright, partially sheltering him, but he was engulfed in rubble and unable to move. From the intense pain he felt in various parts of his body he thought he had a broken leg, a broken arm, and some broken ribs. His breathing was shallow and he could see nothing. But he was alive, and not mortally wounded. He wondered briefly whether anyone would ever be able to find him.

And then he heard the sound that would haunt him for the rest of his life: the voice of his son, muffled but clearly screaming in pain, "Daddy, daddy!" He tried to shout in reply, but his own voice was swallowed by rubble and his son was beyond hearing. Gradually the screams became moans. Then they stopped, and there was silence. The Iraqi was alone with his tortured thoughts. There had been no sound from either his wife or his daughter - they must have perished in the initial collapse. He thanked God that at least it must have been quick. And then he began to slip away.

After what must have been hours, he became aware of vibrations as the rubble and debris were removed and the dim voices of his rescuers became clearer. They lifted him carefully from his near-burial place and placed him in the back of a makeshift ambulance. In a voice that was no more than a harsh whisper he begged his rescuers to search for his family, but they ignored him. They'd already found his wife and two children along with countless other bodies and there was little point in confirming what he must already know. The vehicle took off towards the hospital and The Iraqi lapsed back into merciful unconsciousness.

Some time later he awoke. His body felt as though it had been run over by a steamroller and he struggled for a few moments to make sense of where he was. He was lying in a low stretcher bed in an over-crowded hospital ward. Alongside him was a row of people, shattered and broken, like him. He could hear their low cries and moans of pain and he realised with detachment that one of the moans was his. Nurses rushed from bed to bed. A few doctors were dotted around the ward. More stretchers arrived with a jolt and joined the row next to him.

Then reality flooded back. He remembered the howl of the planes, then the rubble, the dust and despair. The moans of his son. He *wept until he thought his heart would break. A young nurse stopped by his bed, wondering what agony would make a man weep so bitterly. But she shook her head and hurried on – there was no time for broken hearts and sympathy here, too much to do and too many broken bodies to try to hold together.*

The Iraqi spent two months in this and other hospitals. After the chaos immediately following the bombings and the rapid defeat of the Iraqi forces, a semblance of order was restored. The rubble of the apartment building was searched and the bodies of his wife, son and daughter were found. He was too ill to move from his bed so they were buried without him being present - he didn't find out until well after the event.

He was treated for his wounds, which were severe and eventually he made a complete physical recovery - but his mind would never be the same. The anguish and despair he felt every time the images of his family flashed into his mind were more than he could bear - never to hold Hamidah again, and make love to her, never to hug Afwida and Kamil, or play with them and hear their delighted shrieks as he chased them around their apartment.

After two months of such tortured thinking The Iraqi was a changed man. He had been a quiet and contented man, well-educated and brought up in a respectable God-fearing family with strong values, qualities he inherited and practised. Now he was consumed with hatred for those who had slaughtered his family and destroyed his life. He swore a terrible oath, that he would devote the rest of his life to finding ways to avenge his family, and all other Muslim families who were victims of his enemy. And his enemy was any citizen of the coalition countries from the West who had illegally attacked and invaded his homeland - men, women and children - he made no distinction.

Chapter 1

Yusuf had never considered the possibility that death would come to him at the age of 25, but now it was minutes away. And he was going to welcome it, or so he kept telling himself. He looked out the window and down to the eastern suburbs of Sydney, bathed in the fading light of a typically beautiful late summer sunset, and he thought about the fact that it was the last one he would ever see. Suddenly it was all so much more beautiful than he'd ever remembered. He was overwhelmed with the wish that he could turn back time, that he'd never met Malek, that he was at home, that he wasn't facing death.

He pushed that though aside and began to pray. Soon he'd be in Paradise, surrounded by beautiful women. The Qur'an said so, so it must be true. His colleague sitting opposite him was also praying, his lips moving, his hands on the automatic rifle he was holding shaking slightly.

What Yusuf was about to do would have been unthinkable three years earlier. As a young graduate he'd got a job as a telecommunications engineer, earning good money, with a close circle of Muslim friends and on good terms with his workmates. Once in a while someone would make a crack about Islam and Muslims, but generally they were friendly enough. He even got on with his parents, who had migrated to Australia from Lebanon in the early nineties. Their obsession with fitting into their new country sometimes got on his nerves - they were so desperate to adapt, he felt they were compromising their own religion. His mother refused to wear a veil and his father regularly missed

Friday prayers at the mosque. But then, they hadn't had the advantage of having the sort of education they'd been able to give him. He'd been to an Islamic school with excellent teaching - his religious teacher was from Saudi Arabia, so he was an authority on the Qur'an and the obligations that went with being a pious Muslim.

For Yusuf life was uncomplicated and comfòrtable. Until he met Malek.

When Malek first appeared at Yusuf's mosque he'd kept to himself. Malek spoke little, exchanging a few pleasantries but not giving much away about where he came from or why he was in Australia. He said his prayers with great conviction, and knew all the correct procedures, better than most of his fellow worshippers who had been home-schooled in their religion. To Yusuf he had the look and mannerisms of a true Muslim, from the Middle East, the homeland of the Prophet Muhammad, where Shari'a rules.

Then one day Malek approached Yusuf, smiled at him and began a conversation. He was charming and handsome, with a worldly air about him. They talked about their background, their work - the usual small-talk. As Yusuf had guessed, Malek was indeed from the Middle East – Iraq - fleeing from what he described as the tragedy that came after the US invasion. He said he was, like Yusuf, an engineer, working for a United Arab Emirates company selling communication equipment, and was stationed in Sydney for what was planned to be a three-year posting. They parted, agreeing to meet for a coffee during the following week. Thus began the grooming.

Over the next eighteen months Malek educated Yusuf about the many indignities inflicted on the Muslim community by the West – the colonisation of most Muslim-majority countries and the suppression of their cultural and religious practices; the propping up of corrupt dictators post-colonisation; the overthrow of the democratically elected prime minister of Iran in 1953 and the re-installation of the hated Shah; the setting up of the Israeli state and support for the Jews in the wars that ensued; the placing of their military on holy lands to wage the Gulf War; the invasions of Afghanistan and Iraq; and the meddling in Libya and Syria.

Before long, under Malek's careful guidance, Yusuf began to spend many hours searching out and reading websites that highlighted how Islam everywhere was 'under siege' by the West. He became ultra-sensitive to any real or imagined slight against the Muslim communities in Australia, and to feel that the government, let alone the general population, was Islamophobic.

Malek had been sent by Allah, Yusuf decided, to further his religious education, making him more aware of the details of the Qur'an and Shari'a, especially the concept of jihad and the responsibility Muslims had to defend Islam and the world-wide Muslim community. He had gradually emphasised how Allah values and rewards those who fight for the Islamic cause, and how those who die in the process go straight to Paradise, with no need to be subject to Judgement on the Final Day. "Chapter 22, verse 58-59, promises this" he would say, and quote:

"Those who leave their homes in the cause of Allah, and are then slain or die, on them will Allah bestow verily a goodly Provision: Truly Allah is He Who bestows the best provision. Verily He will admit them to a place with which they shall be well pleased: for Allah is All-Knowing, Most Forbearing."

It took eighteen months but by then Yusuf, against all logic, was totally radicalised, and ready to be persuaded by Malek that it was his duty to strike a major blow for Islam.

Many weekends during the next eighteen months were spent in combat training, mainly in the use of automatic weapons. These were conducted by another man whose identity was never revealed – he always wore a mask - and he was clearly an expert in the art of battle. He had access to a secluded property in the Blue Mountains which was covered with forest, so there was little chance of them being disturbed. Even though the weapons were automatic they only ever fired off one shot at a time, to avoid attracting the attention that bursts of gunfire might bring.

Two other men of about Yusuf's age were also in Malek's team. They had been recruited by him from the same mosque. Prior to the commencement of their training there'd been no contact between the three of them, but soon they became like brothers, aware that they were going to fight and die together in a glorious cause. Malek would constantly remind them that they were in the front line of an international grand strategy to protect their religion and culture.

"Muslims in the West are getting soft" he'd say, "and being won over by the infidels and their hedonistic lifestyle. Remember how I told you about Sayyid Qutb, about how after he'd been to America, he said this is the biggest danger facing us, the subversion of our religion and culture. It's even more true today. Your sacrifice will demonstrate the true spirit of jihad, and remind our fellow Muslims who they are, that they are part of a world-wide community that has been trampled on by the West for too long. It's time to fight back." They were young and impressionable, it appealed to their vanity, and the argument worked.

Two weeks earlier, Malek had summoned the three of them for a meeting and told them he'd been contacted by the leader in Australia of the international liberation group he represented – the mission for which they'd been recruited, and which had been meticulously planned and developed over a three-year period, was ready to execute. During the following days they made their final preparations, including the farewell videos that explained the rationale for what they were about to do.

And now here they were, about to realise what had been sold to them as their glorious destiny. There was no turning back, their fate was sealed. One of the team had been trained to fly a helicopter, and the three of them were now winging their way towards their target, which now loomed ahead, its instantly recognisable roof soaring like the sails of a fleet of gigantic yachts, silhouetted against the sunset sky – the Sydney Opera House.

*

Meanwhile, more than two hundred and fifty people mingled and chatted over drinks in the main hall of the Opera House, where an exhibition was being held, hosted by the city's top dealer in modern art. It was early evening on a Friday, and everyone was relaxed and in a good mood. In addition to the usual art set, most of them from the well-heeled eastern and north Sydney suburbs, a group from the leaving class of one of Sydney's premier private girls schools was present, having their horizons expanded by exposure to the latest crop of Australia's avant-garde work. Waiters moved amongst the guests, serving sparkling wine, and the place was a hubbub of chat and laughter. One of the schoolgirls, Rachel Johnson, charmed one of the waiters into giving her and her friend a glass, which they managed to hide from their teacher.

Charlotte Scott, art enthusiast and modest collector, was talking to a distinguished ex-judge. He had known her since she was at law school when he was a tutor.

"Honestly Neville, I don't know why I invite you to these events – you're a complete Philistine. You hardly looked at all those wonderful paintings."

"I admit it. I don't know what you see in this stuff – it makes no sense at all to me. I only come for your charming company, and the champagne. But anyway, how's that son of yours, the one who's the professor at Sydney University? The one who's always being asked about terrorism on TV? He'll end up getting his head chopped off one of these days if he's not careful."

"Don't be silly, Neville. He's just an academic, and I'm sure the terrorists wouldn't bother with such small fry, that's if we had any terrorists. Now a famous judge, that's another matter. But David is fine, still single though. Thank God for his sister who's given me a couple of grandchildren – I'm giving up hope with David, although he's got a girlfriend at the moment. Really pretty girl, from Malaysia, I think."

And so Rachel, Charlotte, the judge and the other guests chatted on, oblivious to the terror about to be unleashed upon them.

*

The helicopter was now very close to the Opera House, and the pilot began to manoeuvre his craft over the centre of the roof, where the largest and the third largest sails connected. Yusuf slid open the door and he and the second member of the team positioned themselves behind the huge bomb that was sitting on set of rails at the edge of the now open doorway. The pilot finalised his positioning, slowly raised the craft directly upwards a further two hundred feet, then tipped it slightly on its side while the other two released the catch that held the bomb. It slid slowly out the door. The pilot violently turned the craft to get as far away as possible before the anticipated explosion. The bomb hurtled down, crashed into the outer skin of the roof, tore through to the ceiling below, and then exploded with a mighty boom that could be heard for miles. The men who'd planned the operation had done their homework well – the bomb inflicted massive damage to the roof, with two of the sails virtually destroyed. A large area of the ceiling below collapsed, with large chunks of debris crashing to the floors below.

The helicopter pilot struggled to control his craft as it was slammed violently by the explosion, but it was far enough away to avoid damage. Once it was stable, the pilot turned back to the Opera House, and in a very short time landed on the main deck close to the entrance. Yusuf and his two companions gathered up their automatic rifles, fastened the backpacks containing spare magazines and leapt out of the helicopter to run towards the main doors. A small number of people had already stumbled outside onto the main deck, but the team ignored these and ran on - the overwhelming mass of the attendees were still inside.

Inside it was bedlam. People were dazed and shocked, hearing impaired by the deafening explosion, some injured by falling debris, most instinctively heading towards the entrance. Malek had told his team: "You've got to move fast. It won't take the police long to get there. But you won't need too long – you can kill a lot of infidels in just a few minutes with the weapons you have. Make sure you make every bullet count."

He was right - as the three burst into the main hall they were confronted with a solid mass of humanity, presenting a target that was virtually impossible to miss. For an instant all three hesitated, as though the enormity of what they were about to do had suddenly hit them, then one of them pressed the trigger of his weapon and the bullets streaked towards the closest group. This propelled the other two into action and then it was like a scene from hell - at first the bodies fell like ten-pins, then terrified people began to scatter, forcing the team to pursue them, firing as they went. All around the main hall, then up stairs to the surrounding balconies, people fled, only to be cut down by a spray of bullets. Every so often the firing from one of the team would stop as he threw out the used magazine and replaced it, but then the firing would continue, and the bodies would fall. At intervals each member of the team would shout 'Allahu Akbar', as instructed by Malek, to make sure that any survivors would report that an Islamist group was responsible.

For the first few minutes the closeness of the crowd had provided easy targets but then people had fled away from the front of the hall to find temporary sanctuary, behind pillars, rooms adjoining the balconies – anywhere out of immediate sight of the killers. The team were forced to search for their victims and as Yusuf slowed down, flashes of doubt began to assail him. Some of the people he'd shot were schoolgirls, one was a woman with a veil, undoubtedly a Muslim. Was this really going to help the Muslim cause? Would Allah really approve of this? But it was too late, he couldn't take back the bullets. And now he could hear the wail of sirens, heralding the arrival of the police. There was no choice but to trust in what he'd learned in the last three years and carry on – it would soon be over, and he'd meet his Maker.

Earlier, one of the security guards who'd been posted around the building, had been able to contact the police and quickly explain the situation. Less than ten minutes after the firing began a heavily armed team of ten police was on its way to the Opera House. By the time they arrived, and entered the main hall, the firing had become intermittent, and it wasn't hard to identify the location of each of the gunmen. Within minutes Yusuf and his brothers had died in a hail of bullets - the police knew better than to attempt to take prisoners.

Yusuf's death would forever be seared into the mind of Rachel. She'd fled up a flight of stairs at the onset of the shooting, her champagne glass clattering to the floor. She crouched, shaking behind a pillar, listening as the shooting reduced in frequency. As the minutes passed, the shooting became more intermittent, and she guessed that the killers were searching for more victims. She held her breath hoping they would pass her by, but suddenly Yusuf appeared directly in front of her. She recoiled in terror expecting a rain of bullets, but Yusuf hesitated for a moment and she lifted her eyes to look defiantly and directly back at him. A look of confusion came over his face. The next moment his body was thrown aside like a rag doll as the bullets smashed into his body. The armed policeman looked briefly at her, assessed she was unhurt, and moved on, weapon at the ready.

After the last bullet was fired, the police lowered their weapons to look around them at the scene of carnage. People lying at awkward angles, covered in blood, were strewn over most of the main hall and the balcony areas. Most were dead, but many were wounded, some crying out from the pain of their injuries. There were people who'd clearly flung themselves in front of a wife, husband, child, friend, in a vain attempt to shield them from the bullets, mostly to no avail. But now and then someone stirred from underneath a body, alive, sometimes injured, sometimes unscathed. The police found the other security guards, who'd rushed into the main hall to try to do something, anything, but they too had been cut down. In a very short time the ambulances started to arrive, with paramedics swarming everywhere, tending to the wounded, placing them on stretchers and carrying them outside.

When the final tally was made, ninety-seven people were dead and sixty-three wounded. Two of the sails of the building had been destroyed, leaving a gaping hole in the roof – the unique and beautiful skyline of Sydney had suddenly been altered, in the most tragic way. And the message had been clearly sent - Australia was no longer immune from the violence to which much of the rest of the world had become accustomed. Big-scale Islamic terrorism had arrived.

Rachel Johnson walked out of the building on her own two legs, physically unharmed but shocked by the terrible images that would remain with her forever, as well as the haunting and never-to-be answered question: Why did the terrorist hesitate for those few seconds that saved her life, while brutally executing so many others?

Charlotte Scott was not so lucky. She was found lying in a pool of blood beneath the body of the elderly judge, a gentleman to the last, trying vainly to save the woman he had known since she was a girl.

*

Within thirty minutes of the terrorists being killed, the scene around the Opera House was pandemonium. The police had cordoned off all the walkways that led to the building, but large crowds of people, which swelled by the minute, were gathering around Circular Quay, trying to see what was happening. TV crews had arrived and were filming and interviewing anybody they could get hold of. Dozens of police were shepherding survivors who had not been hurt to an area away from the general hubbub and were questioning them about what had happened. Meanwhile the ambulances continued to arrive, loading up with the injured and speeding away to the nearest hospital. Police helicopters flew overhead, searching the central city area for any sign of potential further terrorist threats.

In the midst of this turmoil, three members of the Australian Federal Police, headed by Detective Superintendent Jason Blake from the Counter Terrorism unit, arrived and immediately headed to the area where the Sydney police were talking to the survivors of the slaughter. Jason took aside the most senior of the police, introduced himself, and asked for a quick rundown of what had happened.

"Well, first the bomb. You can see the damage that's been done. It seems that they dropped it from the helicopter that's parked over there. Then they came back, landed, and ran into the building. There were three of them, now all dead, and they had automatic weapons, with stacks of spare ammunition. It was a massacre. They tell us that they were shouting about Allah as they were shooting, and when you see the bodies you'll see that they were all wearing Arab headgear. Islamic terrorists, for sure."

"I guess so," Jason replied, "but for the moment I think we'd better keep that to ourselves."

"Sure, I get it," said the policeman. "Our boys will keep their mouths shut, but there's no way we can stop all these people talking."

"You're right, but we just need to delay it a little. Give the government a bit of time to work out how they're going to handle this. Will you tell your guys that people need to hold off talking to the press for now? Don't forget this is a matter of national security. Now, where are the three guys?"

They moved into the main hall, where all the injured had now been removed, but many of the bodies still remained, with blood seeping in ever-widening pools around them.

"Jesus Christ," breathed Jason, "How many?"

"Ninety-seven dead, sixty-three wounded. Some of them probably won't survive."

"Bloody hell, they knew what they were doing. That's a high kill ratio. Someone trained them well."

They moved up the stairs, where the three terrorists lay in quite widely separate locations.

"They're young, probably mid-20's," observed the policeman. "They all look as though they come from a Middle Eastern background. I wonder if they're foreigners, or brought up locally. Surely they couldn't be."

"Don't count on it. We'll find out soon enough."

He had a long look at each of the weapons that lay alongside the three terrorists, taking photos with his mobile phone.

"I'm going to need these weapons ASAP."

"Sure. They'll be there in a couple of hours."

"Good. You carry on. I have to go and brief a few people. I don't envy you having to handle this."

He and his two fellow AFP colleagues made their way as fast as they were able, through the dozens of helpers and officials trying to bring order to the chaotic scene, then through the onlookers, to the car that was waiting on Macquarie Street. Once they were in the car, Jason turned to them:

"My guess is there'll be an announcement from an overseas terrorist group claiming the credit. But I need to know who those three guys were. Jesus, if they're home-grown there's going to be hell to pay. This is bad, probably the worst violence in Australia since the bombings of Darwin and Broome. Get on to the Sydney police and find out who these guys were, fast."

*

When he heard the explosion, Prime Minister Steven Madigan was working in Kirribilli House, his official residence, in the beautiful leafy suburb of the same name, directly across the water from the Opera House. He rushed to a window overlooking the harbour and stood open-mouthed. "Fucking hell, I don't believe it." Half the roof of the Opera House had disappeared. Then he saw a helicopter landing on the main deck, and shortly after the sound of rapid gunfire.

"Mike," he yelled to an assistant sitting in the next office, "Get hold of the police and find out what the hell's happening. They probably won't even know yet because we're probably some of the first that are seeing this. Stay on the phone and keep me informed as you find out."

He went back to the window and watched as events unfolded before him: the police arriving shortly after the cessation of the gunfire, then the dozens of vehicles, ambulances and police cars arriving and leaving the scene. God help us if this is what I think it is, he thought.

Over the next hour he continued to receive updates, all of which convinced him that his worst fears were being realised. The killers were almost certainly Muslims, so it was almost a given that this was an act of Islamic terrorism. And this was huge, not as big a death toll as 9/11, or the Bali Bombing, but 97 dead and 63 injured was still horrific. And this was on Australian soil. And the Opera House! The symbolism was enormous - along with the Harbour Bridge it's one of the most iconic images in Australia, recognisable around the world.

Ninety minutes after the explosion, the Premier of New South Wales, Amelia Petkovic, appeared on TV, on all stations, to give a brief run-down of what had happened, emphasising that the situation, while clearly a catastrophe, was under control, and that there was no further danger to the public. While explaining that three terrorists had been involved, she said nothing about the fact that they appeared to be Muslims, saying that the police were currently investigating to determine their backgrounds, and that more information would be provided as it became available.

Shortly after the telecast, the PM rang the Premier: "Thanks Amelia. Let's hold off letting people know that this is an Islamic thing as long as possible."

"We can't keep this under wraps for long. My office is being besieged by the press, and politicians from both sides, demanding to know what really happened. They know I'm stalling."

"I know, but keep stalling a bit longer. It'll take the police and the AFP the best part of a day to find out who these guys were. That should give me time to think about what the hell I'm going to say. Jesus. If they're local, how did we not see it coming? And if they're not local, how did we not see it coming? But God, if they're local, I hate to think…"

"We've already had plenty of locals going over to fight for IS. It's not like people don't know about home-grown terrorists."

"Yeah, but they did it over there, not in Sydney. Nearly a hundred people dead, over sixty injured, it's a nightmare. I'll let you know more as soon as the AFP get back to me. Talk to you soon."

One hour later his assistant called out to him: "The Editor of The Australian is on the phone. Says it's urgent. I'll put him through."

"Ted. You know about what's happened?" asked the PM.

"Of course I do. How could I not? I can actually see what's happened. Besides, I've got journalists crawling over the place, and the cops. Anyway, I've got news. We've just received a notification from a mob called Jaysh al-Tahrir al-Islamii, which is Arabic for The Muslim Liberation Army, claiming credit. I'll read you what they said:

'You were warned to stay out of Muslim lands, yet you persist. Australia should stop being America's lapdog, and look after your own problems, including the discrimination our brothers and sisters in Islam face in your country. You may have thought you were safe, but nowhere is beyond our reach.'

We've looked them up. They're an offshoot of al-Qaeda, but we don't know much more. Looks like they've been around for about ten years, but they're pretty shadowy. If it is them, they must be damned well organised."

"Christ. I never thought something like this would happen here. I can't believe it, but I look out the window and there it is. Ted, I'm going to address the nation as soon as I get confirmation on who these guys were. I need you to hold off on this until then."

"C'mon Steve, that's asking too much. This is huge."

"We'll work fast, less than twenty-four hours. And you'd better not jump the bloody gun on this. It's too serious.

"OK, OK. But I'm going to have it ready for publication straight after."

"Fine. Look Ted, we're in new territory here. This is bad enough, but if they're local we're going to be in for some rough times."

"Don't worry, I get it. Talk soon."

The PM put down the phone with a heavy sigh. As if running a country wasn't hard enough without this sort of madness, he thought. I wonder how someone like the Prime Minister of Pakistan manages, where dozens of ordinary people get massacred by terrorists what seems like every other week? And they're killing their own people, fellow Muslims. What a crazy world we're living in. He prepared himself for bed, dreading what the following day would bring. Normally he enjoyed Saturdays, but not today.

*

The next afternoon the Head of the AFP rang the PM's office and was immediately put through.

"Prime Minister, our people have tracked down the three terrorists. I'm afraid it's bad news. They were all born and raised right here in Sydney. Parents all came here in the early nineties, two families from Lebanon, one from Iraq."

"Bloody hell! Do they know anything about them? Were they on any suspect list?"

"No. At this stage we know next to nothing. No run-ins with the law, nothing to draw any attention. Just seemed like normal people. But we'll be crawling all over this, and we'll find out a lot more about them, people they were mixing with, whether there were any signs of radicalisation, the usual stuff."

"I guess that'll take time, which I don't think I have - I can't delay addressing the nation. I've got the key facts, so I might as well get it over with. Anything else you can give me?"

"Sorry. I wish I could. I've got the feeling this isn't going to be easy. This has all the signs of being a very slick, professional operation so they'll have covered their tracks pretty well. But I'm putting my best people on this and we'll throw everything at it."

"OK. Well, keep me posted."

"I'll send my man over to brief you Monday if that's okay, sir."

"Fine. Best to meet face to face."

Here we go, the PM thought, as he put the phone down. Time to face the music.

*

That same evening, at 6.00pm, the PM sat behind his desk at his Kirribilli office, with a bank of cameras facing him, about to give a live address which was to be aired across the nation. He was conscious that the audience would not only be Australian, but that the telecast would be international news, shared with broadcasters around the world. He'd spent the previous two hours composing something that he hoped would both allay the fears about more attacks and forestall any violent reaction against the Muslim communities throughout the country. Nevertheless, when he began he was nervous, despite the countless hours he'd spent in front of the cameras throughout his long political career.

"My fellow Australians. It's with a heavy heart that I have to confirm what most of you probably already know, that a terrible and cowardly act has been committed against us. Terrorists have bombed our beautiful Sydney Opera House, and then murdered over one hundred of our fellow country men, women and even children. The terrorists stole a helicopter, somehow managed to load it with a powerful bomb, flew directly over the roof of the Opera House, and dropped it at a carefully chosen position which would inflict maximum damage. They then landed, went inside, and proceeded to open fire with automatic weapons on the dazed and helpless people who'd been innocently enjoying an art exhibition. After the initial onslaught, when those who were unhurt fled to try and find safety, these men callously hunted them down, and shot them without mercy.

"I want to commend the brave and professional members of our police forces who responded to the alert about the attack within minutes and were able to prevent the atrocity from being even worse than it was. There were three terrorists, and all were killed at the scene.

"It pains me considerably to have to report that all three terrorists were Australian citizens, born and raised here, and that they were members of the Muslim community. Let me make it very clear that many senior representatives of numerous Muslim community groups have publicly expressed their horror at and condemnation of this terrible act and disassociated themselves and their communities from whatever agenda these terrorists had. Let me also tell you that we have had a communication from an international terrorist group in which they claim credit for this act. So, this is not an Australian initiative, but an international one, where a group has cynically made use of young, impressionable people to carry out this heinous act to further their political agenda. This is clearly about politics and not about religion. Like the Christian religion, Islam is a religion of peace, and just as the Christian religion has at times in the past been exploited for most unholy purposes, Islam has been so exploited. This is such a case.

"Let me also assure you that our police forces, both state and federal, have begun to search for any other possible source of terrorist violence, and to take precautions against any such act. Public places are being patrolled, and airports are on alert for the entry of any suspicious people. I therefore urge you to carry on with your usual activities, and not let this incident affect the way you go about your normal life, particularly in the way you interact with your fellow citizens. We're all Australians, we all reject the mentality of the people behind this crime.

"As I speak, there is a special team of investigators engaged in finding out how this happened, and I and your parliamentary representatives, whether in government or in opposition, are going to work together with a wide range of groups, in the police, the public service, academia, and community groups, to ensure whatever circumstances have allowed this to happen change, so it never happens again.

"Our thoughts go out to the families and all those affected by this terrible event, and we pray for the swift recovery of those who were injured.

"Thank you."

The cameras stopped transmitting, and the PM got up and walked to the window, looking out once again to the stricken building across the harbour. Our innocence is gone, he thought. I don't think we'll ever be quite the same again.

Chapter 2

"Professor Scott, I take issue with the fact that you're even sitting on the Panel. You're not a Muslim and yet you're advertised as an expert in matters that are directly affected by our religion. How can you possibly relate to what the Muslim community thinks or feels if you don't practice our religion? You're like a Catholic priest, giving marital advice when he's obliged to be celibate, and can't marry. He has no experience in what he's giving advice about."

David Scott found himself experiencing a feeling with which he was quite unfamiliar – discomfort and a tinge of embarrassment. Over half the audience was Muslim, and he could feel their eyes focusing on him, challenging him to come up with a credible answer to this questioning of his credibility. Well, bugger it, he thought, who are they to question me, one of the top people in my field in Australia, my advice sought by governments - the best defence is attack.

"Well, I'm glad to say the analogy doesn't extend to my being celibate", was his first response, which brought a scattered laugh. That's a good start, he thought. "Look, I totally disagree with you, and I think all you're doing is betraying your own insecurity. One doesn't have to *be* something in order to study it and be knowledgeable about it. Physicists have never seen an atom, and yet they can lecture about them and write books about them. Some psychologists are experts in the behaviour of psychopaths, yet they're not themselves psychopaths. Well, not generally, anyhow." Another laugh. "I'd suggest to you that there are some significant advantages in being detached somewhat from one's subject, particularly in matters involving human behaviour. Someone within a religion can be so close to the issues that sometimes you can't see the wood from the trees. And forgive me for making the point that it's common for Muslim scholars to throw up this criticism of anyone outside their religion daring to make any comment about it. That's why I made the comment earlier that I think it's about your own insecurity. Anyway, I've never claimed to be an expert in Islam the religion. My interest is in the politics of Muslim communities and the impact that the religion can have on those politics."

There were some murmurings from the crowd, and the person who'd raised the objection didn't look at all pleased, but he chose not to say anything further. The discussion, about immigration, ended without any further contention. Afterwards David mingled with the crowd and engaged in the usual small talk. Despite there being three panellists, as was generally the case David was the centre of attention. His slightly arrogant air notwithstanding, people, especially women, were attracted to him. He was tall, quite handsome, clearly very smart, and could be very charming when he felt like it, which to be fair was most of the time. So, he was forgiven his put-down of Muslim scholars and peppered with questions, until his host shooed the audience away and allowed him to make his escape.

As he drove towards his home in Rose Bay, David replayed in his mind the bit of interplay with the audience member. Had he been fair, or did he go a bit over the top? Maybe, but someone needed to start saying things like that. Everyone tiptoed around anything that smacked of even the slightest criticism of Islam, and long-term that was going to do everyone, Muslim and non-Muslim, a disservice. If they're going to live here as Australian citizens we're all going to have to come to grips with some real issues involving Muslim communities and their relationship with the rest of Australians.

He continued with this train of thought as he drove, because this was becoming an increasing preoccupation with him. Someone was going to have to lead the way, and who was better equipped than me, he thought (humility was not one of David's greatest virtues). But how to get peoples' attention? The academics were generally too politically correct to agree there was a problem, at least not on the Muslim side – any fault had to be the government's, particularly this conservative government. And the government people seemed to think money was always the answer – that way they didn't have to think too hard about the real issues and face up to them. As he pulled off Victoria Road and headed down Cranbrook Road towards the water the thought crossed his mind: Why do I want to take this on? Life's pretty good at the moment, why do I want to rock the boat? There's lots of people who'll give me lots of grief if I push this one hard.

And life had indeed been very good to David. His father had been the CEO of one of Australia's biggest private companies, and his mother had been a senior partner in one of the top Sydney law firms. He'd therefore had what is described as a privileged upbringing – attendance at one of the most exclusive private schools, and holidays in the UK, Europe and the US. He was very bright, and good at sport, and his parents instilled in him the classic Protestant work ethic, so he sailed through school. There was discussion about whether he should go to Oxford or Cambridge, or one of the Ivy League universities in the US - his exceptional results plus family connections made this a realistic possibility - but he was adamant that he wanted to stay in Australia. He loved his parents and adored his one younger sister, had a lot of close friends, and besides, he'd been fortunate enough to have seen quite a few countries, and knew Australia really was the 'lucky country'. So, he went to the University of Sydney and continued on his high-achieving path. Except that instead of following his parents into the private sector as a lawyer or banker or business executive he chose academia – he was fascinated by history and politics. By the age of 25 he had his doctorate, by 35 he was a full professor, and now at the age of 43 he was regarded as one of the top people in the country in his main area of speciality, Political Islam. His opinion was regularly sought by the mainstream press, and television news, and every now and then he would appear on one of the current affairs programmes on television.

As he pulled into the driveway of his apartment building his heart lifted as he saw Dina's silver BMW 330 sedan parked on the road outside. Dina was his latest girlfriend, and he was crazy about her - maybe she was going to be the one to finally take him out of the singles circuit. He parked his car and ran up the one flight of stairs to his apartment.

*

Dina Kassim had been upstairs for an hour, and as had been happening frequently lately, was thinking about her relationship with David. She couldn't hide it from herself any longer – she was falling for him, big time. He was no longer someone she could have a great time with for a while, enjoying the sex and the intelligent conversation, until she judged that it was all getting a bit serious and walk away with her heart still intact. Once bitten twice shy – she'd had no intention of getting tangled up again with someone who would undoubtedly eventually cause her grief. She had a good life, she was in control, life was uncomplicated. And then along came David, with his good looks, his brilliance and his charm, and here she was, in grave danger of having her life becoming very complicated indeed. As if that wasn't bad enough, he wasn't even a Muslim. In fact, he was a complete unbeliever - her *ustatz* at the mosque would say he was definitely headed for hell. Mind you, with all this sex outside marriage so are you, she thought to herself ruefully. Deep down though, she didn't really believe in hell – a loving God and hell made no sense to her.

Dina had lived in Australia for seventeen years, initially to attend the University of New South Wales. There, like David, she studied history and politics, with honours, and then a Masters in Education – she'd decided that she wanted to be a teacher. Like many Malaysian students she stayed on after graduation, gaining her Permanent Residency and later becoming a citizen – she loved her adopted country and was a very proud Australian. She even succeeded in persuading her parents to emigrate when they retired – they didn't like what was happening politically in Malaysia – and they too were now very happy in their new country, living in Gosford, north of Sydney.

After working in three public high schools she'd recently landed a position at one of Sydney's most prestigious Church of England private schools, co-educational, where she taught history to the two senior years. The students were motivated to do well so she enjoyed teaching them, the girls in particular, who were generally the most industrious. Nearly all the boys were smitten by her, so they kept in line. Work's been pretty good, she thought, but her love life hadn't been quite so successful. When she was 25 she'd married another Malay from Malaysia, but it lasted less than two years. In the early days of their relationship he was the epitome of a moderate Muslim, making no comment about her very Western approach to life. Once married he began to expect her to behave more conservatively, even at one stage pressuring her to wear a veil. She flatly refused, and this began a downhill slide. They managed to part company in a reasonably amicable way so both of them went on with their lives with a sense of relief, each believing they'd dodged a bullet. She had a few brief relationships in the next few years, nothing serious, all nice guys but not for her. Then six months ago David entered her life, and it began to take a new and slightly scary path.

They'd met at a University of New South Wales function where David was the guest speaker, and his speech was followed by the usual cocktails and nibbles. With a glass of wine in his hand, he was surrounded by attendees who were plying him with questions, some of the ladies undoubtedly with un-academic thoughts on their minds, but during his speech he had spotted Dina in the audience and was determined to meet her. While fielding questions he kept looking over to where Dina was herself the subject of continuous attention from a series of men. Eventually he saw his opportunity, made his excuses to the current group of questioners and made a bee-line for her. Out of the corner of her eye she'd seen him coming but of course pretended she hadn't, turning as though to get another drink.

"Hello, I'm David Scott", he said, having gained her attention by standing directly in front of her. "Mind if I join you?"

"Sure. Of course I know you're David Scott. You're the big star, why we're all here. I'm Dina Kassim."

"Very pleased to meet you, Dina. Does that mean 'love' in Arabic?"

"Yes, I'm impressed. How did you know that?"

"Well, there was a lady who wrote a good book I've read who had that name, so just for fun I looked up the meaning. So, I'm not really so smart. I understand very little Arabic."

They chatted on, with David cleverly eliciting a lot of information from her about herself, and amusing her with some of his anecdotes. When they parted he asked her point-blank if he could call her and perhaps have a coffee, or lunch. A man who listened more than he spoke was off to a very good start as far as Dina was concerned, so she said yes. The first coffee was followed by a lunch, which was followed by a dinner. The third dinner after that was followed by an extremely pleasant night in his bed, and after that they were an item, going out together at least twice a week, and she generally staying the night. Before long she decided that she liked him, a lot. He was a bit full of himself, but she'd seen him with his family and friends and how they reacted to him, and it was clear that at heart he was kind and good-natured. It was rare to see him in a bad mood, and he was always quick to snap out of it. So here she was at 34, fancy-free, with a challenging job that she loved, earning a good living, and with a handsome, charming and very successful boyfriend who was a lot of fun and great company. Why then did she have a sense of unease, that things weren't quite as rosy as they appeared? Deep down she knew what it was – parents, and religion.

Dina was often conflicted. She'd spent the first seventeen years of her life in Muslim-majority Malaysia, but now she was living in secular Australia. As a child she'd been deeply immersed in the culture of her Malay community, within the wider culture of the country where the three major ethnic groups, Malay, Chinese and Indian, co-existed in a state of general, although at times precarious, harmony. She was one of a generation of Malays who were raised in an environment where the issues of race and religion had become political footballs. Being a Muslim had become the major identifier for the Malays, the ultimate sign that they were the original inhabitants and deserving of the special privileges that had been enshrined in the Constitution and expanded in the New Economic Policy. The Malay political parties vied with each other to be perceived as the most Islamic, which meant that the version of Islam practiced in Malaysia became increasingly conservative. Along with this came considerable peer pressure to conform to what were becoming the Islamic norms – most Malay females, even schoolchildren, wore veils, and those that didn't came under considerable pressure to do so, not so much from the authorities, although that also was present, but from their family, friends and workmates.

Like most Malays, Dina had been sent to Islamic classes outside her regular school classes. Also, she was naturally influenced by her parents who, while not particularly conservative, nevertheless were quite pious and adhered closely to the required Islamic rituals of prayer and fasting. Like most children brought up in a strong religious environment, she was herself quite religious. However, being in an international school with classmates from all Malaysia's ethnic groups, plus a lot of expatriate children, she was not as influenced by the peer pressure that was prevalent in the public schools, where most of the attendees were Malay. She'd never worn a veil, although her mother did, but never pressured her to do so. She was also smart enough, and strong enough mentally, to reject suggestions from some of her Malay girlfriends that she shouldn't become too friendly with non-Muslims, an idea that was pushed by many public school teachers, imams in the mosques, and even some of the politicians. Going to university in Australia, and being exposed to students from many parts of the world, as well as the locals, broadened her outlook considerably, and she relaxed a little as far as adhering to the more overt aspects of Islam, but she still considered herself a good Muslim, and believed in the fundamentals of the religion. Previously it would never have occurred to her to marry a non-Muslim, and she knew her parents would be very unhappy if she did. What would they say if they could see her now, in a Caucasian unbeliever's home, about to commit yet another sin with him, and not only that, to even be considering getting more serious with him? *Alamak*, what to do, she thought?

At that moment the front door opened, and there was the object of both her desire and her confusion. Her heart lifted, and like Scarlett O'Hara, she thought: 'I'll think about that tomorrow.'

*

Later, they came down to the lounge and sat down to have a glass of wine, and chat about the day.

"I might have offended a roomful of Muslims today" he said, and explained his exchange with the questioner at his talk.

"You're so arrogant sometimes. I can see why they call people like you Infidels. I don't know why I go out with you" she said, but with a smile on her face.

"Such harsh words, to the love of her life. And I thought I was going out with a refined and gentle Muslim girl, who respected her men."

"I've been around Aussies like you too long – it rubs off. But seriously, do you really believe what you said to him, or was it just a put-down that you thought of on the spur of the moment?"

"Alright, to be serious, yes I do. I know it's true that I don't know a lot about the intimate details of how Muslims practice Islam and live their lives, but I don't think that prevents me from being able to see the effects of their collective behaviour in the public arena, and in their politics. There's stuff going on right here in Australia that I reckon I can see that they can't, because they're only looking at things from their point of view. What about how other people in the community think? And yet when I say this, a lot of people, not just Muslims but a lot of non-Muslims, especially a lot of my academic colleagues, shout me down because they say I'm not qualified to talk about issues involving Islam, and even that I'm Islamophobic. I find that bloody insulting."

He stopped, and looked at her. "Sorry. I'm getting het up. But it does annoy me. What do you think? Am I being unreasonable?"

"Well, you're not Islamophobic, I know that. But the rest, I don't really know. I think there's a lot of negative stuff about Islam in the press. Every time some crazy people somewhere else in the world do something terrible the impression we get is that too many

Australians think we're all like that deep down, that we secretly support them, and it's not fair."

"I agree with you, but there's clearly a major communication problem between the Muslim community and the rest of Australians, and if someone like me tries to open up the conversation about these issues we get shouted down, mostly by people who appear to be speaking for the Muslim community."

Dina gathered breath to retort when a very loud noise stopped her. It seemed to come from far way, but the deep thudding boom suggested something massive, like a huge explosion.

"What on earth was that? It sounded like cannon fire, only much bigger." David exclaimed. "It seemed to come from the west, maybe in the city centre."

"I think it sounded more like a bomb. But how could it be, in the centre of Sydney."

"If it's some sort of accident it'll be on TV in no time" said David, as he got up and switched on the news. Before long the programme was interrupted, and a presenter announced in shocked tones:

"Less than ten minutes ago the Opera House was bombed, apparently with a bomb dropped from a helicopter directly overhead. At this moment there is gunfire coming from within the building, but it's not clear what's happening. Our camera crew is heading to the scene and we'll get a picture on screen very shortly."

Fifteen minutes later David and Dina watched in horrified silence as the news channel's team arrived near the Opera House and began filming. They saw the smoke rising above the building, and the shattered sails beneath, the police cars and vans on the road directly adjacent to the outside decking, the helicopter parked on the deck, and heard the scattered gunfire coming from within the building. The TV presenter described how the police had arrived a few minutes earlier and had rushed into the building. They assumed that a firefight was currently in progress, with whom they didn't know.

They continued to watch the chaotic scene onscreen, where by now the gunfire had ceased and the ambulances were arriving. They could see crowds of people being led out of the building and moved to a section of the deck outside of the view of the cameras. Then, to their further horror, they saw paramedics carrying stretchers with people lying on them and taking them to the ambulances. Suddenly, with a strangled cry, David leapt to his feet: "Mum was there."

"What do you mean?" asked Dina, as she also stood and took him by the elbows.

"She was going to some sort of art show. I just remembered. She mentioned it to me the other day when I had lunch with her. She was going with an old friend, Judge Mitchell. My God, I don't believe it. A bomb, guns, people being carried out on stretchers. It looks like this was a bunch of terrorists, shooting up the place like that guy did in Christchurch."

He paused, and his voice trembled. "I can't believe this is happening. She could've been shot. She could be dead."

"Try and call her. The police got there very quickly. Maybe she's fine."

David dialled her number and listened. It rang, but his heart sank as it eventually went to voice mail.

"No joy. I've got to get down there and find out if she's alright."

"I'll come with you" said Dina, and they rushed out of the apartment and down to David's car.

*

When they neared Circular Quay they found the roads adjacent had all been blocked off, so they parked the car in the nearest space and ran towards the Opera House. Already the crowds had gathered, and it was difficult to force their way through, David pleading with people to make way because his mother was in the building. Eventually they arrived at the end of the street leading to the main deck of the building, and this was guarded by six police who regularly made way for an ambulance or police car but steadfastly refused to let any pedestrians take a step closer. David went up to them and explained the situation and eventually they let them both through. When they got to the edge of the main deck their way was blocked by a sturdy barrier that surrounded the entire building, with a large number of police standing on the other side. This time they were not so accommodating.

"I'm sorry, mate." said the policeman he spoke to. "We understand the situation but at this stage it's impossible for us to give any details about what's going on inside, other than there's been an explosion, some shooting, and there are some casualties, as you can see for yourself. We have many of our people inside and they're clarifying what's been happening and who's been affected. But even for family members we can't tell you anything more. I'm really sorry. I know you're upset. I promise you, if you give me your contact details, and the name and address of your mother, we'll let you know as soon as there's information."

"How long do you think that will take?" David asked.

"It could take a few hours" the policeman replied. "You don't live that far away, so I think it would be best if you went home, and we'll contact you."

David thanked him, and reluctantly turned away. He dialled his mother again, but still there was no answer. With a sense of foreboding he took Dina's hand and walked with her back to the car, driving back to his apartment in silence and settling in for a long wait. David had decided not to call his sister, Beth - there was no point in worrying her, hopefully unnecessarily. They'd switched on the television, in the hope that there would be an announcement of some sort explaining what had happened. Shortly after the Premier came onscreen and gave the bare details, including the fact that three gunmen had been involved. But they learned nothing about their identity. Almost three hours later David's mobile rang and he answered.

"Is that Professor David Scott?" asked the male voice at the other end of the line.

"Yes, that's right."

"You were at the Opera House earlier and informed one of the policemen there that you thought your mother was attending a function at the Opera House, is that correct?"

"Yes, that's correct."

"Professor Scott, I'm terribly sorry to have to tell you that she was at the function, and that she was one of the casualties of the shooting that occurred after the bombing."

There was a brief silence as the policeman waited to see how David would respond. David's mind reeled as he tried to absorb the news, that his mother was gone, that he'd never be able to speak to her again. After a full ten seconds, as the policeman waited patiently, he collected himself, and managed to reply: "Thank you for telling me. What do you want me to do?"

"Tomorrow we'll need you to identify your mother's body - someone will contact you in the morning to arrange a time."

"Yes. Yes, I'll do that. Were there many other people killed?"

"I'm sorry that I can't say anything at this stage. It will be made public very soon. Again, I'm very sorry to have had to bring you this news."

"Thank you, Officer. I appreciate that. I'll be there tomorrow."

He hung up, turned to Dina, and broke down. He didn't have to say anything, it was obvious what he'd been told. She hugged him, and tried to comfort him, and seeing him so upset broke her heart – she knew how close his family was. My God, she suddenly thought. Beth. It's going to kill David to have to tell her. When David finally collected himself, it was clear that telling Beth was uppermost in his mind also.

"This is going to be the hardest thing I've ever done" he told Dina. "I'll go into the bedroom to do it – it's not going to be pretty."

"Of course, I'll be here."

It took quite some time before he emerged, but he was able to tell her that Beth was OK, although understandably horrified, and terribly upset. She in turn was going to have to give the news to her two children, a girl of seven and a boy of five, that their Gran was gone. But she was lucky to have a supportive husband who'd help her through.

She'd asked him: "Who were these monsters? Were they terrorists? Muslims?" He'd told her that at this early stage no news about the killers had been released, so he didn't know, but that he was sure by the following day something would be said. They'd agreed that he would go around to her place the following morning.

"Do you want me to stay tonight?" asked Dina.

"Thanks, darling, but you'd best go home. I need to get my head around this. I'm seeing Beth in the morning – do you want to come over tomorrow evening?"

"Of course I do. I'll see you then."

She gave him a kiss and a long hug, after which he accompanied her out the door to her car and watched as she drove off. With a sigh he turned and walked slowly back upstairs.

*

The next morning David drove to his sister's house in Bondi, where they had a tearful reunion. His niece and nephew looked sad, but it was perhaps a blessing they were still so young that it was all a bit much for them to comprehend - they were soon back into a normal routine of watching television and bickering over who had the remote.

"Thank God Dad wasn't here to see this – it would've broken his heart" said Beth. "It's such a waste. She was in such good form, the life of the party, enjoying retirement, healthy. She'd probably have lived another twenty years." She broke into tears again, and David held her until she recovered her composure. After they'd finished the tea Beth served, he explained that he had to leave to identify the body, upon which Beth looked as though she would burst into tears again. But she took a deep breath and held herself together. She was mentally tough, a lawyer like her mother, and she knew she had to get over this – she had a family to care for.

David's experience at the morgue would be one that he'd never be able to get out of his mind. The staff there were understanding, and he was grateful for how gently they guided him through the difficult task he had to perform. But seeing his mother laid out, so still, was enough to bring tears to his eyes. He leaned forward, stroked her cheek, and kissed her, confirmed that it was indeed his mother, Charlotte Scott, and walked out of the building.

That evening Dina came over, and they sat and chatted sombrely over a glass of wine. They had the television on in case the announcement they were waiting for came on, and sure enough, at 6.00pm, the Prime Minister appeared onscreen. They listened with horror and incredulity as he described the extent of the atrocity, so many killed, so many injured. Then, when he explained that the three terrorists were Muslims, and that they were born and raised in Australia, Dina felt David's body stiffen, and saw his face tighten. He'd been holding her hand and he squeezed it so tight that it hurt. Suddenly, a terrible feeling of apprehension came over her. I'm a Muslim, she thought. Is he going to blame us all for this?

The PM's announcement finished, and for a little while they sat in silence. "What are you thinking?" she eventually asked.

"I don't know what to think. Deep down, I've been dreading something like this for a long time, that Australia couldn't stay immune to Islamic terrorism. Sooner or later someone like Al Qaeda or Islamic State would do something like this just to show the world that nowhere on earth was safe. You know - if it can happen in Australia it can happen anywhere. And I was right about the Muslim community here – they're in denial, while terrorists are being nurtured in some of their own homes."

"But David, you know that it's only a tiny minority of crazy people. It's not the whole community." Dina protested.

He paused. "Yes, I know it's not the whole community. But how many are really pushing back against the sort of thinking that allows this to happen? Too few, in my view."

About to give an angry response, Dina thought twice. *He's really upset, and he's every right to be. Now's not the time to argue. Let it go.*

"Darling, let's not talk about it right now. Don't be angry. You know how much this has upset me too."

David bit his tongue and held back on what he was really thinking. *Don't say something you'll regret,* he thought, *especially to this girl you love. You know she has nothing to do with all this.*

"You're right" he said, and smiled at her. "I know I'm not thinking quite straight at the moment." They sat down together, arm in arm, but both knew something had just happened that threatened to poison their relationship, and it wasn't going away.

*

Iraq: 1969 - 2003

The Iraqi was born in 1969, in Baghdad. His father was an imam, a religious leader in the Sunni community, so of course he was steeped in Islam and practiced it diligently. As an imam, his father was well off financially, and able to afford to send him to the UK to study, where he qualified as an electrical engineer from a very respectable university in London. He enjoyed his time there and got on quite well with his fellow students although, as is quite typical with students from Muslim-majority countries, he tended to spend most of his time with fellow Muslims. In this way they managed to largely adhere to the requirements of their religion, in particular the prayers five times per day, and the avoidance of eating pork and drinking alcohol. But The Iraqi was human, and now and then had a drink or two. He was tall, strongly built and quite good looking in a tough sort of way, so he was frequently tempted to take advantage of the approaches he regularly received from his fellow female students, particularly those from Western countries who were attracted by the slightly exotic air he had about him. He excelled in sport, and became quite expert in martial arts. When he completed his studies he returned to Baghdad, with largely positive views about his UK experience. He'd quite liked the Brits, the Americans and the Europeans he'd mixed with, even though he felt most of them suffered from a lack of religion, and the sort of purpose that Islam provided him. And his English was fluent, although still with a slight accent.

With his excellent qualifications he readily got a job with the country's main electricity supplier and progressed through the ranks rapidly. This was during the regime of Saddam Hussein, who was President from 1979 until his overthrow in 2003. While Saddam was from the Ba'ath community, and while the various sects of Islam largely kept to themselves, in those days there was little interference from the ruling regime unless anyone did something to antagonize them. If one was careful – and The Iraqi was - life could be quite good. Saddam was no religious fanatic, and Islam in Iraq was practiced in a quite moderate way. Women were not forced to veil, were able to receive tertiary education, and were generally treated well, in contrast to many other countries in the Middle East, notably Saudi Arabia.

In his late-20's The Iraqi married Hamidah, a girl he'd actually sought out for himself rather than it being an arranged marriage, as was more common in Iraq. They were in love and it was a happy union. Hamidah had also studied at university so they were intellectual equals and The Iraqi was quite modern in his thinking

- probably because of his time spent in the UK. He didn't push the patriarchy issue too hard and if he ever tried she pushed back and he generally relented. Before long they had a daughter, Afwida, and then a son, Kamil, and life was good. Because he worked for the government and had become quite senior in his profession, his family weren't severely affected by the sanctions imposed on Iraq after the Gulf War from 1990 until shortly after the 2003 invasion. But he could see the effect it had on those not so well off, and he found this troubling. But there was nothing The Iraqi could do, so he just got on with his own life.

Then 9/11 happened, and people in Muslim-majority countries waited with considerable apprehension to see what the American reaction would be. The invasion of Afghanistan was almost expected, and it was hoped that it would be enough to satisfy the American public that the Taliban had been sufficiently punished for harbouring the people behind the atrocity. Perhaps it was, but it wasn't enough for Paul Wolfowitz, Donald Rumsfeld and the rest of the Neo-Cons who had infiltrated into President George W. Bush's administration. To the initial bemusement, and then gradually increasing apprehension of Iraqis, accusations by this group that Saddam had developed weapons of mass destruction (WMD's, as they became popularly known) were taken seriously by the US press, and gradually by the governments and press of other Western countries. Tony Blair, the Prime Minister of the United Kingdom, took it so seriously that he staked (and consequently ruined) his career on these accusations being fact, and talked his parliamentary colleagues into supporting whatever punitive action the US decided to take.

Before long the US, in the form of a most reluctant General Colin Powell, the Secretary of State, was presenting embarrassingly suspect evidence at the United Nations that suggested Saddam did indeed possess WMD's, and requesting approval for a US-led alliance to invade Iraq. Saddam's denials were in vain – the Neo-Cons had always wanted to invade Iraq and now was the chance. They were going to have their war, no matter that the facts were false, and that they knew it. The Iraqi and his fellow-Iraqis watched this tragedy unfold with horror, but were powerless to stop it, as were the myriad Middle Eastern representatives consulted and subsequently ignored by US representatives. On 20th March 2003 Operation Shock and Awe was unleashed on the Iraqi population.

It could be argued that the 2003 invasion of Iraq was the greatest foreign policy blunder ever made by the US when one considers the long-term, unforeseen (at least by the US administration) consequences – the unleashing of hitherto repressed tribal forces, the rise of ISIS, the hundreds of thousands of people killed, the millions displaced, and the trillions of dollars spent by the US. But that's all macro level. As in all wars, the real tragedies are felt in the micro, at the family and individual level. The Iraqi was one such individual.

CHAPTER 3

It was Monday morning, and the great city was alive with people, moving into the centre in various modes of transport. Pedestrians hurried along the streets, steering away from the barricades that shut off all entrances to the Opera House area. Circular Quay was as busy as usual, with ferries coming and going every few minutes. The Harbour Bridge was crawling with cars, and every so often a clattering train, so that at least one of Sydney's two iconic structures was its usual self – the other was bare, and silent. Every person coming into the city from the north shore, or from the water, couldn't help but gaze at the huge, gaping hole in the Opera House roof - a glaring reminder of the horrors that had been unleashed just a few days earlier.

Steven Madigan was doing the same, standing at the window of his office in Kirribilli, and mentally preparing himself for the first of what would undoubtedly be many meetings to discuss the implications of the terrorist attack. I wonder what the next few weeks will bring, he thought. How bad will the backlash be? He thought about George W. Bush after the 9/11 attack, and how he at least was able to identify some form of target to unleash his forces upon and demonstrate to the American people that he was 'taking action'. What the hell are we going to do, who is it that we can attack? People are going to blame us because we didn't see this coming and stop it. And why the hell didn't we? What were the AFP people doing? And so his thoughts ran on, until he finally said to himself: Snap out of it. You can't sort this out by yourself. There's a whole team waiting in the other office who are going to, so let's get going. With that he strode out, walked down the corridor a few paces and entered a large office where the Cabinet of National Security was gathered. They all stood as he entered.

"Good morning, everyone. Thanks for coming in. You'll notice that I've invited Andrew to join us – I think this is bigger than politics – so welcome, Andrew, we look forward to your input. Let's get started." he said as he sat down. He looked around the table at his six fellow members of the Cabinet, plus the Leader of the Federal Opposition, Andrew Atkinson, the Premier of New South Wales, Amelia Petkovic, and Jason Blake.

The Head of the Australian Federal Police, Manfred Ryan spoke first: "Prime Minister, I have with me Detective Superintendent Jason Blake, who I've placed in charge of this investigation. He's had some experiences that I believe make him the best suited for an operation of this nature. I think he should attend any of these Cabinet meetings that you have. He'll keep you all updated as to what's happening."

"Thanks Manfred, and welcome Jason – you've got a big task ahead of you, but we're counting on you to get to the bottom of this. Anything you need, just ask for it, from me, Manfred, Amelia, any of us – this is absolutely top priority. You all understand that?" He looked around the table, and there were nods all round. "Now first things first – Amelia – what's the situation in the street? Any incidents?"

"Not much so far" the Premier replied. "The police are out in force patrolling, and they've seen a few cases of verbal abuse, but no violence. But I think it's only a matter of time."

"I agree" said Paul Davies, the Minister for Home Security. "The more media coverage this gets, and of course there's going to be mountains of it, some idiots are going to say things which will get some other idiots out there all fired up, and that's when things could get nasty."

"I'm afraid I agree" said the PM. "Remember the Cronulla Riots – and what motivated them was nothing compared to this. This is like someone's declared war on us." He paused for a moment, and then went on. "You know, earlier I was looking out at the Opera House, and thinking about 9/11 and what George Bush would have been thinking. He lashed out, and started something that's turned out really badly – more than badly, catastrophically. And we've been drawn into it. Whatever we do about this, we've got to be smarter, and not make the same mistakes. But what that is, I've got to be honest, I have no idea. But I think there are a couple of things we need to be doing in parallel. We've got to find out how this happened, and get the people behind it. That's what Jason is going to be working on. But we've also got to find out *why* this happened, and how it could have involved people who've been born and raised right here in this country. And then somehow we've got to fix it, once and for all." He paused again, and then asked: "Jason, what can you tell us?"

"Well, sir, obviously it's very early days, but here's what we know so far. The three terrorists hired a helicopter, with a pilot, for what was supposed to be a joy ride around Sydney, for two hours. It was all done properly, with all the required paperwork. What must have happened is that when they were in the air the pilot was put out of action, and one of the terrorists, who was a qualified pilot himself, took over the controls. By the way, the pilot has not been seen since. We assume that they killed him and dropped him in the sea a little way off-shore, so I'm betting a body will be washed up soon. Anyway, they landed somewhere, we don't know where, and set the helicopter up with the bomb and the means to easily slide it out the door when the time came. They then flew straight to the Opera House, and you know what happened then."

He paused, but the Prime Minster nodded for him to go on.

"Now, a few things about all this that I find particularly disturbing. Obviously, the guys that did this really knew what they were doing, but it's the planning behind it that is the most impressive. The three terrorists were home-grown which means they were radicalised. That takes time, years probably. And they weren't just some crazy young guys who got all fired up and did this themselves – they were university educated guys, and there were obviously people behind them. For starters, I'll bet you there was someone who got to them and started the radicalisation. But the bomb was big, and sophisticated. How did they do that? It would be very difficult to smuggle it in, and would involve a number of people if they did. I'm guessing they didn't – I think it was made here, and once again, that takes a lot of doing. Why I think that is that the weapons they used in the Opera House were hand-made, and I'm sure they would have been made here. If the weapons were going to be smuggled in there's no need to hand-make them, they could just get them off the shelf. And the other thing, it's very hard to get hold of weapons like that here, and any attempt to do so has a real chance of attracting attention. Making the weapons here is a very smart move. But it also means that they've got access to some real skills. All this means that first, this group is very professional, and very patient, willing to wait a long time to be sure that what they plan works. And second, there's some sort of operation out there, with a number of these guys involved. Which means they could do something like this again."

He paused, and then added: "I don't want to labour the obvious, but if people like this are smart enough, and patient enough, and they're prepared to die, it's very difficult to stop them before they've managed to do at least some damage."

There was silence while the others digested this very unwelcome news.

The Prime Minister eventually asked: "So what's happening? Have you got any leads?"

"We've identified the three terrorists, and spoken to their families. They seem very normal, and appear quite devastated at what's happened and that their sons were involved, as well as, of course, that in the process they've been killed. I believe they're genuine – I don't think there's any extremism there. We've also identified the mosque that the three attended, and have started interviewing regular attendees. That's in the early stages, and after this meeting I'll be meeting with my people on the ground for updates. We want to get a feel for whether there's any support for extremist views or anyone out there who could have been doing the radicalising. I reckon there's a good chance the mosque is where these three young blokes met the person or persons who did it."

The Premier chipped in: "We've got as many police as we can release from key duties to patrol the most likely targets of another attack - any places where large numbers of people gather, like big shopping centres, and places of worship like Christian churches and so on. But it's needle in a haystack stuff, really. They could target anywhere. But we've got to make the general public feel they're safe, so they can go about their normal business."

Next was the Head of the AFP, Manfred: "In addition to the very specific investigation Jason is leading, we've got a large team interviewing anybody who's on our radar as a potential extremist. The Muslim community won't like it, as it's inevitable that we're going to sweep up lots of innocent people in the process. We don't have the time to run around getting search warrants, but that's too bad – this is too serious a situation to pussy-foot around. Amelia, do you agree, as far as New South wales goes?"

"Normally I'd be protesting, but I agree with you this is an emergency. I'm pretty sure the other Premiers would agree."

"OK", said the PM. "Manfred, I was going to ask you how it is we didn't identify these guys before they were able to do this thing. The public are going to want to know, they'll be after blood. But I know the answer. I know you guys are doing as much surveillance as you can, but it's impossible to watch everybody."

Manfred nodded his thanks for the PM's understanding and the PM went on: "But it's imperative we deliver. We have to find these people, and we've got to stop this happening again. One last thing before we adjourn - I'd like to have an expert on this Political Islamic stuff. We need a better idea of what we're dealing with. I don't want anyone who might be sensitive about all this, somebody more neutral, a non-Muslim. Maybe an academic in the political field. Who can find that sort of person?"

The Premier spoke up: "I'm sure I can. Leave it to me."

"Great. Swear him, or her, to secrecy and all that stuff. When you've got him lined up, I want Jason to meet him. I figure he's going to have to work closely with him, so Jason, I'd like you to meet him before he comes to brief us, which should be as soon as possible. I know you've got a million things to do, but I think this could turn out to be really important. OK?" Jason nodded.

"Amelia, that means you have to get this person lined up fast." He stood up. "Alright, let's get on with it. See you all soon."

*

A short time later Jason was back in his office, where three of his team leaders were waiting to brief him about their latest meetings with members of the Muslim community. The first, Mike Anderson, began:

"We've been meeting people who are regular attendees at the same mosque the three attackers attended. Most of them said they were shocked to discover three of their neighbours could be capable of such a thing. They said there was no sign of it - they hadn't changed their behaviour, hadn't said anything out of the ordinary. In fact, no-one at all told us anything that suggested they'd been radicalised. It was interesting though, the different types we spoke to. Most had either been born and raised here, or had been here quite some time and seemed to have settled in pretty well. Their English was pretty good, and they appeared to have jobs and so on, and they seemed to be genuinely upset about what had happened. Some were fairly new, and they were sometimes a bit different. Didn't have much to say about the terrorist act, you know, didn't make a thing of condemning it. Some of the young ones in particular almost seemed a bit hostile."

"But it's interesting that the three terrorists all came from the first lot you described" the second team leader, Gavin Smith, interjected. "We spoke to their families, and they all came to Australia quite a few years ago, and seemed to have settled in, with jobs, and made a pretty good life for themselves. So why would their sons go off the rails like this? It doesn't make much sense. You'd expect it would be the young ones you mentioned, who perhaps have some sort of chip on their shoulder."

"Did anyone mention someone the three attackers had been talking to, who could perhaps be the one who set them off down the radicalisation path?" asked Jason.

"No" replied Mike. "It's a big mosque and while there's a fairly big congregation who are regulars, there's also quite a large transient population of attendees who come for a while and then they don't see them again. So, if they met him at the mosque he could be one of those."

"What about the families? Did they mention anyone that their sons had met, or any change in their behaviour?"

"Not really" replied Gavin. "But, each family did mention that every few weeks their son would go on a trip with friends over a weekend, somewhere up the coast, camping and fishing. They didn't know exactly where. This has been happening for about eighteen months or so. I wonder whether they actually met up with their terrorist mates and learned how to handle weapons?"

"I think that's very likely" replied Jason. "But where? They'd have to have a property that was pretty secluded, and of a decent size. I guess it could be anywhere within about a 200-kilometre radius, and that's a hell of a lot of properties to check."

Speaking to the third team leader, Jim Callaghan, he said: "Jim, get your team on to this one. It's a pretty good guess that there has to be a place like this, and if we could ever identify it, it could hopefully lead us to the owners, and maybe to the people we're looking for. It's a bit of a long shot but we've got very little to go on at this stage, so let's get started on it. I also want you to look at those weapons too. Remember, they're hand-made, and I reckon they were probably made here. Check out who's got the capability to do something like that. I know it's another needle in a haystack, because they could have been made anywhere, not just here in Sydney. But when you've got bugger all to go on you have to follow up everything. If we can find out who made them, we may be able to get them to admit who they did it for."

Winding up the meeting, he said: "OK. Keep meeting people, get them talking. You never know what might come out. Let's meet again tomorrow."

He watched as they filed out of his office, then sat back and thought about what they'd told him. These guys have covered their tracks completely, he thought. The three young terrorists, all university graduates, clearly pretty smart. It makes sense that once they were radicalised there's a good chance they'd be able to be educated as to how to behave, and have the discipline to stick to it. These guys are really good, better than anyone I've come up against before, he concluded, and that really scares me.

Jason had been chasing after Muslim terrorists, one way or another, for much of his career, which was now over twenty years.

He graduated in law from the University of Western Australia, then joined the Federal public service and was posted to Canberra, in the Department of Foreign Affairs. After a few years based in Australia he was posted to Malaysia, working with the area of the High Commission that was concerned with the gathering of information, particularly about security issues. He was essentially a spy, but of course he had a very innocuous title, and had to be quite inventive in describing what he did at the Commission at cocktail parties. He was then moved across to the Australian Federal Police, and was posted to Jakarta, where he was involved in the investigation following the Bali Bombing, in which 88 Australians had been killed. This was his first taste of real terrorism, and he gained a little familiarity with the mind-set that can rationalise such horrific acts. He was then posted to Manila, and worked in conjunction with Philippine counterparts in various pursuits of Abu Sayyaf terrorists in the southern regions of the country. By the end of this posting his education about the violence some men are prepared to inflict on others was complete. When he was posted back to Australia he was determined he'd do everything he could to make sure major terrorism would never reach its shores. And now this.

*

Shortly after lunch on that same day, he received a phone call from the Premier.

"Jason, I've got us an expert who I think fits the bill the PM was talking about. He's been briefed, sworn to secrecy, the whole works, and he knows that he has to be available whenever we call on him, for meetings, advice over the phone, whatever. I've told him about you, and that you'll be calling him very soon."

"OK. Who is he?"

"I've just e-mailed you his name and contact details. I'm sure you'll have seen him on TV. Professor David Scott, from the University of Sydney. He's spent most of his career studying Muslim populations, mainly in Malaysia and Indonesia, but around the world as well. He's fairly young, in his early-40's, bit of a glamour boy, but seriously smart, and knows this field really well. Now, one thing you need to know, and be sensitive about. His mother was in the Opera House, and was killed."

"Jesus" breathed Jason, "that's terrible. Are you sure this isn't asking a bit much, to do this in those circumstances?"

"I know, it's a real imposition. But this is an exceptional situation. I believe he's brilliant, and is going to be more focused on this event than almost anyone you can think of. I know it's a bit awful to be taking advantage of that but it's like wartime, everyone has to do whatever it takes. I've got a feeling he could end up being very helpful."

"OK, fair enough. No worries. I'll call him. Thanks, see you next meeting."

He hung up, and checked his In-Box. Sure enough, there was an e-mail from Amelia Petkovic. Bloody hell, I can do without having to baby-sit some glamour-boy academic, particularly one who's going to be grieving over his mother. I don't know that this is a good idea. But, orders are orders. He dialed the mobile number it contained, and after a few rings there was an answer.

"Yes, this is David Scott."

"Hello, this is Jason Blake, from the Australian Federal Police. I believe the Premier's office has been in touch with you, and that you'd be expecting a call from me?"

"That's right. We're supposed to meet?"

"Yes, and I know this is an imposition, but it has to be very soon."

"I understand. Shall I come to your office?"

"Great. Say at 10.00am tomorrow?"

Next morning David was seated in Jason's office, with a cup of coffee in front of him, the initial introductions having taken place, and the expressions of sympathy regarding the death of David's mother. He described to David the setting up of the Cabinet of National Security by the Prime Minister, and that the PM had requested an expert on Islamic politics to join one of the next meetings. He also gave David a brief run-down of his credentials to be leading the investigation into the atrocity.

"What exactly are they after from me?" asked David.

"Well, I guess some of us know a little bit about Islam and it's politics, and the Muslim community here, but we don't know that much, and some of them know next to nothing. So, we're flying a bit blind, and we'd like a better idea what's going on, what we're up against. He doesn't want an Islamic scholar, but rather someone more neutral who understands the politics. He doesn't want anything held back, no political correctness, no worrying about offending anyone – this is too serious."

"Tell me about it" David said sadly. "OK. I'll help as much as I can. But I've got to tell you, I might be considered an 'expert', and I suppose it's true to an extent, but that's really about the big picture stuff, the history, the politics. I don't really know a lot about how Muslims actually live day-to-day, how their mind-set may be a bit different to ours - I'm not what they call 'an Islamic scholar'". By 'ours' I mean those of us brought up in a largely Christian, Western environment, which by the way is everyone in that Cabinet Group you've described. Also, I know a little but not a lot about what's going on in the Muslim communities here, how they're settling in, the problems they're having, things like that. I should probably know more, but I'm afraid I don't. No point kidding you. Pretty quickly we're going to have to get some input from people in the Muslim community."

"I agree, and that will happen. But right now that group needs a crash course in this stuff, and you're miles ahead of all of us. As far as the Muslim community goes, my people are speaking to lots of them right now, although what they're covering is fairly superficial, you know, who did the three terrorists mix with, any changes in their behaviour, and so on. I'm going to see if I can identify some community leaders we can speak to, not the religious types, not yet anyway, maybe senior business people who've clearly settled in well, but are still very involved with their communities. That's how investigation works – you meet lots of people, they put you onto others who they think can help, and generally you slowly start getting somewhere."

"By the way" Jason added, "there's two aspects to what's going on here. I'm obviously focused on finding the people who did this and stopping them doing it again. That's a crime investigation, and clearly that's the top priority of the Cabinet Group. But the PM also wants to try and understand what the underlying issues are here that could result in home-grown boys being willing to kill large numbers of their fellow-Australians. That's the area he thinks you can be most helpful."

"That's the million-dollar question" David replied, "not just here, but all over the world. I'll try and help, but it's a tough one, and there's going to be a lot of feathers ruffled."

He added bitterly: "Speaking for me, after what's happened, I actually don't give a stuff how many feathers I ruffle. And I'll help in any way I can in the short-term investigation part. I really want to see the guys behind this put away, permanently, and I don't mean in jail."

"I understand, and so do I." Jason stood up, and held out his hand. "OK. Thanks for agreeing to help. I might get in touch now and then to bounce ideas off you – I'm sure we'll work well together."

"Of course, anytime. I'd be pleased to help. And good luck with the investigation. I'll see you on Thursday at the PM's office."

After David left, Jason thought: He's not quite what I envisaged, a bit more down-to-earth. Seems to be handling his mother's death pretty well – must be fairly resilient. Let's see how we get on.

*

Later that evening Dina came around to David's apartment. After giving him a perfunctory kiss, she removed her jacket, threw it over the back of a chair and flopped down on the sofa, with a dark look on her face. David, who was not feeling in the brightest of moods himself, sat down beside her, and asked: "So, how was your day?"

She turned and looked at him, and eventually burst out: "I've had a shit of a day. I suppose I shouldn't be surprised, but I wasn't expecting it."

"Why? What happened?"

"At school. I was in the Common Room at lunch time, and two of the other teachers started getting in to me about what's happened, asking me why so many Muslims are violent. They actually asked me whether many of the people I knew would have secretly sympathised with those three terrorists. They were probably wondering whether I did. By 'people' they meant Muslims – they probably assume I don't mix with anyone else. I can't believe they could talk to me like that – I've been with them almost every working day for nearly six months, and I thought they accepted me just like any other Aussie. But I think I've been deluding myself."

"Come on Dina, don't be like that. Not everyone thinks like them – they're just a bit ignorant. And they're probably pretty upset, and scared, like most people will be."

"So, does that excuse them from jumping to the conclusion that all Muslims are the same, that we're all violent? They probably think that we secretly hate all you white people."

"I'm sure they don't. They probably don't know any other Muslims so you're the only one they can ask about things like this. If they didn't like you they'd probably never ask you."

She snorted in derision, but didn't answer. After a moment she turned and looked at him closely: "Honestly, I wouldn't blame you if you felt a bit like that, after what's happened to your mother, but you've got good reason. But do you? Do you feel angry at all of us?"

He looked at her, and saw that her lip was trembling, and he quickly reached for her and held her. "Of course I don't. I'd never feel that way about you. But I am angry, but only with the bastards who are behind this. I know they're only a tiny group. OK?"

"OK". She snuggled up to him, and was quiet, her outburst over. He was also quiet, thinking about what she'd said, and wondering whether deep in his heart he really believed what he'd said in reply to her. Was it really only a tiny minority, or was it a lot more pervasive? Maybe there were only a few who would ever become terrorists, but maybe there was a widespread climate of distrust of non-Muslims that nurtured those few. One thing was for sure, and that was he wanted to find out, and his role in the PM's Cabinet Group would give him a chance to do so.

Chapter 4

It was a blustery autumn morning as Farrah Haris made her way down Denison Street in North Sydney, hurrying because she was in danger of being late for work at one of the many coffee shops that catered for the large population of commuting office workers. The wind whipped her long dress around her legs and caused her veil, which she wore loosely around her tied back hair, to continually slip back, so that she was constantly having to put it back in place. It was early and there were few people on the streets, particularly a small side street like this one, but about thirty metres ahead of her she noticed two men leaning against the wall of the rear of what appeared to be an abandoned shop lot. They were quite young, white, stubbly faces, very short hair, wearing jeans and short coats with hoods hanging at the back. Apprehensive, she quickened her pace, hoping to pass them quickly, but her heart jumped when they casually moved forward and blocked the pavement.

"What's the hurry, lady?" one of them asked.

"I'm late for work. Please let me pass."

"Going to your halal shop, are you? Can we come and buy some pork?" the same one asked, and they laughed. The other one continued: "Why are you wearing that stupid veil?" He stepped closer and looked her up and down. "I think I could go for you if you let that hair down. And that long dress – why not show off that pretty body of yours? Maybe you're saving it for your terrorist boyfriend."

"Just leave me alone, and let me go" she said, as she tried to press pass them. Instead, they moved towards her, preventing her from moving forward, and then manoeuvred her back towards the wall. Now, becoming genuinely frightened, she raised her voice: "I don't know any terrorists. I just want to go to work. Please leave me alone."

"Come on. Don't give us that. You all hate us. Why did you come here in the first place? Why don't you go back where you came from, and you can blow up all the people you want?"

"I was born here" she screamed at them. "I'm as much an Australian as you are. Why do you think we all want to blow people up? Just because of a few crazy guys?"

"If you're so Australian, why do you wear that stupid thing?" one of them asked, and then leaned forward and ripped the veil from her head. Shocked, she screamed, and burst away from them, and started to run, praying they wouldn't pursue her. To her enormous relief they didn't, contenting themselves with yelling 'Muslim bitch' after her. She kept running, until she reached her workplace, in tears, hurrying past the few customers who were already enjoying their morning 'heart starter', and into the rear of the shop and out of sight. One of her workmates rushed after her, and asked "Farrah, what's wrong, what's happened?" Between sobs she explained, and cried: "Is this how it's going to be now? Is everyone going to think all Muslims are terrorists at heart?"

Her workmate, Jane, a non-Muslim, leaned forward and hugged her: "No, they're not. Those guys were stupid, ignorant idiots. Not everyone's like that."

Farrah looked at her, tears still on her face: "Maybe not everyone, but I think a lot. There's been plenty of stuff before, but it was just annoying, not scary like this. Now, after the Opera House, I'm really afraid of what could happen."

Jane just hugged her again, but said nothing. Deep down she thought Farrah could well be right. She worked with her and knew she didn't have a mean bone in her body, but even so she was angry and resentful about what had happened at the Opera House, and couldn't help but feel there had to be something wrong with the Muslim community for such a thing to happen. If she felt like that, what about all those who didn't know people like Farrah, and just relied on what they read in the media, or what they saw on TV? Things could get really nasty. After pursuing that thought for a few moments she decided she didn't want to go too far down that track, so stepped back and said:

"Let's try and forget what happened. We'd better go, customers are probably waiting. Are you OK?"

Farrah smiled weakly and nodded. Jane started to walk towards the front of the shop but stopped and turned to Farrah, and said with a smile: "By the way, your hair looks great – I've never seen it all before."

*

David was in his office at the university, but had the TV on, one of his ways of keeping up with the latest developments in his field of interest. At the moment, of course, the news was all about the Opera House atrocity. He flicked between the channels, searching for something interesting. The ABC morning programme reported there had been a spate of incidents of Muslims, mainly women wearing veils, being accosted and abused. Some of these involved veils being ripped off, but other than that there were no reports of any serious violence. Most of the abuse was verbal, with Muslims interviewed describing people yelling at them to 'go back to where you came from', or various forms of insult involving the words 'Muslim' and 'terrorist'.

He turned on his radio and listened to one of the popular talk-back shows hosted by one of the more intelligent, although quite right-wing, 'shock-jocks'. The callers had a variety of agendas, although most involved negative comments about the Muslim community. A favourite was the suggestion that Muslim immigration should be curbed, or even stopped completely.

"Don't you think that's a little extreme?" asked the host of one of the callers, who had made that suggestion.

"No, I don't. We've had thousands of immigrants come to Australia over the years, and they've all settled in fairly quickly. Look at the Italians, Greeks, Vietnamese, Chinese, Indians. By the second generation they were dinkum Aussies and were never any more trouble than the rest of us are. But this lot are different. They don't want to settle in. They want to ban Christmas and get us to shut our swimming pools so their women can swim by themselves. Who do they think they are? No, I say only let people in who want to be Australians, and not just have their own little bit of their home country here."

"But what about refugees, don't you feel sorry for them?" the host asked another caller.

"Of course I do. But there's lots of refugees around the world. They don't have to be Muslims." was the reply. "The risk is too great. Some of them want to do us harm, and the others are just difficult."

One caller suggested that the government should deport all Muslims, like Donald Trump had talked about doing in the US. The host took a responsible stance and replied: "Actually, I don't think the President said to deport them – I think he just talked about stopping or slowing immigration. But do you realize that there are over 600,000 Muslims in Australia, and some of them have been here for generations? Can you imagine the difficulty of doing that, and the uproar internationally? And where could we deport them to?"

"Well, it's better than being blown up or shot" replied the caller aggressively. "See what the families of the people killed in the Opera House think."

A little to David's surprise, one caller suggested that it was completely unfair to generalise about the whole Muslim community on the basis of what a small number of people had done, and that overwhelmingly most Muslims just wanted to have a decent life, free from the poverty and danger that some of them had left in their home countries. But few of the callers shared that view.

Eventually David turned off both the radio and the TV, leant back in his chair and sorted through the various thoughts that came into his mind about this whole dreadful event and the issues around it. For starters he was devastated that he'd lost his mother, when she was still relatively young and healthy and great fun to be around. It was made worse by the fact that she played a major role in his life – they met at least once a week, and she was more frequently on the phone with him. He felt a surge of rage when he thought about the pitiless and brutal way she'd died, and all those others as well, and swore to himself that he'd live to see the day when the people behind the atrocity were made to pay, hopefully with their lives. He calmed himself down a little, and then thought about the conversations he'd just seen and listened to, and probed his own feelings about Muslims – did he blame them all because they were in some way complicit? Surely that would be unreasonable, surely it was only a tiny few who were to blame. But how could those three young men get so easily radicalised? There must be something going wrong somehow in the wider community, that creates some sort of climate where people are susceptible to that sort of thinking. David knew from his academic studies that uneducated and poor Muslims in many Muslim-majority countries were in fact extremely susceptible to unscrupulous people who invoked Islam to provoke offence and outrage, which often resulted in mass murder. But these three weren't poor and certainly weren't uneducated. But he also knew that many Islamists in many countries were in fact well educated, generally from some sort of science discipline. So, what the hell is going on, he asked himself.

Almost reluctantly, he began to think about Dina. How did he feel about her? She couldn't possibly be complicit in this. But did she, deep down, have some of the same resentments he knew - or rather, to be truthful to himself, he'd read - that many Muslims, even Westernised Muslims, had about the actions of the West against Muslims, not only in colonial days but currently, with the invasions of Afghanistan and Iraq, and the ongoing support of

Israel? But that's fair enough, he thought. He was very public in his condemnation of the Iraq invasion, in particular – in his view it was possibly the greatest foreign policy blunder the US had ever committed, and he said so. But disapproval of Western actions is one thing – secretly approving of people who retaliate against Western targets is something else altogether. But he couldn't believe Dina would be guilty of that, even sub-consciously – she was too gentle by nature, and smart enough to think through the nuances involved in what was a very complex issue. No, he concluded, Dina is totally innocent, and he wasn't going to let this mess up their relationship. An image of his mother flashed into his mind, and again he felt a surge of rage – Dina's OK but the jury's out on the rest of them.

*

Meanwhile Jason had been busy, working the phone to track down some senior people in business who were Muslims and active in some way or the other in work for their own community (that is, from the same country of origin as them), or for the wider Muslim community. He'd been assured that these people, mostly men, were very sensible, responsible citizens who would be as helpful as possible, and he wanted to pursue every avenue to get help on what was an extremely difficult investigation. Enjoying getting out of the office into the sunshine, he'd driven to meet the first and most highly recommended, Fariq Hashim, over coffee. He was the MD of his own importing business, and the coffee shop was nearby to Fariq's office in Crow's Nest, one of the smart commercial suburbs of Sydney's lower north shore.

As he walked in a man seated at the side of the room stood up and smiled at him: "Mr Blake?" he said enquiringly. Jason took his proffered hand, confirmed he was indeed Jason Blake, and sat down. Fariq was tall and lean, a full head of silver hair, moustache, and strong features – a cliché desert Arab. Jason was relieved to see that he was dressed in a very conventional business suit, which nowadays was a sign of an old-time conservative, although he guessed Fariq was only about 50. He looks like Omar Sharif, the film star, he thought. Lucky bugger. Jason was a big man, strongly built, and clearly very fit, but he was no film star, with a tough, slightly forbidding face. Most people were a little wary when they first met him, as he was short on words and could even appear a little abrupt. But in fact, he was a kind man, with a quiet, wicked sense of humour, both qualities which eventually showed themselves when people got to know him well.

"It's very good of you to see me, Mr Fariq" he began, "and at such short notice."

Fariq smiled and replied: "These are special times, Jason, and troubling ones, I'm afraid. You're from the Australian Federal Police, I understand. Should I be nervous?"

"Of course not" laughed Jason. "I'm here to seek your help."

"That's a relief. How can I do so?"

"Well, I'm leading the investigation to track down the people behind the three killers. My colleagues are interviewing all sorts of people, from the mosque they went to, their families, friends, and so on. But I want to get a better understanding of the Muslim community generally, to try and get a feel for how this sort of thing can happen, you know, three young men born and raised here obviously totally radicalised. I thought that people like you, leaders of your communities, would have insights about it." He paused for a moment, then said: "I also figured you'd be as keen to sort this out as I am – I'm afraid this is going to cause a lot of grief for Muslims here. I know it's unfair, but it's bound to happen."

"It is happening, already. Just watch the TV news or listen to the radio – the backlash is starting, and I agree with you – I'm very fearful about what's going to happen. So, I'll help you any way I can. And there are others, like me, who I'm sure will also help. Perhaps I should first explain my background, but before I do let me clarify something about the 'Muslim community', as everyone refers to it. Actually, there's no such thing – there are lots of Muslim communities, that essentially are people who come from the same country, or even the same region. I'm from the biggest one, the Lebanese. I came from Lebanon when I was in my 20's, although I'm a Palestinian by background. I was lucky. I'd had an education, and my parents had a bit of money, so I was able to start a business here, and do OK. So now I'm an Australian citizen, I've got kids at university, all very normal. But, I'm a practicing Muslim, I go to the mosque pretty regularly, say my prayers, all that sort of thing. You'll find most of us are like that – there's not many Muslims who aren't pretty religious – it's part of being a Muslim."

He paused for a moment, so Jason asked: "What's your take on what happened? Do you think there are many out there who are anti-West, anti-Australians - I mean non-Muslim ones?"

"Unfortunately, there are some, I don't think all that many, but they're certainly there. Mostly they sound off about all the terrible things they think the West has done, and that Australia is part of the West, and that Muslims should stay away from them, comments like that. They complain about the attitude Australians have to Muslims, how racist they are, you know the sort of thing. But I haven't come across any that actually suggest violence."

"You seem to be, if you don't mind me saying it, very moderate in the Islamic sense." Jason stopped for a moment, and asked: "Is it OK to say that, or does that imply that I think lots of Muslims are mad fundamentalists?"

Fariq laughed: "It sort of does, but I know what you mean, so don't worry. Yes, I'm what you'd call moderate, in the sense that I think religion is a private matter, and I don't try and impose my beliefs on anyone else. And I think there are many paths to God, not only Islam."

"Are you suggesting there are many out there who don't think like you?"

"Well, I think you'll find that many Muslims believe Islam really is the only true religion, and that the rest of you are on the wrong path – a bit like Catholics used to be – I understand they've wised up a bit nowadays. A lot of Muslims believe the Qur'an must be taken literally, and can't be contextualized, and that can cause problems sometimes, especially when the fundamentalists start invoking Islam and saying that people should do this or do that or they're not good Muslims. But generally, this is all pretty harmless. But there are a few who practice some pretty extreme versions of Islam. Do you know about Wahhabism?"

"That's what they practice in Saudi Arabia, isn't it?"

"Yes, it is. And it's very extreme. You may be surprised that there are Wahhabists here in Australia, and that it's on the curriculum of some of the Islamic schools here."

"I did actually know that, and I've always found it a bit disturbing. Do you think the people behind the terrorists could have come from this group that practice extreme versions of Islam?"

"Well, they came from somewhere, but I must say I never thought any of these people would actually go that far, certainly the ones that I've met. They seem more like 'all talk and no action' to me. But I will say this: young people who have lots of exposure to people sprouting all this rubbish could be more susceptible to someone getting inside their heads and radicalising them. So maybe in that sense these people are potentially dangerous."

Jason considered that, then commented: "Well, we've had enough young men go off to fight for Islamic State in Iraq and Syria, that what you say has to be true. And if you recall, a couple of them over there have called on Muslims in Australia to carry out acts of terrorism, here."

He paused again, then looked at Fariq, and asked: "I've heard and read some people say that there's a fundamental problem with the religion of Islam that makes it susceptible to violence. Do you think there's any truth at all to that? I know that's a pretty heavy question to ask a Muslim, so I hope you're not offended, but I'd really like to know what you think."

"Unfortunately, it's probably a fair question, when you look at what's going on around the world, not just this incident. I don't think I'm really qualified enough to properly answer you – I do know it's an incredibly complex issue. Muslims seem too often to be prone to get all fired up about their religion or their politics and doing crazy things. But I can't pinpoint exactly what causes them to behave like that – you'll need to talk to an expert and maybe they might have a better idea."

"It's very interesting you think that, and I'm grateful you were willing to share it with me. Tell me, do you think there are many people who think in a similar way to you?"

"I'm not sure" said Fariq, "but I suspect some of the businesspeople I mix with might. I've spoken to a few of the in the last few days, and they're extremely concerned about what's happened. Some of them have said that 'something has to be done', but what that something is no-one seems to know."

Jason thought for a moment, then said: "I've just had an idea. Do you think you could get a group of your friends together, people you think have the same sort of thoughts you have, to meet with me and another chap, an expert, who's helping look at this whole question?"

"I probably could. What sort of timing are you thinking about?"

"Probably in the next week or so. Would that be possible?"

"I could try. Probably."

"That would be great. Thank you. I'd better go, lots to do, as you can imagine. I really appreciate how frank you've been with me. I'll give you a call in a few days and see how you're going with getting some people together, and we'll arrange a meeting."

As Jason walked to his car he felt very encouraged about the meeting. In truth, he knew much of what Fariq had told him – he wouldn't be much of a senior AFP person with the experience he'd had if he didn't – but he was surprised at how frank he'd been, and how helpful. And maybe the group Fariq was going to put together could be open to the idea of having a hard look at their religion, and how it affected their communities? Now that would be something. Even the great David Scott would be impressed with that, he thought, with some satisfaction.

*

Later that evening David met Dina at the Royal Sydney Golf Club, where he was a member, for a squash game. After getting into their squash gear in their respective change rooms, they met on the court. David looked admiringly at the very short, pleated skirt Dina was wearing.

"What are you looking at?" she asked him teasingly.

"You know very well. It's just one of your tricks to distract me. You'll do anything to beat me, won't you?"

"Hah. I don't need to distract you – sheer ability is all I need."

They had a strenuous, hard-fought game. David was strong and fit but squash was not his first sport and Dina was an exceptionally good player, so she did in fact manage to beat him, but only just, to her obvious enjoyment.

"Told you" she said. "Brains beats brawn every time. Let's shower and have a drink upstairs."

Half an hour later, after David had showered at leisure and wandered slowly upstairs, but still having had to wait the usual ten minutes while Dina completed her beautifying, she joined him at a table directly overlooking the eighteenth hole. David loved that view, with the elevated green directly in front of the clubhouse, and the fairway sloping away down the hill, the scene of many a heart-stopping finish to a major event involving some of the top players in the world. A few years earlier he'd watched Rory McIlroy pip Adam Scott by one stroke, thanks to Adam overshooting the green with his approach and bogeying the hole, much to the largely Australian crowd's disappointment.

"So, what's been going on with you today?" Dina asked, after their drinks had arrived.

"I've just been at work, a couple of lectures, usual stuff. I didn't tell you last night because you were upset but I've been asked to join Prime Minister's Cabinet of National Security, which is meeting regularly to look into the Opera House attack. They apparently want me to brief them about Islamic matters because none of them know much at all and they want to make sure they know the basics."

"Wow. That's quite an honour. Who else is on it?"

David ran through the list and mentioned how he'd met Jason, who was also one of the group and in charge of the criminal investigation.

"But how do you feel about being that involved after what happened to your mother? Are you sure it's not a bit close to home, that it might be upsetting going through all that?"

"No, I'm fine. It's a way that I can try and do something, try and find those bastards who did this. Also, to see if there's any way of getting to the bottom of how this happened in the first place and stop it happening again."

Dina thought about that for a moment then said, smiling as she did so but with a slight edge in her voice: "So they've called on a white non-Muslim man to advise a bunch of white non-Muslim men about Islam, and the Muslim communities?"

"Well, they've got to start somewhere, and I guess they feel more comfortable with me – they don't want to offend anyone with embarrassing questions" he answered, a little defensively.

"Maybe they think a Muslim couldn't be Australian enough, that they can't talk openly in front of one. Perhaps he could be a closet terrorist." she said, still smiling, but with more than a little sarcasm. She saw his face tighten and said: "Don't worry – I'm only teasing. It's great they've asked you. But what sort of things do you think they want to know?"

"Jason told me they're tackling two things. First, they want to catch the guys behind the terrorists. But they also want to understand what's going on in the Muslim communities that could result in three local young blokes doing something like this, and what can be done to prevent it happening again, not just immediately, but long-term. I don't think I can help much with the first one, but maybe I can start thinking about the second."

"You've been studying political Islam for a long time now, and you are at least a little bit clever - you must have some thoughts about it already?"

David paused for quite a few moments, and then replied: "You know, I don't think I want to go into that right now. It's very sensitive, and I'm not comfortable with talking about it to a Muslim, even you. I know you have beliefs that I don't, and some of the things I might end up saying you won't like. Let's just leave it, at least for a while."

"But you're going to say what you think to those others. What's so sensitive? Are you going to start interfering in the way we practice our religion? No-one, here at least, interferes with any other religion."

"Maybe because they haven't had members of their religion killing people in the name of God" he snapped, but immediately added: "I'm sorry. I shouldn't have said that. Look, I don't know exactly what's going to come out of this group, on this longer-term stuff, but hopefully I can keep it sensible. There are people out there saying the government should do some extreme things, like stopping all Muslim immigration, and closing Islamic schools, things like that. I don't think the PM would go for that sort of thing – he's no Donald Trump."

Dina didn't look pleased, but she chose to stay silent. Inside she was angry, but at the same time she conceded that David had every right to be very upset, and it wasn't entirely unreasonable for him to be thinking negatively about Muslims. And there was no getting away from the fact, no matter how much Muslim spokespeople denied it, that a huge proportion of terrorism was carried out by Muslims, often invoking Islam. But still, she was a Muslim.

She finally said: "David, I'm going to say something you mightn't like, either. You've got every reason to be upset, but you're now going to be in a really influential position, with the Prime Minister and those other Ministers listening to you. Please be objective about what you say and recommend. You'll probably be upset that I could even say that to you, but you wouldn't be human if you didn't have your mother in the back of your mind."

David was annoyed, but he was old enough to have learned to have a quick mind and a slow mouth, certainly with important matters. And Dina was very important. He took a deep breath and said: "It's a fair comment, and I promise I'll remember to do that. When I'm clear in my mind I'll bounce it off you before I suggest anything to the PM. But if you can't convince me I'm wrong then I'll still do it. OK?"

She thought about it, still not entirely happy, but she wanted to make peace, so said: "OK, that's reasonable. Now, enough of all this serious stuff. Let's go to your place, have dinner and watch a movie. And if you really behave yourself, I'll stay the night."

"You sure know how to make an offer I can't refuse. Let's go."

*

Iraq: 2003 - 2007

The Iraqi watched while his country collapsed around him. The economy was in tatters, and society was rapidly unravelling. The

US-installed governor made the fatal mistake of disbanding the Iraqi army and police, acting on the premise that they'd served under Saddam so couldn't be trusted. He thus unleashed thousands of bitter, unemployed men who had military training, were armed, and hated the invaders. They were quickly recruited by various 'warlords' commanding militias who began fighting over the spoils which are always available when a country descends into chaos, the spoils being both power and money, with the latter being guaranteed by possession of the former. The Shia sect of Islam was the majority community of Iraq, but Saddam was a Ba'ath, a minority group that was more Sunni than Shia. Now the Shias were determined to redress this situation, and the Sunnis equally determined to try and preserve the status quo. The conflict was bloodthirsty - it was an almost everyday occurrence that the lifeless body of a member of one sect would be found, with signs of terrible torture. As well as fighting each other, the militias had a common enemy, the Western invaders, who found it increasingly difficult to maintain control. The result of these various conflicts was that the fabric of Iraqi society broke down, and people were reduced to a struggle to survive.

When he finally emerged from the hospital, he quickly concluded that it was well-nigh impossible to recreate his previous life and he had little motivation to do so. His heartbreak over the deaths of his wife and children would never leave him, and the initial rage continued smoldering, never waning, continuing to feed his cold determination to get his revenge on those he saw as their killers. He was quickly identified by one of the militia groups who were proliferating in the chaos as an intelligent and educated man with a huge axe to grind, a man who was not interested in making money but rather on carrying out his private vendetta, the aims of which reflected their own. Because they were the Jaysh Altahrir al'Islamii, an offshoot of al-Qaeda, but acting independently of the original group. Their aim was to take the fight against the West to the West, the strategy preached by Osama bin Laden, and the chaos into which Iraq was descending was heaven-sent. As well as the immediate opportunity to kill Americans and their allies, it provided them (and other such groups) with a huge supply of recruits to their bigger cause, men whose lives had suddenly been upended. They took him under their wing and trained him over the next few months in various aspects of combat, including the use of automatic weapons and the making of explosives.

For the next one and a half years he conducted many operations directed against American and allied soldiers. He refused to attack fellow-Iraqis, and his handlers were happy to allow him to focus his efforts against their main enemy. They watched with great interest as he showed an outstanding ability to plan increasingly sophisticated attacks and carry them out effectively - and particularly, an ability to survive. Eventually they decided that he was suited for bigger things and approached him with the idea of leaving Iraq and taking the fight to the enemy, in one of their home countries. He agreed, but he was advised that to increase his chances of being accepted for immigration he should appear to resume his old profession, and start an engineering business, using his real name. With their help he did so, and again with their help behind the scenes the business grew rapidly, so that he was able to employ a manager to run the business day-to-day, leaving him the free time to continue with his terrorist activities. That he managed to do this without detection was a tribute to his outstanding ability to plan meticulously, execute with great efficiency, and lead a double life.

After eighteen months, it was decided he had built up a sufficiently successful background that it was now time to apply for immigration to a new country. Given the choice of the US, the UK and Australia (because of his very good English) he chose the latter - he was particularly infuriated at how Australia faithfully followed the US on their various military adventures but appeared to never suffer any consequences. With further help and guidance from his Jaysh Altahrir al'Islamii superiors he applied for conventional immigration to Australia, citing his qualifications, his ability to bring sufficient funds to be able to start a small business, and desire to leave the chaos that was now Iraq. After three months he was granted approval, and a further few months later, in mid-2007, he was in a Qantas plane on the final leg of his journey to his new home, Sydney.

CHAPTER 5

'Muslims Claim They're Under Siege' blared the page one headline in the Sydney Telegraph. 'The President of United Muslims of NSW (the state representative body of the Australian Federation of Islamic Councils) hit out at extremist white Australians who are making life a misery for ordinary Muslims who just want to go about their affairs without being subject to abuse for the sins of a tiny group of fanatics. "Islam is a religion of peace, and we are a peaceful community. Yet we are all being branded as terrorists, and being abused in public, as though we are all responsible for what happened. And the biggest offenders in this abuse are white Australians, who are simply exposing themselves as bigots and racists."'' The article continued in this vein, with descriptions of incidents where Muslims had been accosted by individuals or groups in the street and on public transport, quotations from accusers blaming the Muslim community for nurturing terrorists in their midst, and quotations from Muslims defending themselves, often aggressively.

Jason sighed, and put the paper aside as he saw David enter the coffee shop where they had agreed to meet - the quaint Two Good Eggs Café, which was just down the street from Jason's office in the Sydney Headquarters of the AFP. He had suggested to David that they meet, both to satisfy the PM's request that they work together (he was privately concerned that this could slow him up in his pursuit of the terrorists), and to inform him about his meeting with Fariq. He also thought that he might as well get some value out of David's knowledge of political Islam. After the initial pleasantries, he ruefully observed: "Just been reading the

Telegraph. Predictable, depressing stuff. It'd be nice to have some people with some constructive things to say instead of all this blame game. But someone in my profession should know better, I guess."

"Well, you can't blame people for being very angry, and most Aussies know very little about Islam, just what they get on TV and in the papers. And that's mainly about wars, or suicide bombings, so they're fearful. I know lots about Islam, and *I'm* very angry. But I know I'm not very objective at the moment. I'm still struggling to believe that someone in my family could be killed, in Australia, by Muslim terrorists. That's something that happens somewhere else, on TV, not here."

"Of course, you're right. And you've got every justification to be very angry. It must be tough to put that aside, particularly given what you're being asked to do."

"It's OK. I know I've got to put it behind me, or I'm going to be no help to anyone. And I want to help try and fix this. And anyhow, what they want me to do is nothing compared to what you guys are up against. I imagine the people behind this must be really scary, and you've got to find them and tackle them. I wouldn't want to do that, that's for sure. I'm just a theory man, not an action man."

Jason smiled: "You never know what you can do until you have to, but you're right – theory's a lot safer."

There was silence for a little while, each lost in his thoughts, then Jason told him about Fariq, and was gratified to see that David was very impressed. "That should give you something to get your teeth into" he suggested (and keep you out of my hair, he thought to himself). He then went on: "In my job, when I was in South East Asia, I learned a little bit about Islam, and terrorism, but really I don't know much. I was hoping you could give me a bit of a fast-track education about what makes these terrorists tick, what we're up against if we want to stop something like this ever happening again."

"Are you sure? Once I start on this stuff I get into lecturer mode. Well, OK, but I hardly know where to begin. It's of course a really complex situation, and there are no perfect answers that explain everything, but I'll have a go."

David paused for a moment to collect his thoughts, and then began to speak. "I'll probably jump all over the place, but let's start by considering why terrorists do what they do – why do they want to kill so many people, sometimes other Muslims, their own people? I think there's a few reasons. A very obvious one is when they think of themselves as victims. Their lands were colonised by the terrible Westerners, which is why they're now in such a bad state, with poverty, illiteracy – it's not their fault, if they'd been left alone all would be well. And even though colonialism is over, the West still interferes in Muslims lands in one way or the other - you know, oil, invasions of Afghanistan and Iraq, and so on. So, this sort of terrorism is simple payback. 9/11 is the most dramatic example of this. The Opera House is perhaps another, at least that's what the terrorists are saying. I'm not sure I buy that, but let's leave it for the moment. So, this sort of terrorism is very directly aimed at the West, retaliation for our past sins. You'll get variations of this, like the Charlie Hedbo massacre. That was in retaliation for the cartoons which they said insulted the Prophet Muhammad, but it was Westerners that did it, so in a sense is just more punishment for what they see as general Western antipathy towards Islam."

"What about the Lindt Café incident?" Jason asked. "Was that about punishing the West, or was he just a mental case?"

"I think that's a bit more complicated, but let's come back to that one later. So, all those incidents, like the men who killed those people in London, on the bridge, the one who drove down the road in Nice and killed all those people, the stabbing here in Sydney by that young bloke, all of these are sort of punishments of the West, although the guys concerned are probably not really clear in their minds what they're doing. But they often invoke Islam when they're doing these things, so I guess in their minds it's a battle of Islam against the West. This is where it gets complicated, where they mix up religion with what are really politically inspired acts. Someone invades your country so you retaliate – what's that got to do with religion? But they make it so, and then people start thinking that it's Islam that's behind it all."

"Are you saying that Islam has nothing to do with it?" asked Jason.

"No, that's what makes this so difficult, because to an extent Islam is actually involved. But let's keep going, and I'll see whether we can draw it all together later and make sense out of it." He laughed ruefully: "Actually, I'm not sure I'll be able to. I don't think anyone has. Anyway, let's look at what goes on in Afghanistan, and Iraq, and Syria. There, you've got a situation where one group of Muslims is continually massacring other groups of Muslims, on a scale that makes what we've experienced in the West look like almost nothing, except for 9/11. The Tehrek-e-Taliban (that's the Pakistani Taliban) have killed hundreds of innocent Pakistanis and

Afghanis in single attacks, and what's that got to do with the West? The Islamic State essentially declared war on two Muslim-majority countries, again resulting in the massacre of thousands of fellow-Muslims. Again, what's that got to do with the West? Some people will say that we started it, by invading Iraq in the first place, and so created the conditions that allowed the Islamic State to thrive. That may be true, but it doesn't explain their actions, why they killed so many other Muslims, as well as others of course, the Yazidis, Christians and so on. This is where Islam does actually come into it. ISIS believe in a very extreme and conservative version of Islam, where anybody, Muslim or not, who doesn't agree with that version is a heretic, and deserves to die. Is this Islam's fault, or is it just politics using religion to justify a war to set up their 'Islamic State', and expand it as far as they possibly can? It's probably similar to the Christians in the Middle Ages using religion to justify the Crusades."

He paused again to think about how to take his 'lesson' forward. "The Taliban in Afghanistan are another story. The Americans booted them out of power after 9/11, so they've got plenty of reasons to hate them, but I don't think that explains all the massacres they've been guilty of since. They'll say it's all about getting the foreign invaders out of their lands, because we're still there, albeit in quite small numbers. But nearly all the killings are aimed at their own people. At times they'll look like they're upholding their religion when they attack people. Like that case in Pakistan, when the Pakistani Taliban shot Malala, because they said females shouldn't be educated, it's not Islamic. But most of their attacks are really aimed at the government, you know, the army, the police, so I think what they're really trying to do is destabilise the country to such an extent that they can take power again."

"I see that" said Jason, "but what about here, in Sydney?"

"Well, as I said, it's perhaps a bit about payback, because Australia has supported the Americans in all their wars in Muslim lands. Remember Osama bin Laden warning Australia about being involved, how'd we'd be made to pay? And of course, that's what the group said immediately after the bombing. But I think there could be another reason, and that's the destabilisation thing. It's possible that they're really trying to set the rest of the Australian communities against the Muslims here, so that they'll withdraw into themselves, and unite in defence. It's like what the Telegraph said this morning, that they're claiming they're under siege. So, a classic defence is to become more Islamic, in a sort of defiance, as well as a way of uniting communities that really are quite different culturally. You know, the Muslims from the Middle East are not the same as those from Southeast Asia, or from Africa. But they're all Muslims, even though the different sects in another environment could actually be at each other's throats. That's why wearing a veil is such a big issue – it defines their Islamicness. Muslim women are often used to be the front-line in these situations."

"Do you really think that's possible, here in Australia? It's hard to believe that all those Muslims who've been going about their business could get sucked in to something like this. Surely it's only a tiny percentage of the population who could think like this?"

"Well, hopefully it is actually impossible. But don't forget those three young men that did this were Australian born and raised, and from what we've been able to find out were perfectly normal, well-educated and in decent jobs. You'd think it'd be impossible for them to be so brainwashed that they could not only give up their own lives but take so many innocent people with them. Yet they did. So, I don't know, anything's possible. If they were trying to isolate the Muslim community and get everyone else opposed to them, they're off to a good start. But maybe that's not it at all. But even if that wasn't their intention, there's a risk it could happen anyway."

David had a mouthful of his coffee, then looked at Jason and said: "What would really scare the shit out of me is if there were more incidents, because then I'd think that's what this is really all about. And then we've got a real problem. What we've seen so far would be nothing compared to what could happen if the population became seriously scared. I'm sure you'd appreciate that better than me."

"I certainly do. It's one thing to chase after a few criminals, because once we've got them everyone can relax, but if you get communities at each other's throats then we're into a whole different ball game, a lot harder to tamp down." There was a pause for a few moments while both thought about the consequences of what they'd been discussing, then Jason asked: "You said a bit earlier you'd come back to the issue of Islam's role in all this – can you say something about that?"

"Ah well, now we come to the really hard stuff. There are lots of debates about whether there's something about Islam that results in all this violence. Some people wade through the Qur'an and quote statistics about how many times violence is exhorted and rest their case. But of course, you could say the same things about the Christian Bible. And then you get all that business about how

'Islam is a religion of peace', immediately after some terrorists have slaughtered a stack of people while yelling about how great Allah is. So, it's all very mixed up. One of the most sensible quotes I've seen is from an ex-Islamist, Maajid Nawaz, who said, in this context, Islam is not a religion of war or of peace - it's a religion. What he means by that is that it's got its good points and bad points, like any religion, and can be used for good or bad."

David paused, and looked at Jason closely before deciding to go on with what he was about to say: "But now I've got to make a confession that I'm asking you to keep to yourself. Despite my being a so-called 'respectable academic', which means I should be objective, deep down I have real concerns about how so many people interpret and practice Islam. I think there's something going on that makes it particularly vulnerable to being exploited for violent purposes, which of course have an underlying political motive. Bad men invoke Islam and get impressionable people to go along with what they want them to do, because if they don't, they'll be a 'bad Muslim', and they hate that. Christianity has had its problems too, but nowadays you rarely see instances of Christianity invoked to justify violence. There's been some really interesting stuff written about this, about how Islam's history is so different from Christianity's, how right from the beginning religious, political and military issues were in the mix, and the implications of this.

"Having said that, one thing I'm convinced about, and always have been. People are pretty much the same everywhere, it doesn't matter what country, what race, what religion – ideally, they just want to live their lives in peace, bring up their kids to have a better life than they had, the usual things. They don't want to hurt anyone. But some are more impressionable and vulnerable than others – if they're very poor, have little education, or for some reason their lives are not turning out well – and then bad people can exploit them, and religion has always been a great way to influence people. And around the world, a lot of Muslim-majority countries are very poor, and the people are low in literacy. And so you get those lynching situations because someone accuses someone else of some insult to Islam - often complete rubbish - and gets a mob involved.

"The other thing about Islam, and I think this is really important, is that overwhelmingly Muslims believe in God, that the Qur'an is truly the Word of God, and that it has to be interpreted literally. So, in Muslim-majority countries, when someone quotes the Qur'an, even highly intelligent and educated Muslims are reluctant to say anything, and so people go along with it. That's a huge reason why there's a world-wide Islamic revival – people are too scared to speak up about it so it rolls on inevitably. I think until that situation changes – the bit about so many people believing the Qur'an has to be interpreted literally – Muslim communities will continue to have problems."

He paused, laughed a little self-consciously and said: "I really am lecturing, aren't I? But you asked, and that's what I really think. Not very politically correct, am I?"

"I'd love to see you appear on the TV talk shows and say all that, they'd tear you to bits. But even though I don't know anywhere as much as you about this, it make sense to me, all the bits and pieces I've picked up from reading and living in South East Asia. That stuff about people invoking Islam to get people to go along with them is very true – I've seen it in action in both Malaysia and

Indonesia. But last thing, the Lindt Café siege – what was that about, do you think?"

"Ah yes, I put you off earlier. Well, this has been debated a lot. At the time the police said it was a terrorist incident, but I think the general consensus now is that the guy was a mental health case, and it was a little bit political, and also just plain criminal. Not really Islamic terrorism."

Jason shifted his chair back and got to his feet: "Well, thanks for that. It's been very enlightening. I've got to head off for a meeting. I'll get the coffee – your fee. I'll let you know about the meeting with Fariq."

"OK, thanks. Probably see you next at the PM's office – we're meeting them all on Thursday, remember."

*

Jason dropped in briefly to his office to check on progress, but there was nothing of consequence to report. His people had interviewed more people from the Muslim communities who frequented the same mosque as the three terrorists, but they hadn't been able to shed any more light on who may have made contact with them. He then drove to his next meeting, which was with the President of The Muslim Association of NSW, Abdul Rashid, who had been quoted in the Sydney Telegraph article he'd been reading before he met David, and some other members of his organisation. He'd looked up the UMNSW's website, and noted that part of its role was to bridge the gap between Muslim communities and the wider Australian society and the Australian government. He'd also done some research on Abdul Rashid and discovered that he'd gained some notoriety with public comments about women that were blatantly sexist. Also, that there were rumours (unsubstantiated) of corruption within his organisation, with Abdul the person claimed to be most at fault. Jason wasn't sure what he could gain from such a meeting, but felt he was obliged to meet with people who held senior positions within the overall Muslim community, to try to enlist their help with his various investigations, and to see if they had any advice for him. Given what he'd found from his research his expectations weren't high.

His destination was a suburb about twenty kilometres south-west of central Sydney, mainly residential but with some commercial buildings, one of which housed the MANSW. With much to think about the journey went quickly, and before long he was seated in the Council's main meeting room, on one side of a large oval table, with Abdul Rashid and three others ranged on the other side of the table. I feel like I'm in an interview for a job, Jason thought to himself. Despite his inner misgivings he smiled, and opened up with:

"Thank you very much for meeting with me. I appreciate it, because I'm looking for all the help I can get."

"It is our pleasure. You have a tough job, and if we can help, we will. This is a terrible act that has been inflicted on the Muslim community."

On *your* community? What the hell is he talking about, Jason thought to himself. "I don't quite understand what you mean by that" he said. "I thought it was very clear that this massacre was aimed at the non-Muslim community."

"Come, Mr. Blake. That's what it may look like from where you sit, but who's going to end up being the most affected by this? The Muslim community. Look at what's happening. Muslims are being abused in the street, and this is only the beginning. Do you think that there won't be violence? It's just a matter of time. And there'll be calls for all sorts of discrimination against us – stopping immigration, stopping us building mosques, stopping us living our lives according to our religion and culture."

Bloody hell, Jason thought. Maybe David was right about the real motive of the terrorists, setting the rest of the Australian community against the Muslim community. Aloud, he said: "I wouldn't have immediately thought of that, but I see what you mean. So, particularly considering that point, what do you think the motivations of these men were? Do you really believe that it's about Australia's role in the wars in the Middle East and Afghanistan, like the terrorist group said?"

"Maybe, because certainly the West has a lot to answer for, and Australia has chosen to be squarely in the camp of the anti-Muslim forces." I'll let that go, thought Jason, as Abdul went on. "Maybe as well as killing lots of Australians, non-Muslims, they thought additional punishment is to set our communities against each other, which will cause long-term harm to the country."

"Do you have any ideas about how we could find who in Australia is behind this?" asked Jason.

Abdul Rashid looked around at his colleagues, who each slowly shook his head. "Not really. I'm afraid to say there are some Muslims here who are very anti the West, and also critical of

Australia, and some of them will say a lot of inflammatory things, but all of these are just loud-mouths who couldn't, and probably wouldn't, pull off something like this. But there'll be some who have those feelings but stay quiet – they're the ones to worry about. And I don't how you identify them."

"I see. That's not very comforting. Tell me, do you think there are many here who actually have some sympathy for what these men did, or stand for?"

"Yes, there are some, but I don't know how many. I don't think many people would condone the violence, even if they agree with the politics."

"On a different tack, are there many people who would like to be able to live under Shari'a law here, and not under normal Australian law?"

"Ah, that's a different matter. Yes, I think there are people who would think that, including me, and my friends here" Abdul Rashid said, gesturing around the table.

"But wouldn't that separate the Muslim community from the rest of Australia? Would you still think of yourselves as Australian?" Jason asked.

"We'd certainly be Australians, but just living in the way we've been brought up to live. Isn't that what multi-culturalism is all about?" Abdul Rashid answered, with a smile.

"I'm not sure about that" Jason answered, "but let's leave it there. Thank you again, and I'll hold you to your offer to help. If you think of anything, will you please contact me. And I hope I can meet you again if there's anything else I think of."

"Of course. We wish you well in your investigation."

As Jason walked out of the room and made his way back to his car, he had more questions in his mind than when he arrived. Are these blokes really with us, or against us? Are they representative of the whole Muslim community, or are they a small minority? Shari'a law – are they crazy? I wonder what Fariq and his friends would think of that? I'll have to find out. And I've got to meet more Muslims and see what they think. And how the hell are we going to track down the people behind this? With more than a little consternation he accelerated away and headed towards his office.

*

The sun was close to setting, casting long shadows through the trees in Garigal National Park, in the northern outskirts of Sydney. This is the most beautiful time of the day, Evelyn Myers thought, as she made her way down a path that led eventually back to the road where she'd parked her car forty minutes earlier. Twice a week she did this, taking almost exactly one hour to complete the round-trip from her car, around the oval-shaped walk and back again. Apart from the exercise, Evelyn found it a wonderful way to relax and unwind from a busy day's work at the primary school where she taught the first grade. She loved the children, but they could get pretty taxing sometimes, particularly in recent years when almost all young parents considered it barbaric to physically discipline their kids. And for a teacher to do so would have dire consequences. So Evelyn and her colleagues did their best, but regularly joked to each other that they should be eligible for sainthood. Evelyn laughed to herself as she thought about this and reminded herself that despite it all she loved her job, and now and then those incorrigible kids did or said something that made it all worthwhile.

A twig snapping behind her startled her out of her reverie and she turned to see what had caused it. It was a man, about forty metres back. She resumed walking but stepped up her pace slightly. After another fifty metres she rounded a corner and saw another man, stationery, about fifty metres ahead. She turned back for another look at the man behind her, and he was now only thirty metres away. Disturbed, but not yet panicking, she continued walking, but when she got close to the man in front he moved in to the centre of the path and blocked her way.

"What do you want?" she asked. "Let me through".

There was no answer, and she became conscious that the second man had now moved up and was immediately behind her.

"What do you want?" she asked again and couldn't keep the panic out of her voice.

Again, there was no answer. As both of them moved closer to her she noticed that they were fairly young, in their early-thirties, and looked as though they were of Middle Eastern origin. She also became aware that they were wearing rubber gloves. In terror now, she thought: My God, those are surgical gloves. What the hell? Then the man behind clapped one hand over her mouth, shutting off the scream that was forming in her throat, while his other arm wrapped around her upper body. The second man grabbed her two legs and the two of them lifted her and carried her off the path into the bushes, far enough that they could not be seen. Still holding her fast, they laid her down on the ground, and gagged her with a cotton scarf. Thoughts raced through her mind as to what was about to happen. Are they going to rape me? Will they kill me afterwards? Then the second man drew a long knife from beneath his coat, grabbed her by the hair, and with a flash of horrified insight Evelyn knew what was coming.

*

At 8.30 the following morning, the Prime Minister was sipping his tea, and wading online through the four newspapers he checked first thing every day – the Australian, the Sydney Telegraph, the New York Times and the Times of London. The local papers were still full of items about clashes between non-Muslim Australians and people they perceived as Muslims, and calls from right-wing spokespeople for all sorts of actions against Muslims, most of which, apart from being offensive and provocative, were illegal. Where are the voices of reason, he asked himself in frustration? I'm not hearing or seeing much of that. Don't these people understand how much they're playing with fire? But he knew he was being unreasonable in his expectations. Everyone's confused, and scared, and most people don't think all that logically anyway, so they say the first thing that comes to their mind, and don't think through the consequences.

The landline phone interrupted his thinking, and he picked it up. "Yes, what is it?"

"Sir, I've got Jason Blake from the AFP on the line. He says it's urgent."

"Sure, put him through."

"Hello Jason" he said. "How're things going?"

"Good morning sir. Not so good. I'm afraid I've got some bad news."

"I've just been reading the papers. Things are bad enough. What else have you got for me?"

"I hope you're sitting down. Early this morning, in a park in North Sydney, some walkers discovered the body of a young woman. She'd been beheaded, with her head placed on her chest, and a note pinned to her T-shirt. It's the same mob, saying the same thing. They're going to keep attacking us until we remove our troops from Muslim lands."

"Bloody hell", the Prime Minister exploded. "This is outrageous. They're animals." He paused, and then said quietly. "This is disastrous."

"Sir, I'm afraid that's not all. Two more bodies have been discovered, exactly the same circumstances, one in Melbourne, one in Brisbane."

"My God" breathed the Prime Minister. "So, it's beyond Sydney. There's no more doubt. This is a well-organised campaign."

"That's right, sir. And it would seem it's not going to stop. They're going to keep doing this until we find them. And what they're doing is what's always been my biggest fear about terrorism. Picking out what I'm sure are completely random victims, anybody they can grab safely, without being seen. It's impossible to work out in advance where they're going to strike next. But at least now we know they're still here, there are people we can definitely chase."

"Well, I agree, but it's small comfort. This is a really terrible development. The impact out there's going to be massive. Coming on top of the Opera House there's probably going to be real panic. This could really split our society, between Muslims and the rest. We're going to have our work cut out, trying to keep people from doing stupid things. And you're going to have to find these guys fast and put a stop to these killings – we haven't got a hope of fixing the big picture until you can do that." After a pause, he said: "Anyway, we're scheduled to meet later this morning for one of our meetings. We're going to have a lot to talk about. See you then."

"Yes, sir. Sorry to bring you such bad news."

"Not your fault, Jason. I know you'll do your best to get these guys."

The PM hung up, and thought: Five minutes ago things were bad – now they're catastrophic. Am I up to handling this? He sat back in his chair, and for a few minutes was lost in some serious reflection. One of his strengths was he was able to be very honest with himself – he had no self-delusion. Like David Scott, things had always come easily to him. He was a gifted student, and very competent sportsman, and as a consequence had won a Rhode Scholarship, like a few of his predecessors. After a meteoric rise through an investment banking career he entered politics quite early, and steadily rose through the ranks of his party. He was ambitious, and it never entered his head not to campaign for the Prime Ministership. Inevitably, he achieved that ambition. Now, in this moment of crisis, he asked himself, why had he so eagerly sought this job? Was it to serve his country? Deep down, he knew that wasn't the case – it wasn't that he didn't care, but it was certainly not top of mind. He was in it for his own satisfaction, to achieve a life-long ambition. But he'd never expected to be faced with something like this. Madigan, this is your moment of truth, he told himself, because now your country really does need you, and you'd better deliver. At the same time, with totally honest unconscious arrogance, he thought: It's terrifying, but thank God it's me in this job, and not one of those other dills it could have been.

CHAPTER 6

The following morning the newspapers all around the country were full of articles about the beheadings - photos showed taped-off areas, with large numbers of policemen combing for clues and shepherding curious onlookers away from the scene. Similar coverage was provided by the television news programmes throughout the day. Media commentators - some credible, some not - provided opinions about who was behind the atrocities, why they were happening, and what should be done about them. One theme dominated – that the Muslim community was guilty of harbouring too many people who were fueled by highly problematic Islamic ideology, who hated the West and who were capable of resorting to violence.

Politicians of various stripes also weighed in on the topic. The leader of Australia's most right-wing party, Penelope Hartfield, featured in the following exchange in an on-air interview with a television Current Affairs reporter:

Reporter: "What's your reaction to what's happening?"

Penelope: "Well, it's clear to me that what I've been saying for years is coming true, that all this immigration from Muslim countries is going to bring us trouble. A lot of these people come here, with their own culture and expect to be able to have it all here. They don't respect our laws and want to have their own Shari'a laws. It's all so they can subjugate their women, like, having four wives, and keep them all under control."

Reporter: "But why do you think all this violence is happening, what are they trying to achieve?"

Penelope: "I think they're telling us that we'd better let them have what they want, or they'll keep attacking us."

Reporter: "So what do you think should be done?"

Penelope: "Well, it's difficult now, because so many of them are already here. But I think we should definitely consider stopping any further immigration from Muslim-majority countries, or at the very least have very stringent screening."

Reporter: "Do you think all Muslims are guilty of this kind of thinking?"

Penelope: "No, of course not. But I think too many of them have some sympathy for those points of view, and don't speak up. They're sort of guilty by inaction, you know? My real worry is that too many come from such a different culture and way of thinking that they just won't fit in to our culture and won't ever as long as they believe in all that Shari'a law."

The President of The Muslim Association of NSW featured in an article in one of the mainstream newspapers in which he managed to be both conciliatory and aggressive. He began by saying how abhorrent the beheadings were, and how actions like this were repugnant to Muslims and very un-Islamic. He then went on to berate the authorities for waging a campaign against the whole Muslim community in their search for a tiny number of people who were not at all representative of the overall community. This caused a predictable negative reaction from callers to the radio 'shock-jocks', who generally did little to calm the increasingly inflammatory comments. Most common were suggestions that immigration of Muslims should cease - a few callers actually suggested that all Muslims should be deported.

The Federal Leader of the Opposition, Andrew Atkinson, was interviewed, and he took a generally responsible, bipartisan stance:

Reporter: "How do you feel the government is doing in handling this situation?"

Andrew: "It's a very difficult situation, one of the worst that we've faced in very many years, and I think that so far the government is doing all they can. It's early days, but they need to apprehend these criminals fast before they can do any further major damage, and we'll of course be monitoring very closely what's happening. But we also need to think about the important underlying issue here, and that is the conditions that have allowed a situation where Australian-born young men can carry out such terrible atrocities. The government needs to address this as well, and again we'll be watching this very closely. But in such difficult times it's highly desirable that parliament is unified in supporting the government in getting this situation fixed, for both the short and the long-term."

Meanwhile, the Prime Minister's most trusted assistant, Janet Mitchell, was beginning to brief him about what was happening throughout the Australian community, across the country.

"I guess it could be worse," she began, "but it's not good, and it's likely to get worse. I'll give you and idea of the things that are happening, in pretty much every capital, although Sydney, Melbourne and Brisbane are the worst, as you'd expect. First, there's the usual harassment of Muslim women who are wearing veils. Generally, it's verbal, but there's a lot of instances of people grabbing their veils and trying to rip them off."

"Has anyone been hurt?"

"No, but you can imagine that most were given a real scare. Then there are hundreds of reports of nasty verbal abuse of Muslims generally, mostly on the streets, or on public transport, in shopping centres, shops, pretty much everywhere. Even some cases of spitting. In Brisbane they say there are vigilante groups in some suburbs that are bailing up anyone who looks 'Middle Eastern' and questioning them. There's vandalism on Muslim-owned businesses, mainly shops and cafes, generally graffiti, but smashed windows, and minor stuff like that. No arson, yet. But we're also starting to get data about the hiring of Muslims being dramatically reduced."

"What about the media, what's the general feeling out there?"

"Well, there's the usual stuff on radio, some real rubbish, but again, it could be worse. A few minutes ago I watched Atkinson being interviewed, and he was pretty good, you know, supporting the government in these difficult times and so on."

"That's good. Let's keep talking to Andrew, and make sure he stays on side. What about cases of Muslims retaliating? That's got to be coming."

"Nothing so far, but I think it's only a matter of time… We could end up with another Cronulla."

"Jesus. We have to find who's behind this so we can tell the public it's all over and stop this sort of violence. But I'm worried about the bigger issue - I think big part of the population is mistrustful of Muslims, generally. They have been, for a long time, but this has just made it umpteen times worse."

"These beheadings have really got people scared. They've got *me* scared. It's just unbelievable that this can be happening here."

"I guess I've got to make another address. I've just got bugger all I can say that suggests we're getting anywhere. I'll just keep reminding people this is all being done by a tiny minority of the Muslim community, and for people to keep remembering that. It's so damned frustrating."

"I know, but what you've just said is really valuable, and lots of people will react well to it."

The PM sighed, and said ruefully, "Most people are sensible, and will behave pretty well. It's the stupid ones, and the nutters who are the problem. I'll try and come up with something positive. OK, on with the show. What's on for the rest of the morning?"

*

That evening Dina and David were sitting in the lounge in David's apartment watching the evening news. The Prime Minister was being interviewed and had been asked his reaction to calls from many quarters for an immediate halt to all Muslim immigration, and other punitive measures against the Muslim communities.

"Look," he said, "whatever the terrorists have done, or could still do, it'll be even worse if we start over-reacting, and setting different groups in the community against each other. We're all Australians, and these terrorists are a tiny fraction of the Muslim community. Don't forget, terrorists can come in all forms, not just Islamic – remember Christchurch."

"You're not going to tell us Islam is a religion of peace, are you? We've been hearing that from leaders all over the world, always straight after some terrible atrocity committed by Islamic extremists."

"It's no more or less a religion of peace than Christianity or Judaism. All their books have some violence in them, which bad people can use to rationalise the bad things they do."

"I think some people could take issue with that line of argument, but let's leave that. Getting back to the situation we're facing, what tangible steps is the government taking to tackle it?" the journalist asked.

"The Australian Federal Police are heading up a massive effort across the country to track down the people behind these atrocities. In doing that, they've sought and received cooperation from a wide variety of Muslim community organisations. It's unfortunate, but these are exceptional circumstances, the police have had at times to take quite forceful measures to get access to people they wish to question, and we apologise to any innocent people who have been affected by those measures. The police are also questioning senior members of various Muslim organisations to try and gain an understanding of how it's possible for

Australian-born young Muslims to become so radicalized that they would commit such terrible acts against their fellow Australians."

The interview continued in this vein for a few more minutes, then the news channel switched to other topics, at which point David turned off the television, and asked Dina,

"So, how's your week been?"

"Not great. I've been getting more questions from my students about Islam, and terrorism, and while it's not too bad it's starting to get a bit uncomfortable."

"What are your family and friends saying about it all?"

"I think everyone's scared, worried that things are going to get worse, that there's going to be more and more incidents where Muslims are targeted, and eventually people are going to start getting hurt."

David paused for a moment, "Has anyone suggested any ways the Muslim community could respond, any changes they could make to improve relations with non-Muslims?"

Dina looked at him, then asked, a little icily, "What sort of changes did you have in mind?"

David could see that he was heading for troubled waters, but nevertheless persisted.

"Well, I can think of a few things that'd be good PR that could be publicized. Like, no more funding from Saudi Arabia for Islamic schools. Like, have your own Australian-born and raised imams, rather than importing them from conservative countries like Saudi Arabia, and Egypt. Making sure all the Heads of the various Muslim Councils can actually speak English."

Dina privately agreed with what he was saying, so replied, "Okay, you've got a point I guess. What else?"

"Why do so many of the women have to wear veils? Surely you all know it freaks some people out, and they're not obliged to do it anyway – I've been assured it's not in the Qur'an. They're in Australia now, not back in their home countries. How about adapting to our culture, like they expect us to do when we're in their countries?"

Predictably, this raised Dina's hackles even further, and she reacted angrily, "Why do you think the entire Muslim world should change to fit in with a Christian way of thinking? Only Westerners could be so arrogant."

"You're in our country," he replied, "why shouldn't it be you that makes an effort to fit in, rather than we having to bend to suit you?"

More harsh words were exchanged, until both fell silent, each inwardly fuming.

Eventually David asked her, more calmly, "I've never really understood, perhaps because I'm not religious anyway, what's so great about Islam? Why are you so keen on it?"

"It's probably hard for you to understand, because I guess you wouldn't understand why Catholics like their religion, or Buddhists, or anyone who practices a religion. But for me, I find it comforting. The five prayers we have to do each day, for example – for me it's like a discipline, like going to the gym. It makes me feel good about myself. And the discipline of fasting one month a year – same thing. And the importance it places on giving to charity – you *have* to do it, it's so important. And it's got all the good things that Christianity has, like kindness, helping strangers, helping the poor. It's just a recipe for a good way to live."

"And it's also got lots of violence," David pointed out.

"Sure, but so does Christianity. There's lots in the Bible that's just like the Qur'an in that department."

"True. But doesn't that make you question the whole thing, that the Qur'an is the literal word of God? Christians nowadays don't believe the Bible is literal."

"I'm a bit confused about that. I've been brought up to believe it, never to question it. It's hard to ignore that. But I definitely believe that Muhammad had revelations from God, just like Christians believe Jesus is the Son of God."

"So, do you believe I'm going to hell, because I'm an infidel?"

"I don't even want to think about that! Besides, maybe I can eventually save you. That's what all Muslims believe is their duty, to spread Islam across the world to help ignorant people like you get into heaven. Just like you Christians used to do with all us poor, ignorant natives," she added sarcastically.

He laughed briefly. "Also, if you still think the Qur'an is the word of God, why don't you wear a veil?"

"God, you're back on veils again. Why are you so obsessed about that? I guess deep down I think I should. I can empathise with women who do. In fact, they're probably showing that they're prouder of their religion than I am."

"Well, at this moment I think they're crazy. Wearing a veil is like a red rag to a bull to lots of people out there after what's happened, and what's still happening."

This was clearly an inflammatory statement, and the exchange went downhill from there. David knew that he should back off, and be more sensitive to how she felt, but he was still feeling very raw about his mother and he was taking it out on Dina. He knew this intellectually, but his emotions had taken over, and he couldn't stop himself from continuing to goad her.

The argument culminated in Dina shouting at him, "So, you think all of us are to blame, that we all think like those bastards. Is that what you think?" She gathered up her things and stormed out of the apartment.

After she'd left, David sat back on the couch, closed his eyes and reviewed what had just happened. Why did he push her so hard, what was he thinking? What's going on? Is it really Mum? He forced himself to systematically analyse what his feelings were, and with a certain amount of shock he soon realized just how antagonistic he was to Islam, and consequently, to Muslims. And this despite his years of study and awareness of the nuances involved with the way Islam was practiced, how diverse a religion it was, and how different Muslims in different parts of the world were.

He told himself that he could be forgiven for feeling this way – his mother had just been slaughtered by a Muslim terrorist. It was only natural for him to react. But intellectually he knew this was pointless, and wouldn't achieve anything constructive, and it risked ruining his relationship with Dina. But still … He went to bed that night a confused and conflicted man.

*

Later that same night a black car with four men inside idled slowly past a small mosque in one of Sydney's outer suburbs. It continued at the same pace to the end of the street, turned the corner and returned to the rear of the mosque where it came to a halt. No-one was about, the street was deserted. The men got out of the car, each carrying a leather bag. It was a moonless night and they were clad in dark clothing, so they were quite inconspicuous as they slid through the gate and walked around to a side entrance. They'd checked earlier and knew the mosque had no security cameras or alarms, so they simply picked the lock and entered, making their way to the main prayer area. There they split up and conducted a detailed investigation of the whole building before meeting in the main hall to share their findings and agree the plan. They installed two sets of explosives in the positions they'd identified, each fitted with a timer set to go off at 7.00 o'clock the following morning. They left by the same door, taking care to lock it behind them before getting back into their car and leaving as quietly as they had come.

The men were members of a group calling themselves the AFA, Australians For Australians. They were right-wing extremists, previously members of a more mainstream organization, which was opposed to Islam's presence in Australia, but now it was a splinter group, with a commitment to using violence to achieve its ends. AFA clearly knew what they were doing, because at exactly 7.00am the explosives detonated and the subsequent blast largely destroyed the entire building, killing seven of the twelve people who were inside, and injuring the other five. Clearly the killers were sending a message rather than aiming at wholesale slaughter, because they chose not to set the explosives to detonate at a time when the mosque would be full of worshippers. But for the twelve people unfortunate enough to be in the mosque at the time it was a lethal message.

In what was becoming a depressingly familiar sight, police cars converged on the scene within minutes, shortly followed by ambulances. It was clear the perpetrators were no longer at the scene, so the police directed the paramedics to the injured and cordoned off for the scene for further investigation. It wasn't long before Jason was contacted by a senior member of the NSW Police and informed about the bombing and the outcome.

"I know that you're the Senior Investigating Officer of the Opera House incident," she said, "and I figured this has got something to do with it, so you'd want to know straight away."

"Thanks for the heads-up. I'll let the PM know. We're going to see more of this, I'm afraid."

As soon as he hung up, Jason dialed the PM's office and got through immediately to the PM's assistant.

"Hi Janet. Is he available? I need to speak to him urgently.'

'Hang on, I'll put you straight through."

A few seconds later the PM came on the line. "Jason. What've you got for me?"

"I'm sorry to say it's more bad news. A bombing of a mosque, seven people dead, five injured."

There was a brief silence before the PM said, very quietly, reflecting how much this news had disturbed him, "It's escalating, tit for tat. Any ideas about who did it?"

"Well, it seems to have been pretty professional, so it's probably not some isolated nutter. There was enough explosive to suggest more than one person was involved. My gut says it was one of those right-wing extremist groups. There's plenty of them, although not many go in for this level of violence. It could be an offshoot of one of them."

"What are your chances of finding them quickly, before they can do this again?" the PM asked.

"Well, we've got a pretty good handle on most of these groups. I'm a lot more confident about getting this lot quickly than the ones behind the Opera House."

"I hope you're right. It feels like things are starting to unravel... Look, we've got another meeting of the National Security Commission of Cabinet tomorrow. Can you get that expert – I want to get a better handle on what the hell we're up against."

"I will, sir. If that's all, I'll get going."

"Thanks Jason. Good luck."

After he hung up the phone, the PM said to Janet, who'd come into his office, "Don't worry, I know what you're going to say. Schedule a briefing with the press for later this morning. I might as well get in first. I've really got to hammer the point that small groups of people are doing this, and if the general population doesn't understand that and keep their cool it will lead us all down the road to disaster."

"Righto Boss, I'm on it."

After she left the PM reflected for a few minutes about the situation he and his country were facing. Civil society is a fragile thing, he thought. We take it for granted because we in the West have been blessed with it for so long, for a few hundred years, actually. We feel safe because we've built up the institutions that protect us. We've got water and energy and sanitation, and just as importantly we've got the police and the armed forces and the judiciary. But when something like this happens, and suddenly people are really frightened, that civil society is threatened. With a sudden flash of compassion, he thought about what it must be like for the ordinary citizens in places like Syria, whose lives have been completely upended and shattered, the world they took for granted gone. We're a long way from that, he thought, but we don't want to go even a little way down that path. But someone seems to want us to…

*

Sydney - 2007 to the present Day

When he arrived in Sydney The Iraqi was immediately contacted by a member of Australia's settlement services for new migrants. Finding that he spoke excellent English, was financially secure, and had well-developed plans for starting his own business, they put him in contact with one of a number of Sunni-based community organisations and left him to his own devices, undoubtedly with considerable relief that here was a migrant well able to take care of himself.

He did in fact contact the community organisation and introduced himself, seeking advice on mundane matters, such as desirable places to live, locations of mosques, and so on. He also let it be known that he was going to open a halal store and would be welcoming customers. Over the next few years he worked hard on creating the image of model citizen. It turned out that he had a nose for business, and his halal store was very successful, so much so that he was able to open stores in Melbourne and Brisbane using generated funds (as opposed to the alternative of funding from his overseas masters, which carried risks of detection.) After waiting the requisite four years, he applied for and was granted, citizenship – he was now a real Aussie, but one with a terrible agenda.

The strategy he'd agreed with his masters in Iraq was to become a 'sleeper', to blend into his new environment, and take his time evaluating how best he could strike a major blow against the enemy. This he did, watching and learning as the years ticked by. He noticed the pace of Muslim immigration to Australia increasing, to the point where Muslims were becoming a significant minority group, growing faster than any other. It occurred to him that if this continued, and enough years went by, Australia could even become a Muslim-majority country. But what he feared was that the Muslim population would become just another group of Aussies, with much the same culture and no desire to set up an Islamic state.

Almost a century earlier the Egyptian Sayyid Qutb, one of the heroes of the Islamist movement, had spent time in the US and had concluded that absorption of the infidel culture was more threatening than military conquest by them – it was seductive, and had to be resisted at all costs.

The Iraqi had been in Australia long enough to acknowledge that it was indeed a 'lucky' country, with a lifestyle for the majority of the population that would be the envy of most countries in the world, particularly those in the Middle East. But it was an infidel lifestyle, with little thought to the spiritual side of life and little thought to the hereafter. He had been brought up to believe that for a Muslim, the next life was far more important than this temporary time on earth. He saw a way to strike a blow against the enemy, while also protecting his fellow Muslims from themselves, ensuring that they and future generations of Australian Muslims stayed on the right Islamic path.

The Iraqi's strategy was simple: he would pit Muslim Australians against the rest of the Australian population, not just to extract a measure of revenge by chaos and bloodletting, but to separate the

Muslim population from the majority. This way they would continue to practice their faith and way of life without the contamination of western thinking. He looked to examples in the UK and France, where whole suburbs had become Muslim-majority, with cultural norms from the home countries perpetuated. The authorities were reluctant to interfere, sometimes for security reasons, but as much for fears of being termed racists, and anti-multiculturalism.

Once the Muslim population got to a critical mass, he reasoned, they could start to gain political influence and encourage more immigration from Muslim countries, thus further increasing the rate of growth. Who knows, he thought in his more fanciful moments, maybe in a hundred years Australia could be an Islamic State. For the next few years he watched and waited, during which time he identified seven Muslim men who shared his mindset – one was Malek, the Recruiter, and the other six he installed in his three stores. This was his core cell, and he was now ready to implement his plan. Malek did his part well, finding three young men who were ripe for radicalising, and The Iraqi did the rest.

Over the years he at times had periods of doubt about the justification for what he was planning to unleash. But as more news emerged about the ever-increasing violence in his home country, and as credible analyses were published in the West making it clear that the invasion of Iraq and the ensuing death and misery had been justified by lies, his resolve was strengthened. The later events in Libya and Syria further strengthened this resolve, and he came to the conclusion that his targets had what was coming to them. He comforted himself with what he interpreted as justifying verses from the Qur'an, such as Surah 22, Verse 29:

> *'Permission to take up arms is hereby given to those who are attacked because they have been oppressed – Allah indeed has the power to grant them victory – those who have been unjustly driven from their homes, only because they said: "Our Lord is Allah".'*

When he judged that the time was right, he gave the orders to proceed with the attack on the Opera House without compunction. And it had gone so well, he thought, even better than he'd dreamed. He was proud of what he'd accomplished. But it was not over - he and his remaining co-conspirators now had to evade the authorities for as long as possible - the longer they could do so the more effective the plan would be, as more beheadings further terrorised the non-Muslim population and widened the gulf between them and his fellow-Muslims.

Chapter 7

Grim-faced, aware that they were facing an unprecedented crisis, the members of the National Security Commission of Cabinet, plus the Leader of the Opposition, the New South Wales Premier and Jason filed into the meeting room in Kirribilli House. Shortly after the PM entered and took his seat at the head of the table. He glanced out the windows and thought fleetingly how incongruous the bright sun and blue sky that could be glimpsed between the leaves of the trees surrounding the house seemed as a backdrop for the sort of discussion that was about to commence.

"OK, you've all heard what happened last night. We're entering a new phase of this crisis, and it's not good. Amelia, have the police made any progress on finding out who did the bombing?"

"Not yet, Prime Minister, but they're combing very quickly through the list of known right-wing groups and getting a lot of feedback. All the mainstream ones completely disown the bombing, saying that while they're against groups such as Muslims, they don't resort to violence. I think that's generally true. So, our police have been probing them for any more extreme members they've had who might have set up offshoots and they're now following up on those. It may take a little while but I'm confident they'll get them."

"The issue" the PM said, "is whether they'll pull off any more such acts in the meantime. Each one is going to make this situation so much worse. So far, on both sides, I'm sure that what's happened has been done by a tiny group of fanatics, but the longer this goes on the more likely it is that more ordinary people are going to start retaliating, and then it's going to be very hard to stop. So, I know you're giving this all your attention but please do even more. Jason, any more from your team?"

"No real progress, sir. We've interviewed a lot of people, but we've uncovered nothing of real importance. The fact that these terrorists have covered their tracks so well makes me even more convinced that we're dealing with a highly professional group. This is serious discipline. There's a couple of hunches I've got that might lead to something, and we're putting a lot of time into them. It'll take a while, but I think there's a good chance it'll reveal something. It's a hard grind, but that's what these situations generally take. By the way, remember the pilot of the helicopter that the terrorists stole? As I guessed would happen, the body of the poor guy was washed up on one of the beaches south of Sydney. It was found last night so won't have hit the papers yet. Not much left of him, I'm afraid."

"Another victim of these beasts" the PM said, then turned to the Minister for Home Security. "Paul, anything?"

"Our people have been combing through Muslims who've entered Australia in the last few years to see if we can identify anyone who's suspicious, and while we've found a few it's not led to anything. One thing I need your approval for, because it's going to get a lot of flak, is that we want to seriously increase the rigour with which we process Muslims wanting to enter the country. We'll be accused of profiling but considering the situation I think it's warranted."

"You're right, it'll get a lot of flak, but it is indeed warranted. The Muslim communities will scream blue murder and the Rights groups will complain, but I think the majority of Australians will agree it's prudent. In fact, if we don't do something like this they're the ones who'll probably start to scream blue murder. So, unless anyone can convince me that this is a bad move, I'd say go ahead."

He looked around the table, but there was no dissent.

"OK Paul, do it. Now, at our first meeting I asked Amelia to find an expert who could give us a better understanding of what this Muslim extremism is all about, what motivates people to do this sort of thing. He's here this morning to give us a briefing and do his best to answer any questions we've got. Janet, can you get him in here?"

Moments later David Scott was seated at the far end of the table and gave the group a very short precis of his background, and credentials. Because he was a regular contributor to The Australian newspaper and regularly consulted by the news journalists, most of the group had been exposed to him and were satisfied he knew what he was talking about.

"Now David" the PM began, "I think you know why you're here, but let me be specific. We've got a situation here that I think is worse than anything I've ever experienced in Australia. They thought the Whitlam Dismissal polarised society – well, I don't think that was anywhere near as dangerous as this. This could result in a real fracture of society if we can't contain it and fix it. I don't think anyone in here knows much about Islam and Muslim societies and what makes them tick, except maybe Jason (who immediately indicated non-verbally that he was no expert), and it would help us to have some idea of what we're up against. So, assume we know nothing, and you tell us whatever you think is relevant to the situation we're facing. You've got about 15 minutes, because this is terribly important. If I think you're going off-track I'll let you know, so please don't be offended if I do – there's no time for niceties. Also, we promise you that nothing you say will ever leave this room, so don't hold back in your opinions. Don't give us politically correct stuff. We want the truth, as you see it. Is that OK?"

"Yes sir, I get it." David replied. He paused for a few seconds, gathering his thoughts – this was no easy task he'd been set, and he wanted to make sure he didn't make a fool of himself in front of this very senior group.

"Alright, can I make a couple of things clear before I start. First, while I may be a so-called expert in Political Islam, that's really the macro view, and it's primarily about the politics and impact on societies. I don't know a lot about how individual Muslims live their lives. I've tried to read the Qur'an - it's extremely difficult to understand, let me tell you - and obviously I've picked up a bit about the religion of Islam, but I'm no expert in it. Second, I have to confess that I've got concerns about how Islam is often interpreted and practiced, and the way this impacts on societies. I really believe people are fundamentally the same the world over, with very similar aspirations, but I think the way the religion is presented to them can often mess up Muslim's thinking – I'll explain this a bit later. Added to that, I think you're all aware that my mother was killed in the Opera House atrocity, so that's made me even more negative. But I'll do my best to be objective.

"If you'll bear with me, I'll start by covering three areas, and then you'll probably have questions. First, I'll explain why there's been an international revival in Islam, with people all over the world becoming more pious, and the growth of more extreme groups. Second, I'll explain why I think Islam is susceptible to being used for bad purposes. Finally, I'll give you an idea of the Islamic scene in Australia.

"The modern revival really started in the late nineteenth century, as a sort of push-back against colonialism. Nearly every Muslim-majority country was colonised, or if not, greatly affected by it. A few centuries earlier Islam had ruled the roost, and now it was conquered and humiliated. A group of 'thinkers' in different parts of the Middle East decided that part of the problem was that people were no longer practicing Islam in the right way, and that if they could get back to the early days of Islam, when the Prophet and his immediate successors were still around, they could get rid of the colonial usurpers and regain Islam's former glory. So, you started seeing women putting the veil on again and men wearing beards, and the general population becoming more pious. This didn't really achieve much, and then of course the First World War intervened. After the war ended the Allies carved up the Middle East in a pretty disastrous fashion, including paving the way for the later setting up of Israel. A whole pile of dictators ended up running the countries, often puppets of the colonial powers, and tried to introduce a secular way of organising things. That generally involved suppressing the Islamic movements. And this predictably resulted in a new batch of thinkers emerging who tried to energise the populations with a more aggressive approach, and an even stronger reversion to old style religious thinking. This is when the Muslim Brotherhood was set up, for example.

"In the second half of the twentieth century the dictators started being toppled, and a lot of countries adopted a form of democracy, but one which still resulted in very strong Presidents running the show. Think of Sadat, and later Mubarak in Egypt. In 1979 we had the Iranian Revolution, which served as a real spur for the Islamist movement worldwide. For the first time, the people had kicked out the colonialists and their puppets, and an Islamic State had been set up.

"One thing I should emphasise, and this is going back a bit in history. In the eighteenth century Wahhab, a really extreme cleric, rose to fame in what is now Saudi Arabia, started a religion called Wahhabism, and formed an alliance with a leader from the House of Saud. Together they united a whole lot of tribes and conquered lots of territory. The Ottoman Empire people put them down eventually, but in the 1920's the same alliance formed again, and this time it resulted in what is now Saudi Arabia. Very importantly, it cemented Wahhabism, which is about the most extreme version of Islam, and gave it a powerful sponsor. This became a major factor after about 1970 when the oil crisis resulted in lots of Middle Eastern countries becoming fabulously wealthy because of the vast reserves of oil. And none more so than Saudi Arabia. Because the ruling family badly needed the legitimisation provided by the clerics, they allowed them pretty much free rein to export Wahhabism around the world, by sending Qur'ans everywhere, funding the building of mosques, setting up Islamic schools, funding academic scholarships, exporting their imams - the equivalent of our priests - and training imams sent to Saudi Arabia by other countries. Wahhabism is now a major influence all over the world and provides a rationale for terrorists.

"So, the result of all this is that generally Muslims are more conscious of their religion and practice it more seriously. Also, there's a bit of a feeling that Islam is under siege, with first colonialism, then the setting up of Israel and the dispossession of the Palestinians, and the more recent invasions, particularly Iraq. To some extent, Muslims all over the world have feelings of solidarity with their fellow Muslims - the Ummah, they call it - so when one group is attacked by non-Muslims the rest feel it as well. That's why the Israel/Palestine issue is so bitter, and why Muslims from all over the world came to Afghanistan to fight against the Russians, and then Iraq and Syria to fight against the Allies. I think even when they emigrate to Western countries they're a bit defensive and quick to feel they're being discriminated against. This is all gross simplification of course, but it reflects a fair bit of the reality."

David stopped, and looked around. "That's enough for the first part, I think, although the academics would probably have a fit if they could hear me. How are we going? All OK?"

The PM nodded, and said: "That's fine. One question. You said Wahhabism is being exported all over the world – what about here in Australia?"

"I'm afraid so. I was shocked to find out a few years ago that some of the Islamic schools have bits of Wahhabism in their curriculum. You see, it's a quid pro quo. The Saudis donate money, and the schools have to play along by having some Wahhabism."

"That's just great", the PM said sarcastically. "OK, please go ahead."

"Alright. Now why do I have concerns about the way Islam is often, perhaps generally, practiced. There are two things I think are key to understanding why Islam, to us, seems backward and prone to extremism. First is that Muslims believe that the Qur'an is truly the Word of God, and very many of them believe it has to be interpreted literally. Now I'm sure you've heard that the Qur'an has both good and bad stuff in it, just like the Christian Bible. That means that bad guys, like ISIS, al-Qaeda and all the other terrorists can cherry-pick and find verses that they argue endorse what they do. Of course, there are other verses that will say the opposite, but they ignore those. But it's not just about terrorism – this fact also tends to inhibit any discussion about interpreting the Qur'an to suit the time and place. In other words, to contextualise it, so for example one could start cutting out the really patriarchal stuff, women's rights and so on. If someone makes a sensible suggestion along this line someone else will argue that it's against God's will as expressed in the Qur'an, and how do you argue against God? I believe this is certainly true in Muslim-majority countries, and while in countries like Australia there is some such discussion, I haven't seen much evidence that it's had much effect.

"Now, Muslims use both the Qur'an and the supposedly verified records of what he did and said as their sacred scriptures – they call it the Sunnah. Muhammad died in 632, and these documents were finalised in about the ninth or tenth century. So, they obviously reflect life in Arabia in medieval times. No matter how enlightened Muhammad was for his time, the way they lived back then was a whole different world than what we have now. But in about the eleventh century the clerics, who were very powerful, decided that they'd thought of everything that people would ever need to live their lives, and that there was no further need to update their laws. These laws were based on the Qur'an and the Sunnah and consolidated into what they call Shari'a. That's why they refer to them as 'God's Laws'. So, in a sense, Islamic thought was stuck at that time and hasn't been allowed to progress much. Of course, they eventually got into the new technologies, but socially they're pretty well stuck back there. That's the favourite reason given for why the Islamic world was overtaken by the West, and conquered.

"Please remember that I'm giving you a very brief, simplified version of all this – it's actually far more complicated, but I think it gives you the general idea.

"The second thing, in my view, facilitates the inhibition of any discussion about reforming Islam. If you look around the Muslim-majority world, the big majority of people are both very poor and very poorly educated. They've been taught the rudiments of Islam by an imam who is also pretty basic, and so when anyone they perceive is senior to them, or knows more about Islam, tells them some fact about Islam they'll go along with it. That's why it's so easy to get them stirred up and acting like an out-of-control mob. That's how you get those lynchings you read about in India, and Pakistan. Someone accuses some probably quite innocent person of a violation against Islam and the next thing you've got a mob tearing them to pieces. So, in most places people are actually scared to stick their necks out and propose change. You'll find that almost the only places you'll see intelligent, forward-thinking Muslims arguing openly that it is quite in order to contextualise the Qur'an are Western cities, like New York and London. And even there there'll be lots of people who'll try and shout them down."

"How are we going so far? I'm doing a lot of talking, but I don't think I can make it any shorter."

"It's fine" the PM replied. "It's extremely interesting. I've read a bit about Islam but never had it explained like that. Please go on."

"OK. The last thing I'll cover before getting into some questions, is the scene here in Australia. The Muslim population here is climbing up towards 3%, but growing very fast, mainly because of immigration. By the way, all those stories about Islam taking over the world just by having a greater birth rate are pretty much rubbish – just alarmist stuff you get on the internet. And it's quite diverse. There's no such thing as 'the Islamic community' – there's lots of them, and they'll have different cultural backgrounds, and often even different versions of Islam. Like Christianity, Islam has a lot of different sects under its umbrella. Some came here a very long time ago, but that was very few. Then in the 1960's and 70's came the first wave of new immigrants, mainly from Lebanon, and mainly into Sydney. You'll all remember the Cronulla riots a few years ago – they were Lebanese. But since then, people have come from all sorts of places – Somalia, Sudan, Iraq, recently Syria. I think the situation now is that 50% of Muslims in Australia were not born here. And it's a real mix – some are well-educated and settle in pretty well, and some are very poor and not well educated, and they struggle.

"There's a lot of community organisations, and they do a lot of good work helping people settle in, learn the language, try to get them jobs, and so on. The government does a fair bit as well. But one still reads and hears about a lot of Muslims here having a difficult time settling in and being accepted. I think there's a lot of wariness on the part of the average Australian towards them, and personally I don't think they help themselves by emphasising how different they are. This is very politically incorrect, but I've got a real issue about women wearing veils. The truth is it's not mandated in the Qur'an that they have to, but they nearly all believe it is. There's no more obvious way to trumpet the fact that you're different than by wearing a veil.

"There are various official Muslim organisations, the top one being the Australian Association of Islamic Communities, and there are state bodies as well. These have got a very chequered history, with some of the Heads of these organisations not even able to speak English, who make inflammatory statements, and are generally very unhelpful. But some have a good reputation, like the main association in Victoria, I believe. There are women's groups, and a lot of others I won't try and list now. As I alluded to earlier, there's lots of mosques and Islamic schools here, and again I'm very suspicious about what goes on in some of them."

"Look, I think that's enough of an overall background – you'll all fall asleep soon. Is there anything specific I can perhaps try and answer?"

The Attorney-General, Anthony Simpson, spoke up: "You said that Muslims are susceptible to being influenced by fellow-Muslims with strong, maybe extreme, views. I've got a few Muslim acquaintances and they're highly educated, successful people – I just can't see them going along with things they don't agree with."

"Well, maybe not, but what often happens is that even people like that don't want to be seen by their fellow Muslims to be opposing things that involve invoking Islam, even if they privately think it's not appropriate, or too extreme. Of course, if someone started explicitly suggesting violence then I'm sure they'd speak up. But short of that they're likely to say nothing, and so the more extreme view gets carried. In this way a community can gradually be shifted towards accepting things that privately most of them disagree with. No-one wants to be accused of not being a 'good Muslim' – they hate it. But it's true that there are quite a few Muslims here who do regularly speak out and push ideas like contextualizing the Qur'an, but there doesn't seem to be any evidence that they're having much of an impact, particularly with the newer arrivals who have often come from quite traditional societies."

The PM then asked the obvious question: "What's your guess about why this group is doing this? What can they gain from it? Surely they can see it's going to be bad for the Muslim communities. The backlash has already started."

"That's the million-dollar question, and I can only guess at it. The most obvious answer is that it could be some sort of revenge, just like 9/11 in New York, a strike against the Allied forces in their home countries. After the Opera House that's the first conclusion I came to. But when the beheadings started, I wondered if there's some bigger agenda. The fact that it's not a one-off like 9/11 means there are people out there who are continuing with whatever plan they've got. Maybe it's just as much revenge as they can get before they get caught, but I'm not convinced."

He paused, and looked around, and then said: "Look, this might be a big stretch, and I hope I'm wrong, but what if these guys are trying to set the Muslim population here against the rest of the country, to create a complete rift? If things get so bad that both sides completely reject each other what would happen? There's too many of them to deport them all, and to where? What could happen is that the Muslims set up their own communities, apart from the rest of the population, and push to have their own laws and so on. You could argue that this is already happening in parts of Europe, so it's not a completely crazy idea."

There was silence while the meeting digested this very unpleasant possibility, then the PM asked: "But why do that, what's to gain from it?"

"It could be that whoever's behind this thinks that Muslims are gradually straying from the way Islam should be practiced, and that this is only going to get worse the longer they stay in this, what they think, is an infidel environment. If they can be left completely to their own devices then they can enforce the traditional ways of doing things, via that process I mentioned to you earlier, where most people won't speak up against them. Now, I'm not convinced that this strategy would work – I think there are too many sensible people who'd just refuse to go along with it. But it could still be what's behind this. And the longer it goes on, and the more the tit for tat stuff goes on, the better chance it has of working, even if it's only to a limited extent."

The Defence Minister then said: "But surely that's a completely crazy idea. You can't have two populations living in the same country with different laws, separated from each other, certainly not in a country like Australia?"

"Maybe not as crazy as you think. Do you remember in 2008 the Archbishop of Canterbury actually suggested that Britain should legalise Shari'a law, simply because there were so many Muslims clamouring for it? It didn't happen, but the very fact that someone so senior in the establishment could even suggest it is telling. And it's a fact that whole swathes of northern England have Muslim-majority populations who pretty much do as they like socially – the authorities are reluctant to interfere. Look, this is just an idea. I'm probably completely wrong, but I think it's at least a feasible possibility."

The PM then spoke: "We asked you to give us the benefit of your expertise, and to tell us what you really think, and that's what you're doing. I think what you're saying is not crazy. Right from the start Jason here has made the point that whoever's behind this is very professional, very calculating. I think we should take any idea David comes up with very seriously, even if it's not what we want to hear."

He looked around the table, but there was silence. He went on: "Now David, another question. The three terrorists who did the Opera House were home-grown – do you think the people master-minding this could also be home-grown?"

"My guess is, no. I just can't see anyone local having the background and experience to be able to plan and manage something this big. My guess is that it's someone who's come from a country that's been or is at war, and that they learnt their trade there. If so, it could be a number of places – the Southern Philippines, Afghanistan, Pakistan, Iraq, Lebanon, Syria, Libya, Algeria. Jason, what's your guess, you've had more exposure to real-life terrorists than any of us?"

"I think you're right" Jason replied. "One of the things we started doing immediately was checking out Muslims who've arrived in Australia, starting recently and working backwards, to see if any of them have a questionable background. The trouble is, if this guy's as smart as he appears he'll have a very innocuous background – it'll be very hard to pick him out. We're going to need some other link, and I've mentioned in here before that we're pursuing a couple of leads, long-shots, and they'll take quite a long time to work through, but it might give us that link."

The Deputy Prime Minister, Michael Williams, then asked: "How do you think the general Muslim population feel about what's going on? After 9/11 there were reports of Muslims in different parts of the world clearly rejoicing about it – do you think that could happen here?"

"There'll always a few real extremists, in any population, and who knows what they might do or think. But I absolutely believe the overwhelming majority of Muslims here will be horrified with what's happened, both from a human point of view and because the last thing they want is to have the non-Muslim population here even more negatively disposed to them than they already are. Don't forget, the ones that emigrated here did so to get a better life, to become Australians – this could put that in jeopardy. The scenario I painted earlier could only happen if the retaliations and the tit for tat gets so bad that it seems like the only choice. It's not what people want, I'm sure of it."

The PM glanced at his watch and said: "I think our times up. Thanks everyone. David, that's been very helpful. In fact, I'd like you to attend these meetings from now on, together with Jason. You're both out there actually talking to people, so I want your updates and insights. In fact, I'd like you two to collaborate on this, which means you, David, putting in a lot more time. Can you organise that with the university? It's an emergency, tell them I've asked you. Is that OK?" David nodded his assent. With that the

PM stood up and left the room, with the others filing out after him, leaving David and Jason alone.

Despite his misgivings about having to work with David, Jason was impressed. "You really stuck your neck out and gave them something to think about. Do you really think that scenario is possible?"

"God knows, but he asked me to tell them what I think, and I think it's better to warn them of possibilities. Makes sure they don't under-estimate what's going on, although to be fair, I don't think they are, certainly not the PM."

"Fair enough. I think you're right about the PM. I've actually been pretty impressed with him. I always thought he was a bit of a glamour boy, but there's some steel there. So, you're now part of the team. How do you feel about that?"

"I don't mind. Anything I can do to help get those bastards is fine with me. I'm also seriously worried about the longer-term implications."

"OK. We'll have to catch up regularly and compare notes. By the way, I've arranged that meeting with Fariq and his mates. I'll text you the time and venue."

*

That evening David met Dina for a drink and dinner. He'd made a special point of booking a table right against the windows, at Sails on McMahon's Point, Dina's favourite restaurant. She especially loved the fact that it was situated right on the edge of the harbour, with the Opera House in the background framed by the Bridge in the foreground - in her eyes it was like a beautiful painting. But tonight, even as she gazed at the view and as always thought how stunning it was, it didn't lift her heart the way it usually did. She was troubled, and it showed, in the shadows under her eyes. The terrible terrorist acts, the blowback against the Muslim communities, and the fact that it seemed even David felt the same way, even if he tried to hide it. But tonight, she thought, let's try and forget it.

On David's part he felt like he was walking on eggshells. The briefing he'd given earlier in the day had further convinced him that there was a real problem with the way Islam was practiced, and that Muslim communities were oblivious to it, even Dina, much as he loved her. But he was torn. If he expressed these thoughts to her he'd already had experience that she didn't take it well, that she was very sensitive about her religion and the culture that seemed inevitably to go with it. On the other hand, if they were going to get married, they couldn't avoid the topic forever. There was no way in the world, for example, that he would ever consent to becoming a Muslim, a requirement in the Malaysian version of Islam if he was to marry a Muslim, even if it was only a token gesture.

So, with the memory of their last meeting and the unpleasant argument that had ensued in their minds, for the whole meal both were determined to avoid the topic, and they kept the conversation on safe ground – some of David's more annoying colleagues, Dina's more boisterous students, the latest triumphs of Australia's cricket team, and the like. For two hours they navigated the treacherous waters until the meal was finished, and David was able to ask the question he had been thinking about all night –

would she come home with him and spend the night? That's safe territory, Dina thought to herself. I think even if I hated him I'd still want to go to bed with him. So, she smiled, and said yes, of course. They left the restaurant, got into their respective cars, and drove to David's apartment a little faster than they should have.

CHAPTER 8

Sydney: Present Day

"Welcome back" the lady at the check-in counter, Jenny, said brightly. "I've got your booking here. Back to Brisbane again?"

"Yes, got to check on my business there, make sure the staff are behaving themselves and not wasting all my money."

"I'm sure they're not" she laughed. "Here you are, Seat 2A, a window as usual. Have a good flight."

"Thanks Jenny, see you next trip."

As he walked away Jenny watched him for a few moments, thinking as she had many times before what an interesting looking man he was – tall, lean and fit-looking, a hard but not unpleasant face, with a scar running across the left side that gave him an air of mystery. I wonder how he got that, she thought, before turning back to the next customer who had appeared in front of her.

The Iraqi made his way from the check-in counter through the maze that is Sydney's domestic air terminal to the Business Class lounge, where he stood in the queue to collect a coffee. He then found a seat near one of the windows so that he was able to see the planes coming and going, framed against an almost startlingly blue sky, a feature of Australia for much of the year. There he sat, blending in with the dozens of other businessmen (not so many women) who, like him, were waiting to board their flight to another part of the vast country, the very picture of a model citizen, in his case a success story of the assimilation of an immigrant Muslim into Australian society. His three stores, one in each of Sydney, Melbourne and Brisbane, were all busy, serving the rapidly increasing Muslim populations of each city, selling halal products to Muslims and to those non-Muslims who believed in the ethical aspect of what halal was all about.

"It's not all about pork", he regularly explained to non-Muslim Australians, "it's also about not dealing in products that in any way are associated with things my religion considers bad for society, like cigarettes, alcohol, gambling, and so on. Pretty sensible, don't you think?" He'd sometimes joke with them that they should become customers, that it would be good for their soul. He'd usually get a laugh, as most people found him quite personable.

Each of his stores, managed by his trusted lieutenants recruited by Malek, employed between four and six staff, depending on the season. So, he provided employment for about fifteen people, and paid a considerable amount of tax every year, always on time, and scrupulously accurately. He belonged to the Chamber of Commerce in Sydney, and to the Institute of Directors, was a regular attendee at his local mosque, and a regular contributor to a number of worthy Muslim charities. Except for his mosque attendance, his public appearances were work-related, and while he was not at all gregarious, he was quite popular, with a quiet sense of humour. Nevertheless, outside work he kept very much to himself. He had no family, apparently very few, if any, friends, and did not appear to seek female companionship. He bothered nobody, and more importantly, nobody bothered him. His fellow business-travelers would have been astounded to know that the man next to them was not quite the model citizen he appeared – in fact, he was any Western country's nightmare, a textbook case of a normal man converted by circumstance into a hate-driven purveyor of terror, directed at the West.

Sitting in the Business Class lounge, he watched as the ABC morning programme on television focused almost exclusively on the atrocity committed the previous evening on a number of Muslim businesses, the premises burned to the ground, the employees killed. *I'm sorry for the victims,* he thought, *but this is just perfect – they're playing right into my hands, just as I prayed they would.* At that moment, the cameras switched to a street interview where a journalist introduced a Professor David Scott, explaining that he was an expert in Political Islam at the University of Sydney. The Iraqi immediately sat up and listened carefully.

"Professor Scott, what do you think the implications of this attack are?" the journalist asked.

"They're very worrying" David replied. "We've already seen a lot of harassment of Muslims, but this is the first time we've seen this level of violence, with people being killed. This was clearly a professional job, obviously carried out by a well-organised group, and I'll bet they've got more such acts planned. They don't realise it, but they're playing right into the terrorists' hands."

"Why do you say that?"

"I believe the terrorists are trying to set non-Muslims and Muslims against each other, to sow chaos in the country. They're hoping that non-Muslims will retaliate against the atrocities that we've already seen, and which seem to be set to continue until the police can stop them, and this is exactly what these extreme right-wing groups are doing. It's crazy."

"Do the authorities have any idea who these right-wing groups are?"

"There are some well-known groups, so the police will know who to start investigating. Let's hope they can identify them quickly."

The call came over the loudspeaker for The Iraqi's flight to board, so he stood up and began to make his way to the departure lounge, leaving David and the interviewer still talking. *I don't like this David Scott*, he thought. *He's cottoned on to what's going on a bit too quickly.* He boarded the plane, not quite as satisfied with himself as he had been a little earlier.

*

"It's nice to see you again, Mr. Blake, and so quickly" said Abdul Rashid, the President of the Muslim Association of NSW, as he shook Jason's hand. Jason had arranged another meeting with Abdul Rashid and his three colleagues, on the off-chance that they may have something to offer him.

"Well, I said when we parted last time I'd hold you to your offer of help, so I'm hoping maybe you have something for me" he replied, as he sat down, and nodded hello to the other three.

"I'm really sorry to have to say that we haven't come up with anything, and we've genuinely tried, Mr. Blake, I can assure you. This situation is going from bad to worse, and we're getting very worried about the long-term impact this is going to have on Muslim communities in this country."

"I presume you're in touch with your counterparts in Melbourne and Brisbane. What's the feedback from there?" Jason asked.

"Just the same. Whoever these people are they know how to keep their activities very quiet. Is it normal in your experience for criminals like this to be so disciplined?"

"No, most criminals have real weaknesses, and it's not usually too long before they make a mistake. But it's a common experience around the world that a lot of Islamic terrorists (Jason used the sometimes regarded as inflammatory term deliberately to see whether he'd provoke a response) are extremely well-trained and disciplined. Perhaps that comes from believing fanatically in a cause."

A little to his surprise there was no response to his provocation. Maybe they're beginning to get how serious this is, he thought. As if in reply to his thoughts, one of the other three, Adzhar Hassan from the NSW Association of Imams, responded: "We agree with you that these people are fanatics, and there's no doubt they've been very well prepared, which makes them terribly dangerous. We've been trying to work out what they're trying to do, and it certainly seems like they're trying to get the Muslim and non-Muslim communities at war with each other. But why? It's not like Australia is Iraq or Libya, where the terrorist groups try to get the state to collapse so that they can move in and take over like ISIS did. The state here is too strong, and the institutions are well established. It's not going to fail."

Remembering what David had said at the briefing for the PM and Cabinet, Jason put the question to the group: "Last time we met you suggested that maybe setting our communities against each other was additional punishment for Australia, for it's role as an ally of the US – do you think maybe it's something else, that they want the Muslim communities to become completely separate from the rest of Australians, like some of the places in the UK and Europe, and live according to Islamic laws, not Australian law? If I recall, you said then that the four of you, and lots of others, would welcome that."

Abdul Rashid looked shocked when he replied: "We did say that, but it seemed a very hypothetical scenario, and certainly not one brought to reality like this. None of us want to be alienated from the rest of Australians."

"Well, things aren't looking too good at the moment. If we can't find and stop this group soon I fear the violence is only going to escalate. We've had one instance of extreme right-wing violence, and there's bound to be more. I think it's only a matter of time before some of the ordinary members of both communities are going to start tit for tat attacks, and God knows where that will end."

Abdul Rashid looked around at his three colleagues, then said to Jason; "I can assure you, Mr. Blake, whatever you may think privately about us, that's the last thing we want to see. Have you got any suggestions about what we can do to help?"

"Thank you, I welcome that. As I've said, priority one is to find and stop this group, before the situation gets too much worse, and that's largely up to me and the rest of my police colleagues. But of course, any lead you and your people get, no matter how inconsequential you think it is, please let us know immediately. But I think this is going to stretch for a little while longer before we can find them, and I'm afraid more damage is going to be done. This'll mean there's going to be a big repair job needed, and this is where I think you need to think hard about what you can do."

"What do you mean exactly by that?" Adzhar asked.

Jason knew he was venturing into sensitive territory, but thought what's there to lose? "Look, even before all this happened the relationship between Muslims and non-Muslims in Australia was not very good. I imagine you've seen the survey results about the level of mistrust non-Muslims here have towards Muslims – they're scary. And now it's going to be miles worse. I think you're going to need to think creatively about what you can do to make non-Muslims feel more positive about you. What is it that makes them distrust you? You need to find out and see if it can be changed."

After a brief silence Abdul Rashid said: "That's not very palatable, but I guess there's something in what you say. But can I just make one point – I think it works both ways. I think a lot of Australians have a lot of misconceptions about us, and that needs to change as well."

"That's a fair comment" replied Jason, "and I'll certainly make that point to the government, if they haven't thought of it themselves."

He looked around and thought to himself that this had gone better than he thought it would – they were at least thinking about what he said. "Gentlemen, I think it's time for me to go. Thank you very much for listening to me, and hopefully taking it on board. Let's stay in touch."

He shook hands with them all, this time feeling there was a little more warmth coming from them and left.

*

When Jason got back to his office it was after 6.00pm. Many of the staff had left for the day, but Mike Anderson was waiting for him, looking grim.

"I don't like the look of this" Jason said, "what's going on?"

"More bad news, Jason. Two more bodies have been found, one in Melbourne, one in Brisbane. Both beheaded, heads sitting on the torso, with the same message."

Jason looked at him, the fury building up inside him. "Bloody hell. I've been waiting for it. I knew there'd be more, but it doesn't make it any easier."

Mike waited a little while Jason calmed down, then added: "The victim in Melbourne was a Chinese man, an Aussie citizen, the one in Brisbane a young Indian woman, also Aussie."

"So, this is their sick version of diversification, making sure they get people from all sorts of ethnic backgrounds." Jason paused for a few moments, then asked: "What about Sydney? No body found?"

"Not yet, but I bet there will be, very soon."

"Are the press onto it yet?"

"Of course. It'll be on the news tonight and in the papers tomorrow. And you just wait. I'll bet we'll see another extreme-right attack within a few days, and it will all start spiraling."

They looked at each other, contemplating that scenario in silence. Finally, Jason got up and headed to the door. "Let's go home and get a good night's sleep, because we're going to be facing the music tomorrow. But Mike, we're going to get these guys. Sooner or later, something's going to break – they'll make a mistake, or we'll find something. I don't believe they can stay hidden forever. And then we'll get 'em."

*

Jason hadn't been home any longer than having had time to down a quick beer when his mobile rang.

"Sir, it's Jack Thompson of the NSW Police. There's been another beheading, and we thought you'd want to know immediately."

"You're right, I'm going to be there. Where are you?"

Minutes later he was racing to the crime scene, a park not far from the cliffs over the ocean north of the city centre. When he arrived he found six police securing the area for a radius of over ten metres around the body, which was covered in a blanket.

"Show me" he ordered.

One of the policemen moved the blanket back, revealing a headless torso, with the head stacked on top of the chest. It was a man, Caucasian, probably in his forties. Attached to his shirt was a sheet of paper, with the same message that had been found on the bodies from the other beheadings. He examined where the knife had sliced the neck and was surprised at how clean it was – the knife must have been incredibly sharp. He noticed a red weal on the man's skull, probably the result of a heavy weapon to put him out of action so he could be easily dragged away from the path about forty metres away. He carefully examined the area around the body, keeping away from the faint footprints that had been preserved by the police team. They were very flat, with no patterns that would often be present, particularly with rubber soled footwear.

"Looks like they could have been wearing something over their shoes so that no footprints were left" he remarked.

"That's what we thought. These guys were very careful, very thorough. I'll bet we don't find any fingerprints – they're bound to have been wearing rubber gloves."

"Is there anyone who was around who may have seen something?"

"No, only the couple that found the body. No-one else appears to have been here."

"The paper the message is on – anything identifying?"

"No. It's plain old A4, probably a million sheets sold every day in Sydney."

Bloody hell, Jason thought. It's going to be like looking for a needle in a haystack. No clues, nothing. This is not like most murders, where's there's people with a possible motive. And they're usually committed by amateurs who make mistakes. These guys are well trained, and the victims are bound to be completely random. The only way we're ever likely to find them if one day they're seen by somebody, who survives to identify them. Just great!

"OK Jack. I'll leave it with you. If anything comes up, let me know straight away."

Jason left the scene and drove back to his apartment, furious at the brutality with which the murder had been committed, and with the fact that he was, at least for the moment, helpless to do anything about it. And he was sure there were more to come.

CHAPTER 9

That same afternoon David was in the Players Lounge of the Royal Sydney Golf Club having joined three of his close friends for a drink after they'd played 18 holes in the regular Wednesday afternoon competition. The violent death of his mother, the rocky state of his relationship with Dina, and continuing to have Muslims and terrorists top of mind due to his work with the Cabinet, was getting to him. He badly needed some cheering up and some interaction with old familiar faces, and these friends from his school days were always good company.

"David", one of his friends said, "we didn't expect to see you here."

"Well, I've been having a shit of a time, and I missed you silly buggers. You can buy me a drink."

They laughed sympathetically. They'd known him for over 35 years, and they could tell that he was very depressed. For a little while they focused on light matters, relating their golf course woes, cracking a few jokes, trying their best to help him forget his problems, but inevitably the conversation steered towards the atrocities and the whole issue of the relationship of Muslims with the rest of Australians.

"I just can't see them fitting in here" said Charles Murphy, a lawyer. "Even before these terrorism incidents there were lots of problems. Remember the Cronulla Riots? And that bloke from the Islamic Council, always complaining about things, wanting laws changed. One of them made that comment about women wearing revealing clothes were like fresh meat – remember that?"

"Yeah, but you can't judge them all by him" countered Frank Brady, a real estate developer. "I've dealt with a few in real estate deals, and they were fine. Mind you, I didn't go out for a beer with any of them, but they seemed like good blokes from what I saw of them."

"That's one of the problems," said Charles. "They don't drink, so it's a bit hard to do much socialising with them. I guess it makes us all seem like alcoholics, but it's a big part of how we all get on together, so it's just another thing that makes us different. But you're talking about the better off and better educated of them – so many of them have come from places like Sudan and Somalia, or Afghanistan, where they've had very little education and they've been in this very conservative culture, and they want to live the same way here. Remember that mob that wanted the local council to shut the swimming pool so that Muslim women could bathe there alone? It's just not on."

The conversation continued in this vein for a few minutes, and David chose to remain silent and listen. He was always a little surprised at how these friends of his, and so many more of his acquaintances, most of whom were intelligent and well educated, knew so little about Islam and had so many ill-conceived notions about them. But he couldn't help himself when Geoff Lucas, the owner of a metal fabrication business, made the claim that so many Muslims had four wives and consequently had so many kids that they were going to swamp the world demographically.

"Jesus, Geoff, you always were bloody hopeless at maths. Think about it. There's only a set number of women in the world, so it doesn't matter if some blokes have lots of them for wives, there's still the same number of women, so they can only have so many kids."

Geoff contemplated this for a few seconds, then laughed. "Shit, you're right. That was pretty dumb." The others all laughed and agreed, and insisted he buy a round of drinks as a fine for making such a ridiculous comment.

Charles then continued with his argument. "But Geoff does have a point. Isn't the Islamic religion around the world growing faster than any other, upwards of two billion now? And the Muslim population in Australia is growing like topsy. And I've read there are lots of Muslims who believe it's their duty to convert the rest of the world to Islam. With all their Islamic schools, and the attitudes they bring from their home countries, do you really believe they're interested in becoming real Australians? It seems to me like lots of them just want to have their little Afghanistans and little Somalias here, with their own laws so they can keep their women under the thumb, and so on. And now this terrorism. I think we're taking on real problems that we don't need. But David, you're the expert – what do you think?"

"Well, I must admit I'm not feeling very positive about Muslims at this moment." The others nodded silently, all aware of how much the death of his mother, and the manner of it, had affected him and his family, many of whom were well-known to them. "But I'm trying my best to be objective about it. By the way, keep it to yourselves, but the Prime Minister has asked me to sit in on all the meetings he and his National Security Commission have about this whole matter. It's not just about trying to find the terrorists, but what to do about the whole relationship with the Muslim communities." He added, with venom that shocked them, as he'd always been the most affable of people, as long as they'd known him: "I know it's not my job, but I'll be doing anything I can to help get those sons of bitches that killed Mum and all the others." After a brief silence, his friends murmured their congratulations on him being given such an important task.

Regaining his composure, he went on: "So, I've got to take all these issues about Muslims very seriously, and really try and be constructive about it. What do I think about what you've been saying? Well, first, I've always believed, and still do, that people deep down are pretty much the same, all over the world, with the same sort of aspirations, for themselves and their families. And I think they all want to get on with other people – they don't want wars, and terrorism. And so, I think the same about the Muslims who are here, those who were born here, and those who've emigrated here. I'm guessing most of them do actually want to settle in here, and pretty much become Australians like the rest of us, albeit with a few different ideas and ways of doing things. But there do seem to be more issues with Muslim communities than we've had with the other groups who've emigrated here – the Italians, the Greeks, the Vietnamese, the Chinese, the Indians. The reasons for this are really complex, and I'm not going into it now. That's something I've really got to try and find out and see if there's a way to fix it. And these terrorists are stirring things up so that it's going to be much more difficult.

"Bottom line? I'm not sure at the moment what to think. There's a fair bit of truth in what you're saying, Charles, but what do we do about it? People are saying deport them all, but that's crazy –

it's inhumane and impossible anyway. Others are saying stop all immigration of Muslims. That's not impossible, but it's also rather inhumane, and would make us a pariah internationally. So, the answer is we've got to fix it, somehow. My job is to help work out how to do that."

Shortly after the group broke up and David made his way out to the carpark, full of thoughts about what his friends had said. Maybe the only way the Muslim community is ever going to fit in and be accepted by people like his friends is that there needs to be some significant changes, but what? He thought about the Christian Reformation and wondered if such a thing is possible. Maybe Australia could be the first place where a Muslim community takes a giant step away from Traditional Thought. But that's a huge ask. Even if the women stopped wearing veils it would be a big help. He started his car, and headed towards his apartment, where he hoped Dina would shortly be arriving to join him for dinner.

*

Meanwhile, in a low-rise building in West Street in North Sydney, a Meeting of the Australia Arab Chamber of Commerce was about to commence. As is customary at these events the attendees were milling around greeting other members, introducing themselves to those they didn't know and doing their 'networking', the prime justification for most of them being there. Fariq was there, as expected, since he was a member of the Committee. He looked around the room, spied a face he didn't see all that regularly and walked up to him with hand outstretched.

"Mazlin, I'm pleased you've chosen to honour us with your presence" he said with a smile, to indicate he was jesting with him. "It's not often we see you at these meetings."

Mazlin Muhammad replied in kind. "I thought I'd been neglecting the Chamber, and that I'd better show up or you'd kick me out. But actually, I'm interested to hear what these Qataris have got to say, given how they're still persona non grata with half their neighbours."

"Yes, I agree. I'm looking forward to it. Actually, I'm glad you're here, because there's something I think you may be interested in. I and a few friends are meeting with a couple of representatives from the government, to talk about how we can help with all this trouble that's going on resulting from the terrorism, how we can prevent it from happening again, and I thought you might like to join us. There aren't many, I just wanted to get some people who represent the more senior businesspeople from the Muslim community and, if I may say it, who've got their feet well and truly on the ground. There's a lot of people you meet, even at these things, who've got some pretty crazy ideas."

"Sounds OK. When's it on?"

"On Monday. Would that suit?"

"Yes, I think that should be alright. Who are the government people?

"There's one from the Australian Federal Police who's heading up the investigation into the Opera House bombing, Jason Blake. And the other's an academic who's advising the PM and his

National Security Commission about Political Islam, Professor David Scott."

"That sounds interesting." He took out his phone, consulted his Outlook Calendar, and said: "Yes, that's fine. I'll be there."

"Hey. There's Imran Ismail. He's someone else we don't see too often. Excuse me, I've got to nab him too." Fariq made his way over to Imran, went through the same explanation, and they then made their way together into the meeting room.

*

That same afternoon Jason was meeting with his three team leaders at the AFP Sydney Headquarters in Goulburn Street, just up the road from where he and David had recently met for coffee. The feedback was not encouraging. Despite pushing hard into the various Muslim communities and following up on any report of individuals who had any sort of police record, or who had ever been under surveillance, nothing of real interest had been identified.

"The most important investigating we've done" said Mike Anderson, "is interviewing anyone who knew the three men who did the bombing and shooting, and there's still nothing. No indication from any of them about anything that would've led them to think they were even contemplating something like this. And that's worrying, that they were able to keep something so big under their belt so no-one had a clue. That's serious discipline."

"That's right" chimed in Gavin Smith. "Like we've found all along, there are quite a few who have some negative things to say about how they're treated in Australia - the discrimination, even though they were born here. But they're probably not the ones who'll do something like this – they'd never advertise it if they were. But actually, the big majority of the people my team have spoken to were positive about Australia and really shocked about the terrorism."

"But still" said Mike, "those ones who've got negative things to say, who knows whether, if the right person got to them, they couldn't turn them. Just like it appears they turned the three who did the bombing. They didn't appear to have any history before."

The third Team Leader, Jim Callaghan, then offered a thought: "You know, maybe there's some sort of environment in which lots of these young men have been brought up in, that if the right trigger comes along they can switch from being quite normal citizens to suddenly seeing all sorts of things they resent about the West, and Australia, and think they have to fight back."

"You never know" Mike replied. "I've been doing some research and it seems there's certainly some ammunition for them. Do you know that a survey in 2011 showed nearly half Australians have a negative view of Islam? A quarter have anti-Muslim views, and this is five times higher than for any other religion. On the one hand, one side of politics gives Muslims the message that multi-culturalism is great, and that they're free to practice their religion and live according to their cultures, and the other side, people like John Howard and Peter Costello, give quite opposite messages. And the general public tend to back the Howard/Costello view. And that survey I mentioned, I bet if they did the same survey now the results would be at least twice as bad."

At this point Jason intervened. "Getting back to the investigation, from what you're finding I'm guessing that we're highly unlikely to get any clues about who's behind this terrorism by interviewing these people. Not that I think we can afford to stop – you never know what you might stumble over. But I think we're more likely to get a result from other ways. So, that property in the Blue Mountains? And the guns? Jim, you were looking into that - how are they going?"

"We're certainly pursuing them both, but we've been putting more effort into the interviewing so far. We did find a property that could have been a possibility, but it was a dead-end. I could switch some people and put more onto them if you like?"

"Yes, I think so. I said before it's a long shot but we're not getting anywhere with the other stuff, so go for it. OK guys, that's it. I know you're trying but we're going to have to try even harder. Good luck."

He watched as they filed out of his office, thinking, we really do need to get a break.

*

It was a Thursday evening, and Dina was heading to a friend's apartment in Pymble, an up-market suburb about half an hour's drive north of the centre of Sydney. Once a month she and five of her friends, all Muslims, met to catch up and compare notes about what they'd been up to since they'd last seen each other. They'd been friends since university days, and this was their way of ensuring they didn't lose touch. It was also comforting to be able to share problems and ideas with people they knew they could trust, and who'd be sympathetic and helpful. With what was happening since the Opera House bombing there was lots to talk about, and this was the first time they'd be meeting since it happened. She parked in the street outside the apartment building, walked into the lobby and caught the lift to the sixth floor. With only two apartments per floor, her friend Farida had left the front door open so that her visitors could walk straight in. Dina was the last to arrive, so Farida shut the door behind her, and they joined the other four in the lounge room. The apartment overlooked the Pymble Golf Course, so they were able to look out onto the tree-lined fairways that were dappled with long shadows in the soft early evening sunlight, a beautiful view of which they never tired.

For a short time they exchanged notes about their latest doings, but inevitably they turned to the subject of the bombing, beheadings and the retaliations, expressing shock and disbelief that such things could happen here in Australia.

"What I can't believe" said Farida, "is that this could've been done by Muslims who were born and bred in Australia. I mean, you read about young guys being radicalized in places like Pakistan, but here? It just doesn't make sense."

"Your boyfriend David would know all about this, wouldn't he?" another friend, Fauziah, asked Dina. "What's he got to say about it?"

"He hasn't said a whole lot, but the other evening he did ask me whether I knew anything that had been suggested in the Muslim communities about things we could do to get us better accepted by ordinary Aussies. It annoyed me, actually, because it seemed like he was suggesting that it's all our fault. He said if we didn't wear veils it would be a big step, and I thought that was so insensitive. Why should anyone care about whether we wear a veil or not?"

There was a general chorus of agreement with her, particularly as three of them did actually wear a veil. However, one of them, Norani, giggled and said: "You know, I wouldn't mind taking it off. In a way it really bugs me, but I'd get so much disapproval from my family, my boyfriend – it just wouldn't be worth it."

"But don't you think you really should, that it's in the Qur'an, that it's God's command, that it's a sin if you don't?" asked Farida. "I know I don't wear one, nor does Dina or Marina, but I actually feel a bit guilty about it. I tell myself that one day I'll do it."

"Maybe, maybe not. I'm not really convinced. I've read where some experts in Islam say that it's not in the Qur'an at all, that it was just a bunch of men imposing Middle Ages culture on us all" replied Norani.

"That's exactly what David says" said Dina. "He told me once about a group of clerics about a thousand years ago, the Mu'tazilites, who believed that the Qur'an could be contextualized to suit the place and time. He said that was the accepted version of things for awhile, until there was a big fight between them and the Traditionalists, who were very conservative, and they won. So ever since that's been the orthodox thinking, that the Qur'an has to be interpreted literally, and so you can't question it. Or the Sunnah, or Shari'a law. He said that's one of the reasons Muslims around the world are so backward, that they're stuck in Middle Ages thinking."

"Well, I've read that also" said another friend, Marina, who was one of the three, together with Dina and Farida, who didn't wear a veil. "It makes you think. It's pretty convenient for men to have us believe that it's all God's word, so it must be right. So, we have to wear veils, and they can have four wives, and all that other stuff. What do you all think, do you really believe it's true?"

"I'm really shocked that you can be saying that" said the sixth friend, Azizah. "It's fundamental to our religion, we've learned that since we were little kids. If you don't believe that you can't be a Muslim."

"We might have had it drummed into us all our lives, but that doesn't necessarily make it true" retorted Marina. "Sometimes I think that lots of Muslims are too focused on all these peripheral things, and not on the spiritual side, which is what I think a religion is supposed to be about. Surely, it's really about being kind to our fellow human beings, and not about doing things because we're scared of being punished if we don't, like going to Hell. Do you really believe in Hell? I don't think I do."

There was a shocked silence for a few moments while the others digested what Marina had said, then there was a furious debate that went on for some time, but it didn't result in any consensus. Azizah was quite convinced that Marina was completely wrong (she told her, good-humouredly, that she'd have to start praying for her to save her from Hell), but the other four were not sure what to think. They all admitted that deep down they felt that some aspects of what they'd been taught didn't ring true, but that it was very difficult to go against what they had believed since they were little children.

"Anyhow" said Marina, "just think about what it would be like if all Muslims agreed that the Qur'an could be contextualized. Think how it could change the way women are treated, no more excuses quoting the Qur'an. We could be truly equal like women are here."

"But they're not totally equal, even here" argued Farida.

"Maybe not, but they're light years ahead of most Muslim communities" retorted Marina.

"But there's one thing that really worries me about all this" said Farida, changing the subject, "and that is you read about those suicide bombers who apparently are indoctrinated to believe that they'll go to heaven, and have forty virgins, and all that rubbish, because what they're going to do is justified in the Qur'an, and that's the word of God so it must be right. If Muslims didn't believe that the Qur'an had to be taken literally, then the ones that do the indoctrinating couldn't get away with it. That's probably how they got the guys who bombed the Opera House to do it." The others all murmured agreement, even Azizah.

"Getting back to the Opera House, have any of you had any bad experiences - there's lots in the news about things happening, and then there was that bombing of the mosque the other day?" asked Norani.

Dina mentioned about the boys in her class questioning her, and all three of the ladies who wore veils recounted how they had been verbally abused a few times in the street. Norani asked angrily how on earth people could associate what had happened with ordinary Muslims. "It's like they're all against us, that they don't want us here" she said.

"I don't think it's all of them" ventured Dina, "but I have to admit there seems to be a lot of negative feeling. I think even David's a bit that way, but you must remember his mother was killed in the Opera House."

"Oh my God. I didn't realize that" said Azizah in a shocked voice. "I guess it's hard to blame him."

"Yeah maybe. But even so, I think he of all people should know better than to blame a whole society because of what a tiny few did. I can't help myself feeling angry with him."

A short time later it was time to go, and soon Dina was back in her car heading towards the Harbour Bridge to meet David at his apartment. As she drove, she thought about the conversation they'd had, and was amazed at the very idea of them seriously discussing changing the way they thought about the Qur'an – it was so fundamental. And yet, it was a tempting thought. As Marina had said, think how it could change the way women were treated in Islam. But it'll never happen she concluded – the men would surely resist it. What motivation would they have to change things – they've got it made, she thought bitterly. Anyway, right now all that didn't matter – what mattered was what was happening between Muslims and the rest. It was getting ugly, and somehow it all had to be stopped. But who, how? And it was making things uncomfortable between her and David. And she was beginning to really resent having to feel so defensive about being a Muslim. With such troubled thoughts she continued on her way.

*

When Dina arrived at David's apartment he was already there, with an open bottle of wine. After kissing her hello, he poured her a glass and she took it readily, but was suddenly struck with a thought: If I was a good Muslim I wouldn't be doing this. I've really strayed from the path I was taught as a kid. But would God really care whether I have a drink or not? She shrugged off the thought and sat down, while asking David how his day had been.

"I met Charles, Frank and Geoff at the Club for a drink. Just catching up."

"What did you talk about? Anything interesting?"

"Oh, all sorts of things. The bombing, beheadings, what the government's doing and saying, all the usual things you'd expect at the moment."

"I'll bet they had lots to say - they can be a bit redneck sometimes."

"They're OK, just don't know much about Islam, so they've got some preconceived notions. You know that silly bugger Geoff reckoned that because Muslim men can have four wives they'd end up out-populating the rest of the world. Cost him a round of drinks for being so stupid."

"That's really crazy" Dina said. "But I've seen rubbish like that on the internet, how Europe is going to be Muslim in fifty years. And your friends are professionals, they're supposed to be well-educated! If that's what they think, imagine what the not so educated think. What chance have we got?"

"Come on Dina, they're not all that bad" David responded, but even as he said it, he was thinking that actually, a lot were. There was so much distrust, especially now.

They moved on to safer subjects, watched the news, and then David cooked up a light meal. As they were clearing the dishes Dina asked him: "What time's the funeral tomorrow? Where do you want me to meet you?"

David hesitated, took a deep mental breath, and started a subject he knew was going to turn out really badly. "Look, I wanted to talk to you about that. Some of the family think it might be awkward for you if you come to the funeral, given how Mum was killed. There's likely to be a lot of people there, and we mightn't know lots of them, and there might be a bit of hostility."

Dina was silent for a moment while she digested this, something which she hadn't even considered as a possibility. "You say some of the family, what about you?"

"No, of course not. We argued, but they came on pretty strong. It got a bit nasty. I can't believe that they'd think like this – they know how I feel about you, that we're engaged. I think it's just that everyone's feeling pretty raw, and all this stuff that's happening is making it worse."

Dina could feel the tears building up. She felt as though she was being betrayed, by people she thought had accepted her as part of their family. Is this the way it's always going to be, she thought bitterly? Maybe her parents were right, and that she should stick to her own kind. But she loved David, but was that enough?

"And what do you think?" she eventually asked. "Do you think I should stay away?"

"No, absolutely not. I told them that if you didn't go then I wouldn't either. They all knew that wasn't a tenable scenario, so they backed down. But I just wanted to warn you, so that you'd know what to expect, if anyone behaved strangely."

There was a long silence, and eventually Dina spoke, sadly: "This is the last thing you want when you're burying your mother. I don't want to have you worrying about me, when you should be thinking about her, and your family. It's best that I don't go."

"No, I won't hear of it. You're my fiancé, I want you there."

"I know you do, but it's best this way. I won't go."

They didn't speak for some time. David had given up trying to dissuade her and deep down, even though he was ashamed of the thought, he felt maybe it was indeed for the best. Eventually Dina turned, started to gather up her things: "I think I'll go home. I suddenly feel very tired."

David reached for her and put his arms around her: "Darling, I'm sorry. I can see this has really hurt you. It's the last thing I wanted."

"I know. It's not your fault. It's just the way things are. I'll see you in a couple of days when you've done what you have to do with your family."

David walked her to her car, they kissed goodnight, and she drove off, struggling to hold back her tears. He walked back to his apartment, thinking about what had just happened. It began to become clear to him just how awful this situation was for Dina, and how it could even raise questions about their relationship. Surely they were too far down the track with each other for this to seriously affect them? Or were they? The more he thought about it the more he realized that his family pushing his fiancé away at such an important event as the burial of his mother was a serious rejection of her – and he'd always assumed they all got on so well. And he hadn't tried very hard to persuade her to come – he'd taken the easy way out. Christ, I'm a selfish prick, he berated himself. When this was all over he'd have to fix this – it suddenly hit him how much he needed Dina, and there was no way he was going to lose her. But first he had to bury his mother.

*

Sydney: Present Day

The Iraqi was on the phone to the Manager of his Brisbane halal store.

"Good afternoon, Abdul. How are things going this week – is business good?" he asked.

"Yes. Despite all the fuss our people are still going out shopping."

"That's good to hear. It's the same in the Sydney and Melbourne stores. Maybe our people are coming more to our stores and less to the ordinary supermarkets. So, I think we need to order in a bit

more stock – we don't want to run out. Check out the fastest-moving items and get some more of them, OK?"

"Sure. We'll get right on it."

Abdul hung up and looked across at his Co-Manager, Hamid. "That was the boss. It's time for another round."

That evening, just after 6.00pm, the two of them drove to the outskirts of Brisbane to a national forest that was a favourite of the fitness brigade due to the wide choice it offered for jogging tracks. Over the previous two weeks they'd made a number of visits and explored the various tracks and observed how frequently runners used them. They'd decided on one which was a little further from the main car park than the other tracks, and which was a lot less used. They parked at one side of the main car park, left the car separately and headed into the forest in different directions. Both were in running gear, although with a light jacket on top of their T-shirts. After going some distance into the forest, they both made their way to the track they had chosen, to a particular spot they'd agreed offered good cover so that they couldn't be seen by a runner, no matter from which direction he or she came. They then settled down and waited patiently, keeping a close eye on the track in each direction.

At much the same time a quite similar routine was being followed by their colleagues from the Melbourne and Sydney stores. The Iraqi's phone calls to them all had, of course, been a code to swing them into action - it was time to give the terror cauldron another stir and push an already unsettled population closer to breaking point.

The following morning Jason received a phone call giving him the unpleasant news that three more beheadings had occurred, one in each of the same three cities and with the same note affixed to the bodies. And predictably, as sought by The Iraqi and his co-conspirators, the media exploded with sensational coverage, with increasingly inflammatory comments on talk-back radio. The Iraqi watched the TV coverage, and listened to the radio, and smiled with grim satisfaction – his men had pulled off another series of attacks, apparently had gotten clean away with it, and the media was reacting as he had hoped. Things were proceeding very satisfactorily he thought – he couldn't hope for anything more.

But if he wasn't hoping for more he received it anyway. That night an extreme-right gang, possibly but not necessarily the same one that had bombed the mosque a week earlier, carried out another bombing. This time it was a larger mosque, and this time with far more casualties – over twenty people were killed, and another thirty injured, some severely. This time the media coverage was different, with more than a few talk-back callers suggesting that, while it was a terrible act, it was perhaps understandable. Some of the talking-heads on the TV panel shows followed a similar line, tut-tutting about how such violence could never be justified, but nevertheless suggesting the non-Muslim population was losing patience and that more of the same was likely. But the politicians, both government and opposition, emphasised how dangerous the situation was becoming, and that it was imperative that people remain calm. The word had leaked that David was working with the Prime Minister's Cabinet emergency group, so he was now being perceived as the 'expert' on what was happening. He was called up by a number of TV stations to comment, and he made the point again and again that these retaliatory acts were simply playing into the hands of the terrorists, that this was the very response they were after. But it was becoming clear the general population was beginning to panic, and things were close to getting completely out of hand.

Chapter 10

It was the following morning and Dina had had a restless night's sleep, thinking about what had happened with David. The reaction of his family had really shocked her, shaking the foundations of her carefully constructed life in her adopted country. She'd assumed that she was now considered a real Aussie by all who met her, with her good education, excellent English, willingness to have a drink or two, and generally her ability to fit in to any social situation in which she found herself. It no longer occurred to her that anyone would care one way or the other if they knew she was a Muslim. And now, when put to the test, all that counted for nothing – she was a Muslim, therefore she fell into the stereotypical category of being part of a group of crazy people who followed medieval laws and who were sympathetic to terrorists. If that's the way they think, then am I wasting my time going to all this effort to fit in? In fact, am I a traitor to my faith and my fellow Muslims by doing so? I've been hiding the fact that I'm a Muslim so people will accept me more. Maybe I should make it clear to them that that's what I am – take it or leave it. Such thoughts went around and around in her head until by morning she'd made what was for her a radical decision.

After she showered and dressed and put on her makeup, she opened one of her drawers and pulled out a veil from a choice of two different types that she kept for occasions when wearing a veil was a must. One type was what is known in Malaysia as a *tudung,* which is similar to the headgear worn by a Catholic nun, which covers the hair completely but doesn't cover the face. She'd wear that when she was on holiday in Malaysia and at a function where it was expected, even insisted upon, by her relations. The other she wore in Australia when she attended a mosque, which was much more revealing, a very light scarf actually, which was placed loosely over the top of her head and which left much of her hair revealed – the same style favoured by Benazir Bhutto, the glamorous two-time Prime Minister of Pakistan. Dina never wore it anywhere else other than at the mosque - but not today.

Thus attired she sallied forth, drove to her school and parked in the spot reserved for her. When she passed the security guard at the front entrance, he gave her a quizzical look but didn't say anything. When she walked into the teachers' area where she had a locker it was a different story.

"Hey, Dina. What's the story with the veil?" one of them asked her, Joan, a woman with whom Dina got on particularly well.

"Well, I'm a Muslim, and we're really supposed to wear a veil."

"But you've never done so before. Why now?"

"I guess I just think it's right for me. I've been thinking about my religion a lot, and I think it's time."

"You've picked a hell of time to do it, if you don't mind me saying so. Surely you've read about all the incidents where women in veils have been harassed?"

"Yes, I have. I just don't think I'm being true to myself if I pretend I'm something different to what I really am."

Joan looked at her for a moment, then said: "I think you're being very idealistic, and also I think you're kidding yourself. That's not really you. This is the wrong time to be making a stand like this." She walked towards the door to go to her classroom, with a final comment: "Dina, sorry, but I think this'll end in tears."

Joan's reaction left Dina a little taken aback, although she'd expected that her veil would prompt some sort of reaction. But the seriousness with which her friend had spoken to her unnerved her slightly. But she shook it off – what did you expect, she thought. If you want to stand up for your faith, you'd better be prepared to take a bit of heat. She then went in to her first class, and as soon as she walked in there was a total silence from the 25 or so students who would normally not quieten down so much at her usual entrance. But despite some whispering among themselves no-one made any direct comment. The reaction was much the same for the rest of her classes. But, after her last class she was summoned to the Principal's office. What on earth is this about, she thought, with a little apprehension? She was one of the best-performing teachers and was a particular favourite of the Principal.

The Principal, John Hargreaves, was in his early 50's, a kindly man who ran a very successful school and was very popular with staff and students alike. When Dina walked in he stood up and smiled and gestured to her to sit down.

"Hi Dina. How are things with you?" he asked.

"Fine thanks, John" she replied, a little apprehensively, "although I'm wondering why you wanted to see me. Is there any problem?"

"No, not a problem. But I heard that you've chosen to change your appearance, and it made me wonder if there's anything that's happened to bring that about. I was worried that maybe you're having some sort of difficulty that you'd be willing to share with me."

"No, John. I just felt that I'd come to a stage in my life when my religion should be more important to me. You know that strictly speaking we Muslim women should wear some sort of veil."

"Yes, I know that, but I also know that lots of practicing Muslim women choose not to. I gather there's some debate as to whether it's really mandatory, or just something that reflects culture more than religion."

"That's true. I think for me it's more about being more positive about my faith, being proud of it rather than hiding it from view."

The Principal studied her for a few moments, and then asked: "I don't suppose it's got anything to do with all this trouble we're going through at the moment, the terrorism?"

She hesitated, then replied: "Perhaps it has. A lot of my fellow-Muslims are getting abused just because they happen to be Muslims, and I think it's so unfair. It seems to me a little cowardly to hide the fact that I'm a Muslim too."

Again, the Principal studied her for quite a few moments, before saying: "I understand where you're coming from, and I don't want to suggest to anyone how they should practice their religion. We're a Church of England school, but I was very happy to take you on because I believe strongly that all religions should get on with each other, and that having teachers from religions other than Christian is good for our students. You didn't wear a veil, and I'll deny saying this if you ever repeat it, but that made it a lot easier for me. I happen to think religion is a private matter, and that making a constant public statement about what religion one practices is promoting difference, and I don't think that's good. I can't do anything about it if you insist on wearing a veil – all I can say is that I'd prefer it if you didn't. I'd say the same if we had a Jewish teacher who wanted to wear a skull cap to class."

After a pause he went on: "But there's another thing, and this is simply advice for your own good. At this moment, with what's going on out there, choosing to put on a veil is inflammatory. I know it shouldn't be so, but it is. I'm worried for your sake that you could get hurt by some idiots who think they're standing up for their version of what they think Australia is."

Dina was silent, and simply looked down, avoiding his eyes. He waited for a few moments, but clearly, she was not going to respond, so he stood up, signaling the end of the meeting.

"OK, you don't need to say anything, I just want you to think about what I've said. If you want to talk again about this, I'm available any time. Understand?"

She smiled her thanks, and left his office, again slightly perturbed at what had John had said. All this fuss over a veil, she thought. Why does it cause so much aggravation? What are people scared of? She gathered her things and walked out to her car, her first day of 'going public' at an end, and her mind a little confused as to how she felt about it. I wonder what David's going to say, she thought? He'll probably freak out, but that's just too bad. In that defiant mood she set off towards home.

*

That same morning, David, his extended family, and over two hundred other mourners gathered at the Waverley cemetery to bury his mother. The service had been held at St James Church in King Street in central Sydney, and David, his sister, and one of Charlotte's close friends delivered eulogies, all of them full of praise for the way she'd pursued her life, her considerable professional success, and her ability to brighten up any gathering she joined. There were tears on the part of David's sister and the friend, but David remained stoic, although in his speech he didn't hide his anger and hatred for the people who had committed, and were behind, his mother's murder.

He did not, though, articulate his resentment against the culture that seemed to go hand-in-hand with Islam that provided the rationale for what they'd done. He couldn't stop himself asking the same old questions: Is it really just a tiny few, or are they all tarred with the same brush? As long as they all go along with what Islam espouses are they all guilty, at least to some extent? Why is it that a huge majority of Muslims say that Islam is a religion of peace and yet these terrorist monsters continue to commit their crimes in the name of Islam? How do I feel about Muslims generally? Do I want to keep interacting with them, or am I going to stay away from them? But what about Dina? I don't want to stay away from her, and if I'm with her then I have to put up with her family, her friends, and all the rest of them. Even as these thoughts flashed through his mind, he knew he was very confused, and didn't really know what to think. Better forget it all for the moment – get through today and then think it through a bit more carefully. I'm an expert in Political Islam – I can't keep on having these thoughts and still be a real professional.

At the wake, which was held in a large room at the golf club, he calmed down a little after a couple of glasses of wine. He talked to many of the guests, all of whom expressed their deep and genuine condolences for a woman they knew was exceptional, and with whom David had been very close. Eventually, he found himself alone with his sister, Beth.

"How are you going?" she asked.

"I'm OK" he replied, "I guess as much as I can expect."

"How did things go with Dina – I thought yesterday you said you wouldn't come if she didn't also?"

"I did, and I told her that, but she said it was probably better if she didn't." He hesitated before adding: "I'm ashamed of myself, but I was sort of relieved, and didn't make much of a show of insisting."

Beth looked at him closely, before saying: "You know, I didn't agree with what the others were saying. I think it's a terrible slap in the face for her, to be discouraged from coming. And I think you should've insisted. She's the nicest girl you've ever been with. And that's a hell of a big choice" she added, digging him in the ribs. "Don't mess it up and lose her. I hope she hasn't taken it too much to heart, though. This was a really big deal, you know – don't under-estimate how upset she may be. You guys are so bloody insensitive. You're probably going to have to do a hell of a lot of fence-mending."

"Yeah, I probably will. I'm not looking forward to that. Anyway, let's get through today first."

With that, they went their separate ways to mingle with more of the guests.

*

The next morning David was sitting in the waiting room of the President of the Australian Association of Islamic Communities, in a suburb about four kilometres south-east of the city centre, preparing himself for what he envisaged could be a very difficult meeting. The Association described itself on its website as 'The No. 1 Body for Australian Muslims', but in fact had been set up to represent the Sunni population. However, as Sunnis represented the big majority of Muslim populations globally, the claim was probably fair. The Prime Minister's office had set up the meeting so the people attending would know David was representing the National Security Commission of Cabinet. He had persuaded the Prime Minister's advisers that he should go alone as he felt it would lessen any embarrassment that might ensue if the conversation got too heated. Right now he was glad he had done so, as he knew he was in a combative mood. His mother's funeral had rekindled his rage at what had happened and hardened his resolve to try and make sure such a thing could never happen again in Australia, and he was still apprehensive about how his next meeting with Dina would go as they hadn't seen each other the previous evening. He looked up as the receptionist (a woman, in a veil) approached and informed him the other members of the meeting had all arrived and were ready to see him. He followed her into a quite spartan board room where six men were standing to greet him, two of them wearing Islamic headgear and all with beards of one sort or another of Islamic style.

The President of the Australian Association, Reza Muhammad, came forward and introduced himself with a welcoming smile, then introduced the other four, giving their names, the organisation they represented, and their position. Each of them came forward and shook David's hand as their name was mentioned. After the introductions were completed and all were seated, Reza began the meeting.

"Gentlemen, I think you're all aware of Dr Scott's background, that he is a distinguished Professor in Political Science at the University of Sydney, specialising in Political Islam. He's been asked to advise the Prime Minister and his National Security Commission of Cabinet, which is meeting regularly to deal with this crisis of which we are all painfully aware. He is here to seek our help and I've assured him that we'll give him every assistance. I'll now hand over to him to explain."

"Thank you very much, Reza, and thank you all for coming here today. I'm going to ask for your patience and understanding in advance because I think some of the issues I want to raise are going to be quite sensitive and may not be to your liking. But they're critical issues that we have to face and find some way of dealing with them. But let me get to it. You all know the three terrorists who committed the Opera House bombing and shooting were born and raised in Australia, and that fact, over and above the atrocity itself, is giving us a great deal of heartache." He looked around the table, and they all nodded acknowledgement.

He went on. "There are two things we're trying to do, in parallel. The first, obviously, is to find who's behind the Opera House bombing and the subsequent atrocities and put them out of business. The longer these things go on the worse the situation out will get, and it's already spiraling out of control. The extreme-right is now involved, and it's odds on that retaliation back and forth is going to happen. The AFP and the state police forces are pulling out all stops on this, as I'm sure you'll be aware, because they're putting big pressure on your communities. I imagine you're getting a lot of feedback and complaints about it." He looked around the table, and again there were grim nods of acknowledgement. "We can come back to that later."

"Difficult as that situation is, I think the second issue is much more so. If young men, born and raised here, could commit an act like this then it appears something has gone seriously wrong with how they've been brought up, what they've been taught, how they view the non-Muslim communities here. As part of what the PM is tackling with his National Security Cabinet, he's asked me to try and get to the bottom of this, and see whether there's any way to tackle it, and fix it, so it can't happen again. I'm hoping that you'll help me by facing up to what's happened and see if we can agree what the underlying causes are."

He stopped and gave them time to digest what he'd said and waited for some sort of initial reaction. It came shortly, from Zaid Hamid, the Head of the Australian Association of Imams.

"Dr Scott, I'm getting the feeling already that you think this a Muslim problem, that there's some fundamental flaw with Islam, and I totally reject that sort of thinking. We're talking about three men, out of a Muslim population in Australia of about 600,000. And as for suggestions that there's some problem with how Muslims here view non-Muslim populations, what about the man that did the Christchurch shooting? He was a non-Muslim, born and raised in Australia, and he killed over 50 Muslims. There are bad people in any community, Muslims just like any other."

"True, but if you take the Christchurch man, it still reflects a problem between Muslim and non-Muslim communities. But as for those three terrorists here just being an isolated aberration, there are obviously people behind them. The police have established that they were radicalised – they were perfectly normal a few years earlier. And someone had to train them and get them the equipment they used. This is a far bigger operation than just those three men. And let's face some hard facts. This is not just some terrible, isolated incident. Things like this are happening all over the world. Young men are radicalised to become martyrs while attacking Western targets – Copenhagen, Nice, London, Paris."

"But Dr Scott" Zaid replied, "you know there've been many academic studies about this, and the conclusion is that the reason these people do these things is to fight back against the atrocities the West and its ally Israel have committed, and are still committing, against Muslim populations. Look at the invasion of Iraq. I don't agree with what they do, but it's not Islam, it's political."

"It's one thing to do that in a war zone" David shot back, "when a perceived enemy is right in front of you. But against civilians? And here in Australia? Look, there are things going on here that I think are just not right. Your Islamic schools have got Wahhabism on the curriculum, and we all know how extreme that is. You import your imams from countries that have vastly different cultures to Australia. And not just imams - a recent Head of your Australian Association couldn't even speak English. And look at what your 'Mufti of Australia' said, about women asking to be sexually assaulted – he called them fresh meat."

"He was extreme, and we don't agree with many of the things he said. But the other things. Why shouldn't we bring imams from countries where they've been properly trained? And Wahhabism – if the Saudi government is good enough to fund the building of schools and mosques it seems only fair that we teach our students about how the religion is practiced in Saudi Arabia, the birthplace of Islam."

David's hackles were beginning to rise: "And let's look at where most of these imported imams have come from, and the sort of environment they've been brought up in. Saudi Arabia, Iran, Pakistan – women severely subjugated, no pluralism in religion, polygamy. And Wahhabism, the most extreme of all sects of Islam, the inspiration for terrorists everywhere. If this is the sort of influence some of your children are getting, then they're going to have the same sort of attitudes as in those countries I mentioned. Is that what we want in Australia?

"Are you saying that we're not allowed to practice our cultures and religion here. I thought Australia was all about multi-culturalism?"

David could see that the discussion was starting to turn into an argument but pressed on anyway: "Multi-culturalism is all very well, up to a point, but we don't want little Somalias or little

Afghanistans or little Pakistans here, with all their own rules. This is Australia, and you have to live by Australia's laws, and ways of doing things."

Zaid was also not about to back down: "You can't expect people who've been brought up in a certain culture and way of life to just change overnight. You've got to be sensitive to our cultures."

At this David exploded, unable to stop himself, the words spilling out: "You guys just don't get it. You carry on as though you're still living in Pakistan or Afghanistan or wherever. You're not – you're here in Australia, and it's not a Muslim-majority country. You have to fit in here, just like we have to if we want to stay in your country. You complain about lack of sensitivity to your culture – what about your lack of sensitivity to our culture? Women wearing veils – it reminds people of what they see on TV from the Middle East and Afghanistan, and all those negative associations come back. Our women change how they dress when they go to your countries so why can't your women do that here? How can you be so arrogant as to expect our councils to shut swimming pools to the general public just so your women can swim in private? And it's all so ridiculous, convincing women that all this modesty is about religion."

He paused for breath, and looked around at his audience, aware that he'd broken all rules of civil discussion. After a stunned silence Reza said gently:

"Professor Scott, I think you're being overly harsh."

David paused, took a deep breath, and replied: "I'm sorry. You're right. That was out of order, but I've had this bottled up for a long time, and these are exceptional times where some hard truths have to be faced. Look, there's something I think you all need to realize. You mightn't like what I've just said, but I'm afraid it reflects the reality of what a hell of a lot of Australians really think, but they're too scared to come out and say it. There's a minority of people, generally academics and others on the left of politics, and many in the mainstream media, let alone social media, who'll shout you down if you dare say a negative word about Muslims, or Islam. They'll accuse you of being Islamophobic, an Alt-Right, whatever. They'll make your life hell, you could lose your job, because few people are brave enough to come out and support you. It's not just Australia, it's everywhere. But deep down they agree, and that's why they elect people like Donald Trump, and Geert Wilders and Pauline Hanson, because even though most of what they say is rubbish, they articulate some of the fears that lots of people have. So, what happens? There's no intelligent, reasoned debate about very real issues that have to be tackled and sorted out if the relationship between the Muslim community and the rest of the Australian population is going to be what it should be. Can you get that?"

After another long pause Reza said: "OK David, you've made your point very strongly, and while it's not what we want to hear I think at least you're giving us the hard truth. Generally, when we hear anything like this it's in the form of abuse, from very uninformed people, so we don't take a lot of notice. But we can't say you're uninformed - you're highly educated, you have a fair bit of knowledge about Islam and Muslims, and I believe you mean well. So, let's have that reasoned discussion. What else have you got to say, what do you suggest?"

David had calmed down by now and thought to himself that maybe losing his temper mightn't have been such a bad thing – it seemed they were prepared to listen, at least the Council Head anyway, and that's really important: "Well, thank you for that invitation. First, something fundamental. As I said earlier, during my rant – again, I'm sorry about that - people can't come here to Australia and aspire to live in just the same way they did in their home country, where the laws reflected a fair bit, or a lot, of Shari'a law. So, like I said before, I don't think it makes sense to bring imams here who've been trained in those sorts of countries – they're going to perpetuate that thinking. I think you've got to train your own people here, who've been born and raised here, and who really understand this country, its laws, it's general culture. It especially doesn't make sense to have any of your schools including Wahhabism in their curriculum – it can't help but have a bad influence on your children. There are thinking Muslims all over the non-Arab world who bemoan the 'Arabisation' that's happening in their countries, all because they've been seduced by Saudi money."

Reza responded: "I do see your point about those issues, and we've been having discussions recently about them in our own circles. We're not all in agreement" – he looked meaningfully at the Head of the Council of Imams – "but I think the direction in which we're heading is along the lines you've just described. Any other ideas?"

"OK, another important one. It would seem that both of us – by that I mean your various community organisations and the government organisations – need to do even more to settle in new Muslim arrivals into the country. I know a lot of work is already being done, by both groups, but it's clear we need even more. It's critical that all new arrivals learn to speak English as fast as possible, and we need to put more effort into this. And perhaps even more important, we need to do everything possible to ensure people get jobs, especially the young people. We all know that unemployment is a major reason young people can go off the rails, particularly young men."

All the meeting participants nodded their heads in agreement with this suggestion, Reza saying: "As you said, we're already very conscious of this, but clearly we have to do more. And we'd welcome more input from the government. Anything else?"

"Well, I do have a couple of things, but while I think they make eminent sense, they're extreme. I almost hesitate to raise them, because I know that some of you, probably all of you, will hit the roof, but after what I said earlier, I don't think I can offend you any more. So here goes. The first one is veiling, the point I so rudely made earlier. It really invites attention and is a major differentiator between Muslims and non-Muslims, and for what purpose? Surely you'd agree with me that it's a cultural thing, and not really about religion? You're now in a culture where women wearing veils is frowned upon, so why do it? Already lots of Muslim women here don't wear a veil, so what's the harm? It would just take one item of difference off the table, and a big one."

Abdul Rashid, the President of the Muslim Association of NSW, responded strongly: "Dr Scott, first, you're making a big assumption when you say that we'd agree with you that veiling has nothing to do with Islam. And secondly, these women want to wear a veil. And thirdly, surely it's the Australians who should accept that this is our culture, and have some understanding?"

"On that last one, I thought I'd already made the point that you're the ones who should be accepting that you're in a new country where the culture is quite different and make adjustments accordingly" David responded. "And as for women wanting to wear the veil, they might think very differently if they hadn't been brought up to believe that religiously and culturally it's what they should do. Some very enlightened and qualified Muslim women, and men, argue that wearing a veil is a purely cultural issue, and not only that, it reinforces the idea that women are second-class citizens in Islam. Women can't be second-class citizens here."

Before Abdul Rashid could reply, Reza intervened: "It's a logical argument, Dr Scott, and as you rightly point out, there's a lot of debate among Muslims about it. We'll discuss and debate that privately. You mentioned a second contentious suggestion?"

David paused for a moment, debating with himself whether he was really going to proceed with what was on his mind. We're never going to get anywhere if we keep pussyfooting around the issue, he thought, and you reckoned you were going to try and fix it, so here goes.

"We talked earlier about why terrorists do the things they do. Zaid said it's because they're fighting back against the West. Does that explain why they do the same things to other Muslims? Look at Iraq and Syria. And ISIS, worst of all. And you can't keep saying it's got nothing to do with Islam – they invoke Islam all the time. You can't possibly say that every terrorist is just cynically using Islam as a saleable explanation for what they do – a lot of them really believe it, and that's backed up by respectable academics. I agree with you that a great deal of the violence committed by Muslims has very complex motivations and that a lot of these are to do with politics, and that the West is certainly very guilty of lots of bad things. But I also think that Islam is an enabler for terrorists – it seems to be very susceptible to be used by certain people to influence others, who are true believers, that they should commit some atrocity or other because Islam says it's OK to do so."

Zaid broke in: "Dr Scott, you're not about to come up with that old chestnut about how Islam needs a Reformation, an Enlightenment, are you? I'm surprised at you, a supposedly respectable academic."

"I don't think it's academic heresy to raise it as a possibility. A lot of Islamic experts, including Muslims who live in countries where they're free to express their views, have done so. Don't forget the Mu'tazilites. They raised the idea of the Qur'an being able to be contextualised for time and place a thousand years ago, and that was orthodox thinking for a time. So, there's precedent. I'm convinced that as long as Muslims believe the Qur'an has to be interpreted literally, bad people will use it in bad ways. Don't forget that the majority of Muslims around the world live in very poor countries and so are poor and not well educated. They're very susceptible to people who want to influence them in all sorts of ways, from keeping women under their thumb, to stirring them up to lynch innocent people, to persuading them to become martyrs."

"Dr Scott, are you actually seriously suggesting that we change one of the most fundamental beliefs of our religion just to be accepted by Australians?" asked Zaid incredulously. "That's an outrageous idea. I can't believe you said that."

"I know it's outrageous" David replied, "but if it's been done before why not again? Think what an amazing difference it would make to how Muslims could live their lives. If it happened everywhere in the world it would undermine the whole terrorist argument. Australia could be the place where an Islamic Renaissance started, and perhaps influence people elsewhere. And what difference would it really make to the fundamentals of what Islam is about, the spiritual side, and leading a good life? It wouldn't change your Five Pillars. It could definitely change some of your Shari'a laws, but there's a strong argument that they've got nothing to do with real religion anyway, like women's rights. And you could stop having to tie yourselves up in knots trying to defend things like cutting off hands for stealing, and stoning for adultery."

Before Abdul Rashid and Adzhar Hassan, the Head of the NSW Association of Imams, could furiously respond, Reza again intervened: "Once again, Dr Scott, we'll go away and think about that one. It certainly is a very controversial thought, but we're in difficult and strange times, so no idea should be dismissed out of hand. Have you got any other thoughts, perhaps something not quite so extreme?"

"Only two, and the first is something I think you'd welcome. Some of our schools have a bit of education about all the main world religions so that students have at least some understanding of what other people practice. I think it would be a great idea if it was made mandatory that all schools, whether government or private, had to do that, so that over time every Australian had a reasonable understanding of what the major religions were about, and what different people believed. I think one of the problems right now is that too many Australians know very little about Islam."

"Yes" replied Reza, "that would indeed be an idea that we would welcome. And what's the second thing?"

"Gentlemen, I know that notwithstanding what I've been saying, particularly about contextualization, there are quite a few of your fellow-Muslims who are saying similar things. But I don't see it having any significant effect, and I don't think it will until the official bodies like yours take up the cause and publicly help them. Then I think real change could happen. As the representative of the National Cabinet, I'm asking that you seriously consider this."

Reza paused for a moment as he digested this request. "As I said a moment ago, these are strange and difficult times, so it's only right that I give you an undertaking that we'll give this a lot of thought. Alright, I think we can conclude there. Thank you very much for sharing all this with us. I know your intentions are good, even if you gave us a bit of a hard time back there. Actually, we know that you have extra reason to be upset about what's been happening, so we understand you sounding off a little. Don't think any more about it."

At that point, the Head of the Association of Victoria, Mustafa Sulaiman, who had not uttered a word throughout the meeting, said to David: "Dr Scott, I think some of your ideas are very interesting, and I'm going to take them back and discuss them with my Association. We do need to think outside the box a bit. (Abdul Rashid, Zaid and Adzhar looked at him disapprovingly) Thank you, and I look forward to meeting you again soon."

David left the building with a spring in his step, feeling that the meeting had gone far better than he'd dared to hope. Perhaps he was kidding himself, but he thought it was just possible that he might have an ally in Reza, and maybe even Mustafa. Who knows, maybe there were a lot of Muslims like them who were just looking for an excuse to seriously look at change in Islam but were scared to stick their necks out. Maybe it took a crisis like this to jolt them into action. But don't get carried away, he told himself. If this really happened it'd be massive. Let's see what the next few weeks hold.

CHAPTER 11

That same morning Fariq had arranged the first meeting of the group he had described to Jason some time earlier, one he described as 'sensible, moderate businessmen and women' who were desperately keen to help stop the madness that was engulfing Sydney and the other capitals. Jason had asked David to join him, both to hear what this group had to say and to give them better qualified input than he was able to provide. And seated among the rest, one of Fariq's circle of 'respectable businessmen', was The Iraqi, very keen to hear how this group was responding to the way his plan was unfolding. Having received the news of both sets of atrocities earlier in the morning he was hard put to conceal his satisfaction when he greeted Fariq and the fifteen others in the boardroom, instead murmuring the expected expressions of shock at the appropriate times. When all were seated Fariq stood at the front and reminded them why he had called the meeting, although he'd explained this to each person when he first contacted them.

"Ladies and gentlemen (it was a measure of Fariq's open-mindedness that there were two women present), thank you all for coming here today. I've spoken to each of you about the purpose of our meeting, and the terrible news this morning just confirms why it is so critical for people like us to help address what's going on and do anything we can to help stop it."

He then introduced David and Jason, explained their respective roles, and suggested that Jason first give them a brief update on how the search for the terrorists was going, and then David would explain how he thought this group might be able to help. Jason very quickly explained that an intense effort was underway, but at this stage no definite leads had been identified. He figured he would keep the fact that he was pursuing two long-shot possibilities to himself. After he'd finished speaking David stood up and addressed the group.

"Thank you, Fariq, and good morning everyone. I have to say that I was very gratified when I heard about Fariq's offer to get this group together and consider what I'm now going to suggest. I'm sure you understand that we all, that's the entire community, face two fundamental challenges. First, we have to find these terrorists, both groups, I might add, but particularly the Opera House bombers who I think are far more dangerous. That's the task Jason here is charged with, and while I'm sure you'd pass on any lead you may stumble over, we're not expecting that there's much you can do on that score. The second thing is to get to the root of how this could occur, how a group of young Australian-born Muslims could get so radicalized that they could become involved in atrocities like this. How were the conditions created that nurtured such a possibility? Can we change things so that it's a lot less likely to happen again?"

David then proceeded to pursue the same line of argument he used when speaking to the senior group of Muslim Council members a few days earlier, although this time he kept himself well under control and was a model of diplomacy, notwithstanding the fact that the topic was so potentially fraught with the possibility of offence. The suggestions about imams being home-grown rather than being imported, and banning Wahhabism from school curricula, were well-received – in fact there appeared to be universal and enthusiastic agreement that these were ideas that should definitely be implemented. The Iraqi made no comment but didn't indicate in any way that he disapproved.

The subject of veiling created far more discussion, although it was not heated. No-one seemed at all insulted by the suggestion, and various pro and con views were put and debated in a reasoned way. David had not said too much at the outset of this discussion, rather simply throwing in the idea and seeing what resulted. Eventually he gave his justifications for saying that veiling was a completely cultural rather than religious issue, and that it was not, despite what many Muslims and particularly clerics maintained, laid down as mandatory in the Qur'an. Finally, Fariq spoke up, making the point that neither of the women in the room wore a veil, and that virtually all the wives of those present also didn't wear a veil. He confessed that he privately had thought for many years that veiling wasn't compulsory, and that he agreed with David's point that in a Western environment it unnecessarily highlighted difference between Muslims and non-Muslims, and that this was clearly counter-productive. There was a general, although not universal, murmur of agreement around the room.

With a little trepidation, David raised the most sensitive of the issues he had discussed with the other group, namely, the idea that there were many respectable scholars of Islam who maintained that it was not heretical to believe that the Qur'an did not need to be interpreted literally. This time there were several expressions of dismay at such a thought.

"This is one of the most fundamental beliefs of our religion" one of them, Mazlin Muhammad, said. "You can't be a Muslim if you don't believe that." Most of the others indicated their agreement. David then explained about the Mu'tazilites, and the fact that there was historical precedent for such a belief being the orthodox view. He also quoted various well-known Muslim scholars based in various Western countries who supported this view.

"Just think about the implications if this became the orthodox view" he put to them. "Terrorists would find it far more difficult to rationalize their actions on the basis that it's in the Qur'an and therefore must be right. Impressionable young men would not be so readily persuaded that if they committed some or other atrocity that it was sanctioned by God and that they would be martyrs and go to Heaven. Women wouldn't have to feel that they were obligated to wear a veil. The list goes on." He also made the point that it would make no difference to the spiritual aspects of Islam.

Mazlin again made an objection: "But Dr Scott, whatever you say, you're talking about essentially dismantling our religion. This is going too far. I'm sure the normal Muslim would reject such an idea out of hand. In fact, they'd be horrified." Several of the others nodded their agreement.

"I understand why you would feel this way. It's a radical idea, for most people. But honestly, I think you'd be surprised at how many of the intelligentsia who have the freedom to think what they like and express what they like actually believe this. They wouldn't do that lightly. But here's another way of looking at it, and I hope you're not offended by this line of argument. I'd put it to you that this is a matter of belief. Some well meaning and intelligent people think one thing, and another similar group thinks something else. Who's right? Who's to say? But here's the thing. What has the Traditional way of thinking brought the world of Islam? I'd put it to you that much of that world is still locked in an almost Medieval mind-set, where people think more about what they think is the next world instead of getting on with this one, with women being pretty well second-class citizens, with populations that are poor and ill-educated. Why not try the other view, the way the Mu'tazilites saw things, and see what happens? It's like when a tennis player is losing a match – he changes his game plan, because keeping on with the current one will guarantee that he'll lose." David realized that he'd started to speak a little more passionately than he'd intended, so he paused for breath, and had a good look at his audience. To his surprise he saw that some of them were smiling a little and nodding their approval.

Fariq again said his piece: "David, I think you've struck a chord with some of us at least. I've felt what you're arguing for a long time, since I was quite young, actually, but I didn't dare come out and say it. But things are different now. We can't afford for things to stay as they are. We've got to change, I think not just because of what's going on right now because of this terrorism, but for our long-term good. This is going to be a very difficult thing to persuade most of our fellow-Muslims about, but I think we should give it a try. It might take years, if we succeed at all, but we should try."

There was a little more discussion, with a few people confirming that they had similar thoughts to Fariq and others saying that they felt this was treading on dangerous ground. But no-one was now completely condemning the idea – after his initial objection even Mazlin seemed to have gone along with the mood of the rest of the group. Eventually Fariq made the following observation: "I'm getting the impression that quite a few of you don't believe the Qur'an has to be interpreted literally, and the rest are in two minds about it, so why do we keep on letting the conservatives have their way, bullying people into going along with what they say? Look at what happens in places like Pakistan."

One person spoke up: "It's not so easy. The whole Muslim world believes it, and if you don't go along with it, they'll say you're a blasphemer."

"We're in Australia, not Saudi Arabia or Pakistan" Fariq responded. "For too long we've let the conservatives have their way, and if you know your history, as we do, we know they don't have a monopoly on how Muslims should practice their faith. We don't have a Pope, we can have our own interpretation and be just as good a group of Muslims as they are. And we can get ourselves out of Middle Ages thinking and into the 21st century. Most Muslims here are well educated and are not going to get whipped into a religious frenzy by the clerics and lynch us. They can be talked to and reasoned with."

There was no further comment, so Fariq suggested that they should call it a day. "Let's think hard about what's been said today and meet again soon to discuss it further." David and Jason waited with Fariq until the others had left, and then thanked him profusely for getting the group together.

"I'm amazed at the reaction" David said. "I was hoping that it would at least be given a fair hearing, but I never expected any of you to actually agree with the idea."

"I think you may be surprised at how many educated Muslims harbor these heretical thoughts" replied Fariq. "You've rightly pointed out that it doesn't mean we're no longer believers – it simply means we feel our religion has to modernize and leave that

Traditional thinking behind. If we don't, we're fearful that Muslim populations will be forever condemned to be poor and/or backward. Maybe something good can come out of this terrible time."

*

Sydney: Present day

"May Allah curse that interfering kaafir", The Iraqi said to himself in his own language, so incensed that he said it out loud, as he drove away from Fariq's meeting. David was the focus of his fury, the one he saw as the person guilty of planting the seeds of blasphemy in the minds of his traitorous fellow Muslims. And they were so ready to be led astray, he thought incredulously. How could supposedly good Muslims, pillars of the community, allow themselves to consider such outrageous ideas that struck at the heart of what Islam was all about? In his view if one didn't accept the Qur'an as the literal word of God and interpret it accordingly then one couldn't be a Muslim. In fact, if a Muslim, who should know better, rejected that belief then he was the enemy. In a flash of anger, the thought entered his head that all the people who attended that meeting deserved to die, particularly Fariq, Jason and David. But David was the greatest enemy, the most dangerous.

By the time he'd reached his home that thought had crystallised to the point that he decided to seriously consider doing something about David, and maybe Jason as well. He was skilled at research, and with the access that Google, Facebook and the other social media provided, it was not difficult for him to build up a fairly comprehensive picture of both men.

Considering what he'd found out about Jason, he debated whether or not he needed to do anything about him. How much risk did he pose to his plans? He cleared his head of the fury he'd been feeling about the meeting. Then, in the manner in which he had become adept since he had become (in his mind) a revolutionary, thought dispassionately about Jason, whether it was necessary to eliminate him. It didn't take him long to reach a decision. Jason was indeed a clever and formidable adversary, and he had no doubt that, with the considerable resources he had at his disposal, he would soon crack the case. He didn't resent this, in fact he quite respected Jason who in his mind was a soldier doing his duty. He had always been resigned to the fact that one day he'd be found out and killed, and he decided now that it might as well be Jason who was the one to do it. If it wasn't him it would be someone else, and so the difficulty and risk involved in killing him just wasn't justified. So, Jason was in the clear – he would leave him be. If Jason had been able to read The Iraqi's mind he would have been very relieved. Pursuing terrorists always involved risk, and he had no illusions about the dangers his job sometimes involved, but being at the top of the 'hit list' of whoever it actually was who was masterminding this particular terrorist programme would fill anyone with dread.

Having made that decision, The Iraqi turned his attention to David. He found it a little harder to remain cold and dispassionate about this kaafir swine who was potentially posing a serious threat to the major purpose of all his plans. All his efforts, the bombing, the beheadings, and the reaction they were generating from the right-wing extremists and other hotheads in the non-Muslim population were meant to encourage his fellow Muslims to retreat into their own communities with the solace of an even more traditional version of Islam. And here was this peacock with his so-called academic expertise putting that in jeopardy. After a thorough check of David's background and career, the biggest trouble with him, The Iraqi had to reluctantly concede, was that he was convincing. He did indeed know about a lot about the history of Islam, and about the politics associated with it. And he was very articulate, and intelligent, so that he could put his point of view across very persuasively. On top of it all, he had the ear of the Prime Minister and his Cabinet which gave him the aura of authority, and The Iraqi knew that his fellow-Muslims respected authority. That was the sealer – he had, if at all possible, to be eliminated. And unlike the situation with Jason, if David was out of the picture, it would be far harder to find another 'look-alike'. And then maybe all this talk of 'reform of Islam' would die down.

While doing his checking of David, he had also discovered that he had a fiancé, and that she was a Muslim. He duly carried out an investigation of Dina, and concluded, unsurprisingly, that he strongly disapproved of her. She was engaged to an infidel, she was teaching in a Christian school, she didn't wear a veil, and there were photos of her drinking wine. However, this didn't concern him – she was not important in the whole scheme of things, unless she provided an opportunity to get to David.

By this time, he'd arrived at his Sydney store, and after a short time doing his usual checking of how things were faring business-wise, he called the two managers into his office, and shared his thoughts with them.

"There's a man, you might have seen him on the news, Professor David Scott. He's becoming a real threat to our cause, and I've decided that, if it's possible, he should be eliminated."

"What's the problem with this guy?" asked one of the managers, Ashraf. The Iraqi explained, and both his managers agreed that he was indeed dangerous.

"But we'll only do it if it's perfectly safe. We can't jeopardise the bigger game we're playing. There's still some more stirring of the pot that we can do, and I believe is still very necessary, and we can't do it if we've been caught trying to kill this son-of-a-bitch. So, what I want you to do is to watch him for a few days, see if there's any pattern to his movements, so that we can work out a plan to take him out. But be careful, make sure he doesn't catch on that he's being followed. He probably won't – he's a civilian, not trained in this sort of thing. Understood?"

They both nodded. He then gave them all the details he had about David, including photos. He also explained about Dina, and that it was likely that David would be regularly seeing her, so that one of his visits to her, or her to him, could possibly provide an opportunity. They decided that they'd follow him each morning, and evening, when he was going from and to his home, as these were the most likely times in which he would possibly have some sort of routine. Then, during the day, they could look after the store – they had three helpers, but they needed quite close supervision. With that agreed they filed out of the office, leaving The Iraqi to his own thoughts, which were becoming uneasy. Things had gone so well up until now, in fact better than he'd dared to hope. The extreme right-wing people had reacted exactly as he had predicted, and he found it interesting to speculate what their motives were. Was it outrage at what had happened, or did they also want to stir things up between Muslims and non-Muslims to the point of causing a permanent rift between them? If that was *the case, they had a shared objective. How ironic that would be, he thought.*

But now he had a sense that his time was running out, that Jason and his people would soon find some connection between him and the atrocities. Going after David put him at further risk of exposure. But it's going to happen anyway, he thought, and David is a real danger. No, I'll still do it. And I think I'd better get ready for the final act. In contemplating this he had a combination of fear, and relief. His fear was more that of not wanting to fail at what he was attempting – he had little fear of death, as he truly believed he would be going to a better place, where he would see his wife and children again. The relief would be to have it finally over, all these years of planning and waiting – he'd had enough.

*

The Prime Minister was in his Kirribilli office, switching between TV channels to see what the latest coverage of the two sets of atrocities was showing, when Janet interrupted him to say that the Cabinet group was waiting for him in the meeting room. He immediately rose and joined them. They were all present, including David and Jason.

"OK, first up, Jason. Any new developments?"

"Well, you know about the two latest cases, the beheadings and the extreme-right bombing. We're no further with the Muslim terrorist group, but we're pursuing a fairly solid lead regarding the extreme-right people. With a bit of luck we might have them in the next day or two."

"That's good news, but of course it's the first group which is the biggest worry. You've said before that you were pursuing two long-shot ideas of yours – any progress?"

"We're grinding through both of them, sir. I really believe that they'll eventually uncover something, but I'm afraid I can't even guess exactly when. It could be any day, or it could be a month."

"Let's pray it's not a month" the PM retorted, a little impatiently. He went on: "What's the latest in the street? How are people reacting?"

Paul Davies answered first: "As we all predicted, things are hotting up. There are more incidents, and they're getting more violent, and that's in all cities, but as you'd expect, Sydney and Melbourne are worst. There are cases of gangs of young non-Muslim males beating up Muslim males. Muslim women wearing veils are increasingly getting accosted, generally just verbal abuse, but sometimes physical. By that I mean, ripping veils off. There haven't been any beatings of women. Muslim shops are being vandalized, with paint, and sometimes objects thrown through windows. We're also getting anecdotal evidence that Muslims are getting discriminated against in job hiring."

"You mean more than usual?" observed Amelia, the NSW Premier, with a grim attempt at humour.

Paul ignored her interruption and went on: "Each city is pouring police onto the streets, day and night, patrolling, attempting to keep things under control. But these extreme-right attacks are really making things extra difficult, as if they weren't difficult enough. We're just waiting for another Cronulla – I hate to say it, but I think it's almost bound to happen."

"Remind me, what exactly happened then, how big was it?" asked the PM.

"Well, you know it started after a Cronulla beachside brawl between some young Lebanese and some Life-Guards - Caucasians, of course - which in turn was after accusations against the Lebanese about sexually abusing some non-Muslim girls. The following weekend a huge crowd gathered, over 5,000, and it eventually ended up in fighting, some stabbings, and so-on. It spread to other suburbs, with more violence. No-one was killed. But it kept going over a few days, and lots of people were arrested."

"And that was over something relatively minor, compared to what we've got now" pointed out the Attorney-General, Anthony Simpson. "But still, how likely is it that what we've got now could lead to some sort of mass riot? I would have thought it's more likely that we could have an increasing number of isolated incidents, like what's happening right now. Not all the crowd at Cronulla were involved in fighting – just a big crowd that turned up to see what was going to happen."

The PM looked around the table and asked: "Do you think Tony's right, that it's unlikely that we'll have large numbers of people all fighting each other?"

After a short silence Manfred Ryan gave his view: "I think he is, but we don't know. We haven't had a situation like this before. If we were in a country like Afghanistan or Pakistan I'd say there was a very good chance of mass rioting, but I think people here would be generally reluctant to get drawn into an all-out brawl where they could be badly hurt or killed. I think it's more likely that they'd count on the police and the army to keep the peace. But if we don't find the people who are doing all this soon, I think there's going to be a hell of a lot more isolated incidents and a lot of people are going to get killed – just not all in go."

"I don't think I want to even hear the word 'army'. If we have to involve them then Heaven help us" said the PM. "Manfred, Jason, Paul, you've just got to find these people, both groups, fast. I don't care what you have to do, who you have to offend, just get it done."

He then changed the subject: "Now, we all agreed that longer-term we've got to do something about improving the tension between the Muslim and non-Muslim populations, or incidents like this could keep on occurring. We've got four leaders of the Muslim community outside waiting for us, so I'm going to call them in and see if we can start a conversation about it."

Very shortly after four men filed in – Reza, the President of the Australian Association, Zaid, the Head of the Australian Association of Imams, Abdul Rashid, the Head of the NSW Association, and the Head of the Victorian Association, Mustafa. "I gather some of you have already met Dr Scott, and maybe Jason Blake" the PM said, "but you probably don't know the rest of this group." He made the various introductions and then began the meeting.

"Gentlemen, I'm sure I don't have to tell you how serious a situation we're facing. I'm also sure you know that we're doing everything in our power to find the people who are doing this – both groups – and stopping them. We're also doing all we can to stop the isolated incidents of violence that are happening. But you and all your institutions can help on this one, if you can get the message to your communities to be patient, and not retaliate. If that starts happening in any sort of big way, then things can get right out of control very fast. We don't want any more Cronulla's, do we, a 'war' between Muslim communities and the rest?"

The four nodded their agreement, and Reza assured him: "Prime Minister, we certainly don't, and we're already in touch with every community organisation we can identify to get that message across to them. Of course, we don't have any jurisdiction over them, we can only suggest things. But we'll do all we can."

"Thank you, we appreciate that. Now, something that's rather more difficult. There's no getting away from the fact that there's a problem between Muslim communities and the non-Muslim communities here. It's been that way a long time, but I don't think we've ever seriously tackled it. In fact, I'd suggest that every time anyone even touches on the subject all hell breaks loose, and they're accused of Islamophobia, and goodness knows what. But it can't be avoided any longer. We've got to do something to try and make sure these sorts of atrocities can never happen again. Would you agree?"

"We're listening, Prime Minister. What do you have in mind?" Zaid asked cautiously.

"I think you know Dr David Scott here. He's been briefing us about Islam, some of the history, some of the issues, and he's made some suggestions to us."

"We're already familiar with Dr Scott's suggestions" said Abdul Rashid, "and what he's doing is interfering in the way we practice our religion. That's not the role of governments in a Western democracy, is it?"

"Well, that may normally be true" the PM replied, "but when the Sydney Opera House gets bombed and dozens of people are slaughtered, then the situation changes. There's a hell of a lot of people here who are arguing for us to take drastic action, stopping Muslims coming to Australia, even deporting those that are here, and that's the last thing we want to do. But I don't think it's unreasonable for people to expect that we don't just sit on our thumbs and hope everything will turn out right. It won't, and you and I know it. We have to take some positive action that people can see, make changes that give us a chance to improve the situation."

Reza broke in: "Prime Minister, we understand your position, and I for one agree, even if my friend here doesn't, that we have to be ready to make some changes. Dr Scott came to see some of us the other day, and he put the same argument you're making to us - very strongly, I might add" he said with a smile. "But something you must understand, and that is we don't have a 'Pope', who can say 'This is how it has to be' and everyone has to do as he says."

"I think we can help you with that. On some of the things David suggested to us, the government can just make it mandatory" the PM said. "We of course would talk it through with representatives like yourselves, but at the end of the day we'd say: 'This is going to happen', and that's it. I'm talking about things like having to have home-grown imams, no more Wahhabism, and the like.

People may argue whether we have the right to take such action, but right now I guarantee you they won't win the argument."

There was silence while everyone in the room, especially the four Muslims, digested these quite aggressive points the PM had made. Eventually, Reza said: "Prime Minister, I understand your position, and your need to take firm action. We'll consider what you've said very seriously and come back to you with our own suggestions."

"Thank you. That would be very welcome. May I suggest that you liaise with David on this, and together you can come back to us with what you've agreed is a way forward. Is that OK?"

Abdul Rashid looked very unhappy with that suggestion, but the other three nodded their agreement.

The PM then added: "Gentlemen, I should mention that we all understand that this can't be all just one way – we've got to do our part as well. I'm sure you've noticed how the politicians, from all parties, are consistently urging restraint and understanding in their interviews with the press. We've asked church leaders, from all faiths, to preach the same message to their congregations. And we'll keep on thinking whether there are other ways that we can get that message out to the general population. Be assured of that."

With that he called an end to the meeting and the four Muslim leaders left the room. After they were gone the PM turned to the others and asked: "Well, what do you think? Will they play ball? What do you think, David?"

"I think they will. I had a pretty tough session with them, but the Head of the Australian Association and the Head of the Victorian Council both reacted pretty well, and I think they're very influential. Something else I should tell you. Jason arranged for the two of us to meet with a group of very senior Muslim businesspeople. We discussed some pretty daring ideas and to my surprise they didn't throw us out of the room. And I think they'd be quite influential too. So, I'm optimistic that we might be able to get some important changes to take place in Muslim communities. That's a good idea you had, getting them to accept having me work with them. Let's see what we can come up with."

"Good. OK everyone, let's get back to work. And Jason, we're counting on you. See you next meeting."

*

The lights were dancing on the water in Rose Bay as David watched from his window table in the Catalina Restaurant in New South Head Road. He was in good humour following the meeting with the PM and the others earlier that afternoon. Despite the news being generally bad, he felt that at least he might make some real progress with the senior Muslim community and bring about some changes he'd been thinking about for years. He was waiting for Dina who was, as usual, a few minutes late. He was a stickler for punctuality and this aspect of her character frustrated him, but he was resigning himself to the fact that he'd better get used to it – he wasn't going to not marry her just because she was always running late. This would be the first time he'd seen her since the disastrous conversation they'd had the night before his mother's funeral, and he was very nervous. He hoped desperately that she'd gotten over it and that they could carry on as though nothing had happened. Just as he was thinking this she appeared at the door, and the eyes of nearly everyone in the restaurant turned towards her. David was used to Dina attracting the instant attention of most men, but this time it was women as well. To his shock she was wearing a veil, a very fashionable one to be sure, but one that advertised that she was almost certainly a Muslim. He stood as the waiter showed her to his table, and after she was seated sat down opposite her, still having not said a word.

"Has the cat got your tongue?" she asked, unable to keep a slight note of defiance out of her voice.

"N-n-no" he stammered. "I was just surprised, that's all. I've never seen you in a veil before. It's thrown me off a bit."

"You shouldn't be so surprised. I'm a Muslim, after all, as you so well reminded me the other night. So, I've decided I might as well look like one."

"Look Dina, I'm so sorry about that. You know that I don't care about all that. I should've argued the toss with you then and made sure that you came with me. The whole thing had me a bit fazed, and I didn't handle it well."

"Even if you don't care, it's clear that your family do. How do you think that makes me feel?"

"They're not all like that. Beth got stuck into me at the funeral, singing your praises and saying that I should have made sure you came."

"Beth's a nice lady, and I appreciate that, but the whole thing's left a very bad taste in my mouth."

There was silence for a while, David not sure what to say next. He had a good look at her and thought to himself how it was actually quite ironic, that veils were supposed to maintain a woman's modesty, to make her not so attractive to men, and yet if anything this style of veil made her look even more alluring than usual. Eventually, and with a lot of trepidation, he said: "I don't blame you for being mad at me, but you surely know that at this particular moment wearing a veil is perhaps inviting trouble."

"Maybe so. At least I'll find out what it's like for all those other women who aren't ashamed of their faith and culture, who wear veils all the time."

David decided to stick to the old 'quick mind, slow mouth' adage to avoid getting into even more trouble than he was already in, so changed the subject to mundane matters, like what would she like to drink, had she seen the menu, and so on. In this way they got through the evening without any harsh exchanges, but at the end of the meal, when David asked her if she would come back to his place, she looked at him coolly and replied: "I think not. I need to think about things, and going back with you will just mess with my mind. So, I'd prefer to just go home."

Dina didn't respond to the light kiss David gave her as they parted, but just drove off without another word. The good humour David had been feeling, and the excitement he'd felt at the prospect of seeing Dina again, and hopefully spending the night with her, had evaporated. With a tinge of panic he was suddenly hit with the unpleasant thought that maybe Beth was right, and that he was in danger of losing her. And Dina was equally unnerved. Was she cutting off her nose to spite her face, just to make a point? Was she really prepared for the backlash she knew deep down was going to result from her defiant choice of dress? Just yesterday evening she'd had a drink with her friend Marina, and when she saw Dina's veil Marina had actually said: "What the hell is this? Are you crazy?" And was it fair to punish David for his family's insensitivity? She would have loved to have gone home with him and spent the night having him make love to her. Instead, she was going home to a lonely apartment and a cold bed. It was a sad end to the evening for both of them.

*

Two days later, unlikely as it seemed, David was convinced that he was being followed.

He was a very careful driver, not in the sense of driving slowly, but concentrating very hard on what he was doing, constantly checking the rear and side mirrors to check where other cars were situated, alert to something out of the ordinary happening which would require him to react quickly. This was in marked contrast to his general observational abilities, as he generally had his head full of ideas about history and politics and was regularly teased about being oblivious to his surroundings.

On the previous day, driving back to his apartment, on one of his regular glances in the rear vision mirror he noticed a silver Toyota Camry three cars back. This didn't particularly register, but five minutes later, he saw the same car. Then he turned off the major road and went off to the left down a side street. Looking back a few seconds later he noticed the same car was still there. Going to the same suburb, he thought, and that was it. But the next day, he noticed the same car. That's strange, he thought. Surely I'm not being followed. Why would anyone want to follow me? But, as an experiment he deliberately took a more circuitous route to his university, and sure enough, for much of the journey the same car was there, always three or four cars back. Then that was it. On the journey home, and all the next day, the car was no longer there. Nevertheless, he was convinced that for two days it had definitely been tailing him.

Should I tell Jason about it, he wondered? No, he's got enough to worry about. I'm sure he thinks I'm a bit of a pain, an ivory tower academic, having to keep me in the loop and listen to my crazy theories about the terrorists. He'll think I'm imagining things. And I wasn't able to get the number plate, so he'd have nothing to go on. So, David kept his thoughts to himself. But he was worried, and he began to take a lot more notice of what was going on around him, not just in his car, but all the time.

CHAPTER 12

Jason pulled up in front of a nondescript shed in Penrith which had quite modest signage proclaiming: 'Werner & Werner, Specialist Metal-Workers'. This was the thirty seventh such business that had been visited since Jason had asked Jim and his team to try and find the makers of the weapons used in the Opera House shootings. When he had a bit of spare time Jason would sometimes visit one himself to speed up the process. It was a frustrating task, even though they knew from experience that such investigations were generally a long, hard slog. Often there was no result, but sometimes they got a break-through and this was why they were all persisting, especially in this case where the stakes were so high. There was a slight drizzle, even though it was late summer, so Jason hurriedly clambered out of the car and ran into the building.

Inside it was quiet, with no other customers present. Behind the counter stood a middle-aged man, examining a metal object with keen interest. He looked up as Jason approached and asked: "Yes, what can I do for you?" He spoke with a slight accent, Jason guessed German, especially given the name on the sign.

Jason flashed his credentials and explained: "Mr. Werner, is it?" Werner acknowledged with a nod. "We're doing an investigation, nothing to worry about, but we're trying to find the company, or companies, that might have been involved in making this" at which point he placed the weapon he had been holding discreetly down his side, almost out of sight, on the counter.

Mr. Werner looked down at the weapon, and said, with appreciation: "This is a fine piece of work, clearly not mass-produced, and done by people who know their stuff. May I?" He picked it up and looked closely at all the components for some time, before putting it down again and looking at them, now appearing a little apprehensive.

"Mr. Blake, as it happens, I made the barrel for this weapon. I hope it hasn't been involved in anything serious?"

Jason struggled to keep the excitement out of his voice: "Don't worry, Mr. Werner. What the weapon's been used for is nothing to do with you – we're simply trying to identify who placed the order with you. Was it only the barrel, no other component?"

"No, just the barrel. But it wasn't just one, it was ten."

At this news Jason tried to hide his surprise and asked: "Can you tell me anything about the person who placed the order, and picked them up?"

"Sure, I remember it because this was quite a sophisticated request. The order was placed by correspondence, hard-copy, with a phone call to go over the detailed specs."

"What about picking up the finished products?" Jim asked.

"A chap came in a taxi and picked them up."

"Can you describe him?"

"He was quite tall, big guy, had a beard, dark glasses and a hat. Looked as though he might have been in disguise. He came and went in a taxi, so I can't identify a car."

"What did he sound like? Did he have an accent?"

"He wasn't born in Australia, although he speaks excellent English. Clearly well-educated. I'd guess there was a slight Middle Eastern accent."

"That's very helpful" Jason assured him. "One last thing. You say this is a sophisticated specification – would you know any other people here who could conceivably have made the other components?"

"Yes, I would, because there aren't many who could do work of this quality. Give me a few moments to think about it and I'll list them down for you."

Ten minutes later he had supplied a list of only five companies, their principals, and their contact details. Jason thanked him, again assuring him that there was nothing for him to be concerned about, left the shop and made his way back to his car. He speculated briefly about whether Mr. Werner may have been involved with the terrorists but concluded quickly that it was very unlikely. He wouldn't have had a clue about what it was all about, he thought, although he seems smart enough to know that it could be possible there was something shady about it. But he has to make a living – we can't blame him. He decided that it was imperative that he check the other five companies immediately - forget the diary, this takes top priority. With that he sped off towards the nearest address.

By the end of the afternoon he'd visited all the names Mr. Werner had supplied and had hit paydirt. Between them, four of them had made all the components required to assemble the weapons. In every case it was for ten items, and the manner of order and pick-up was the same as described by Mr. Werner. With this information in hand he returned to his office to brief his three Team Leaders.

"At least one piece of the puzzle is solved. The only thing is we still don't know who the bloke was who ended up with these ten weapons. But maybe something else might come up so that we can link them." He paused and looked at them before going on: "But now we obviously have another major problem. Ten weapons - we know what three were used for, but what about the other seven?"

Jim spoke up: "We know there are more of these guys in each of Sydney, Melbourne and Brisbane – they're the ones who've been doing the beheadings. I'll bet it'd take two people to do that, so that could mean at least six people in total, spread over the three cities. They could well have these other seven weapons."

"Which means they intend to use them at some stage" Jason added. "But when, and for what?"

"I think we know the 'for what'" Jim said. "More Opera House style events."

"Exactly. Even more reason we've got to find them fast, before they have time to put whatever plans they've got into action. Anyway, this is the first bit of genuine progress we've made, so maybe that's a good sign. Perhaps other things will start to fall our way. God knows we've all been putting enough effort into it." Jason waved them out of his office and thought to himself: If only we could link somebody to those gun purchases. Then we're really on our way. But we need some luck, and we sure haven't had much so far.

*

It had started innocently enough, a schoolboys' soccer match between teams from two suburbs in the south-west of Sydney, well-known for having large Muslim populations. One team was from an Islamic school, whereas the other was from a conventional government school with a predominantly Christian players. Late in the game an argument broke out between the supporters of each of the teams, and within minutes pushing and shoving degenerated into full-scale brawling, with racist and religious slurs being traded. The accompanying shouting from the men and screaming from the women attracted dozens of young men from nearby streets who enthusiastically entered the fray, and the brawl began to resemble a full-blown riot. Dozens of police converged on the scene and managed to break up the worst of the violence and arrest some of the clearly identifiable ringleaders. But dozens fled the scene and began to rampage around the streets, overturning trash cans, and even a few cars.

Jason had received the news mid-morning, the day after the breakthrough with the weapons, and decided to drive to the riot scene to see for himself what was happening, how bad it really was. As he began to pass through the streets that were near the soccer field where the riot had started, he encountered increasingly large gatherings of people, generally just standing around, talking. But one such group surrounded his car, shouting at him and banging on the sides and roof. He kept his car moving until at one point at least a dozen men converged directly in front of him, leaning on the bonnet and trying to force him to stop. Some of them had weapons such as steel bars, even machetes, in their hands. They look like they mean business, he thought, time to get serious. He drew out his handgun and waved it above the steering wheel so they could see it clearly, while at the same time beginning to accelerate through them, making it very clear he was not going to slow down. They backed away hurriedly and he sped away from them, towards a big bank of police cars that were spread around the soccer field.

When he reached them, he stopped, got out, introduced himself to the policeman who appeared to be in charge, and asked for a briefing.

"I think the worst is over, for the moment anyway, but a hell of a lot of people have come here, and a lot of them are looking for trouble."

"That's for sure", and Jason recounted the incident he'd just experienced. "Those guys had weapons, and they could do a lot of damage with them."

"They already have. There are three guys we know about who've been killed, and a stack have been pretty badly beaten up."

"How long do you think it'll take to get this under control?"

"I reckon hours. And then the trouble is that this could carry on, and spread to other suburbs, like happened at Cronulla. It could go on for days. I think we're going to need to get really heavy to tamp this down. Might even need curfews."

"I think you're right. This could easily get way out of control. Look, thanks. I'd better get going."

Jason then headed back, this time taking extra care to avoid streets that had many people and driving fast enough to dissuade anyone from trying to get at all close to his car. This is really worrying, he thought. The overall situation between Muslims and non-Muslims is far worse than it was when the Cronulla Riots happened, so what's happening here could really get widespread. Like that guy said, we may be in for curfews, and we're going to need huge numbers of police patrolling the streets in some of these suburbs. Christ, we need to find those bastards and put a stop to all this.

When he got back to his office he found a report on his desk containing more disquieting news, an attack by a knife-wielding Muslim youth on a number of pedestrians in a busy central Sydney street, in broad daylight. Two people were killed and three others seriously wounded, before the attacker was shot by police, not fatally. During the attacks the young man had shouted 'Allahu Akbar', to make it clear to all concerned that he was carrying out God's will. Under aggressive questioning by the police (patience was fast-running out) he confirmed that he was Australian-born and was inspired by the Opera House attack, not ISIS or Al Qaeda, to do his part to further the Islamic cause. Damn, thought Jason, this is the first case of an Islamic terror attack inspired by something that happened locally and carried out by a local group. How many more of these are we going to see? At that moment his phone rang, and when he answered it was Janet Mitchell to say that the PM wanted to speak to him.

"Jason" the PM said, wasting no time for pleasantries, "Are you aware of the riots in south-west Sydney?"

"Yes, I was just there."

"I'm getting recommendations that we need 24-hour patrols by the police, maybe even the army. What do you think?"

"I think it's justified, Sir. But just the police, not the army. That's a last resort."

"Have we got enough to do the job?"

"We have, if this is given top priority. There's bound to be a stack of investigations the police are doing about things that aren't life-threatening that could wait. We could even co-opt the traffic police – anything but the army."

"But they're not trained for this sort of thing. It might not even be legal."

"Sir, this is an emergency, like war-time. What we want are bums on seats in patrol cars, as a deterrent. Hopefully, they wouldn't actually have to do anything. And we could have a conventional police person with each one of them to show them the ropes or do what's required in an emergency."

There was silence at the other end of the line as the PM thought about what he'd said. "OK, I think you're right. I'll speak to

Amelia. And what about the lone-wolf incident? I suppose you've heard about that?"

"Yes, I've just read a report about it. It's on a different scale, of course, but very worrying, nevertheless. A local kid inspired by a local event. We'll have to lean on our senior Muslim friends to pull out all stops to get through to their communities that they've just got to find a way to stop these retaliatory attacks, or we're going to have an all-out war. And we'll all lose, but they'll lose even more. Leave that to me and David – we're getting to know these gentlemen a little."

"Thanks, please do that. Use my name all you want. On that score, I'm going to have to do another address to the nation about this and try and calm people down. It's starting to unravel, just like we've been fearing."

The PM hung up the phone, and Jason sat and thought: Maybe I should have told him about the weapons makers – he needs a bit of good news, the poor bugger. He's got the weight of the nation on his shoulders, one catastrophe after another. But it's still too early, we're still too far from getting the answer. He cleared his mind of that conversation and thought: OK, I need to talk to those Muslim leaders again, and scare the pants off them. He picked up the phone and punched in some numbers.

*

There was a buzz of excitement among the two dozen or so journalists gathered on the landing of the Opera House as they waited for the Prime Minister to appear. In the previous few days there'd been numerous incidents of violence reported around the country, directly related to the terrorist incidents. There'd been another round of beheadings, as always one in each of Sydney, Melbourne and Brisbane. The riots in south-west Sydney were continuing, although spasmodically, with reports of brawls between gangs coming in from nearby suburbs. And now there was the stabbings incident in the middle of downtown Sydney. The situation was clearly degenerating, and there was a sense that it was getting beyond the ability of the authorities to contain it, let alone stop it, so the journalists were agog with anticipation as to what the PM could or would say. As always with a major crisis, as well as feeling genuine concern about what was happening, many of the journalists sensed political blood in the air, and this was to a great extent what they lived for, heightening the excitement. Then, right on schedule, the PM and his party swept in and took their positions in front of the lectern. The PM was accompanied by the NSW Premier, and the Head of the AFP, who stood behind him on either side, with the usual unenviable task of saying nothing but providing support by making the appropriate facial gestures in response to what was said.

"Before I take any questions, I want to say a few words" the PM began. "I don't need to remind you all of the various atrocities that have happened, and the retaliatory violence that is increasingly occurring. This is getting to the point where it's posing a serious threat to the stability of our society, and every one of us has a responsibility to do whatever each of us can to stop it and work together to tackle the underlying issues that are causing all this to happen. But make no mistake, this is being instigated by a tiny bunch of very bad people, who are playing the rest of the population for fools and sucking us in to retaliating against what we see as the other side, the ones we see as being responsible. What's their motive? We think they're trying to set the entire

Muslim community against the rest of the population, so that they'll retreat into enclaves and live separately, keeping to their own cultures and not letting other cultures contaminate them. We've got to show them that we're not going to play their game, that we're going to work together to make sure all parts of our great society get on with each other and together move our country forward.

"Now, let me make a few things very clear. The original atrocity that started all this, the bombing of the Opera House and the shooting that went with it, was an act of Islamic terrorism. There's been a tendency to avoid ever describing these acts as Islamic, which simply meant that the real issues were swept under the carpet and never discussed and addressed. But the fact is that these terrorists have used Islam as the excuse for their actions, and also to try and influence Muslim populations to sympathise with what they're doing. And at times, in other parts of the world, it's working. Now, this is outrageous, that one of the world's great religions is being exploited for such terrible purposes. So, here in Australia we're going to tackle this. We, the government, have begun working with Muslim community leaders to address some fundamental issues that have been causing the ill-feeling that has clearly been present for a long time between the Muslim communities and the rest of the population. There's no point trying to hide from this – it's an unfortunate fact. And this has got to work both ways. There are changes that all parties can make to work towards getting over this problem. From the interactions we've had so far, I'm very optimistic that we can do this.

"Obviously, before we can get anywhere, we have to find and stop these terrorists, not just the Islamic ones, but the right-wing extremists as well. Once we've done this, we have to start rebuilding the trust between communities, in the manner I've just described. And there are many things we can do. While a lot of good things have indeed been done, successive governments of both parties haven't done enough to ensure new immigrants are settled successfully into our country, ensuring they can speak English and that they can rapidly be employed. We need to do more to increase the understanding between the different communities in our overall population. Gone are the days when Australia was overwhelmingly Anglo-Saxon and Christian, and communities were pretty much the same wherever one went throughout the country. We are now a very diverse population, and we have to recognize this, and learn to adapt as appropriate.

"Back to the short-term challenge, we're getting closer to identifying the people behind both the Islam terrorism, and the right-extremist terrorism. And we're putting an enormous effort into containing the violence that's happening in the wider community. We have large numbers of our police forces, right around the country, patrolling the areas where it's felt that this violence is most likely to occur, and we ask for your understanding in giving them the discretion to do what they think is necessary. Sometimes they may go a bit overboard in doing what they believe is necessary to prevent a violent act occurring, but that's better than the alternative.

"I've spoken to the leaders of the other political parties and we are all unified in our response to this crisis. And please, I ask all of you to understand, this is a major crisis, representing a huge threat to our society.

"Now, any questions? …"

Twenty minutes later the press conference wound up, and the PM, the Premier, and the Head of the AFP walked back inside the building.

"How do you think that went?" the PM asked.

"I think you're beginning to get through to them" Amelia replied, "but they'll be under a lot of pressure to get stuck into you. We really need to get that breakthrough you've alluded to."

The PM sighed: "How right you are. All we can do is keep plugging away. But I've got a lot of confidence in Jason, and the AFP and the state police are doing a great job of keeping a reasonable lid on things. We'll get there, don't worry."

*

That evening, just after 6.30pm, David pulled up in front of his apartment block to find Dina's car parked outside. As always, his heart lifted at the prospect of an evening, and if he was lucky, a night, with her. But I hope she's in a better mood than last time, he thought – I could do without that. He caught himself and mentally smiled – you really are a selfish prick. He parked his car, ran up the stairs to his apartment, opened his door and entered, looking around for Dina. She was curled up on his couch, and it was immediately evident that she'd been crying. Not only that, to his shock he saw that she had vivid red marks on both cheeks, she was without her veil, and her dress was badly ripped. He rushed over and knelt in front of the couch:

"What on earth happened? Are you alright? Are you hurt?" the words came tumbling out as he reached forward and took her in his arms.

She began to cry again, and after a short time, in-between sobs, she explained what had happened. She'd been at school, then on her way home stopped at a suburban shop that sold Muslim women's fashion wear. While she was in there, a group of four burly young men – all Caucasian – burst in, trashed the shop, and beat up everyone in there – two shop-assistants, both young women, and three customers.

"They tore off my veil, and ripped my dress, then slapped me hard, more than once, and threw me on the floor. They did the same to the others. It was terrifying. I thought they were going to rape me. All the time they were abusing us, calling us vile names, Muslim whores, terrorist bitches, telling us to go back to where we came from, and other stuff like that. Then they ran out, jumped into their car, and roared off. We called the police, and they came after about twenty minutes, asked us lots of questions and took lots of notes, but I suspect they'll never find them."

"That's terrible. I'm so sorry you had to go through that."

"It's not your fault, just your wonderful fellow-Aussies" she burst out bitterly. "They're never going to accept us, or anyone different, for that matter. It's like they think their country is under threat, and they're on one side and we're on the other."

"You don't have to pick a side", David said, desperation in his voice. "We're all on the same side. We're all Australians."

"You think so" Dina said, smiling sadly, "but you're avoiding reality. You people who think you're the real Aussies are on one side, and everyone else, especially us Muslims, are on the other. Unless we ape you, and become indistinguishable from you, you'll continue to think we're not real Australians, that we don't really fit in to your culture."

"But that's not fair. Surely you don't believe I think like that."

"You think you don't, but deep down I think you do. It's not your fault, you can't help yourself, just like our people can't help believing they have to take the Qur'an literally, and that women should wear veils. Maybe it's true that all we can do is work together sometimes, and apart from that stay in our own communities."

"Dina, that's so wrong. We all just have to try harder to understand each other and learn how to compromise."

"Maybe. It'd be nice to think so." She got to her feet and began to move to the door. "David, I need some time to think about all of this, so it's best if we give each other some space for a while."

"Dina, please, you can't be serious. You know I love you like crazy."

"I know you do. I'm sorry. Sometimes it's all too complicated."

With that she kissed him on the cheek, walked out the door and headed down the steps to her car. David stood on the landing, watching her go, his mind reeling at what had just happened. Surely she'd come to her senses, he thought. Surely she wouldn't seriously consider splitting with him for good. He watched her car pull away from the curb and head down the road and then went back into his apartment, feeling that the world as he knew it was crashing around him - the Opera House bombing, his mother, the beheadings, the violence that was becoming an everyday occurrence, and now this. Sitting down on his couch he thrashed things around in his mind for a long time, at the end of which he'd come to a conclusion. There was no point just feeling sorry for himself. He'd been placed in a position where he could influence finding a solution to what was happening so he'd better damned well do all he can to do so. Tomorrow he was going to another of Fariq's meetings – let's see what that brings.

CHAPTER 13

The following afternoon, David was driving to his university. Since his conviction that he'd been tailed for two consecutive days he had been deliberately taking circuitous routes between university and his home. He was now on a long stretch of road that generally had few cars, but he was regularly checking his side and rear-view mirrors just in case. He spotted a car looming up behind him quickly, obviously driving at great speed. This guy's a complete idiot, or something's not right, he thought.

As the car drew near, he saw that there were two occupants. His heart froze when he saw that the passenger window was open, and that the passenger had a gun in his hand. As it drew directly opposite it slowed a little, the passenger raised his gun and fired. At that same instant David threw his body sideways below the height of his side window and pushed his foot down on the brake pedal as hard as he could. Keeping his right hand on the steering wheel he kept the car continuing in a reasonably straight path, as two bullets smashed through his right-side window, passed over his body and out the window on the other side.

Raising his head slightly he saw that the other car was at least fifty metres ahead of him now - he had surprised the driver by braking so violently. Leaning out the window the passenger fired two more shots, as David ducked again while the bullets smashed through his windscreen and embedded in the left rear headrest. Thanks to his car's superb braking system it came to a stop well before the other car, which was now nearly 100 metres in front. David reversed hard, then swung the wheel as he'd learnt as a young student and skidded the car around in a half circle so that it was now pointed in the opposite direction to his assailants' car. He then planted his foot on the accelerator and sped away, rapidly increasing the distance from the other car, which by now had turned and was fast in pursuit.

But it was no contest. David's car was a BMW M5, with a V8 4.4litre engine, a masterpiece of German engineering. In no time he was doing 130km per hour, still in such a panic that he hardly noticed the police car coming from the opposite direction. Its driver immediately switched on its flashing lights and siren, stopped quickly, turned and set off after him. Meanwhile, the other car with the two would-be assassins had seen the police car coming towards them, and had, at normal speed, turned off in a side street, and were now getting as far away as possible.

When he saw the police car behind him, David immediately slowed and stopped, and waited for them to get to him. He was breathing hard, his heart pumping furiously. The police car pulled up diagonally in front of him and both policemen jumped out, one going to each side of his car. "Get out of the car, now!" the one on his side of his car shouted, clearly very angry. "You were doing 130 in a 70 zone. Are you crazy?"

David got out, leant against his car, waited until his heart slowed a little and his breath came back, and blurted out: "Somebody just tried to shoot me."

"What are you talking about?"

Calming down slightly, David explained what had happened, pointing out his two shattered side windows, windscreen, and the bullet holes in the rear headrest. After initially looking very skeptical, one of them examined him closely, and said: "You're Professor David Scott, aren't you? I've seen you on TV, talking about the terrorists."

When David confirmed that indeed, he was, the officer had another look at his car, and confirmed that what David had told him was the truth: "Bloody hell, you were lucky. Did you get a look at the guys who did this? And their car – colour and make?"

"It was all so fast. All I can say is that it was a white sedan, medium size, don't know what make. I'd never recognise the two guys." He was silent, and then said: "I think I need to sit down. I'm not feeling too good."

"Of course. This must be a huge shock. Come and sit in the back of our car."
While David sat there, the policeman made a few phone calls, and then he drove David to a police station in the city, while the other one followed in David's car.

*

At the police station, to David's surprise, he found Jason waiting, who thanked the policeman who had brought him in and took him to a meeting room and shut the door. They sat down at the table.

"He's a smart young bloke. When he realised who you are he guessed this almost certainly had something to do with the terrorists, so contacted me. Are you OK? You were very lucky. Tell me what happened." Jason asked.

David recounted what had happened and as he talked, he began to think that he'd been pretty clever to have managed to thwart the assassins in the way he had, expecting that Jason would be suitably impressed. Then he said: "But it was a different car from the one that was following me."

"What are you talking about?"

David explained, and Jason's face hardened. He was silent for a moment, then asked quietly. "Why didn't you tell me about this? Didn't you think, with all that's going on, that this could be important, that whoever was following you would almost certainly have something to do with the terrorists?"

David suddenly thought, my God, he's right, I should have told him. He started to apologise and explain that he didn't want to bother Jason when he was so busy, that he was worried Jason would think he was imagining things. But he was shocked at Jason's reaction.

"Are you fucking crazy? How could you be so stupid? It's a miracle you weren't killed. I'm amazed you had the brains to react as you did." Jason was so angry that he was shouting. "I would have had my boss, and probably even the Prime Minister after my blood. Letting the great Professor Scott be killed."

By this time David, who for a moment felt some anger at being spoken to like this, realised that Jason was letting off steam because he was so worried about how close David had come to being killed, so he stayed silent. When Jason finally paused for breath, he simply said, "You're right, I'm a fool, I'm sorry."

Jason looked at him for a long moment, then said, "Yes, you are indeed a fucking idiot, but I have to admit, that was a pretty cool stunt you pulled to avoid being shot, and then getting away from them. I suppose you think you're some sort of action hero."

David, embarrassed because he had indeed been feeling pretty pleased with himself, made no reply. Seeing how crestfallen he was, Jason suddenly laughed: "OK, let's forget all that. Sorry for all the abuse, but you deserved it. Now we've got to make sure this doesn't happen again, so you're going to do what I tell you, and I don't want any arguments, OK?"

"Sure." David said, so meekly that Jason laughed again. "OK Arnie, let's go buy you a beer to calm your nerves, and I'll tell you what I've got in mind."

They adjourned to a nearby pub, Jason ordered a beer for them both, and they sat down, whereupon Jason informed him, "I'm going to have you watched, 24 hours a day, until this is all over."

David was silent, as he digested this. He found it very disquieting, as this was the sort of thing he'd only read about, or seen in films or TV shows, something that involved other people, not an ordinary bloke like him. But it does now, you were nearly killed today, he reminded himself.

"That takes some getting used to, but OK."

"And that's not all. Have you ever used a handgun? In fact, have you ever used any weapons at all?"

"I've used a rifle a bit, at friend's farms. But only shooting at targets for fun. I've never been roo shooting, or anything like that."

"How were you? Any good?"

"Not bad, for a beginner, so my friends told me."

"That's good. Because I want you to do a crash course in how to use a handgun, and I'm going to insist that you have it on you at all times. You can put it beside your bed at night, as well. I'll arrange for you to have a license to carry a gun, so it'll be legal."
'Bloody hell. Are you sure that's wise? I might kill some innocent bystander by mistake.'

"I don't think so. I hate to admit it, but after what you did today, you're clearly a pretty cool customer. I think you'll keep your head if there's an emergency. I know how to make judgements like this - you'll be OK. But hopefully there won't be any more attempts, and this was all just a precaution."

"OK. If you say so. When does this start?"

"Tonight. There are two officers waiting at my office ready to go. There'll be a roster, so that there'll always be two of them, day and night. And I'll schedule your shooting lessons so that they start tomorrow. I'll give you a night to recover from today's excitement. One of the bodyguards will train you – all of them are highly competent with firearms. I reckon half a dozen lessons will be enough. Then when this is all over, you'll have another job option."

David laughed at this thought, then said, "Jason, this is really hitting me how close to us this is getting, and I'm grateful to you for thinking about my welfare like this. I'm not sure I deserve it."

"Well, I don't want to see anything happen to you. One in the family is quite enough. But David, you ought to think about this. Given what's happening, you're important. I'll admit I was a bit skeptical at first, but I'm beginning to realise that the way you're trying to get these senior Muslims to change their thinking is a really big deal that could have huge ramifications. Maybe you don't get how important your role is in all that. So, I've got to make sure nothing happens to you, so you can see this through. That's partly why I was so hard on you back there. It was too close for comfort; it scared the shit out of me."

David replied, with more than a bit of embarrassment, "That's pretty sobering. I'm not used to taking myself that seriously. But thanks for that vote of confidence – coming from you it's a great compliment, particularly after what you said earlier."

Jason smiled, "Yeah, sorry about that. When we're finished here, I'll introduce you to your new closest friends and see about turning you into an Aussie James Bond."

"But before I do," he went on, "let me bounce something off you. While you were being driven in just now, I was wondering why anyone would want to kill you. It was an attempted shooting, not a beheading, so it wasn't one of the terrorists' random attacks. You're stirring up the Muslim community to think in new ways - the terrorists are going to hate that. You've already said publicly that maybe the purpose behind their campaign is to get the Muslim community to retreat into their own enclaves and continue to practice Islam the way it's practiced back in the Middle East. They don't want Muslims thinking they can interpret the Qur'an in any other way than the literal word of God. And you've been suggesting that maybe they don't have to. So, they could regard you as a serious threat. They might think they've got to get you out of the way, to stop you before you can do any more damage."

He paused, before adding, "And who are the people you've mentioned this idea to? Fariq and the rest of his mates. And a few of the community leaders, you told me. Now, I've met a few of the community leaders, and they just don't strike me as the types who'd ever pull off anything like what's been happening. But maybe one of Fariq's mates could. Some of them are entirely different sorts of people, self-made successful businessmen. You've got to be pretty smart, and perhaps tough, to do that. So, I'm seriously wondering whether the guy we're looking for is in that group. What do you think? Make sense?"

After some thought David agreed that it did indeed make sense.

"But why would he expose himself like this?" mused Jason. "He must know that we'd put two and two together and think about this possibility. Maybe it shows just how much he wants to get you, which is worrying. And perhaps as well he thinks his time is running out, so what the hell.

"Anyway, I'm going to work on this theory, and investigate that lot. The guys that made the automatic weapons told me that the person who picked them up was a big man, with a slight accent. There's a few I can remember from the meeting who fit that description, so let's see what we find."

*

The next day, followed discreetly by his two minders, David walked slowly through the gardens towards the building where he was shortly to give a lecture. At this time of the year the gardens were ablaze with colour, primarily due to the large clumps of bougainvillea that hung down from strategically positioned trellises. But David was oblivious to the beauty that surrounded him, his mind preoccupied by the string of events that had intruded into his life. First there was the death of his mother, which he was still trying to come to grips with, and which continued to fill his head with both sadness and rage. And all the other people who had been killed alongside her. Then there were the ongoing atrocities, the beheadings and the retaliatory attacks which were becoming more frequent. And the fallout of all this was resulting in Dina slipping away from him. To cap it all off, it seemed the terrorists were now trying to kill him. What's to blame for all of this – Islam's susceptibility to be abused by these awful people, he thought bitterly.

And this was now seriously conflicting him. Even before all this he'd always had an inconsistent relationship with the subjects that dominated his professional life - Islam, and Muslims. It would be reasonable to assume that he'd have empathy with both, given that he was supposed to be an expert in the field of Political Islam, but the reality was that he had always had concerns about the way Islam was practiced, and he actually knew very little about Muslims, as people. Of course, he knew many Muslims – he was engaged to one – but they were all highly Westernised, almost indistinguishable from his non-Muslim friends. He didn't really understand how an ordinary Muslim, from Pakistan say, lived, or what their world view was. He had to admit he was guilty of putting them all in the same mental box, as being very different and prone to irrational thinking caused by being held hostage to a religion that was medieval in some of its teachings. And now, if he was honest with himself, he knew they were being unfairly victimised, innocent women being attacked simply because of the way they looked. He was for the first time becoming aware of them as real people, trying to live their lives like everyone else. He'd of course seen the refugees in the war zones on TV, but it was all so unreal, so alien to the serene life in Australia, that he'd never really related to them. Now it was all becoming more real and despite his conflicted feelings, his previous attitudes were increasingly disturbing him.

It was in this frame of mind that he entered the lecture theatre, and it was with some difficulty that he put those thoughts aside and concentrated on the topic of the day. As always, once he started talking he got caught up in the enthusiasm he had for his field of study and delivered his usual entertaining and interesting lecture. As he was talking he noticed a girl sitting in the front row who was hanging on his every word. He looked at her a little more closely – she's a stunner, he thought to himself, even with those shadows under her eyes. I wonder what's causing those? When he'd finished, after the other students had completed their questioning of him and left the theatre, she was still waiting, and approached him.

"Professor Scott, I'm Rachel Johnson. I wonder if I could talk to you about something, not your lecture?"

"Of course. I'm walking back to my office. We can talk on the way, if that's OK."

"This is a little awkward," she began, "but you and I have something unfortunate in common. I was in the Opera House when it was bombed, and I know your mother was there. I'm terribly sorry about what happened to her. Such a tragedy, for so many people."

"You were there? My God, how did you survive? It must have been a nightmare?"

"It was - I'm not sure I've woken up from it. It's certainly affected me – I don't think I'll ever be the same person again, which is probably to be expected, I guess. But there's something about what happened that I'd like to talk to you about. It's a bit weird, are you sure you don't mind my telling you about it?"

"Of course not. If there's any way I can help I'd be happy to. Especially this. You were there with my mother – that's a connection between us. Look, my office is fairly close. We can sit down there and you can tell me about it."

Rachel haltingly told him what had happened at the Opera House, recounting everything she could remember from the moment the bomb burst through the ceiling - the sounds of the gunfire and the terror she felt when everyone was trying to hide from the gunmen. And finally, the moment when one of the young gunmen failed to kill her when she was helpless before him, and the look of uncertainty on his face as they stared at each other.

'I'll never forget that look, as long as I live. And I'll never stop wondering, why did he spare me? Why me, when he'd killed so many others? What was going through his mind at that moment? Was he really evil, or was there something else going on? I've had so many confusing thoughts going through my head ever since. Do I really hate all Muslims, or do I feel sorry for them because they've got men like this who make us feel they're all terrorists, when really they're just like us and fear them like we do.'

She paused, looking down at her hands, and David gazed at her in increasing amazement as he thought about how incongruous it was, for someone who had been through such a terrifying experience and who had observed such carnage to be expressing the thoughts she was sharing with him.

"Rachel, what you've told me is amazing," he eventually said. "I've had nothing but rage in my heart since this happened, and I've been feeling very negative about Muslims in general, even though deep down I know that's totally unfair. You make me feel very guilty."

"You shouldn't – you've got every reason to think that way. And I know I'm not perfect. But I also know that I don't want to let this spoil my life, to be bitter forever. I've seen enough films and TV shows to know I don't want that to happen to me. I thought one thing I could do is to try to understand a lot more about Muslims and their religion, and their culture, maybe even meet some. That's why I came to this summer school lecture, plus I wanted to meet you. I was going to ask you about coming to this university and doing some of your subjects. I got pretty good results last year, so I was thinking I might be able to."

"Rachel, I'd be pleased to have you as a student, and if your results are good there'll be no problem about you getting in, even though it's a little bit late. Given all the circumstances we'll get through the admin. stuff with no trouble. You need to come back and enroll and I can help you with what subjects you should do for this first semester, and even a rough plan for your whole degree – at least it'll give you some idea about where you're heading.

"I've been thinking about something you said, about maybe meeting some Muslims. I'm embarrassed to admit it but I've had very little exposure to ordinary Muslims - the ones I've mixed with have all been academics like me, or very senior people in government or business, or other professional people, all very Westernised and modern, and relatively well-off. I've been thinking about that too - while I was walking here this morning, actually. But unlike you I've got no excuse. I'm supposed to be an expert, and yet I know very little about all these people that I just group together in macro terms. I've been wondering what I'm going to do about it and I've decided I'm going to visit some Muslim community organisations, the ones that work with new arrivals to Australia, who try and help them settle in and so on. Would you like to see one of those?"

"I'd love to, Professor Scott. Let me know when you're going, and I'll try to come along."

*

"I've been nominated as official photographer," explained a smiling David, as he snapped photos of groups of two and three in Fariq's meeting room.

"Come on, you two, don't be shy," David coaxed, as The Iraqi attempted to move away. He reluctantly joined the group being photographed, forcing a smile at David's insistence. Pushy *kaafir*, he thought to himself - not only are you dangerous, you're very annoying.

David continued spreading photographic cheer throughout the room, where eighteen of Fariq's circle, plus David and Jason, had gathered for their second meeting to discuss possible Islamic reform.

But The Iraqi was fuming – not only was he having to listen to this group talking blasphemous rubbish, but his photo had been taken, something he avoided like the plague, for obvious reasons. Once in a while it was inevitable, no matter how much he tried to avoid it - one couldn't be an active businessman without being ambushed by some enthusiastic event organiser with a smartphone. But striving for anonymity was so part of his nature that having his existence recorded for who knows who to discover was disturbing.

Shortly after Fariq called the meeting to order. "Ladies and Gentlemen, it's three weeks since we last met, and the situation we've been discussing has become even more serious. Even if the terrorists are discovered soon, as I'm confident will be the case, a lot of damage has been done. If we thought people had negative perceptions of Muslims before, then it's going to be a lot worse now. We have to do a lot of fence-mending. So, I think the ideas we explored last meeting are even more justified than we thought. Let me give you a quick re-cap of what we were talking about."

He gave a short summary of the various ideas discussed at the last meeting and then asked the group to offer any thoughts. The ensuing discussion was animated, to put it mildly, with a few of the group expressing grave concerns that they were talking blasphemy if there was any suggestion that the Qur'an need not be interpreted literally. But others argued just as strongly the other way. It was clear as the discussion progressed that the big majority felt that it was long past time that major changes were seriously considered. The general sense was that if the sad history of the entire Islamic world over the past one hundred years was not convincing enough, then the recent events in Australia had confirmed that it needed to adapt.

By the close of the meeting they'd agreed to recommend to the official authorities within the Muslim communities that the more easily acceptable ideas they'd come up with be implemented as soon as possible. For example, banning Wahhabism completely, not just from the curriculum of Islamic schools and only allowing imams who had been trained in Australia to preach. They would also take on what they knew would be a major battle, to get agreement that there should be a gradual education of the Australian Muslim population to accept that it was allowable to interpret the Qur'an in the context of time and place.

After Fariq officially closed the meeting a few people hurried off to their next appointment, but most stayed to continue chatting, generally in groups of two or three. Mazlin and Imran had begun making their way to the door but were ambushed by Jason who approached them with hand outstretched.

"Hello gentlemen. Good to see you again."

Imran smiled, shook his hand and politely replied, "You too, Jason. You should be happy with the outcome today."

"Yes, I think it's very promising. But, of course, this is just a small group. I wonder how these ideas are going to be received by the general Muslim community?"

"Indeed. I think we're likely under-estimating the depth of feeling Muslims have about these matters. I don't think they'll take too kindly to suggestions that they should change their religion to suit the rest of Australian society."

"What about your own feelings?" Jason asked. "Do you think what we're trying to do is justified?"

Mazlin chipped in, "Well, of course, I understand where you and David are coming from, and I support it in principle, but in all honesty, I don't think it's going to work. I worry that it may do more harm than good – a lot of people could be offended at the very idea and become even more traditional as a way of making it clear that they reject this sort of interference. You know, the 'Islam is under siege' mentality."

Jason thought about that, "Well, you've got a point. I guess that's a risk. But from what I've heard from David and others in this meeting the potential benefits from a change in thinking are so great that it seems well worth having a go. And maybe the ordinary Muslims out there are so sick of all the negative things that have been happening for so long that they'll agree."

"Maybe. We'll see. I hope you're right."

They shook hands and Imran and Mazlin moved off to say their goodbyes to Fariq before walking out the door. Jason quickly moved on to the third man who, along with Mazlin and Imran, fell into the category of 'large', and so was a possible suspect, and engaged him in conversation. When that conversation was over he slid his phone recorder to 'Off'. A short time later he left with David.

"Did you get the recordings?" David asked.

"I sure did. And you got the photos. Send them to me and I can go and do some checking.' They walked towards their cars and Jason went on, 'That was a good meeting in more ways than one. I'm no expert, but this has got to be ground-breaking stuff here. If this group can pull it off, it'll be amazing."

"You're so right," agreed David. "It's such a big deal that I'm struggling to believe it could really happen. But you never know. Maybe it's just a case of a whole lot of things coming together at the right time to make people consider things they'd never have dreamed of before - you know, a sort of "perfect storm."

Jason had reached his car, and as he opened the door he said, "Let's hope so. Anyway, you know where I'm going now. Wish me luck." And with that he drove off, a little faster than a respectable policeman should.

David in turn reached his car, got in and headed off towards the university, his mind racing. He was very excited - almost elated - by the result of the meeting, despite the dampening feeling that the chances of it all coming off were almost certainly a lot less than 50:50. Before all this terrorist madness happened, he'd argued at various times and in various forums about the desirability of reform in Islam, but deep down he'd never believed it would ever be a reality. It had always been a bit of an academic exercise, a stance to take that made him seem fashionably contrarian, someone a bit controversial, good for a bit of publicity. But now there was at least a semblance of a chance that it could really happen – he could hardly believe it.

Don't get ahead of yourself, he thought, not for the first time in recent days. This is just the first tiny step, so many people will oppose this, bitterly. We'll be taking on the whole religious establishment, and maybe the whole Muslim population as well. I'd be crazy to put too much hope in this.

But then again …

Chapter 14

'More terrorist killings: Senior Politician a Victim' screamed the headlines in the online media sites of all the major news outlets. Yet again, a beheading had occurred in each of Sydney, Melbourne and Brisbane. But this time the victims weren't only general members of the public – in Melbourne, Daniel Parkinson, the Federal Opposition spokesperson on Industrial Relations, was the unlucky one who had been targeted while on a very early morning run in the bush near Lorne. All the morning TV shows were headlining the story, many of them airing studio interviews with political commentators known to have unashamedly anti-Muslim views. Their street interviews revealed many members of the public expressing extreme solutions to what they saw as an obvious problem.

"The time's come to admit that all the measures the government's tried haven't worked. These people have never settled in properly to this country, so they should go back home where they belong" was the very loud opinion of one person interviewed on Pitt street in Sydney. "How would you propose that could be done?" asked the interviewer. "What about people who've been born and raised here? They're Australian citizens – where could they go to?" The interviewee had no answer, simply saying forcefully that "Something needs to be done. That's the government's job."

Since the first attack, the Opera House bombing, many people had expressed such views, but there were also many voices of reason urging calm, and consideration of constructive actions to address what was clearly a major social problem. But with this latest attack, involving a very well-known public figure, the voices of reason were being drowned out. It was as though suddenly it hit home to everyone that the violence that they'd read about in the newspapers and seen on the TV news wasn't just something that happened to 'other people' - if Daniel Parkinson, who was in the news every second day, could be murdered it could happen to them too. And it was such a horrifying murder – beheading was something that previously had only been seen in the most violent areas of the Middle East. For the first time it was clear that real panic was being felt throughout the Australian community, and it was being amplified by the media broadcasts throughout the country.

As was becoming an almost daily occurrence, the Prime Minister made himself available at about 9.00am to be grilled by the press, who were becoming increasingly aggressive in lockstep with the increasing public panic.

"You said two days ago that the police were getting close to capturing the terrorists, but clearly these people are still able to attack people indiscriminately. What's your response to these latest atrocities?"

"I said that two days ago, and it's still true. The police are closing in, and I believe it's quite possible that we're only days away from getting these people. It's been a grinding slog, and our police are doing sterling work, as they always do. But in the meantime, we all have to stay calm. We have to stay together as a society, we can't let these people drive a wedge between different groups of people, or else we're playing right into their hands. I've been saying this from the beginning, but increasingly people are showing signs that they're not listening."

"But Prime Minister, it's all very well to say that, but people are frightened, and they've got good reason to be. And now a Federal Minister's been murdered. People are losing confidence that their governments can protect them."

"I think that's misplaced. We've got police patrolling the streets in numbers that are unprecedented, in all the capital cities. And yes, some people have been killed, but remember, it's not only non-Muslims – dozens of Muslims have been murdered by the actions of right-wing fanatics, and they're adding fuel to this violence."

"So why haven't they been stopped? Surely they're easier to identify?"

"The police have already identified three groups that have been involved, and they're all in jail, and they'll be tried for murder. But there are many such groups, and violence breeds violence. Now we're getting cases of individuals, not members of any of these organized groups, who are taking it into their own hands to attack Muslims. And of course, the reverse is happening. These crazy people are inspired by the actions of these organized groups which they see on TV. So again, I appeal to everyone to stay calm, and stop making inflammatory comments that just make things worse, because there are idiots out there that listen and convince themselves that going out and committing some violent act is a good thing. And you in the media have a special responsibility to do your best to dampen this mood that's developed."

After a further five minutes of such questions and answers the PM made a final appeal: "So, let me say it again: Stay calm, let the police finish their job of capturing these people, which I think they're close to doing, and then let's put all this behind us." He then turned away and walked towards his car, accompanied by Paul Davies who had been with him during the interview. When they were seated, and heading back to Kirribilli House, the PM turned to Paul, and said:

"It's getting harder and harder to stall them. Do you think they're taking in anything I say?"

"I'm sure they are. I'm sure most people out there know that what you're saying is sensible, but they're scared, and these journalists are just reflecting that. After what's happened to Daniel, they're probably scared themselves."

The PM sighed. "Yeah, I guess that's right. I don't blame them for being scared. What's terrifying, and these terrorists know it, is that these beheadings are so indiscriminate – it could be anybody. And it's such a gruesome way of killing someone. Whoever dreamed up this whole campaign is a diabolically clever bastard. Like David Scott said to us, he was probably counting on the right-wing nutters getting in on the act and inflaming the whole thing, and Boy, have they been co-operative. Jason better catch these guys soon. It's like being under a siege, that goes on and on. And now I'm going to have to say something to Daniel's family. Another great day in the office. Who'd be a politician?"

*

There was a slight drizzle of rain as Jason, with his colleague Jim Callaghan driving, made his way out of the centre of the city to the outer suburb of Penrith, but it didn't dampen his spirits.

Cautious man though he was, he couldn't help but feel he was at last closing in on the Mastermind behind the terrorism plaguing his country. He thought about the men he'd spoken to just an hour before, and wondered: Could I envisage them being capable of pulling off something like this? It's a terrible thing to suspect anybody of. Is it ever possible to discern evil in someone? He'd come across a number of terrorists in his time and some of them seemed most unlikely prospects to be mass killers. So, looks could be deceiving. But Imran, for example, was a hard-looking man, someone, Jason sensed, that I wouldn't choose to cross if I could avoid it. It wouldn't surprise me if he was the one.

Before long they were in Penrith, where Jim switched on Google Maps to navigate his way for the second time to 'Werner & Werner, Specialist Metal-Workers'. Inside, like the previous time, they found Mr. Werner at the counter, puzzling over a piece of metalwork. He looked up at them, and recognized Jason from the last visit.

"Uh oh" he said. "The police again. This looks ominous. Am I in trouble?"

"Not at all" Jason replied. "In fact, quite the opposite. We're hoping you can help us."

Werner then said: "Since you were here, I've seen you on the news. You're heading up the investigation into the Opera House bombing." He looked at them for a few moments, before saying: "I'm very concerned. Do you think those barrels I made were used in those shootings?"

"It's possible, Mr. Werner" Jason replied. "Don't worry. We know you would've had no idea. But the help you may be able to give us is terribly important."

"Anything I can do. I'm so sorry. This is terrible." Werner looked genuinely devastated.

Jason then explained: "Last time I was here you described the man who picked up the barrels. I know you said he could well have been in disguise, but I'm going to show you three photos, and describe the men, and you tell us whether you think it's feasible that any of them could be the one." He showed Mr. Werner the photos David had taken at the meeting, and added: "They're all big, over 185 cms, or six-foot one inch. This one (he pointed to Imran's photo) is particularly strongly built, very fit looking."

Werner looked closely at them, before saying: "Yes, in terms of height and build they're similar. This one particularly (he pointed to Imran's photo). He also was, swarthy, I guess you could say, like this chap."

"OK, that's good. Now, I've got some voice recordings here. Can you remember whether it sounds like one of them?" Jim turned on the phone recording, letting it play for sixty seconds or so for each man before switching it off, and looking at Werner enquiringly.

"Yes, the third one does sound like him. The chap spoke very good English, but there was a slight accent, just like the recording. This really could be him."

"Mr. Werner, you've been very helpful. This could be terribly important. Can we count on you keeping absolutely quiet about this? We're talking about national security now." Jason looked him directly in the eye as he spoke, and there was no doubting his seriousness.

"Sir, I promise you I will never reveal this to anyone. And again, I'm very sorry that I had anything to do with this man."

"We understand. Thank you again." Jason and Jim shook hands with Werner and walked out to their car. Once seated they turned and looked at each other: "I think we might have hit the jackpot" said Jim. "I think so too" replied Jason, "but let's see what the other four say. If even one of them backs up Werner I'd say the probability is high that you're right. Let's go."

Three hours later, after they had spoken to the fourth equipment maker, they again went out to their car, looked at each other, and this time all caution was gone. "It's got to be" said Jim, with unconcealed glee. "Five out of five. That's what I call confirmation."

"Absolutely" agreed Jason. But ever the realist, he went on: "There's a very good chance that Imran was the one that ordered those weapons. He could be involved, but is he the one that's actually masterminding the whole thing? It looks very possible, but we don't know for sure. We've got to get some more confirmation."

Jim looked a little crestfallen, but Jason laughed and assured him: "Jim, this is a huge breakthrough, and I'm guessing he's the one. But now we've got to prove it."

*

There was a buzz of anticipation in the meeting hall that was located off to the side of the main prayer area of the mosque, in Sydney. There were nearly forty people present, including five women. Included were Fariq and twelve of the group who had attended the earlier meetings he initiated; the President of the Federation of Islamic Councils, Reza; the Heads of the affiliated bodies from all states excluding the Northern Territory; the Head of the Council of Imams, Zaid, and three of his colleagues from Sydney, Melbourne and Queensland; and finally, representatives from a range of Muslim community organisations from a number of states.

The meeting had been initiated by Fariq, who'd met with Reza and impressed upon him the need for the whole Muslim community to consider how they were going to do something positive about the social chaos that had been unleashed upon Australia by a group claiming to represent their religion. Both of them had been exposed to David Scott's radical proposals for change, and it was this shared awareness of what was theoretically on the table if there was to be an accommodation between Muslims and non-Muslims, no matter how unpalatable in some minds, that resulted in their agreement to organise and host such a meeting. In fact, Reza, who perhaps sensed the writing on the wall, suggested that Fariq make the opening explanatory address and chair the rest of the meeting, after he had said a very few words to introduce him and essentially give his blessing for Fariq to take over. Reza now looked at his watch, saw that it was 10.00am, stood up and walked to the lectern, silence descending on the room as he did so.

"Assalamualaikum (May peace be upon you)" he greeted the assembly. "Let us begin in our usual way." He then recited a very short prayer while they bowed their hands, held their arms on their laps with the palms facing upwards in the Muslim prayer position, and listened attentively.

"Ladies and gentlemen" Reza began, "we are here today because we are facing the greatest crisis the Muslim community has ever faced in this country. In fact, along with the Corona virus it is perhaps the greatest social crisis the entire Australian community has faced, since the Second World War. We Muslims can all claim that what has happened is the product of a history of discrimination and all sorts of other excuses, but the inescapable fact is that this crisis was started and is being perpetuated by people claiming to be from our community. We have to face up to that reality. Recently a few of us met with the Prime Minister and his Cabinet of National Security, and we assured them that we recognize our responsibility to play our part in doing something positive about the crisis we all face. I suggest to you all that includes facing up to some harsh facts about ourselves that perhaps explain how this could have happened in the first place. You represent a great proportion of Muslims in this country and are all influential in shaping how your communities think and act, and how they are reacting to this crisis. Today we're going to discuss some very serious matters and I'm asking you to keep your hearts and minds open, and to contribute constructively to what I'm sure will be some very heated debates. At the end of it, I hope we'll all have a better understanding of the issues facing us, and some of the options we have to address them. I'm hoping that you will go back to your communities and faithfully recount what was discussed and perhaps concluded here today."

He paused, and looked around the room, satisfying himself that he had certainly gained their undivided attention. He went on: "I'd now like to introduce Fariq Hashim, who was the instigator of this meeting. Fariq is well-known to some of you. He is a very successful businessman and is a prominent and active member of the Lebanese community. He and a number of similar people have been having some discussions very recently about the issues we're going to discuss today and have some suggestions that, while some of us will consider them revolutionary and perhaps unacceptable, need to be taken very seriously. Don't forget, he and his colleagues represent a cross-section of the non-clerical, but highly educated and aware people in our community. They need to be listened to. Please, welcome Fariq." He went back to his seat as Fariq walked to the lectern, to polite applause.

For a few moments he looked around at the audience, quickly sizing them up. He knew his own group would support what he was about to say, and he guessed that the clerics and the representatives from the Muslim Councils would be strongly opposed. The community representatives he just couldn't tell, but he knew his own community people, one of whom was here today, would be open-minded – perhaps the others would be as well. OK, here goes, he thought. Give it your best shot.

Over the next twenty minutes Fariq spoke without interruption. He first re-iterated the situation they faced, confirming just how grave it was, and the long-term threat it posed to all Muslims in Australia. He reminded them that they had either come to this country to start a new life, or had been born and raised here, and should have had no illusions about the way of life here, that it was very different from what they had been used to in their home countries, and that as immigrants it was incumbent on them to fit into their new country and become 'Australians'. He made the point that continuing to behave as if they were in their home countries could generate negative reactions, even fear, from non-Muslim Australians. While they could argue as long as they liked that this was unfair and that non-Muslims should make allowances for them, it was fact, and they'd be better off accepting it. He put it to them that there were a number of steps they could take which would go a long way to alleviating the concerns and fears that many Australians had about them, and that these were not at all threatening to either their culture or their religion. In fact, he believed that these were highly desirable actions for the Muslim community in any situation, not just this crisis. He then described these steps in detail, which were those which had already been discussed in the previous meetings his group had held, with David and Jason present. He argued that these steps would greatly help in reducing the harassment that a minority of non-Muslims were inflicting on Muslims. In particular, he emphasized this point in reference to veiling, making the case as to why veiling was not mandatory in Islam, but was a purely cultural issue. At this point he did not mention the issue of whether or not the Qur'an was the literal word of God.

He then went on to make the point that the steps he'd described did not address the most serious issue, namely, what could possibly have created a situation where young Muslims, born and raised in this country, could have committed so terrible an atrocity as the Opera House bombing, and shooting. What mind-set could they have had to rationalize such an act? Like Islamic terrorists the world over, these men, in the midst of committing mass murder, had invoked their religion. This, he said very sternly, suggested there was something seriously wrong, if our religion can be so exploited. "I put it to you" he said, "that terrorists argue that what they're doing is sanctioned by the Qur'an, and because the Qur'an is the literal word of God, it must be condoned. But we know that's wrong, so what conclusion must we come to?"

He paused and scanned the audience – they were hanging on his every word, waiting expectantly for what he was going to say next. He didn't immediately give them an answer. Instead, he gave them a quick history lesson, the same one David Scott had given his group in their first meeting, namely that of the Traditionalists and the Mu'tazilites. He also explained the fact that many highly qualified Islamic scholars, largely based in what he described as 'free' countries, argued the Mu'tazilite interpretation. "Ladies and gentlemen, I know that the thought of accepting that the Qur'an need not be interpreted literally is shocking to many of you, perhaps blasphemous in your mind, but I put it to you that just because conservative clerics have been propagating this for centuries doesn't necessarily make it right. The Mu'tazilite view was orthodoxy for some time before the Traditionalists won out. The Islamic religion has the scope for all of us to interpret it as we see fit. We don't have a Pope; no individual or group has a monopoly on truth in Islam. So, I and my colleagues believe very strongly that we should all consider what we in Australia want to believe is our truth. We believe that being able to interpret our Qur'an in the context of time and place will remove many of the negative things that result from the way we think currently and help us as a community get on a lot better with our fellow Australians. Not only that, I think it will improve our own lives."

He concluded by saying simply: "I've said my piece. Now I'll open up the meeting for debate. In order to keep control, please direct your comments and questions to me, and I'll answer myself or direct the question to someone else appropriate."

The meeting continued for another hour, and it was, predictably, heated. One person suggested that they should first consider the most practical ideas Fariq had put forward, such as banning Wahhabism, and having imams who were born and raised in Australia, and agree to implement them, and after some back-and-forth argument most people indicated that they would support that suggestion. Particularly convincing was the recounting by the Head of the Victorian Council of Muslims, Mustafa Sulaiman, of the meeting he and a few others present today had attended when Prof. David Scott had spoken. He explained a little of David's rant, saying they didn't like what they heard, but recognized that it came from the heart, it was the truth. "We can't live in our bubble expecting everyone else to accommodate us – we have to look at what we can do to change so that we all fit better into this country. Don't forget, when visitors come to our home countries, we expect them to fit in with us – we can't expect any different when we're visitors in another country."

However, when someone raised the Qur'an issue and spoke in support of what Fariq had said, it provoked some strong reactions. One of the representatives of the Council of Imams was outraged at the direction the meeting was heading. He said he was opposed to most of the ideas Fariq had put forward, in particular the one involving the Qur'an, which he said was definitely blasphemy. "These ideas will never be accepted by true Muslims, and I'll bet most of the people in this room agree with me." He looked around the room, but there were only a few nods of approval. At that point a woman stood up, took the microphone, looked around at the room which consisted primarily of men, and said, with more than a touch of defiance.

"I for one think you're wrong, very wrong. What Fariq has said today is the most enlightened and sensible thing about our religion I've ever heard anyone say out loud in public in my life, and I'll bet that many in this room, certainly all the women, agree with me." At that, all the women, and most of Fariq's group, burst into applause. Encouraged, she continued: "Our religion has always been dominated by men, because it suits them so well. Why would they ever want to change when it allows them to keep us as second-class citizens, expected to do what we're told, and it's sanctified by God? These changes will bring us into the modern world, where everyone is equal regardless of gender, or race, and while a lot of men won't like it, eventually they'll see that it's better for everybody. I'm very confident that most of the people in the community I represent would eventually go along with this, even the bit about the Qur'an. So, I urge you to have the courage to take these ideas out to our communities, and get these changes made."

She sat down, to further applause, and looks of stunned disbelief on the faces of some of the men. After all were quiet, Reza stood up, took the microphone, and began to speak. "I think most of you know me, and I'm sure all of you know *of* me. I was an Islamic scholar, and I've been an academic all my life, in the Islamic space, so orthodox Islam has always been something I've accepted without question. Maybe it's because I'm getting advanced in years, but recently I've begun to think about many of the things that we're told by the so-called Islamic experts, and I've begun to question them. I'm one of those people Fariq referred to, Islamic scholars who are having a serious re-think about our religion."

He paused for a few moments before taking a deep breath and continuing. "This may well cost me the position I hold as

President of the Australian Association, but I have to confess to you now that I agree with almost all the things that Fariq has put to you." There was an instant reaction from some in the room, with mutterings between them, but he raised his voice and continued. "In particular, I agree with the most controversial of his suggestions, that the Qur'an can be interpreted in the context of time and place." He explained how why some scholars like him had come to conclude that they agreed with the stance taken by the Mu'tazilites, all those centuries ago, and concluded by saying: "So, ladies and gentlemen, I'm adding my voice to the calls made by Fariq and his fellow businessmen for some fundamental changes to the way we interpret our religion. From what I've heard today (he nodded to the woman who had spoken out so strongly), it would seem many in our community organisations will be doing the same." He sat down to prolonged applause. Two more people stood up and supported Reza, but as the meeting had been going for over one and a half hours, Fariq strode to the lectern to close the meeting.

"Ladies and gentlemen. I think this has been a most illuminating and productive meeting. I'm surprised but extremely grateful and relieved that so many of you seem to be supportive of what I and my colleagues have suggested. However, I know that it's one thing to have these ideas, but quite another to actually get the majority of our fellow-Muslims to accept them and put them into action. It'll probably take a long time, but I'm confident it can be done. After we part, I'll get together with Reza to agree how we can take this forward, and we'll be communicating with you all. Thank you for coming, and for participating so constructively." He then left the lectern, walked up to Reza, and said, with a smile: "I think we've got a lot to talk about. How about we go right now and have a coffee?" Reza smiled back and replied: "I'd like nothing better."

*

David was feeling elated. He'd just been talking to Fariq on the phone, who'd briefed him about the meeting he'd chaired earlier that afternoon, and how well it had gone.

"You won't believe it, David, but I really think we're going to get a lot of the Muslim community to back us on most of the changes we've been talking about. I even think that, given time, they're going to seriously consider the Mu'tazilite idea."

They both expressed their amazement that such a forum could so quickly take on board such controversial ideas. They'd expected it would be a long, hard slog to even begin to get a reasonable hearing.

"You know" said David, "maybe a lot of Muslims have been thinking about these issues for a long time but have never dared to air their thoughts in public, for fear of being castigated and ostracized for straying from what's considered to be the right Islamic way to think. Now that you've brought the debate into the open they're daring to say what they really think. You've done an amazing thing, Fariq. And it was very brave and statesmanlike for Reza to come out and support you."

After a few more words they said goodbye and David sat back in his favourite lounge chair, thinking about what Fariq had told him, and how satisfying it was to hear that the crazy ideas he'd been sprouting had actually resulted in this turn of events. At that moment the doorbell rang, and he got up and went to the door, wondering who it could be – he wasn't expecting anyone.

Dina had watched the 7.00pm news on the ABC, followed by the 7.30pm current affairs programme. Both were full of reports and discussion about the latest round of beheadings and the increasing number of incidents of violence, committed by both Muslim and non-Muslim groups. She found it both upsetting, and depressing, the overwhelming impression from the increasingly fiery rhetoric being that Muslims were the root cause of all the problems, and that Australia would be better off if they could magically disappear. The strain shown by the Prime Minister from the pressure he was under to take radical action was obvious on the news flashes where he was asked for comment. Ever since she had her last meeting with David and she'd told him she needed time out to think, she'd been agonizing about their possible future. She certainly loved him but was coming to the conclusion that there were too many obstacles in the way of their getting married. By about 8.30pm she decided that there was no point delaying the inevitable, so she drove to his apartment and was now standing outside his door.

"Dina" David exclaimed in surprise. "Why didn't you tell me you were coming? And you don't need to ring the doorbell – you've got a key."

She came in, and he noted that she was still wearing the veil, but more significantly the fact that she didn't give him the usual kiss. That's not good, he thought. I wonder what's coming. She walked past him into the lounge and sat down in one of the single lounge chairs, not the sofa they usually shared. She looked at him and noticed that he seemed quite happy about something.

"You look like the cat that ate the cream," she observed.

"Well, I have had some good news," he replied, and told her briefly about the conversation he'd just finished with Fariq.

"So, we're going to change our religion to make it suitable for Australian consumption now, are we? You really have been busy."

"Dina, that's not fair. You know there's a lot of changes that make a lot of sense and would help to settle this situation down. We've talked about it."

"I suppose we have," she said a little dismissively. "Anyway, it doesn't matter, you do whatever you think best, it's not my concern."

At this David's feelings of bonhomie disappeared completely, replaced by considerable apprehension. Not my concern? he thought, you're my fiancée. Before he could collect his thoughts to frame a suitable retort she continued.

"I've been thinking a lot since we last spoke, about us, about everything that's going on. It was all so easy before, but suddenly things have got very complicated, and I need to sort them all out in my mind. So, I said last time that I needed a little space to do that, but I think I need more than that. I think we should put any talk about marriage on hold as well, and let's think about it again when all this mess is over. I'm sorry, but I think this is the right thing to do."

David was aghast. He hadn't seen this coming. Perhaps he should have but having the sensitivity to read the small signs in a relationship was not a strength of his. Dina knew this, and even in this fraught situation she could see the amusing side.

"Poor David, you're really shocked, aren't you? Darling, I know you can't help it, but sometimes you're as blind as a bat. 'Feelings – ugh, protect me from them' (she acted out the words, dramatically). David, I still love you, I probably always will. But we need some real time away from each other. Maybe then it can work out, but not like things are now. Understand? Do you?"

"Not really. But you seem pretty certain about this. There's probably nothing I can say to dissuade you, is there?'

"No, there isn't."

She rose from the chair, gathered up her bag, gave him a quick kiss on the lips, and went to the door. He followed her, and stood in the doorway, watching forlornly as she went down the stairs to her car, and away. He walked slowly back to his lounge room and sat in his chair again, his feelings of elation turned to ashes. Just like that, he thought. It didn't even take ten minutes. For Dina's part, the tears began before she reached the end of the street and she had to pull over to the side of the road. For all her apparent coolness, she was shattered. She was convinced she was doing the right thing, but oh, it was so hard. She dried her eyes, gave herself a mental shake, and started again towards her home.

CHAPTER 15

Immediately after Jason and David had agreed that it was a distinct possibility that the terrorist Mastermind could be among Fariq's business group, Jason had set his team on investigating the backgrounds of every one of them, starting with those of the bigger men that he could remember. Their task had been made easier by the fact that Fariq had drawn up a list of all the people who had agreed to attend the meeting and given a copy to each one of them as they arrived. David and Jason had also been given the list. The aim was to obtain a brief description of each participant – where they'd come from, their family situation, their businesses, and so on.

The morning after Jason had met with the weapons suppliers, and identified Imran as a very possible suspect, Jim Callaghan burst in to Jason's office, sat down, and said excitedly: "You'll never guess who's got a business that's got an office in each of Sydney, Melbourne and Brisbane?"

"Don't tell me it's Imran."

"Sure is. What are the chances? He's got to be the one."

"There's a very good chance that he is, but we need one more thing to take it beyond the possibility of co-incidence. Let's see what Immigration can find out for us."

While Jim walked out of his office, Jason placed a call to the Head of the Department.

"Mr. Donaldson? It's Detective Superintendent Jason Blake here from the AFP. I'm heading up the terrorism investigation. I need to find out some information about 'a person of interest', as we coppers like to put it, and I need one of your people to help me. It goes without saying that he or she will have to be very discreet – this is extremely sensitive, as I'm sure you'd appreciate."

"Jason, of course, we all know what you're doing, and we're right behind you. We'll give you any help you need. If you give me your mobile number I'll pick the person I think is best placed to help you and they'll give you a ring within the hour."

"That's great. Thanks very much. I appreciate your help."

Sure enough, twenty minutes later his phone rang. "Detective Superintendent Blake? It's Susan Marsh here from Immigration. Mr. Donaldson said you'd be expecting my call."

"Thanks Susan. That was really quick."

"I know what this is about" said Susan, "so I know this is critically important. Also, that it's highly confidential, so don't worry on that score. What can I do to help? I've been told to drop everything and work on this until we get the answers."

Jason explained that he had a person under investigation who had emigrated to Australia, he thought from Iraq, and he wanted to find out as much as was possible about his background. Where he went to school, where he worked, anything and everything possible. In particular, he wanted to know if he had any dealings with groups that practiced any sort of violence, whether resistance to the allied forces, attacks against the Iraqi government, or any other groups.

"I'm guessing that some of this information may be obtained from our own people based in Iraq, but I'm sure they're going to need to lean on their Iraqi colleagues and any other contacts they have. You'll need to impress on them that the authorization for this comes from the PM himself, so they should give it their top priority."

He then sent Susan every bit of information he had about Imran, including the photos David had taken.

"OK sir. I'm right on it. I'll get back to you as soon as I've got something."

"Thanks, Susan. You can get me on this number, at any hour."

As soon as Susan was off the line, Jason put in a call to the PM's office, and was immediately put through.

"Sir, this is not definite, but I believe we're getting very close to finding the Mastermind."

He then explained the linking of the weapons purchase to a person they had under surveillance, and that they were now investigating him thoroughly.

"That's great news, Jason. Why can't you arrest him now?"

"Sir, we've got no real proof. A good lawyer would have him out of jail in no time, and then he's warned."

"I understand. Anyway, that's the first bit of encouraging news we've had. Let's pray you're right about him."

*

It was a beautiful Sydney day, with only a few clouds in the sky, and a moderate 26-degree temperature, the kind of day that normally would lift the spirits, make one think how wonderful it was to be alive, particularly when one was in a car and far enough from Sydney's centre to have escaped the worst of the traffic. But David was feeling very downhearted, still re-living the previous night when Dina had broken off their engagement. Was it all my fault, he wondered, for the umpteenth time, or was it just circumstance, all this chaos and anti-Muslim feeling? But he had to own up to the fact that he'd handled his mother's funeral appallingly, and maybe that was the thing that tipped her over the brink. Yes, it was definitely all his fault, he thought, berating himself for being so stupid. How could I have let this happen? She's the most wonderful woman I've ever been with, and I drove her away. And so it went on, as it does with most people, 20:20 hindsight kicking in to make them feel even worse. Fortunately, he was diverted from his self-flagellation by a question from his passenger.

"Professor Scott, you haven't said a word in ages. Are you upset about something?"

David turned briefly to look at Rachel Johnson, his soon-to-be student, then immediately back to the road, thinking what do I say to that? She's only just turned eighteen, and I'm her professor. A little self-consciously he confessed: "My fiancée gave me the boot last night, and it was a bit of a shock – I wasn't expecting it."

She shot a quick look at him. Crazy woman, she thought. Doesn't she realize how hot he is? If I was a few years older and he wasn't my professor I'd chase after him myself. "I'm really sorry. Had you been together long?"

"About seven months. She's a Muslim, Malaysian. With all that's been happening it started getting difficult, for her anyway. And I didn't handle it too well. Maybe when this is all over we can give it another try." He left it there, feeling he'd said enough. She read his mood and didn't question him any further. Instead, she switched the conversation to the place they were about to visit, the Lebanese Refugee Centre.

"I've read about the place we're going to. There was an article a couple of years ago in The Australian which I found that told the stories of a few of the people who came through there. They were heart-breaking, almost made me cry. The things they'd escaped from, and then had to endure until they were free on Australian soil - it's really hard for us here to comprehend."

"Yes, I've done some reading too. There was a very good book I read where the author interviewed a number of people who'd been refugees, had been through terrible experiences, but made successful lives for themselves here. One point that came through is how often these same people come back to places like we're going to and help new arrivals. It's quite inspiring."

Switching his attention to navigating his way through a number of minor streets, David soon pulled into the driveway of their destination, in Bankstown, parking his car in a visitor's area close to the entrance, his bodyguards parking nearby. They got out and surveyed the front of the Centre, which looked as though it had once been a very large house, but not a grand one, built from wood and corrugated iron rather than stone or brick. It was slightly run down, in need of a paint job, but nevertheless neat and tidy. They walked through the entrance door into in a fairly cramped reception area, where a large, veil-clad woman was sitting behind a counter. She looked up and with a welcoming smile said: "You must be Professor David Scott. We've all been looking forward to meeting you. You're famous - a TV star." She laughed good naturedly, before adding: "Mr. Razman will be out soon so please take a seat over there while you're waiting." They went to the couch she was pointing to and sat down.

In the five minutes or so they were waiting, a few young women came separately into the room from a side door, said a few words to the receptionist, smiled shyly at David and Rachel, then went back. The receptionist eventually said to them, with a big laugh: "See, you're famous. Those girls came out with some silly excuse, but they just wanted to get a look at you. The handsome TV star." She giggled delightedly at David's obvious embarrassment, not helped by Rachel who said softly, with a laugh: "I didn't realize you were so famous. 'The handsome TV star' – I must remember that."

At that point the head of the Centre came out, introduced himself as Razman Munir and led them into his office. It was quite small, with cheap furniture, and lots of files scattered around - on his desk, on bookshelves, on the two sideboards, and even on the floor. "Sorry for the mess. There's not really enough room. One of these days we'll get all this on computer, become a paperless office." He laughed at the thought. He looked as though he was in his early sixties, slightly overweight, with a friendly, open face. "So, Professor Scott, when you rang I was very pleased to agree to you coming out and visiting us, but I'm not really clear what it is you're looking for, and how we can help you."

David explained again who he was, and in particular his role with the Prime Minister's Cabinet of National Security. "Part of what I'm trying to do is find ways to improve the relationship between Muslims and non-Muslims in the longer-term, when all this terrorism is behind us, and I thought it would be helpful if I had a much better feel for what new arrivals go through. We academics can live in a bit if a rarified environment, you know" he added with a smile. "Rachel here is one of my students, and she's very keen also to increase her understanding. I hope you don't mind that she's here?"

"Quite the contrary. The more people who come and see what we're trying to do the better, and it's particularly nice to see you people come. So, Rachel, you're very welcome. OK, let's see how to do this. I think first I should spend a bit of time explaining to you just what the Centre does, or maybe it's more accurate to say, what we try to do." He laughed, then went on. "Then you should meet a couple of the people who come in and help out with the running of the Centre. They can tell you in their own words what they do. Lastly, I'll quickly show you around and you can see some of the programmes we have going. That'll take a couple of hours – do you have that much time?"

"Absolutely" said David. "It's very generous of you to give so much of your time – I'm sure you must be fearfully busy."

"Not at all. What you're doing is of immense importance, so anything we can do here to help you with your task we'll be very happy to do."

He then proceeded to explain the purpose of the Centre, it's history, and what exactly it does. It had been founded in 1998, by a group of Lebanese men who years earlier had themselves been refugees, and who'd become successful in business. They could see the difficulties that many refugees faced and, grateful for the fact that they'd been accepted into Australia and had done well, they wished to help others do the same. Significantly, they opened the Centre up to refugees from many backgrounds, not just Lebanese. "In fact" said Razman, "we even have a few non-Muslims here, but that doesn't happen very often. The intention really is to help Muslims." The centre helped people in a number of ways. Teaching English was the most obvious need, but they also provided limited child-care facilities, and assistance in finding jobs for those whose English skills had developed sufficiently. They also gave some assistance to those in severe financial need.

"Something that's been really successful is offering the teenagers the chance to play sport, particularly soccer, for the boys. In most of their home countries soccer is enormously popular – most boys dream of being soccer stars. We've made arrangements with a few soccer clubs, and they've allowed us to use their facilities during the week when they're not in use by their members. The idea is to give these young kids something to occupy them, and develop an interest in. We also have two basketball courts here, where both boys and girls can play, together. Apart from the sporting aspect, it's good for the boys to be forced to play the same game as the girls – helps to break down the patriarchal culture that they've come from." He looked at them and observed: "I'm sure I don't have to tell you how important it is that these young boys develop healthy interests, and not get sucked into things they get into on the internet through boredom. This is a fairly new idea, but it's really taking off. We're hoping we can create a sort of competition between various Centres like this, and even better, if we can get our boys playing soccer against other groups of Australian boys, from schools, maybe."

"I think that's a brilliant idea" David commented. "Sport's a really tried and proven way of bringing people from all sorts of backgrounds together and realizing that they're not different at all – it's a great leveler. I hope it works out really well for you. ... How do you get funding?" he went on.

"Most of our funds come from donations from the Muslim communities, but the governments, both state and federal, also give us some grants. They're quite generous, actually. I think they realize that we're making life easier for them, helping get these people to be productive members of the Australian community, and not a drain on the taxpayer. But we couldn't do this just on government money – it's the Muslim communities that really underwrite us."

"Anyway, that's enough of the history. How about you meet two of the volunteers who come regularly to help out here. They both came through the Centre before going out to look after themselves, and now are helping others." He stood up, and led them to a slightly larger room, a meeting room, where very shortly two people came in. He introduced the first, a man, as Muzir, and the woman, as Marina. After explaining to them who David and

Rachel were, and the purpose of their visit, he asked each of them, in turn, to tell their story.

Muzir came from Afghanistan, where he fell foul of the Taliban. He was in jail, where he was treated very badly. His family bought his release, but before long the Taliban were after him again. With a loan from his family he escaped, and eventually made his way to Indonesia, where he finally got on a boat and ended up in Nauru. He was there for three years before finally being admitted into Australia. He wasn't married, but had to leave his parents and siblings behind, which was very difficult. He had virtually nothing when he arrived in Australia, but he'd been a plumber in Afghanistan, and he managed to eventually get a job with a small plumbing outfit. Eventually he was able to start his own business and was reasonably successful. So, he now comes back and tries to help others. The Centre helped him a lot. They taught him enough English to get by, helped him find a room to stay, and to get his first job. "They saved me" he claimed. He's now an Australian citizen. He married a lady from Pakistan, and they have two children, now in secondary school.

Marina, who wasn't wearing a veil, also came from Afghanistan, but a few years later than Muzir. After the invasion, and the Taliban were thrown out of power, she became a policewoman, an un-heard of situation previously. Unlike many girls, her parents had made sure she had a reasonable education, so she was keen to try and get a job. She loved the work, but there was tremendous opposition. She was posted to a village that was in Taliban country, and soon she was the subject of death threats. Finally, she was shot, and left for dead. But, she survived, and after recuperating went back to her job. But she was a marked woman. The Taliban made it known that women like her would not be accepted by them, and she knew it was only a matter of time before she was killed. From then on, her experience was similar to Muzir. She escaped from Afghanistan, and came to Australia via Indonesia, and Nauru. The Centre taught her English, and helped her get a job, working in a supermarket. She worked very hard on her English, then went to night school, and got a better job, and finally became a policewoman, her current job. Like Muzir she was very grateful to the Centre and returns to give something back. She was very active in dealing with troubled young people, discouraging them from having anything to do with extremists.

When they'd both finished, David asked: "I know this is very sensitive, but as Razman explained, I've been asked by the Prime Minister to investigate the sort of thing I'm about to ask. How do you each feel about what's been happening, the terrorism, the reactions, why it happened in the first place, what you think the future holds?" He smiled: "Big questions, I know, but please, I'm really interested in your thoughts on this."

Marina answered first and spoke with more than a bit of passion. "It's shocking, and a terrible thing that young men from our own Australian Muslim community were involved. I know it's also bad that others have retaliated, but the truth is that people invoking our religion started it. How could they do this when they know that Muslims already were distrusted by other Australians? It's now so much worse. I saw you on TV, and you said you thought they were deliberately trying to set Muslims and non-Muslims against each other – I think you're right. And the trouble is they use religion to justify what they do, just like terrorists all over. There's something seriously wrong when people can do this. They say it's in the Qur'an, and that's the word of God, so it must be right. The clerics and other men – it's almost always men – say the same thing when they want to justify having things all their own way, like women having to do what men tell them, and to wear veils. Religion is meant to be between you and God, not what these men tell you." She paused, and added: "Sorry, but it makes me so mad. I've done a lot of reading about this, and I think a lot of what's in Shari'a law are extra things added in later by men, for their own purposes. I know that would get me in trouble in some places if I said that publicly, but that's what I really think."

"And what do you think?" David asked Muzir.

"Well, it might surprise you, but I agree with what Marina said. I think a lot of the time our clerics talk a lot of rubbish. They should stick to spiritual matters, not get into advice about how we should live our lives. And there's no doubt that lots of people exploit Islam for bad things. There's something wrong if they can do that. And now we're living with the consequences, getting blamed for what a few crazies have done. To be honest, I don't blame other Australians being angry with us, even though in some ways it's unfair that we're all blamed. In some ways we've asked for it."

"Well," said David, after a long pause while he digested what the two of them had said, "you've surprised me, but I'm impressed with what you've said, and I'm really grateful that you've been so open with me. You've helped me more than you realize with what I'm trying to do. Thank you very much, both for sharing your stories about how you got to this point, and for those opinions." Then, as an afterthought, he added a question: "Marina, I suspect I know the answer to this, and I hope you don't mind me asking, but many Muslim women wear a veil – in fact it seems to be generally thought that it's compulsory in Islam – but you don't. Would you tell me why?"

"Well, firstly I don't accept that it's compulsory in Islam. And another thing, it seems to me that it's creating a difference between us and everyone else for no reason. It's not that I'm ashamed of being a Muslim, but why do we have to advertise it so much?"

"I thought you'd say something like that" David said with a smile. "Thanks again for being so open. One of these days I'd like to get you to speak at one of my classes – you'd be a hit for sure."

Marina laughed, and then she and Muzir got up and left the room. Razman looked at David and Rachel, and remarked: "Well, that was interesting. I've learned something myself today, thanks to you. No-one would normally want to raise those sorts of issues – it's too sensitive for one of us to do so. But you're an outsider, and you're an expert, so you can do it."

"Well, in the same spirit, what do you think?"

Razman smiled: "Don't tell anyone, but I agree with them. But enough of that. Let me show you around."

He then proceeded to take them on a tour of the whole Centre, which was considerably bigger in area than they'd envisaged. There were classrooms where English was being taught. Other rooms were full of food and clothing, and these were being distributed to people who lived in the neighbourhood and were struggling financially. They also went to an area where there were two basketball courts, full of children in their mid-teens, boys and girls, clearly having a great time. "As I said earlier, we set this up to try and keep kids away from crime, and it's been a real success. We got the idea from the Edmund Rice Centre in Perth." They were also introduced to some adults, who were recent attendants at the Centre. Their English was generally quite broken, and they were very shy, but nevertheless managed to explain where they'd come from, and what they were now doing. A common theme was how happy they were to be in Australia, and how wonderful the people in the Centre were, how much they were helping.

When their tour was completed, and they were back in Razman's office, David commented: "You know, one thing that's really struck me, and that's how selfless all the people are who come back here and help. It's really impressive."

"Well, it doesn't surprise me" said Razman with a smile. "The concept of helping others is very much part of our religion. You know about *zakat*, the concept of obligatory charity, one of the five pillars of Islam. It's very easy to extend that to the general idea of helping others, not just with money. So, you see Rachel, Islam's not just about terrorists and cutting people's hands off. There are some good things, too."

They all laughed, and then David and Rachel left, thanking Razman for being so helpful. On the way out they also bid farewell to the receptionist, who told them to come back and see them soon. As they drove back to the city, they asked each other their reactions to what they'd seen and heard. Both were a little overwhelmed at the obviously awful experiences these people had gone through and the selflessness of the ones who came back to help, after they'd settled in themselves. It was clear that extremism and terrorism and religious issues generally were the last thing on the minds of all the people they'd met – they were just trying to build a life for themselves.

"You know Rachel", David concluded "I've certainly learned something today. These people have been through terrible things, and all they want to do is build a life for themselves and their families. But they've been let down in two ways. First, we, the Australians, need to do more to help them settle in. I know a lot is already done, but I think we need to do even more. But secondly, I haven't changed my mind about the way certain people use Islam to bully people like this into believing lots of things which are rubbish, and then to try and influence them to behave in ways they'd never consider if left to themselves. They do these people, and all ordinary Muslims like them, a big disservice. So, I still think contextualizing the Qur'an is the way forward, and the religious authorities and other people in positions of power deal should make this the new orthodoxy. And from what Razman, Muzir and Marina said, I think there's a big disconnect between what's pushed by the clerics and what a lot of ordinary Muslims think deep down, particularly if they've had a bit of education."

They headed back to the city, both of them a lot wiser, and David feeling a little less miserable than he had on the outward journey.

*

That same afternoon David attended another meeting of the PM's National Security Cabinet. For the first time, there was a sense that maybe an end was in sight. Jason shared with the other members the news he'd given the PM a day earlier, that they now had a very possible suspect for the Mastermind behind the various terrorist attacks, and that he was hopeful that he'd soon get the confirming evidence that would allow him to arrest him. He was of course grilled about why he couldn't move immediately, but they readily accepted the logic of his explanation. David then shared the progress that had been made with the senior members of the Muslim community, and the undertakings they'd made to him, and the PM was particularly pleased to hear this.

"When the violence is over, and everything quietens down, this is going to prove to be a long-term blessing, something we've grappled with for a long time and not very successfully. David, you've done a great job to win these gentlemen over – I don't know how you did it."

"Actually, sir, I think Jason deserves a great deal of the credit. He's the one who made contact with the senior businesspeople, who've really been invaluable in setting things up for us to engage with the leaders of the community organisations and the clerics."

"Well, Jason, when you finally get these terrorists, it would seem we all owe you a great deal of gratitude, on a number of fronts."

"Please sir, let's wait until we've got them, before you give us any congratulations. I'm a bit superstitious" said Jason, but it was obvious he was very pleased to get the recognition.

"Fair enough" agreed the PM. "Anyway, we've at least got some reason for hope that this will be sorted out soon, and let's just be thankful for that. Unless there're any other issues to raise, I think we're done for the day. OK? … Alright, see you all in a couple of days."

As it was quite late in the afternoon David decided to head straight home. All things considered he was feeling quite upbeat, with what he'd personally achieved, and with what was going on generally. In fact, he decided, why not give Dina a call? If he could get across to her how much progress they'd been making, maybe he could persuade her that the reasons she was giving for why it wouldn't work between them were going to gradually disappear. In this positive frame of mind, he ran up the stairs to his apartment, threw his briefcase down on the floor, sat down in his favourite chair, and dialed Dina. It rang at least six times before she answered, and then it was in a subdued tone, in marked contrast to David's cheery greeting.

"You're in a good mood about something, aren't you?" she said, with more than a hint of sarcasm, sufficient to bring David rapidly down to earth.

"Well, things have been moving in a very positive way since we last spoke, and I thought you'd be interested."

He proceeded to tell her about the developments in his dealings with Reza, Fariq and the others, trying his utmost to talk up the part they'd played in coming up with suggestions and commitments for change and playing down his own. But he had limited success.

"It sounds like you've succeeded in getting us all to change to suit you and your Aussie mates, doesn't it? Well, it's what you've always been raving on about, so I imagine you're pretty pleased with yourself."

This isn't going too well, he thought with dismay, but he pressed on regardless. "I was hoping that maybe you'd think that this could change the way you feel about us, if things got a lot better between Muslims and the rest of the population." This was met with silence, so he tried a different tack. "You know, I'm missing you dreadfully."

"Maybe you are, and maybe things could be different. But it's all pie in the sky at the moment, isn't it? We've still got terrorists out there, and the thought of Muslim men changing their beliefs in the way you've described is a bit hard to envisage. I'm afraid I'll believe it when I see it."

"So, what if it really does happen? Would you reconsider? Don't you miss me too, just a little?"

Dina hesitated, before she replied: "Maybe I do, just a little. But I'm not going to change my mind about us getting back together. I still think there's too much coming between us. I just can't see it all going away. … Anyway, David, you're starting to get me upset again, so let's just leave it there, OK? Good night." With that she hung up, leaving David wondering: Was that all bad? She said she missed me, a little. I think there's hope there. After he poured himself a glass of wine and sat down again, he concluded: No, I don't think I'll give up just yet.

*

Earlier that same evening, after almost two hours patient waiting, the two would-be assassins, Ashraf and Iqbal, in their car two hundred metres away from David's apartment, straightened up from their slouched positions. Coming from the other direction was David's car, instantly recognizable to them after the days of surveillance, and the unsuccessful assassination attempt. The Iraqi had told them that he was almost certain that after that failed attempt David would have some sort of protection, and their mission was to determine if this was indeed the fact.

As David began to turn into the driveway, the assassins saw another car following immediately behind, and then pull up and park directly opposite the apartment block. Two men got of the car, and moved swiftly into the driveway, following David's car. After about five minutes one of the men emerged from the front entrance of the building and walked over to the car. He got in, but didn't start the engine – rather, he appeared to be settled in, and watching the apartment. The assassins waited a further ten minutes, before Ashraf concluded: "Damn it. It's pretty clear, they're bodyguards. We'd better get out of here. We'll do one more check tomorrow." He did a slow U-turn and headed the car away from David's apartment block, down to the end of the street, then turned left and headed towards the city.

Early the next morning they returned to David's street, in Iqbal's car this time, and parked at least two hundred metres away from the apartment. A car was parked opposite the apartment, a different one from the car they'd observed the previous night. Shortly after 8.00am a man emerged from the apartment building entrance and walked across to the car and got in. Less than a minute later David's car emerged and headed down towards the water. The other car pulled out and followed him. As the little convoy went past, Ashraf and Iqbal observed that there were two men in the second car.

"It's definite, they're bodyguards" concluded Ashraf. "Looks like it's up to the Boss."

A little while later they were in their store, briefing The Iraqi about what had happened.

"OK, that's it. No more assassination attempts. I'll try myself later. So, it's business as usual, for as long as we can."

The other two went out to the front of the store and resumed their normal day job, appearing and behaving not at all like two ruthless assassins who'd come with an ace of murdering a member of the Prime Minister's Cabinet of National Security. Meanwhile, The Iraqi thought about the implications of what had happened. With the failed attempt he was confident that Jason would soon suspect that one of Fariq's group of businesspeople was behind it. If that's true, he thought, it's not going to be long now. Well, I'm ready to meet my Maker, I've been ready a long time.

Chapter 16

The following morning, David welcomed three visitors to his workplace at the university. "Gentlemen, my office is too small to accommodate so many people, so we'll have to go to a meeting room. Please follow me." Fariq Hashim, Reza Muhammad and Zaid Hamid dutifully trailed along behind him as he led them down a corridor off the main reception area to a medium-sized meeting room that looked out over a grassed area behind the main building. They were intrigued by the presence of two large men who had been loitering in the reception area and who were now following them at a discreet distance, trying to look inconspicuous. After they were seated and had been offered and served coffee, David asked: "So, Fariq, you suggested that the four of us should meet. I'm keen to hear what it's about."

"Before I answer that, we're all dying to know who those two large gentlemen are who've been following us. Are we considered potentially dangerous characters?"

David laughed. "No Fariq, it's a bit embarrassing, but Jason – you've met him, remember – thinks that the terrorists might be especially interested in me, and that I need protection. So, I've got those two, or others like them, day and night."

"Now that's interesting. Still, I guess you've been pretty high-profile lately, and probably lots of people know that you're working with the Prime Minister and the Cabinet. So, he could be right. Anything's possible in these crazy times."

Like the fact that one of your fellow Chamber members is very likely the terrorist Mastermind, David thought, but I can't let on about that. "So, Fariq, back to my question."

"Well David, you've met twice with me and my fellow business colleagues, and you've also met separately with these two gentlemen and some of their colleagues, who represent the more establishment Islamic community if I can express it in that way."

Fariq looked enquiringly at Reza who smiled and nodded his agreement. "Now, in those meetings you've put some ideas in our heads which, to put it mildly, are controversial, and which have resulted in some furious debate within our various communities." He smiled: "I gather you expressed yourself in rather strong terms in the meeting with these gentlemen."

David shifted uncomfortably in his chair: "Yes, I did. It was very rude of me, and I apologise again, gentlemen. It was quite out of order."

"Perhaps it was" said Reza, "but you certainly made your point, and it sank in." He laughed a little at the recollection.

Fariq then continued: "Recently, we had a meeting, where my group, Reza's group, and other representatives of Muslim community groups all were in attendance, over forty of us. The purpose of the meeting, which was triggered by what you said to us, was to consider what we could do collectively to help deal with this terrible situation we have. Maybe we can't do much to help catch the terrorists, but as you pointed out, we need to see how to improve the situation between Muslims and non-Muslims when this is all over. Reza, would you like to explain what happened?"

"Certainly. David, to summarise what happened during the course of a long meeting, we generally agreed that many of the things you suggested we should do are reasonable, and we'll do all we can, as people who have quite an influence over what happens in our communities, to bring them about. Some of them, as you suggested, are relatively easy, others more difficult. Locally trained imams, for example, we agree with that, isn't that so, Zaid?"

The Head of the Council of Imams nodded. "Yes, I was initially a little shocked at the idea, but the reality of what's going on made me think a lot harder about it, and I can see that it makes sense. While we're on this, we're also unhappy about the infiltration of Wahhabism into Australia. If one is honest, it's clear from the history of the last fifty years or so that the pushing of this around the world has been good for terrorists, and bad for normal Muslim communities. I think we can get our people to agree with us on this."

"Thanks, Zaid. There are some other things we can do which we think will be helpful, for example, monitoring far more closely what's being taught in Islamic schools, and even being prescriptive about curricula. And this brings us to the most contentious of the suggestions you made, and which have caused us the most internal discord. You said that we should re-visit the old debate between the Traditionalists and the Mu'tazilites regarding whether the Qur'an can be contextualised. The outcome of this debate of course has enormous implications for what's preached in mosques and what's taught in schools. Well, you'll be surprised to hear that in principle we're willing to start floating this thought in our communities, to see what reaction we get. If we find that it's not as big an issue with most of our Muslim colleagues as we've always thought, then we can move down that path at a sensible pace. This isn't the sort of thing one changes overnight, as I'm sure you appreciate, David."

David had been listening to Reza with increasing amazement. He'd been greatly encouraged by the reactions he'd observed at his meetings with Fariq and his colleagues, and even with Reza, Zaid and the rest of them. But he didn't for a moment think they would move this fast.

"Gentlemen," he eventually said, "you've surprised me in the best way I could imagine, and I can't tell you how gratified I am that you'd take my suggestions so seriously. If you go down this path and take your people with you it'll be absolutely ground-breaking. Australia will be the first country in which the Muslim communities significantly revise their interpretation of Islam to respond positively to the challenges of the contemporary world. And I'm sure in time it'll have a huge impact on Muslim and non-Muslim relations."

"That may be so" Reza responded with a grim smile, "and it could also see me, and my colleagues, thrown out of Islam as apostates. But I think it'll be accepted here, and most of our people won't think too badly of us. But overseas there'll definitely be outrage. I don't think we'd better do any travelling for a few years. ... Anyway, David, you can now tell the Prime Minister and his colleagues in the Cabinet of National Security about this meeting, and what we're proposing to do. And I think it would be a good idea if, when your friend Jason catches these terrorists and things hopefully get back to something like normal again, Fariq, Zaid and I should meet them again, and tell them ourselves."

"That would be an excellent idea, Reza, I'm sure the PM would be really keen to make that happen."

"Well," said Reza, "I think that concludes our business, so we should be on our way, before you talk us into some other outrageous idea." He paused and added with a smile: "Come to think of it, I don't there's anything more outrageous than what you've already convinced us to do. God help us." They all laughed, as they rose to head back to the reception area, after which David walked them to the carpark and waved them off. He walked back to his office, forgetting for the moment how miserable he was.

*

It was mid-afternoon and Dina was returning to the city by train after having had two days off work to spend time with parents in Gosford, north of Sydney. Being with them had been a welcome relief from the hustle and bustle of central Sydney, particularly with what was going on as a result of the violence that had been unleashed, initially by Muslims and now involving extremists from both sides of the conflict. Since she started wearing a veil going out in public was hazardous, with all sorts of people ready to throw abuse at her. It still amazed her – all that fuss over a veil, she thought. What was wrong with people? And it also gave her time to think about David. She'd been miserable ever since the evening she told him that it was over between them. She wondered what he was doing and how it had affected him. He's probably already taken up with some gorgeous young girl, she thought, there are so many chasing him. Was she crazy to push him away? What did she think she was going to do now? Last time she had a relationship with a Muslim it ended badly, and that's where she was inevitably heading now if she really believed what she told David. Maybe she'd been a bit rash, painting herself into a corner with the stance she was taking on behalf of her religion. Was it really so important, that she'd give up David, who she knew deep down she loved dearly?

Deep in such contemplation she hadn't noticed the three young men, all Caucasian, who'd entered the carriage at the previous stop. Loud, clearly having had more than a drink or two, they moved up the almost empty carriage and sat opposite her.

"Hey, look at what we've got" one of them said to his companions. "A raghead, and not bad looking, either."

"It doesn't matter what she looks like. She's a bloody Muslim and she'd cut your throat if she had the chance. Wouldn't you, lady? Just like your terrorist mates. You all hate us."

Dina was nervous when the three men sat down and now, listening to the vile things they were saying, her heart began to beat like a drum. The baiting continued, getting nastier, with Dina cowering down in her seat in terror, when they all became aware of a large figure that had suddenly materialized, standing between Dina and the three men. They looked up, and saw a man, not a lot older than them, with fair hair almost down to his shoulders. He was large - he looked as though he could easily be a member of one of Sydney's rugby league teams – and he said in a deep but quiet voice:

"You know, I don't think you really mean all that, do you?"

The three of them stood up, looked the newcomer up and down, and one of them, who appeared to be the spokesman, eventually asked: "What's it to do with you?"

"Well, I object to ladies being harassed, particularly by nasty buggers like you. So, I'm telling you to leave her alone."

"And if we don't?" the same one said defiantly, although his voice was beginning to lack conviction.

"Then you'll just have to bear the consequences. Do you really want to find out? If not, then clear out, right now."

The three of them looked at him, then at each other, somehow mutually deciding that, whatever the final outcome of a conflict might be, it would involve a lot of pain, and it wasn't worth it.

"OK, no need to get your knickers in a knot" said the spokesman, and they proceeded to move off, mustering what dignity they could, before exiting through the door at the end of the carriage. The large man watched them until they'd left the carriage, then looked down at Dina and said: "Are you OK?"

Dina looked up at him, her heart still beating wildly: "Why did you do that? You can see I'm a Muslim. Don't you blame all of us for what happened?"

He looked at her, silent for a moment, then said simply: "No."

She looked back at him and then collected herself: "I'm so sorry, I shouldn't have said that. Thank you so much for what you did,

I'm very grateful. You could have easily been very hurt if things had gone differently."

He laughed: "Maybe, but I think they're the ones you should've been worried about. But anyway, it's nothing. I would've done it for any lady."

Dina was silent for a moment, waiting for her heart to get back to beating at normal speed. "Why don't you sit down?" she eventually said, gesturing to the place beside her. He smiled and did so.

"I'm very lucky you were there. I don't know what would've happened if you hadn't stepped in. Honestly, I can't thank you enough."

"It must have been very nasty for you, but I don't think they would've physically harmed you. They were just stupid young blokes, having what they reckoned was a bit of fun."

"But I can't understand why they do it. Do I look like a terrorist? Why would they want to abuse me? It's just so frustrating that everyone seems to judge us all because of the actions of a tiny little group of crazy people."

"You know, we're not all like those guys. I think most people aren't really seriously anti-Muslim. But please don't be offended, I'm just going to tell you a fact. If you didn't have that veil on, they wouldn't have looked twice at you." He stopped and smiled, and said: "Well, maybe they would, because you're very pretty. But seriously, with a lot of people, when they see a woman in a veil it sets things off in their minds, makes them think of all the things they've seen on TV. And because they're pretty basic, they lash out."

A little taken aback, Dina asked: "Do you feel like that?"

He hesitated, then said: "Well, I have to confess, a little bit. It does bring to mind the negative things we see and hear about Islam. And it annoys me. Why would a woman in this day and age want to wear something that's a symbol of how women are put down in her society? And another thing, it tends to give a message that you don't really want to be part of Australian society, that you're different." He stopped: "I'm sorry. I probably really have offended you now."

She was silent for a moment, then said slowly: "No, I guess I'm not offended. Actually, you've made me think a bit. You're obviously a nice guy, and yet you think like that."

The train was pulling into a station, and he stood up, making ready to leave. "My stop. It was nice to talk to you, and sorry again for being so frank. But, last comment, if none of you women wore those veils, you'd probably get rid of nearly all the hassles you seem to go through when you're out in public." Before she could gather breath for a reply he laughed and said: "Don't worry I'm leaving now."

As he began to walk off, she called after him: "Would you have done what you did if you didn't think I was pretty?"

He laughed again and replied: "I hope so. Yes, of course I would." He smiled at her and walked out the exit door. The train moved off and Dina sat there, thinking hard about the whole incident, and what he'd said. Can a veil really have that much impact on people, she thought to herself. He looked like a typical Aussie, and he proved he's a real gentleman, ready to fight and get hurt to protect me, but seeing me in a veil puts him off. But he still did it. Am I being silly, thinking it's so important to prove to everyone that I'm a Muslim? Maybe if we all changed just a little bit, we'd get on a lot better with everyone. Adding to her confusion, the thought suddenly popped into her mind: I wish I could talk to David!

*

Late that same afternoon two officers from Jim Callaghan's team rushed into his office. In any spare moment they could snatch between interviewing members of the Muslim community they'd been combing various property records for a possible location for the terrorists' training ground. "Jim, we think we might have something. Take a look at this and see what you think."

One of them, Warren Oatley, had brought in his laptop and placed it on Jim's desk, while leaning in behind him and working the keyboard. "We've found a property that seems big enough – 500 acres – as well as being in a fairly remote location. It's quite hilly, so it'd be easy to be hidden, and helps to muffle the sound of gunfire. Here it is on the map." Jim peered in and agreed with them that it did indeed look feasible.

"But here's the thing" Warren went on excitedly, "It's registered in the name of a company, which has three directors, all of whom have Western names. But one of the directors is representing another company. Normally we probably would have just passed this over, but this property looked so ideal, and we hadn't found anything else remotely feasible that had any owners with Muslim names, so we followed up that second company. It's owned by a guy named Imran Ismail, it turns out he lives in Sydney, and wait for it – he owns a business that has three stores, one in each of Sydney, Melbourne and Brisbane. It's the same guy we were investigating yesterday."

Jim drew a sharp intake of breath, his mind racing. Was this the decider? Was it enough? He was silent as he thought through how to treat this potentially exciting piece of information, then said: "It really looks like this is the guy. But we can't just rush down to his store and check him out because if he *is* the one it'll warn him, and at this stage we've got no proof of anything, so we can't arrest him. If he gets suspicious, he may decide to unleash something, whereas if we wait until we've got something definite on him we can arrest him before he's got a chance to communicate with anyone else in his team. Look, I'll talk to Jason about it and see what he thinks. But you two have done a great job. We're getting close."

Warren and his colleague left his office with smiles on their faces – there's nothing like a bit of praise from a boss you like. As soon as they'd left, Jim went straight to Jason's office and explained in detail what his men had just told him. "He's got to be the one" he said.

"I think he is, too. But how to take this further, because you're right about not being able to just charge down to his store. This is still very circumstantial. I need confirmation from Immigration. If we get that we go for them."

*

One hour later Jason received a phone call. "Superintendent Blake, it's Susan Marsh here, from Immigration. I was asked to find out all I could about Imran Ismail, and report back direct to you. Are you free right now?"

"Hello, Susan. Of course. And please, call me Jason, it's a lot easier."

"OK, Jason. Look, I've found out a certain amount, so thought I'd brief you straight away. Now, he emigrated here from Iraq in 2007 – he's an Iraqi. It's a sad story, like so many people who come here from the Middle East or South Asia. He was an engineer, well educated, good job, wife and two children. Then his apartment block was bombed at the start of the US invasion in 2003. His wife and children were killed, and he was badly wounded. Took months to recover. It was chaos there for quite a while, as you know, and the records about him are hazy for a couple of years. The next thing he's started a business, doing contract engineering. He was the boss, apparently wasn't all that active in the day-to-day business. The business seemed successful and carried on like this a couple of years. But it seemed he wasn't happy with the continual chaos and violence that was going on, so applied to emigrate to Australia. He'd accumulated a bit of money from his business, was well qualified (got his engineering degree in the UK – parents were quite well off under the old regime), so he seemed a good candidate. He came here and seems a model citizen. Successful business, a member of various business groups. Never married again and apparently keeps pretty much to himself. So, that's what I've found so far."

"That's great, Susan, very thorough. What do you make of it all? What's your analysis of what this means?"

"Well, it all seems fine. But I wonder. That period of two years when there was no information about him. And he wasn't very active in his business. I wonder what else he was doing?"

"Susan, you'd make a good investigator, you're thinking like one of us. You should come and join the AFP."

She laughed. "If I don't get a promotion soon, I might take you up on that."

Getting serious again, Jason thought aloud: "Like you, I wonder what he was doing, first in those two years when it seems he was off the radar, and then the two years following, when he was often not at his work. He could have been doing anything. There were so many groups at that time battling each other, battling the allied forces, it's not at all out of the question that he could've been tied up with one of them. And he's got motivation – his wife and children killed by US bombs in an attack we know now was completely unjustified."

"So, you think he's the one behind the Opera House bombing?" Susan asked.

"Yes, he's a strong possibility. He's smart, he's got motivation, he could well have been trained in guerilla warfare. Look, Susan, what you've got so far is great, but we need now to focus on finding out more about what he was doing during those years after he got out of hospital. Go back to your contacts there, use my name, and impress upon them that they need to go a lot deeper, use any contacts they have in the Iraqi forces, and in any of the various militias they can get to. If I can get even a small clue that he was involved with any of the rogue militias then I think it's a virtual certainty that he's the one, and I can move on him. So far, all I've got is very circumstantial, even though I really believe he's the one. It's very frustrating – I can't touch him, not yet."

"Jason, I've already been doing that. Our people there are digging much deeper. They know time is precious so they're pulling out all stops. If there's anything more I'm confident they'll find it very soon."

"Thanks Susan, that would be fantastic. You're doing a great job. Don't forget, if you find out anything, call me, any hour."

"I will. Cheers."

She's got a really nice voice, I wonder what she looks like, Jason thought. In fact, I wonder how old she is? And is she single? He'd been so busy the last few weeks that he'd no time to think about anything than tracking down those terrorists, but something about her voice had reminded him that there are still other things in life. But regrettably, not right now. Maybe when this was all over, he'd do a little bit of investigating on his own behalf for a change.

He turned on his TV set and did some channel surfing to see what was happening on the various news programmes. It was now a daily occurrence, acts of violence committed against Muslims by non-Muslims, and vice-versa. The frequency was continuing to rise, as was the level of violence at the street level. These weren't major attacks, like the mosque bombings, which had clearly been carried out by organized groups of extremists, but attacks by individuals or small groups in plain daylight, in both city and suburban streets. This was occurring despite the large numbers of policemen patrolling the city centre streets on foot, and the suburban streets in cars, but it was impossible to have 100% coverage. The calls by the general public for the government to 'do something' were becoming louder and more insistent. There were brief shots of the Prime Minister responding to an interviewer's question, and he was beginning to look frazzled from the unrelenting pressure. But his key message was clear and consistent: This was the work of a few extreme individuals, and the Australian public must not let itself get tricked into a vendetta against a whole community on the basis of the evil deeds of that small extreme group.

*

At 7.30am the following morning, as he was readying himself to head for the office, Jason's phone rang – it was Susan Marsh from Immigration.

"Jason, I've got the news you wanted, about Imran. You were right about him. Those years we couldn't account for – he was picked up by that terrorist mob his men here have been quoting and trained by them. He hated the West, and when you know his story I guess we can't blame him. Apparently, he was outstanding, and led many very successful operations against the allied troops, a lot of which were when he was leading a double life as a successful owner of an engineering company. That's why he's been so effective here – he's a real pro, battle hardened. That's what you've been up against."

"I'm not surprised. I really felt that whoever he was, he was really good at what he was doing. No wonder his men were so well trained and that we haven't been able to nail them before. Anyway

Susan, thanks very much for this, you've done a great job. You must have been up all night?"

"Yes, the phones between our office and Baghdad have been running hot. But Jason, it was my pleasure. It felt good to be able to help in some way."

"In some way? You're kidding. You've given us what we need to go for him, and his people."

"Well, that's great. Best of luck with that, and take care of yourself."

As soon as he'd finished the call, Jason contacted his three team leaders via a conference call.

"I've just got confirmation from Immigration that Imran was involved with a terrorist outfit in Iraq. Jim, get some men together and go and arrest Imran immediately – at this hour he'll probably still be in his home. Mike, you get a team together and be waiting at his Sydney office. As soon as his guys turn up to open the store arrest them. Gavin, you get on to our colleagues in Melbourne and Brisbane and get them to do the same with the offices there. Keep me posted."

His three lieutenants rushed off, leaving Jason in a mixture of relief and worry – relief that at last they knew who the enemy was, and worry that the enemy may have already been warned. Do I tell the PM now, or do I wait until I hear back from my people? I think I've got to tell him.

*

"Janet, it's Jason Blake here. Is the PM free to take a call?"

"Yes, he is. I hope you've got some good news for him – he's feeling pretty down."

"Yes, I've been watching him on TV. They're really putting the pressure on him. Anyway, at least I've got some good news."

"Great. I'll put you through."

A few moments later the PM was on the line. "Hello, Jason. How are things going with you?"

"Well, Sir, we've just had a major breakthrough, and after watching you on TV I wanted to reassure you that what you've been saying about being close to catching these terrorists was a reasonable thing to say." Jason then proceeded to give the PM a detailed rundown of the investigation of the Blue Mountains site and the weapons manufacturers, their suspicion about a certain individual, and now the confirmation from Immigration that it was almost certain that he was indeed the Mastermind behind the terrorism.

"So, Sir, right now our people are moving in to arrest them."

"Jason, that's fantastic. If we can tell people we've got the Opera House terrorists I think we can contain the rest of the violence. That's great news."

"Sir, there's one thing we need to be ready for. If this man really is the one, the fact that we've been investigating him in Iraq is very likely to get back to the group behind him, and then to him. If he's been warned he'll go to ground, and it'll trigger their final actions, doing something spectacular before they go down in flames, as it were. I think this is very possible. I hope I'm wrong, but it's almost impossible to keep these sorts of enquiries completely secret."

"I see what you mean. That's sobering. Well, bad as that scenario may be, at least it'll probably mean this nightmare is over. Anyway Jason, your chaps are going to find out very soon, from what you've told me. I think I'd better keep this to myself for the moment, would you agree?"

"Yes, I think that would be wise. The moment I've got something definite I'll let you know."

"Thank you, Jason. I hope for all our sakes you get them before they can do anything else. Best of luck."

Almost before he'd had time to draw breath, Jason's phone rang, and it was Manfred Ryan.

"Jason, have you seen the PM being interviewed in the last couple of days?"

"Yes Sir, I have."

"Bloody hell, they're tearing him to pieces. You said a few days ago you were pursuing a couple of very strong leads – any further progress?"

"Actually, yes. I've just hung up from briefing the PM." He then repeated what he had told the PM and added: "I'm sorry I didn't call you first, but I figured he really looked like he could use some good news. By the way, I've agreed with the PM that we should keep this under our hats. Only he, you, my top three people and someone in Immigration know about it."

Manfred, who'd been feeling a little put out that Jason hadn't shared this news with him earlier, decided it was so good that he put those thoughts aside. "That's OK. I agree about the secrecy – this place leaks like a sieve. Hopefully we've got 'em. Let me know as soon as you have anything."

Jason put down his phone. All he could do now was wait, and hope his men came back with good news. But deep down he was very apprehensive. The people behind Imran, he reasoned, if he really was the one, were very competent. They're bound to have got wind very quickly about the enquiries being made in Baghdad, and if so, they'd get a message to Imran immediately.

Chapter 17

Sydney: The Previous Evening

The WhatsApp message looked quite innocuous - the manager of a business explaining that he'd run out of a particular halal product. He was going to a lot of effort to find a replacement and he was sure that quite soon he'd be successful. However, he would understand if his client wished to make alternative arrangements. The Iraqi read the message, and read it again a number of times, but there was no mistaking what it indicated. It was from one of his suppliers in Baghdad, which in fact was a cover for Jaysh Altahrir al'Islamii. He was being investigated in Iraq, which meant that he was under suspicion here and the authorities must have asked their colleagues in Iraq for help. This meant that he didn't have much more time and it was time to prepare for the final action. He took a deep intake of breath – this was the moment he'd both dreaded and looked forward to, for years, but it was hard to take in that it was finally here. But there was no going back now, it was time for him to meet his final destiny - in a few days he'd be dead. He put that thought aside and began to think about the steps he now had to take.

First, he had to give his men their final assignment, which he judged should be carried out as fast as possible. It was now evening, so it would have to be the next day, and they'd agreed earlier that late morning was the ideal time. For each of the three teams he spoke to the man he'd nominated as the one of the two to be in charge when it came to their jihadist activities. As with the WhatsApp message, what he said was quite innocuous, simply *instructions about some actions they should take in the store the next day. However, it was understood that those particular instructions would indicate that the time had come, they knew exactly what they had to do, and that they should proceed with no further contact with him. On his most recent trip to each store he had confided in his men that he felt their time was running out and that it was likely their cover would be blown, possibly within days, and not to be surprised if he called with these final instructions. Just in case this was his last visit, they said their final, heartfelt farewells – they had been working together for nearly ten years and had developed a lot of mutual respect. They all knew they were about to go to their deaths, so despite the fact that they were tough men, there was a certain amount of emotion.*

Much earlier, before the bombing of the Opera House, he'd liaised with them to choose a target in each city, for them to attack as their final action, during which they'd die as martyrs. He'd recently made one change, and it was pure vindictiveness that had motivated him. He'd instructed his Sydney men to change their target, which was a prestigious girls-only Church of England school, to the equally prestigious co-educational school where Dina was a teacher, and if possible, to ensure she was a victim.

"She's a traitor to Islam" he'd informed them, "consorting with an infidel, and not only that, but one who is seeking to destroy our religion. You fix her, and I'll fix him."

He put down the phone from his final conversation with a feeling of relief. He had every confidence that his men would go down in a blaze of glory, striking three last devastating blows that would add considerable fuel to the already raging fires of social conflict.

He thought briefly about Malek, who had done such good recruitment work for him. He couldn't afford to contact him now – there was too strong a chance that his call could be intercepted by the police, which could lead them to both being apprehended. But there was no real need. He'd had no further role in Imran's campaign and it was highly unlikely that he'd ever be exposed – there'd be no-one left alive to confirm his role. He'd be able to carry on with his life, doing what he could to further the Traditional Islam cause. His mind was at rest as far as Malek was concerned.

He now turned his thoughts to his own final plans which he'd developed months before. His idea was to commit two separate acts, designed to continue the tension and fear between the communities. He would first disguise himself as a Caucasian, with blonde hair and makeup to slightly lighten his complexion, and attack a mosque, using the last of the ten automatic weapons he'd so carefully had manufactured. With this weapon he could inflict significant damage, probably at least two dozen deaths before he'd have to flee and avoid the police who would inevitably arrive within minutes. He was quite confident that with only a bit of luck he could get well away – passing pedestrians would have ducked for cover and no sane unarmed person would tackle someone armed with an automatic weapon. He'd found a place at the rear of the mosque where he could leave a vehicle, which could get him very quickly to the shopping centre he'd picked as his next target. On the way he would throw his outer coat out the window, wipe off the makeup and put on an obviously Arabic head covering. Thus, looking the part of an Islamic terrorist, he would shoot as many people as possible in the time before the police arrived, of course shouting the obligatory 'Allahu Akbar' at regular intervals to make sure everyone got the message. But this time he wouldn't flee. He had plenty of ammunition and he'd keep re-loading and firing until the police bullets stopped him. A glorious way to die, he thought, killing infidels and advancing his bigger cause.

He considered this scenario with satisfaction, but then concluded: I have to give up this idea, great though it is. David Scott is really dangerous - he seems to be making real progress in putting doubts in the minds of too many influential Muslims here. I need to stop him, and perhaps without his influence they'll waver and realize how they're risking being traitors to Islam and risking their immortal souls as a consequence. And Fariq, he's dangerous too, but not as much as David. I can't carry out an attack on a mosque, and a shopping centre, then get David as well – that's carrying my luck way too far. Then he had a brainwave. He remembered that he'd received an e-mail from Fariq saying there was going to be another meeting, and that David would be there. The meeting was due in three days time, so this was a God-given opportunity - as well as David he could kill Fariq and some of the other members of that group, in his mind all traitors to Islam. He quickly consulted Google Maps, and saw there was a shopping centre not far from Fariq's office where the meeting was going to be held. After some thought he concluded he could quite feasibly carry out an attack on a shopping centre, as a Muslim terrorist, although he couldn't linger too long, then get away, go straight to Fariq's office and carry out what would almost certainly be his final attack there. He'd have to forget about the attack on the mosque – too much risk, and getting David was a must.

He thought this course of action through for some time – he was a meticulous planner and he tried to envisage everything that could possibly happen while carrying out that action. Eventually, he concluded that it could work, and it's what he would do. The challenge now was that it meant he'd have to wait for three days before he could act, and he had to assume that huge numbers of police would very soon be searching for him. If he hadn't already been identified, then as soon as his people carried out their final assignments Jason would know who was behind them. But he'd thought of just such a scenario a long time ago and had made his preparations, for himself and his teams.

For himself, in the name of one of his employees from Brisbane, he'd rented a small apartment in an old building in the outskirts of North Sydney, which came with a ground level garage. It was enclosed, so that it could be locked. This was his bolt hole. In it he'd parked a small car and a motorbike, both stolen so that they couldn't be traced back to him. Every few weeks he took them for a short run to ensure they'd start when the time came for him to use them. He always did this late at night when he was sure no-one would see him, so that if his photo was ever displayed on TV as a wanted man, his fellow apartment dwellers wouldn't know that the man sought lived in their building. It was also where he stored his weapons - the automatic weapon, and two high-powered handguns, with ample ammunition for each. His three teams had similar arrangements.

Having made his decision, he wasted no time in getting on with what had to be done. He was in his normal home, so he gathered up a few clothes and put some food into two cardboard boxes which he placed in his car. He also disguised himself with the same wig and beard he'd used when picking up the weapons, waited until he was sure no-one was anywhere near the path he needed to take to his car, moved quickly to it and got inside. He drove straight to his bolt hole, again waited until nobody was around, and then moved his clothes and the boxes of food inside.

He then went back to his car and drove it far away from where he lived, parking it not far from a train station. He boarded a train which took him to the city centre, hired a taxi which dropped him a block away from his bolt hole, and walked the remaining distance. Once inside, he sat down and began his long wait.

*

Half an hour after speaking to the PM, Jason received a phone call from Mike Anderson, and it wasn't good news.

"Jason, we're at Imran's place. No answer, so we broke down the door. I'm afraid there's no-one here. Maybe he's out having a walk, but I think that'd be kidding ourselves. Your fears about him finding out could be right, and he's gone to ground."

Mike winced as Jason turned the air blue with his frustration and waited until he calmed down.

"OK, leave a couple of your men there in case he turns up, but you get back here, and we'll wait and see what happens at the offices. If no-one turns up then we'd better prepare for the worst."

An hour later Jason received a phone call from Gavin Smith.

"Jason, I think there's something going on. It's 9.30am now and the stores in Sydney and Melbourne are still not open. A couple of staff from each one were waiting outside for some time. We saw them make some phone calls and then they just left. It's clear they expected to be going to work, like normal. I don't like the fact that it's the same in both cities."

"What about Brisbane?"

"They're an hour behind, so it's just 8.30am there. But they should be open any minute now."

"Stay in touch with them. If they haven't opened in fifteen minutes then I think you're right – they've been warned, and they're likely to make their final play. We'll have to prepare for that. Get back here and while you're on your way think about the most likely targets."

Fifteen minutes later Jason got confirmation that the Brisbane office also hadn't opened. Shortly after, when Gavin and Jim arrived, and all three Team Leaders were seated in front of him, he restated the situation for them.

"Imran's stores in all three cities haven't opened. Staff turned up, waited and then left. So, obviously they expected it to be business as usual. It's now a no-brainer – Imran's been warned that we're on to him and he's now warned his guys, and almost certainly has given them some orders. What are those orders likely to be? I'll bet that they're all going to go out with a big bang, some horrible atrocity that's a final exclamation mark to the programme they've been pursuing these last few weeks, an Islamic terrorist act against a typical Australian group of people. So, what's that likely to be, and what are the targets? Ideas?"

Jim Callaghan spoke up first. "Remember, ten guns were made, and only three have been used so far. We've agreed before that it's almost certain six of them are for two in each of the stores. So, they're going to go on a shooting spree, like the guys did in the

Opera House. Imran almost certainly will have the last one, so he'll do the same."

Jason looked at the others: "Agree?" They nodded. "Me too. So, the targets?"

This time Gavin gave his opinion. "They'll want places that have lots of people, and places that are fairly easy to get into. I don't think they'll be worried about getting out – these guys are going to die doing this. So, I'm thinking shopping centres, or schools."

"I think schools" Jim said. "As well as having lots of targets, killing kids is especially horrifying. If they're trying to get non-Muslims to react against the Muslim population, which is what we're convinced they're trying to do, then this is a perfect way to really get people up in arms. Also, they could pick elite schools, to provoke the wealthier groups in society who are more likely to be able to influence politicians to take drastic action."

They all considered this for a full minute, weighing up alternatives, before Jason concluded: "Jim, of course we don't know for sure, but I think that's a pretty good guess of yours. It's horrible, but with their track record I think these guys are capable of it."

"So, we can't afford to wait. We've got to assume they're going to attack and for all we know they're on their way now. First thing, of course, we've got to hit the homes of the six store managers, in the remote chance they're still there. But I reckon there's Buckley's Chance of that. Imran hasn't come back to his place, and if he did, he probably would've seen our guys waiting and disappeared. In the meantime, we've got to watch as many potential targets as we and the state police have got people for. I don't think we can assume for sure it's only schools they're after – shopping centres are a real possibility too. And it could be something else. We can't afford to put all our eggs in one basket, or even two. But I think Jim's correct – let's put 50% of our people at schools, 25% at shopping centres, and the rest spread among any other places we can think of where lots of people gather. I'll leave it to you to work out what those might be. Jim, will you handle all the communication with the state police here in Sydney, Gavin, you do Melbourne, and Mike, you do Brisbane. And at the same time, get some of our people to check their homes – no fooling around, just break in. I'll alert the PM, and the Premiers, and you tell the Police Commissioners. Now, what do we tell them?"

He thought for a moment, then decided: "Simply say that we've had a credible source alerting us to the distinct possibility that a terrorist action is imminent in each of these three cities, so we have to move quickly. We don't know the targets; we can only make our best guess. No further details. And they're to simply patrol, as discreetly as possible - we don't want panic. Everyone OK? … Alright, let's go."

They hurried out, while Jason prepared himself for what he was going to say to the PM. I'm going right out on a limb with this one, he thought, I'm still not 100% certain Imran's the Mastermind, or that that they're going to commit some terrorist act. But I can't take the risk of being proven right when it's too late. And I'm sure we're right. With that he dialed the PM's office and as usual Janet answered. He told her it was imperative that he speak to the PM immediately and sensing the urgency she did as he asked without question.

"Yes, Jason. What's the news now?"

"Not great, Sir. Our targets appear to have been warned and gone to ground. I'm giving you the heads up that I'm at this moment alerting all our people, the AFP and the state police, in Sydney, Melbourne and Brisbane, and the Premiers of each state. I believe there's a very high probability that our terrorist mates are aware that we're on to them, and that they're going to commit some sort of atrocity as their final act." He quickly explained the events that led up to this moment, finishing with: "We can only guess when they'll do it, and what their targets will be, but I think it'll be very soon, because they'll be expecting us to move on them immediately, which is of course correct. We're getting every person we can get hold of to keep watch on as many potential targets as possible, and we've emphasized just to patrol, as discreetly as possible, to avoid panic. Sir, I'm sorry that I've done this without letting you know first, but we believed every minute counts."

"No, Jason. You've done the right thing – I trust your judgement. But tell me, if you're right, do you think even with all the people you're throwing at this that they can be stopped?"

"Sir, in all honesty, I don't think we can stop them at least starting whatever it is that they're going to do. But if some of our people are nearby, at least they can get there very quickly and minimize the damage. But I fear there'll be quite a few casualties, no matter what."

"My God, this on top of everything else - the public will go berserk."

"They will, but there's one saving grace – we'll almost certainly have apprehended, or more likely, killed, six of the terrorists, probably leaving only the Mastermind, and we'll know who he is. And it'll only be a matter of time before we get him. And then it'll be over."

"That's true" agreed the PM, "but we'll have one hell of a job keeping things under control. But that's my job. Right now, you go and see if you can stop these guys."

After he got off the phone, Jason sat and considered what he should do. It's in the lap of the Gods now, he concluded, not much I can do but pray we get them before they do too much damage. He then had a thought and picked up the phone and dialed David. When he answered, Jason came straight to the point.

"David, I'm sure I'm being irresponsible in telling you this, but we've considered where these terrorists are likely to target, and our best guess is elite schools. I know Dina is a teacher at one of the elite ones – I thought it might be an idea for you to get out there and see her, with some excuse or other. Make sure my men are with you when you go inside the school. It's highly unlikely that her school would be the one they happen to pick – it mightn't even be a school at all – but you never know."

"God, I hope not. All those kids – what a terrible thought. But it wouldn't surprise me – that's the way they think. Thanks for telling me, I'll certainly go. Not sure what an amateur like me can do, but least if something starts happening I might be able to help get her and her kids somewhere safe."

Jason suddenly began to have second thoughts about the idea of David being in the vicinity of two professional killers. "Now whatever happens you keep your head down. Don't take any risks."

"Look, as you said, it's all highly unlikely that they'll be there anyway. And if they do, it will be a huge bonus if your two men are there, as well as the police you'll have patrolling. Anyway, I'm going. Whatever happens, even if there's no attack anywhere, it's going to be on the news that there was a big alert, so Dina will find out something was going on. So, there's no harm in me telling her to be careful."

"That's true. But if anything happens, be sensible – you're a Professor, not a policeman. No heroics. Leave it to the pros. … I'm beginning to wish I hadn't told you."

"Don't worry, I'm glad you did. If nothing else, it gives me an excuse to see Dina. I'm in the doghouse, you know."

"Yes, you told me. Alright, good luck. I hope you don't need it."

As they hung up, Jason thought to himself: Why the hell did I do that? I hope I don't live to regret it.

Chapter 18

As soon as he'd finished speaking to Jason the PM asked Janet to organize a video conference meeting with the Cabinet of National Security, plus the Premiers of Victoria and Queensland. He emphasized to her that it was extremely urgent and that all of them should immediately drop what they were doing to attend. That's one of the interesting outcomes of the Covid-19 Pandemic, he thought to himself – we got so used to having online meetings and discovered that they didn't work too badly that we're now using them all the time and Boy, do they save a lot of time and travel. Within thirty minutes they were all online, arrayed in small pictures along the top of his screen.

"Sorry to drag you away from your busy schedules" the PM began, and then proceeded to tell them about his conversation with Jason and warn them that it may be very possible that another set of atrocities was about to occur.

"If this happens, bad though it'll be, it'll likely mean that we're about to see the end of this whole crisis. We think that if these terrorists carry out these attacks it'll mean that the AFP have definitely identified the Mastermind and his team, and if they're not all killed during these attacks then it's only a matter of time before they're caught."

"Prime Minister" asked Andrew Atkinson, the Leader of the Federal Opposition, "are you sure that the AFP team couldn't have moved on them earlier, if they were so suspicious? If it turns out these are in fact the terrorists, we could get a huge amount of flak from the public for not preventing whatever you think is about to happen?"

"Until this morning it was all circumstantial, enough to be suspicious, but not enough to arrest them on any real grounds. Let's say they did move, and arrest them on some charge or other, it would never have held up, and they'd have to be released within a few days. If we kept watch on them they could claim we were harassing them and get the courts to force us to back off - then we're worse off. And then they could still go and do exactly the same thing, except this time they'd know for sure we were on to them. So, it was a no-win situation. But this morning they got information from Iraq that the person they were suspicious about does have a background in terrorism, so while it's still not 100% it's extremely likely. Maybe we'll get some flak, but I think the actions the AFP took are very defensible. In fact, they've done a great job to identify this guy. The big thing now is that it'll be over."

"OK, I understand. But it's frustrating. I suppose all we can do now is wait and hope the police can minimize the damage."

"Exactly, and don't forget, we have no idea, really, what their targets are likely to be. All we can do is guess and get our police to cover as many potential targets as possible."

After a little more discussion the meeting broke up, with all participants sworn to secrecy, and facing a very stressful wait for something that may or may not happen.

Meanwhile, David had put in a call to Dina, not expecting an answer as she was likely in class. However, to his surprise she answered, "David, what on earth are you doing calling me at school?"

"Listen, I'm going to tell you something, and please don't react, just listen to what I'm saying."

Don't tell me he's going to give me a big story about how we should get back together, Dina thought. Is he crazy?

"Dina, Jason has just told me there's a strong likelihood that the terrorists are going to launch another attack. He can only guess what the target might be, but it's anywhere that has lots of people. So, schools are one possibility."

"My God. That's terrible. But why are you calling me? The chance of it just happening to be this one is pretty remote, surely?"

"Of course, but I wanted to let you know, to be aware. If you do hear anything strange happening, take precautions, get your kids into a safe place, keep your heads down."

"Hell, David, you're scaring me. Aren't you being a bit alarmist?"

"Maybe, but it doesn't hurt to be ready, just in case. In fact, I thought I'd come out, you know, just to pay you a visit, no-one would think anything of it."

"David, now you're being really silly. Don't you dare do that."

"Well, I'm coming anyway. Don't forget, don't say a word – we don't want a panic. There'll be police patrolling the streets around the school, but they'll be as discreet as possible."

Before she could protest any further, he hung up, gathered his things together and headed to his car, followed by his two faithful minders.

*

As he drove the thirty minutes or so to Dina's school, David thought about what he'd do when he got there. She'll give me heaps for embarrassing her, he told himself, turning up unannounced. But then again, maybe she'd be glad to see him. He consoled himself with this thought and then switched his attention to figuring out his possible courses of action if the terrorists really did turn up there. He was still wrestling with this when he arrived at the street on which the front entrance of the school was located. For interest, he drove slowly around the streets fronting on to the school and noticed two cars also slowly cruising. Each had two occupants who had a very close look at him as they passed, but then continued driving, so he deduced that these were police cars and they'd decided he looked harmless. In his rear vision mirror he also noticed his two bodyguards give each car a casual wave which confirmed his deduction. He continued on until he arrived again at the front gates, drove in and parked in a visitor's spot not far from the steps leading into the entrance lobby. His bodyguards' car pulled in immediately after him, parking a few bays away, and then the three of them got together for a brief conference.

"I'm going up to Dina's classroom, which is on the first floor. I'm not sure what I'm going to do, but at least I can help keep them safe if something does actually happen. Where do you want to wait? I think downstairs here near the front entrance would be best. If they do turn up you'll see them quickly and get on to the police we've just seen patrolling."

They agreed that this made sense but impressed upon David that if he heard shooting he was to stay upstairs, look after Dina and her class and on no account come down. He assured them he'd do as they said and hurried inside. He'd been to the school twice before, so he had a good idea where Dina's main classroom was. It was a grand old building, with a large entrance area and wide stairs going up both sides. He went up to the reception desk and told the lady attending that he'd come to see Dina about something. Knowing who he was, and after he explained the presence of his two bodyguards, she smiled and motioned for him to go upstairs. After reaching the first floor, David turned down one of the two corridors that led off the central open area and stopped at the fourth door. Before entering he put his ear to the door and listened – sure enough, he heard Dina's voice. With a little bit of apprehension, he knocked on the door and waited. After a moment Dina appeared, shut the door behind her and turned to him.

"David, you're just crazy" she said severely, although he noticed that she didn't look all that displeased to see him.

"I know, but I just wanted to make sure you were OK. Look, I'll just wander around up here, and you just carry on and pretend I'm not here. It's 10.30am now, I'll see you at lunchtime."

"Alright, but don't make a nuisance of yourself." With the hint of a smile she went back inside the classroom. Fifteen minutes later the door opened, and a flood of teenagers poured through – this class was finished, and another would start at 11.00am. David watched while the boys and girls walked backwards and forwards in front of him, many of them having a good look at him as they passed by, clearly wondering who he was. A few times some of the older girls looked at him carefully and then whispered among themselves, giggling, probably speculating that he was Dina's boyfriend – it's hard to keep a secret in a sizable school. Just before 11.00am the door to Dina's class shut and once again David had the floor to himself. He paced slowly up and down the length of the corridor when suddenly the silence was shattered by the nightmare sound of automatic gunfire, coming from somewhere downstairs. David raced to the door of Dina's classroom and wrenched it open.

"You heard that?" he shouted to the whole room, which in addition to Dina consisted of nearly thirty children in their mid-teens, all of them understandably showing signs of panic. For their whole lives they'd regularly seen news footage coming out of the United States showing scenes of schools, shopping centres, mosques and sundry other places where large groups of people gather, in the midst of a firefight between the police and some crazed gunman – they knew exactly what that gunfire meant. "Don't move, just for a moment, please."

"Dina" he asked urgently, "Is there a store-room or some place close where you all can hide?"

"No, but there's a fire-escape just down the hall, just a few metres away." She was breathless, terrified, but she was holding herself together.

"OK, that sounds good. Wait here a sec – I'm just going to check that it's safe for us to leave here."

He opened the door carefully and stepped through. There was gunfire still coming from downstairs and there was no sign of anyone on this level, so he motioned to Dina to get the children to come outside and run quickly to the fire-escape. In a very short time they'd all rushed through the door, with David urging them as they passed him to go down to the bottom, but not to go out the exit door downstairs, in case the gunmen were still there. When they'd all passed through, he began to move back up the hall.

"Where are you going?" asked Dina.

"I've got to help the other classes on this floor."

"Then I'm coming with you."

Together they rushed down to the next class, where inside they found the teacher was organizing the children to make a barricade of the desks so that they could huddle behind it.

David and Dina quickly conferred with the teacher and told him what they'd done with Dina's class. They agreed that was a better idea, so persuaded the children to come out from behind their desks and follow the teacher to the fire escape.

"You go with them" David urged him, "and you can look after the others who've already gone down. Don't let them try and go out the exit door at the bottom. There's probably a fairly large area down there where lots of them could hide, just in case."

As soon as the teacher and his class had started running towards the fire escape, David and Dina began to make their way to the next classroom, when David stopped.

"Hang on, there's no more gunfire" he whispered. "What's going on?"

They both listened for a few seconds, but there was still nothing. "Stay here" David said, "I'm going to see if I can find out what's happening. If you hear any more gunfire get this class out also."

"OK, but be careful. Don't show your face, alright?"

He nodded, and moved slowly down the corridor, pressing himself against the wall. Before he'd reached the top of the stairs he heard the staccato sound of someone talking on a walkie-talkie, and the voice sounded familiar. He moved forward until he was at the stairs, peered carefully around the corner at the entrance area below and felt a flood of relief when he saw his two bodyguards conferring at the entrance. He stayed put for a few moments and then called out:

"Jeff, it's David. What's happening?"

"David, it's OK. We've got them both. You can come down."

He quickly ran down the stairs and explained to them that the children from two of the classrooms were hiding in the fire escape and that the other two classes were still in their room.

"Leave them for a few minutes. The police who were patrolling are now searching the grounds just in case there's anyone else, but we're pretty sure there were only two."

"What happened? We heard automatic fire, but it didn't seem long before it stopped."

"We were lucky. They came in from the rear entrance – they must have come over the wall – and only managed to get off a few bursts. They weren't expecting us, so we had a clear shot at them, and after some shots back and forth we got them. But they still managed to kill two people, the receptionist, and another adult, who's probably a teacher." David looked around, and saw the bodies, blood slowly gathering on the floor beneath them.

"That's terrible, but imagine how much worse it could have been if you two weren't here."

"Well, everyone can thank you for that, David. We wouldn't have been if you hadn't decided to come out here."

At that moment a voice came over Jeff's walkie-talkie, one of the policemen, reporting that the way was clear – there'd only been the two terrorists, and it was safe for everyone to come out from hiding. While Jeff and his companion Darren each began to move down one of the two ground floor corridors, letting each class know that it was all over, David ran up the stairs to do the same. After quickly informing the first two classes he ran to the fire escape, opened the door and called out to Dina that it was safe for them to come out. The children, uncharacteristically quiet, slowly made their way up the stairs, and looked around tentatively before moving down the hall towards the classroom. Dina was the last to emerge, and as soon as she'd done so threw herself into David's arms.

"Thank God. I was so worried about you. What happened?"

He explained, and her face turned ashen when he mentioned the two people who'd been killed.

"Oh no, poor Jessie. I wonder who the other one was. And no children?"

"No, that was it. It was so lucky my two men were waiting downstairs. The terrorists wouldn't have expected anyone to be there so fast, so I guess they just charged in, got in a couple of bursts and then Jeff and Darren got them before they had time to get to any of the classrooms. Apparently, the police arrived very quickly also, but those few minutes would have made a huge difference. They could have done so much more damage in that time."

"And they were only here because you insisted on coming to look out for me." She hugged him again. "My guardian angel. I think maybe I'd better keep you around."

He smiled down at her: "I think you'd better." Then his smile faded: "I think you should go back and reassure your class and I'll go downstairs and see what's happening. It's probably going to be bedlam, with two dead staff, two dead terrorists and hundreds of scared kids. Your headmaster will probably let you and the rest of the staff know what he wants you to do, so when that's all over, I'll be waiting for you."

"OK." She clutched his face in both hands and kissed him, hard, then ran off to her class. He stopped off at the other three classrooms on the floor and explained to each of the teachers what had happened, suggesting that they stay put until the headmaster instructed them what to do. He then made his way down the stairs to the chaotic scene he'd predicted. The police had found something to cover at least the heads of each of the four bodies and were creating a space around them. Teachers had appeared, one of whom was the headmaster who was conferring with the most senior of the policemen. The other three policemen were making sure that the teachers, who were now being joined by some of the children, stayed well away from the bodies. Jeff and Darren were standing in the entrance to the building, surveying the scene but keeping to themselves. David walked up to them, and shook hands with them both, suddenly feeling the emotion brought on by the after-effects of the trauma they had all been through.

"Thank you, you're both heroes. You did an amazing job. … I'm sorry, but I'm feeling a bit shaky."

"No worries, Prof", replied Darren. "You did really well. It took a lot of guts to come out here and be ready to face this sort of thing. We're trained for it, but it's scary stuff." He stopped for a moment and listened. "Hear the sirens? This place is going to be crawling with cops in a few minutes. I don't think they'll need us. What are you going to do, because of course we'll be staying with you?"

"I'm going to wait for Dina. I imagine all the staff and the kids will be sent home soon, so I'll follow her back to her place, or vice versa." He smiled at them: "I think I've got a fiancé back."

Chatting quietly, they went down the steps and walked slowly around the carpark, waiting for whatever was going on inside to be over. David was still feeling a little shaky, thinking how close he and Dina had come to violent terrorists who would have killed them without a second thought if they'd been in their way. We're safe now, he thought, it's over - no more heroism for me.

*

Back in his office, Jason had been waiting impatiently for news from his men. The first call he received was from Jeff, David's bodyguard.

"Hi. I didn't expect to hear from you. What's going on?"

"Boss, you were spot on. They came to the school where David's girlfriend, Dina, teaches. David wanted to come out here, just in case, so we were waiting just inside the building when the two of them burst in. Of course, they weren't expecting us, so we got them pretty quickly. But they managed to kill two people, adults, before we could get a shot in. The two terrorists are dead, too."

"Anybody killed is bad, but it could have been so much worse. Well done, you two. Is David OK?"

"Yeah, he's fine. He went straight upstairs to where Dina's classroom is and when the shooting started he got all the kids into the fire escape. He and Dina were both starting to help the other classes on the floor when the shooting stopped, and he came down to see what was happening. He's a gutsy guy to come out here and put himself in potential danger."

"Not bad for a Professor, eh? You never know about people. Wow, it's lucky for everyone that he did want to go out there, or else you wouldn't have been there. Look, thanks, you've both done a great job. I'd better get off the line now and see if anything's happened in Melbourne and Brisbane. Cheers."

Five minutes later a call came in from Michael Cullen, Head of the AFP office in Melbourne. "Jason, hi, they hit here, a school, just like you thought. It's not good, but it could have been so much worse. We had two cars out there, and they were close to the school entrance when the first shots were fired, so they got to the scene very fast. But in that time they'd killed two members of staff and eight children before our blokes could stop them. There were two of them, and they're both dead."

"Ten people. Bloody hell. But Mike, you're right, it could have been a lot worse. Were our chaps state police or AFP?"

"State police. They did a great job."

"OK. Thanks Mike, tell them that from me. In Sydney we only had two casualties, which is pretty good, in the circumstances. By the way, it was two of the AFP that got them. They were guarding someone who just happened to go out to the school, so they were there waiting. Talk about luck. Anyway, I've got to see what happened in Brisbane. Talk to you later."

Shortly later the head of his Brisbane office, Bill Masters, rang, clearly very excited.

"Jason, I've got great news. We got really lucky. It was a school, like you guessed. The terrorists decided the way to go was to drive their car flat out into the entrance of the school, so they could get inside quickly and do as much damage as possible before police arrived. There were two cars of state police patrolling the school and one just happened to be pretty much behind the terrorists' car. When they saw it suddenly speed up and turn in the entrance they guessed this was the attack. They sped up too and got inside just a few seconds after the terrorists. They were able to begin firing on them before they'd even entered the school. They had them pinned down, but when the second patrol car arrived on the scene the four police were able to get them. Killed them both, and no school casualties."

"Bill, that is really good news. Not a single casualty. I can hardly believe it."

"I don't think they had any serious military experience or they wouldn't have tried to get in the way they did. That gave our guys time to get to them fast. Has anything happened in Sydney and Melbourne?"

"Yes, we've been lucky, if you can call it that, everywhere. In Sydney two casualties, and ten in Melbourne. Twelve in total – bad, but nothing like it could have been. You've all done a great job. And six terrorists dead. They'll be the ones who've been doing all the beheadings, almost certainly. Anyway, I'd better get on to Manfred and the PM right away. Cheers."

After he put the phone down, Jason sat back for a moment, relief flooding over him. Twelve people dead. That's a tragedy, but he thought about Christchurch, and the Opera House – it could have been dozens of people, in each place. Thank God he made the right call about the schools being the target. But then he thought, Imran's still out there, and he'll know now that everyone'll be after him. He'll go down fighting, for sure. He put that thought aside and put a call in to Manfred Ryan and gave him a detailed account of what had happened in each city.

"So Sir, all in all I think you've got reasonably good news to give to the PM."

"Yes, indeed I have. But I'll leave it to you to ring him. You've lived with this for the last two months and it's thanks to you that this hasn't been a whole lot worse. So, you tell him. And Jason, you and your people have done a great job of detective work on this. Well done."

"You know it's not over yet though, – the Mastermind behind all this is still out there, and he's going to make a mess before he goes down."

"Yes, but we know who he is, so when he surfaces it'll be for the one and only time, and then it really will be the end of this nightmare, even though there may be quite a few casualties."

"Unless we can get him first. But being honest with you, this guy is really good. I don't like our chances. The six we got today were determined, and they were fanatical, but they weren't professionals with military experience, and I think this one is.

He'll be a lot more careful and will have planned things out meticulously."

"I understand that. We'll just have to keep up the patrols and hope we get lucky. You'd better go and brief the PM."

Jason then rang the PM's office and Janet put him through immediately. He repeated what he'd told Manfred and waited for a reaction.

"Jason, that's the best news I've had since this whole sorry business started. I never thought I'd hear myself say that twelve people dead was good news, but you know what I mean. So, we're close to the end?"

"Yes, Sir. Imran can't escape. He'll eventually surface and that will be it. I'm sure we'll get him then, but God only knows how much damage he'll do before we can stop him."

"Well, at least it'll be over, and we can start repairing the damage he's done to us all. Look Jason, you, your AFP colleagues, and all the state police did a great job today. I don't know how you ever predicted the targets so accurately, but you undoubtedly saved a hell of a lot of lives. We're very grateful."

"Thank you, Sir. I think we were also very lucky."

"You know what they say about luck, don't you? Anyway Jason, I'd better start preparing something to say to the press. They'll be clamouring soon, and for once I've got something relatively good to tell them. I'll talk to you again soon, I'm sure."

CHAPTER 19

On the morning after Imran had briefed and fare-welled his three teams, he rose and prepared himself for the wait for the news reports that would inevitably follow the attacks that were about to hit the three cities. He calculated they'd occur at about 9.30am, which was still two hours away. How would they perform, he wondered? They weren't trained in these sorts of operations, as he'd been, so it was going to be a lot harder for them. But they were resourceful, he consoled himself, they'll find a way. He prepared his breakfast and watched the early morning shows on TV as he ate, taking his time to distract himself from the frustration of waiting. At around 10.30am the first of the news flashes began to appear, with breathless journalists reporting of shots being fired at schools, in each city. Where are the details, he thought with increasing annoyance, what's happened? But there was nothing, until an hour later, when the Prime Minister appeared, on all channels, in a press conference held outside the front entrance of Kirribilli House.

As the PM carefully explained exactly what had happened at each school, Imran's dismay deepened with each revelation. Only twelve casualties, he thought, when the account of all three attacks was completed. That's almost a complete failure. How was it that so many police were patrolling these particular schools? He realized that once the authorities were on to him, as warned by his colleagues in Iraq, they would expect some sort of attack. But surely they couldn't cover every place in all three cities where an attack like this just might occur? There just weren't that many police, state and AFP, that could possibly manage to do that.

Jason, he suddenly thought, he guessed it'd be schools, the clever bastard. A flash of rage ran through him, but then, despite himself, he felt a certain amount of admiration for a fellow professional, who in this instance had out-thought him. Damn, damn, damn. But you won't stop me getting David – that'll be my big revenge.

For the rest of the day he continued to watch the news reports which, despite acknowledging the tragedy of the twelve people who'd been killed, were decidedly upbeat. Panels of talking heads discussed the Prime Minister's assertion that this was close to the end of the terrorism that had plagued the country for the last month, and that hopefully the violence that threatened to tear apart society would cease, and reconciliation would follow. Imran considered this, attempting to objectively assess what impact his campaign of terrorism had had on Muslim/non-Muslim relations. There was no doubt they'd been dealt a great blow, but was it enough to irreparably tear them apart? Knowing the progress David was having with senior groups of Muslims and hearing the Prime Minister's consistent urging of restraint, deep down Imran had his doubts. But there was no turning back. He'd done his best and he'd never know the eventual outcome. He had to leave it in the hands of Allah.

The day passed slowly in his forced exile and that night he slept fitfully, waking a number of times and being unable to help himself re-visiting the description of the attacks, feeling intense frustration at their relative failure. But the morning came and once again he rose and began watching the news reports and current affairs programmes. The Prime Minister had mentioned in his address the previous day that the leader of the terrorist group was still at large and that a state-wide search was underway, and that it was only a matter of time before he was apprehended. Imran was very confident that his bolt hole was secure, nevertheless he wondered all day whether he'd hear the sound of approaching sirens, but they never came.

In the early afternoon he assumed the identity of one of the members of Fariq's business group, rang Fariq's office and enquired to confirm that the meeting scheduled for the following day was still on – he was assured it was. So, the plan he'd developed two days previously was still feasible – it was all systems go. When he went to bed that night his mind was at peace and he slept well. There was no more that he could do now except to try and execute his plan, and then he was ready to meet his Maker.

*

The next morning he arose and went through his normal start of day routine. After his morning prayers he switched on the TV to the ABC channel to see what was in the news while he made his first cup of coffee. It was 6.45am and the meeting at Fariq's was scheduled to start at 10.00am. He figured he'd aim at crashing their meeting at about 10.10am, so working backwards it meant carrying out his first act at about 9.00am. That gave him about twenty-five minutes to do the first shooting, get over to Fariq's office, ensure he was undetected getting to the stairs, and then get up near Fariq's floor where he planned to hide in a Men's toilet until he was ready to act. That meant leaving his apartment at 8.30am – a little over an hour and a half to go. He had breakfast, shaved and showered, dressed, and then went to his garage to start his motorbike to make sure it was running smoothly. He then went back upstairs and made his final preparations. This involved packing a shoulder bag with a loose jacket that looked vaguely

Middle Eastern which would fit easily over his normal clothes, and a head-covering which, when it was properly arranged, would look suitably Arabic. Slinging the bag over his shoulder he went downstairs to his garage, picked up his automatic weapon, which was encased in a loose covering that could be easily thrown off, and placed it in a sleeve at the back of the bike. He then tucked his two handguns into his waistband, a spare magazine into a belt slung over his shoulder for his automatic, all hidden by the light jacket, put on his helmet, and was ready to go. Using his remote he opened the door to his garage, idled the bike out, shut the door behind him and eased off at a leisurely pace, not wanting to attract any attention by excessive noise.

*

The Astra café was a popular breakfast and coffee haunt located at the front of an aging shopping centre, in Crow's Nest. It had a large, open entrance at street level that housed a number of coffee shops and food outlets that spilled out almost on to the footpath. At this time of the morning on a weekday most of them were generally packed with people enjoying either a late breakfast, or just a morning coffee. In the Astra, Tony LaPaglia, a budding entrepreneur, was talking animatedly with his friend, Rick Stewart, about his latest project, a small apartment development in Lane Cove.

"The plans have been drawn up, and the bank seems to be happy with the whole idea, so I think it's got a good chance of flying."

"What size are the apartments, and what sort of prices are you thinking about?" Rick asked, and Tony enthusiastically began a lengthy explanation.

While Tony was talking Imran was quietly steering his bike to a small street at the rear, which contained back entrances to the various outlets on the ground floor. Very few people were around, so he idled his bike to an area which was empty, stopped, and proceeded to don the two Arabic-looking garments he had in his shoulder bag. The headgear was the most important, a long cloth that formed a type of turban and then draped around his neck and shoulders, making him look like a member of the Taliban, an image Australians were used to seeing on the news shows and documentaries. Thus attired, he drew out the automatic weapon from its sleeve which he threw aside into the gutter as he had done with the shoulder bag, adjusted the belt holding his spare magazine so that it was easily accessible, settled himself, then accelerated the bike around the corner towards the front of the building.

The Astra was located just before the main entrance to the shopping centre, and there were probably over fifty people seated around the tables, engrossed in their conversations and taking little notice of the traffic that passed along the street just a few metres away. The majority appeared to be businesspeople, like Tony and Rick, engaged in earnest conversation, sometimes with a computer screen in front of them. Most of the rest were middle-aged women, probably retired and catching up with old friends. Incongruously, given his willingness to have his men attack schools, Imran was relieved there were no young mothers with children. He stopped his bike directly in front of the centre of the café and pulled it up on its stand, leaving the motor running. Tony, hearing the bike's motor, looked around briefly, more interested in the bike than the rider, and noted that it was a 500cc Honda with its trademark smoothly running motor. He looked back to his companion and continued talking. Other patrons, turning and seeing Imran in his very Arabic clothing, and then the weapon in his hands, began to shout and get up from their seats, but it was too late. Imran leapt off the bike and immediately started firing at the occupants of the tables nearest to him. He fired in very short bursts to conserve his bullets and to give him that split-second to aim each time and maximise the damage he could cause. For the first few seconds people were stunned, and many of those closest had no chance to evade the bullets that spat out of Imran's automatic weapon. But then the rest, by now realizing what was happening, began to quickly scatter in all directions, so that Imran had to move around to find targets.

Tony and Rick had been seated about half-way back into the café, so they weren't in the first set of casualties. When the first burst of fire shattered the steady hum of conversation they were initially shocked into immobility, but being young and fit their reaction time was fast and they were up and out of their chairs very rapidly, heading for the rear exit, Tony leading the way. He made it to an alcove well back in the café and turned into it, shielded from any further fire. He was surprised that Rick hadn't followed him into the alcove but was fearful of peering around the corner to see what was happening.

Meanwhile, Imran's two magazines of bullets were quickly emptied, although being the professional that he was, the carnage was still considerable. After a quick glance around he calculated that well over twenty people had either been killed or wounded. His decision to restrict himself to two magazines was his belief that it was more important to ensure he could get away safely than try for an even larger number of casualties. Satisfied with what he'd achieved he ran back to his bike, took it off its stand, jumped on and accelerated away. He found a street two blocks away from the shopping centre which was small and largely deserted, and which had a number of large rubbish bins at the back entrances of the shops. He quickly stripped off his headgear and his outer jacket, tossed them into one of the bins, threw the automatic weapon after them, put his helmet on, and then proceeded on his way, well within the speed limit to avoid attracting any undue attention. By the time the sound of sirens heralded the arrival of the police to the scene he was over a kilometre away and safe, for the moment.

After waiting at least twenty seconds after the firing had stopped, Tony peered around the corner of the alcove and was shocked at the sight before him – bodies strewn over the floor of the café, the floor covered in blood, some people moaning in pain, others weeping. There was no sign of The Iraqi, so he emerged and began to search through the bodies to see if Rick was one of the victims. Sure enough, he was lying not ten feet from the alcove, sprawled on his face with a bullet wound in the centre of his back. Calling his name Tony sprang to his side and when there was no response felt his neck for a pulse – there was none. Looking around Tony saw another person, a young woman, lying on her back but moving her hands weakly. He rushed to her and saw that she had a large wound in the lower portion of her left side and was bleeding profusely. He placed his hand over the gaping hole, attempting to stem the bleeding, but it was hopeless. With his free hand he gently lifted her head and spoke softly to her, assuring her that she would be OK, but she was unable to respond. He was sure she was gone, but he was still holding her head when the police arrived, and shortly after the ambulances and the paramedics. When they came to assist her, he stood up, walked unsteadily to the nearest wall and leant against it, in a state of shock. He was still there a few minutes later when a policeman came over to him.

"Are you OK, sir" the policeman asked. Tony slowly nodded, "My friend. He's dead."

"I'm sorry. They'll look after him. I know this is a bad time, but I need to ask you: Did you see the person who did this? Anything at all that we could use to try and identify him?"

Tony paused, trying to clear his mind, but he was still very shaken. "No. I saw him. Can't remember him." Then suddenly: "The bike – it was a 500cc Honda, black."

"You're sure of that?"

"Yeah. I love motorbikes. Honda 500 - great bike."

"Thank you. That's very helpful. Now, are you sure you're OK? You don't need any help?"

"No, I'll be fine soon. My friend. I'm going to have to tell his family."

"If you can identify him now, tell me his name, and some other details, one of our people will contact his family. So, don't worry about that yet. I think it's best if you go home and just take it easy for the rest of the day. And if you give me your name and contact details too, we'll be in touch within the next day or so to see if you're OK. Alright?"

"Sure. Thanks, Officer. I'll leave soon."

After the identification and the noting of Rick's details, the policeman moved on to talk to another shaken survivor, leaving Tony to come to grips with the fact that his long-time friend was gone and to think about what he was going to say to Rick's family.

*

Within moments after the police arrived at the Astra café one of them notified the AFP, and very shortly after that Jason was informed. Together with the nearest colleague at hand he immediately rushed to his car and headed directly for the scene of the shooting. As his colleague drove Jason was on the phone to the police at the scene, asking for whatever details they'd so far been able to glean. His immediate thought was that this had to be Imran, but as yet he couldn't be certain. When he was informed about the make, model and colour of the motorbike he put out a call to all police to be on the watch for a bike matching that description, and to stop and identify the rider. At the same time Imran's photo was sent to them, so that if they were sure it was him to use whatever force was necessary – they were warned he was extremely dangerous.

Thanks to uninhibited use of his car's siren Jason arrived at the scene within twenty minutes and immediately began questioning the police at the scene. They informed him some of the survivors described the assailant as having 'Middle Eastern clothing and headgear', and that he was using an automatic weapon. 'He looked like an Islamic jihadist', some of them said. Guessing that the terrorist would be likely to discard his Arabic clothing as soon as he could, Jason asked the police to search the nearby streets, particularly any rubbish bins. In just over five minutes two of them had returned, holding not only the clothing, but the weapon. Jason grabbed it and looked at it closely - it was identical to the weapons that had been found on the Opera House bombers and the six shooters who had recently been killed while attacking the schools. He was now sure – this was the tenth and last such weapon - the terrorist was Imran.

So, he's finally emerged, Jason thought. But what's he going to do now? Go back into hiding and try and do this again? I don't think so. He's thrown away his automatic weapon, which is almost necessary for this type of attack. I think he's decided that once he comes out, he'll stay out until he's stopped. But what would he try next? His options are limited. He won't get anywhere going after a high-profile target because we're now warned, and they'll all be under close protection. And would he bother just killing a few people randomly? Could be, but doesn't seem like his style. ... What about David? I thought earlier he might go after him. He might figure he could get to him. With that thought Jason put in a call to David.

"David" he said, as soon as the phone was answered, "where are you right now? What are you doing?"

"I'm just about to arrive at Fariq's office. We're having another meeting, starting at 10.00am. Why?"

"Imran's finally emerged. Just shot up a café in Crow's Nest, and he got away on a motorbike. Everyone's looking for him so I'm sure we'll get him soon, but he could still get to another target. It's just another one of my wild guesses, but it occurred to me he could be after you."

"Well, you've been consistent in thinking that. It's a scary thought, but I've got Jeff and Darren with me, and they've shown how good they are at their job. How bad was it at the café?"

"Bad, but once again, it could have been worse. If he'd decided to stay there until he was stopped by police it would have been. But he didn't, so he's obviously got something else in mind, and one possibility is you. So, you tell Jeff and Darren about Imran, and to be on the lookout. And you too, OK? Have you got your gun on you?"

"Yes, I have. And don't worry, I'll be ready, just in case. Good luck with getting him before he gets to anyone else, including me."

"Thanks. And you keep your eyes open."

As soon as David arrived at Fariq's office block and all three of them were out of their cars he briefed his two minders. After a few seconds of deliberation Jeff told him that Darren would wait downstairs, and he would come up and wait outside the meeting room. Together they walked inside, entered the lift and went up to Fariq's floor.

*

Imran had arrived over thirty minutes before them, coasting slowly into the street behind Fariq's building and parking his bike not far from the back entrance. Dismounting, he looked around and saw that nobody was around. He walked to the rear exit to the building, opened the door, and peered inside - nobody was in sight. He knew David now had two bodyguards, so he was expecting them to be somewhere in the building, most probably one on the ground floor and the other on Fariq's floor. There was a reception desk in the front of the entrance lobby, but the fire stairs were out of its sight, so he moved quickly to the door and entered. Once inside he climbed the stairs two at a time until he got to the floor below Fariq's office, opened the door carefully and checked to see if anyone was in sight. The floor was clear, so he moved quickly to the Men's toilet and entered – it was empty. He went to the cubicle farthest away from the entrance door, shut its door and settled down for a forty-minute wait.

Meanwhile, upstairs the meeting participants were slowly trickling into the meeting room. When he arrived at Fariq's floor David decided he'd visit the Gents before the meeting but found that a number of the other participants had the same idea. He knew there was a toilet on every floor, so ran quickly down the fire stairs to the floor below, Jeff following. Smart thinking, he thought, as the room was empty. He went in, leaving Jeff waiting outside.

Imran had been waiting patiently. The time passed slowly but he was highly disciplined and the waiting didn't unnerve him. No-one came into the toilet during the first thirty minutes, then at 9.50am the door opened and someone entered and walked to the urinals which were situated at the other end of the room. He stood up and took out his handgun, leant against the wall to the side of the door handle, softened his breathing, and waited. If the person who'd entered happened to be one of David's bodyguards and noticed that the cubicle was occupied it was possible that he'd want to investigate, just in case. If so, Imran was ready to act. But the person completed his ablutions and went out the door, and Imran would never know how easy it could have been to achieve his objective of eliminating his main target.

Every five minutes or so he had been checking his watch and eventually it showed 10.10am. From his experience of the previous two meetings he was confident that Fariq would have started it on time, at 10.00am, so he judged that today's meeting would have been in progress for ten minutes. He stood up, arranged the two handguns in his belt so that they were readily accessible and walked out of the toilet to the fire stairs. He climbed the one flight of stairs to Fariq's floor, took out one of his handguns, opened the door carefully about ten centimetres, and peered through the small gap.

No-one was near this end of the floor and he knew the meeting room was just around the corner. With any luck he could get to the door without bumping into anyone, which while it wouldn't stop him could possibly be inconvenient. He moved carefully to the corner, pressed himself against the wall and peered around – there was one person, a man, walking very slowly away from him towards the far end of the floor. Imran had a very close look at him, wondering why he would be moving so slowly – usually people in office buildings moved around quite smartly, because they were in there for a purpose. The man was big and looked athletic – it must be one of David's bodyguards, Imran decided. The second was nowhere in sight, so he's probably downstairs, as he'd guessed. At that moment Jeff, for it was indeed him, reached the far wall and turned back, walking slowly towards Imran's end of the floor. He didn't have a handgun in his hand – it was still in its holster - so Imran judged it gave him at least a couple of seconds' advantage. Time to act.

Imran lunged around the corner, moving towards the meeting door and at the same time fired off a round aimed at Jeff's torso – it struck him in the chest and he spun backwards and slumped to the ground. Imran couldn't tell whether or not he was dead, but he was clearly in no state to interfere with what Imran was about to do. He wasted no more time on him, instead moving the last few steps to the door, and wrenched it open. Although he'd judged it unlikely, he couldn't be sure that David's second bodyguard wasn't actually inside the meeting room, so spent a precious two seconds looking around the room to check. As he was doing that he had also subconsciously taken in the overall room. It was large, with four pillars, a lectern up the front, with at least ten rows of chairs facing it.

Fariq was at the lectern, although he was already beginning to move to the side away from the door, towards one of the front pillars. He was Imran's second target and he was exposed at the front of the room, so he fired off a quick shot at him, striking him in the side causing him to fall heavily to the ground, near to the pillar. At the same time everyone in the room began to duck for any cover they could quickly get to, some behind chairs, others behind the pillars. David, more athletic than the rest, had very quickly sheltered behind the front pillar near Fariq.

Imran had caught a glimpse of David when he first entered the room, seated in the front row at the other side of the room, and he'd seen where he'd moved to get shelter. He calculated that it would take at least three minutes for the second bodyguard to get from the ground floor to the meeting room, so he had some time to be thorough. Three men and one woman, all a little elderly and so not able to move so quickly, were still scrambling for shelter from their seats at the front of the room. He fired off three quick shots, all of them hitting their mark.

He then noticed that Fariq was stirring, clearly still alive, on the floor and unprotected, and raised his weapon to finish him off. Suddenly, a shot rang out and a bullet tore through the flesh of his upper left arm, shocking him but not disabling him. He instinctively backed quickly behind the front pillar nearest the door, wondering what had happened. More shots rang out, striking the pillar, forcing Imran to continue seeking shelter. At the same time David, firing as he moved, leaped from behind his shelter, grabbed Fariq with his free hand and dragged him behind the pillar, where he was safe, at least for the moment. Imran, inching one eye around the edge of the pillar, caught a brief glimpse of the shooter just before he disappeared again behind his shelter. David Scott! He hadn't taken this possibility into account. He thought the two bodyguards were the ones he had to worry about, not this show-pony. And there was no doubt – show-pony or not, he could shoot.

For the moment there was a stalemate. David was out of ammunition and was removing his old magazine and inserting a new one, the only spare one he had. Imran was doing the same, thinking fast how he was going to get to David. He had one advantage. He'd always intended that this was his last stand, that he was going to die in this room, but only after he'd killed both David and Fariq. He could storm David's pillar and almost certainly get off at least a couple of shots before David could stop him, and that was all he needed. But he had to move, now, before the second bodyguard arrived. He figured he had about ninety seconds left.

He took a deep breath, preparing to make his final rush, when suddenly Darren appeared at the entrance of the door, gun in hand, sizing up the room, trying to locate Imran. From Imran's position near the front of the room Darren was a sitting duck. David also saw Darren appear, and could see that Imran would have a clear shot at him. Without even thinking he reacted instantly, rushed from behind the pillar towards the front of room so that Imran came into view, hurled himself on the ground and emptied his gun in Imran's direction. An instant before Imran could squeeze the trigger to his weapon two bullets ripped into his chest, throwing him backwards to the floor, still weakly holding on to his handgun. David got to his feet and moved cautiously towards him, his gun pointed at him, ready to fire if necessary, and kicked his gun away.

Imran was still alive, but barely. David knelt down and bent forward so that he could hear if Imran tried to say anything. Imran looked up at him and said, so faintly that David could barely hear him:

"A professor. How ironic."

David could see that he was getting weaker, slipping away, so he asked, urgently: "Why did you do it all?"

Imran struggled to speak, but just managed to get the words out: "To save the real Islam, keep our people on the right path. You're trying to corrupt Islam, you and the rest of your kind. But there'll always be more of us. We'll always fight you. You'll never stop us."

The effort to speak had exhausted him and he fell silent, struggling for breath. A few seconds later his head fell to the side, and he was gone. For a few moments David looked down at him, his mind a jumble of emotions – relief, confusion, sadness – triumph was not among them. He got to his feet and took in the scene around him. Three bodies lay nearby, clearly dead, and a number of people were surrounding Fariq. He quickly joined them and pressed his way through to see what had happened. Fariq was alive, and very lucky to be so. Because he was turning as Imran fired the bullet had entered his upper back, avoiding vital organs, and emerged from his shoulder.

"Are you OK?", David asked Fariq anxiously.

"I'll survive. What happened?"

David explained quickly and Fariq smiled weakly. "Well done, Dr Scott. I didn't know professors were trained gunfighters."

Darren, who had seen Jeff lying on the floor outside the meeting room before he had gone to the door, had called an ambulance and was kneeling at Jeff's side. He was still alive, but in a bad way. One of the meeting attendees informed David, who immediately rushed out to join them. Jeff was conscious, and could speak, but his breathing was very laboured.

"Don't try and speak", David said to him, "everything's OK. Imran's dead."

Jeff struggled to speak, but asked: "Who? Darren?"

Darren answered. "No, it was David. He saved my life as well. Imran had me in his sights just before David got him."

Jeff smiled weakly and started to say something. "No more talking" David said. "The ambulance will be here soon. You're going to be alright."

Jeff fell silent, and David and Darren stayed with him until the ambulance and accompanying paramedics arrived ten minutes later. They carefully placed both Fariq and Jeff on stretchers and took them downstairs, while other paramedics took care of the two meeting attendees who had been killed, covering them and placing them on stretchers which were also taken downstairs.

"How are they?" asked David, referring to Fariq and Jeff. "Will they be OK?"

"This one's fine" one of the paramedics answered, indicating Fariq. "The other one's in worse shape, but I'm pretty sure he'll get through. He looks pretty tough."

"I'll see you in hospital", David called to Fariq, as he was being lifted into the ambulance. Jeff's eyes were closed, so David chose not to bother him, instead walking away and sitting on the steps at the front of the building. He suddenly felt a little lightheaded as the enormity of what had just happened hit him. Darren and the rest sensed this and left him alone. He was still sitting there ten minutes later when Jason arrived on the scene. After a quick exchange with Darren and the police already there, Jason came over to where David was sitting and sat down beside him.

"Good-day, Champ. How's it going?" he asked.

David turned, and Jason could see tears in his eyes. He put his arm around David's shoulders: "It's OK, David. I know it's not easy, but you did what you had to do. He would've killed you and Darren and then gone on and killed a whole lot of others. You saved them. You did an amazing job – I'm really proud of you." David nodded, but remained silent a little longer.

"You were the one who gave me the bodyguards", he eventually said, "and a gun, and got me taught. I probably couldn't have done it if you hadn't warned me that he just might turn up. I was waiting, just in case. You've made the most amazing predictions, all the way through."

"Maybe, but a lot of people are dead because we couldn't find these guys quickly enough. I'm not really sure how good a job I've done."

"You've said to me before that if a bad guy is really clever, well trained, fanatical, and patient, that he's almost impossible to stop, and Imran was all of those. No, I think we can all thank you, and your men, that it wasn't far worse than it turned out to be."

"Well, I hope everyone else sees it that way. Maybe we won the battle. But David, I'm beginning to realize something even more important - you, Fariq and Reza are going to win the war."

Chapter 20

The next morning David and Jason were shown in by Janet to the PM's private office, after being surprised by her giving them both a big hug. "Thank you" was all she said, but her beaming smile spoke volumes. As they entered the office the PM rose from behind his desk and came to meet them, hand outstretched: "Good morning, gentlemen. Please, come and sit here", he said, indicating a settee near the window, while he moved to a single lounge chair opposite them.

"Well, you two should be feeling pretty good about things this morning. Yesterday was quite a day, and the end of quite a couple of months. I hope we never see more like those again."

"I'll drink to that", agreed David. "I'm very happy to retreat to the safe cloisters of academia. I'll leave the dangerous stuff to Jason. But Sir, how do you think things are going to pan out from here, regarding the violence?"

"Well, that's the big worry, but I'm optimistic. The fact that we can say now with confidence that the terrorists behind the Opera House bombing and the subsequent atrocities are all dead will go a long way towards alleviating the immediate fears. I think that alone will stop most of the violence. The really dangerous extreme right-wing groups have been shut down, again thanks to Jason and his people and the state police, so that leaves the general population. There's no doubt there's a lot of ill-feeling towards Muslims out there. It was bad before and inevitably it's worse now. But at least now it's out in the open, and the issue is being debated, and that's a healthy thing."

"I've noticed in the news coverage that politicians from most sides of the fence have been very positive about the need for harmony between all groups in the population, and that's bound to have an effect", observed Jason.

"Absolutely" agreed the PM. "That's something I'm really pleased about. The whole of Parliament has behaved in a really statesmanlike way about this."

"Well, that's something you must surely take the credit for, Sir" suggested David.

"Maybe", the PM said, "but Andrew Atkinson deserves a lot of credit too. He's been a tremendous help in influencing his own people, and other parties too. But he's already warned me that it's back to business as usual now, no more 'Mr. Nice Guy'. But he's a good bloke – I'm actually quite fond of him, but don't tell anybody."

"Now, David", he continued, changing the subject, "the most important thing now regarding this issue is what's going to happen with the work you've been doing with the Muslim communities, and the changes you've mentioned. I really need you to continue heading up this effort, even if it means taking time off from the university. I'll talk to the Vice-Chancellor if need be."

"Sure, Sir, I'll be happy to. There's a lot going on there, a lot of which I've already told you about. But they're actually going ahead with implementing some of them in the very short-term. A big one is taking all the questionable things out of the curricula in the Islamic schools. Also, no more imams from overseas. They'll phase out the overseas ones they've got now who don't fit the new mould, and gradually replace them with local people. They're even going to have some female imams, which will be a first here. Don't forget, as I told you earlier, there's a lot of Muslims who have been quietly pushing these things for a long time, but in my view, not strongly enough. All I did was encourage them to push harder, and this terrorist situation provided a good reason to do so."

"You mentioned in one of our meetings that we need to make some changes as well. What's the plan there?"

"Indeed. A big one is to introduce some education about all major religions in all schools, and we've already started talks with the various education departments about that. I think that'll happen quickly – everyone's very much in favour of the idea. Another one is how much more can be done by way of assistance to new immigrants, to help them settle in, and most importantly, to get a job. That'll be more complicated, but we're starting to talk to the departments concerned. On the other side, we're also setting out to learn more about what the Muslim community organisations are doing on this score, and how we can co-operate more than is happening now. Actually, Sir, I think the government's doing a pretty good job now, but we just need it to be even better."

"What about the really sensitive things you mentioned, you know, veils, and the Qur'an?"

"Ah, well, that's going to take rather longer, I think. The veil issue is easier, and I think there'll be a lot of pressure from lots of the women to move on this. I think we may be surprised about that one. The business about contextualizing the Qur'an literally strikes at the very heart of what many Muslims, particularly many of the newer immigrants, believe is fundamental to their religion, so this'll be a lot more difficult. It may never happen, but again, I'm hoping that we may be surprised. A lot of the very senior Muslims are prepared to push this idea and given what we've all gone through they might have a receptive audience. And one of those people is Fariq, the chap who was shot by Imran while he was addressing a meeting of Muslims. That's made him a bit of a hero, so he'll probably get a really good hearing. The fact that these terrorists were prepared to kill Muslims will probably make people think a bit, as well. So, as I said, you never know."

"By the way, how is Fariq? Was he badly hurt?"

"Not too badly, but he won't be playing any golf for a few months. Incidentally, sir, if I can be so bold as to give you some advice – I think you'd be well-advised to make a big fuss over Fariq. He's been the biggest champion of the changes we've been talking about, and he's a very impressive person, and a very good one, I believe. If you want a poster-boy for the Islamic communities to help win over non-Muslims, he's the one. I don't exactly know how that would work, but some sort of recognition, and endorsement."

The PM chuckled: "David, I think you've got a real political streak in you. We might have to have a chat some time about your future. But I'll take your advice. I'll make a point of meeting him soon and see how we can help him along with what he's doing."

At that point Janet knocked on the door, and entered: "Sir, you have another meeting, remember?"

"Yes, Janet. I'll be right there. Gentlemen," he said, as he rose from his chair, "I have to go. Once again, I can't thank you both enough for what you've done, and what I'm sure you'll keep doing. For you, my door is always open, don't forget that."

David and Jason filed out of the office and went on their way, and as they left the PM thought, what a great pair those two are. They don't know it, but before this year's out they'll each have an Order of Australia. And Jason, if he doesn't end up running the AFP, I'll be very surprised. He went to his window, stared out at the Opera House and thought back to the day two months earlier, just after the bombing, and how apprehensive he'd been at what lay ahead, and how he'd stand up to the challenge. It's been a terrible time, he thought, and too many people have died, but we all played our part pretty well. And it seems we're going to at last make some progress on getting our Muslim populations fitting in better and being accepted. Maybe that could be part of my legacy? That's a good thought. All in all, he concluded, I think history might be kind to me on this one.

"Boss", called Janet, "they're waiting."

Damn, meetings bloody meetings, he thought. But he was humming to himself as he walked out of his office and down the corridor.

That evening David and Dina dined once again at her favourite restaurant, Sails. It was twilight, and the Opera House was still very much in view, framed beneath the span of the Harbour Bridge. The ferries continued to make their way in and out of the dock just beside the restaurant, adding movement to the idyllic scene. This was one of the main reasons she so liked Sails, although the dining experience was also outstanding. At this moment she felt very at peace with the world, a huge change from how she was feeling just a few short days ago. She'd discarded her veil, so that her long, dark hair cascaded around her face – David thought he'd never seen her look more beautiful.

"A penny for your thoughts?" he asked.

"Well, apart from thinking how much I love it here, I was wondering how you're feeling after what happened yesterday."

He hesitated: "I've got mixed feelings. It's great that it's all over, and hopefully no more violence. Now we can concentrate on rebuilding the trust between our communities, and maybe even make it a whole lot better, and I'm really looking forward to playing a part in that. But I never dreamed the day would come when I'd kill someone. I've read about how it feels, and seen movies with people talking about it, but it's all unreal, until it happens to *you*. Even with a bad guy like Imran, it's an awful feeling. I guess I'll never forget it. But it's better than the alternative" he added with a wry grin.

Dina shuddered. "It gives me the shivers even thinking about it. Thank God Jason gave you that gun, and they taught you how to use it. I think I love that man. It could have been you, instead of him."

"Well, it wasn't. It's over now, we don't need to think about it again" David told her firmly. "It's time to think about us. Am I right in thinking that you're giving me a second chance? Or is Jason now the favoured one?"

She laughed, then looked at him and said: "David, when I saw you at the school that day, and the terrorists were downstairs, I realized that I didn't care about religion, or veils, or anything, except that I wanted to be with you. So, I think you'd better hurry up and propose to me, and we can get married on the beach, for all I care."

David leaned across the table and kissed her. "Do you want me to get down on one knee, right here?"

"Don't you dare. Just ask me."

*

A few days later David was sitting in a smart fish restaurant on Circular Quay, waiting for Jason who was joining him for a celebratory lunch, having just rung to warn him that he'd be ten minutes late thanks to an unexpected and long phone call from the Head of the AFP. As it was a bright, sunny day David had ordered a glass of rose as a starter, feeling it was in keeping with both the weather and his mood. Getting Dina back, and now for keeps, had made him happier with life than he could ever remember. And on top of that, it was interesting, he thought, how coming out from the shadow of the terrorist violence that had hung over them for the past two months made one appreciate everything so much more. As he gazed at the harbour scene in front of him, it hit home to him how lucky he and the big majority of his fellow Australians were to live in such a place, with the security and freedoms they all took for granted. He thought about the people he'd met at the refugee centre, and the life they'd fled, and made a mental promise to himself that he'd come down from his ivory tower of academic theory and in some way get involved, to do something useful to help. To be fair to himself, he thought, the high-level issues he was tackling with Reza, Fariq, Zaid and the others probably had far more impact, but still, he wanted to do something more tangible, to meet and work with some real people. His musings were interrupted by Jason's arrival.

"Sorry I'm late. You know what it's like – when the boss calls you have to drop everything."

"No worries, I've got a drink and I was enjoying the view."

"It's really something, isn't it?" Jason ordered a drink, and then asked:

"So, what's it feel like to be a hero? Having all these reporters chasing you, being interviewed on all the news channels?"

Because this is what had happened to David in the previous few days. His dash to the school, and especially his shooting of the terrorist Mastermind, had become the story of the 'post-terrorism' period.

"Hero? You're kidding. I was terrified the whole time."

"Aha, you know what they say. That's why you're a hero. It's a brave man who's terrified but still puts himself in harm's way, because he knows it's necessary."

"Yeah, well anyway, you should be pretty pleased with yourself, too. The news people have been all over you, as well, the man who tracked down the terrorists, who saved so many people. By the way, how's Jeff?"

"He's going to be fine. He'll be off work for a couple of months, but he's going to make a complete recovery. And how's it going with you and Dina?"

"I'm glad you asked. We're going to be married, in three months time, and both of us want you to be there."

A little taken aback, Jason reacted: "That's very nice of you. I'm glad to accept."

"That's great. You know, we'll never forget what you did for us."

"Hey, I was just doing my job. I had to look after the great Professor Scott, the new darling of the Islamic community."

"Jesus, give me a break. Maybe for a small section in Australia. I'll probably have fatwas declared on me all over the world. Anyway, let's drink to what we achieved together, because you're the one who found Fariq, as well as identifying Imran."

"So", David asked, after they'd had their toast, "what's next for you, now that this is hopefully all over?"

"I've had a promotion. One of the chaps above me is going to retire shortly, and is taking all his unused leave, so I'm now an Acting Commander, looking after strategy regarding domestic terrorism. I'll be in the job permanently in about six weeks time."

"Why am I not surprised? That's great, congratulations." They toasted again.

"You probably haven't had a day off since this all began" observed David. "Any plans?"

"Yeah, I've got a small yacht, and I'll take her out on the Hawkesbury a few times. I've just met this lady who seems very nice, and she's going to come for a sail – it'll be our first real date." He laughed: "She doesn't know what a risk she's taking."

"Is this the lady from Immigration you told me about?"

"Yep, she's the one. Susan Marsh."

"Good for you."

And so they chatted on, a friendship forged in a shared battle against a deadly adversary that had nearly cost one of them his life, but one in which both had played a major part in winning. It was a time that would stay in their minds forever, but it was now time to move on and enjoy what had all the makings of being a very bright future.

*

Three weeks later a highly publicised meeting of representatives from a wide range of institutions and community organisations from the Muslim population was held, symbolically, in a large meeting room in the Park Hyatt on Circular Quay, directly opposite the Opera House. More than three hundred people were there, over one third of whom were women, and the mood was one of excitement. The topic of the day was 'An Islam for Australia', and it was expected that there'd be some fiery exchanges between those pressing for change and the Traditionalists who felt that the changes being mooted were heading them down the path of blasphemy. Adding to the excitement was the fact that the Guest of Honour was Fariq Hashim, who'd received an enormous amount of publicity for surviving the assassination attempt by the Mastermind of the terrorist group. His opinion was likely to carry a lot of weight, and there was wide anticipation that in his Keynote Speech he'd be making a strong argument for change. The buzz in the room slowly died down as Reza Muhammad, the highly respected President of the Federation of Islamic Councils, walked to the lectern, and began speaking.

"Ladies and gentlemen, welcome to this historic occasion. Today we're going to discuss and debate some suggested fundamental changes to the manner in which we all practice our religion. The events of the last ten weeks or so have made it very clear that there's a need for us to have a hard look at ourselves – something must be wrong when we continue to have groups like the one here that was terrorising our cities, committing dreadful atrocities, and claiming that it's for the benefit of Islam. That's not the kind of Islam I believe in, nor I think any of you. There'll be a number of speakers, but our first, here to deliver the Keynote Address, is Fariq Hashim, who you'll know as a survivor of the last attack by the leader of the terrorist group. He's going to explain to you why he's in favour of the changes I'm referring to. Please welcome him."

There was enthusiastic applause as Fariq walked slowly to the lectern, his arm in a sling, and clearly still affected physically by his recent ordeal. Since his address to the smaller Muslim audience a few weeks earlier he'd done a lot of research and was even more confident about what he was going to say, although most of it echoed what he'd said at that meeting. For the next thirty minutes he held his audience in thrall, as he related his journey of self-discovery regarding how he felt about Islam, and how he believed that change was necessary. His concluding remarks included the defiant statement:

"If we choose to go our own way here in Australia no-one in Islam has any right to question us. No-one in Islam has a monopoly opinion on how Muslims are to practice their faith."

When he thanked them for listening to him, and finished speaking, almost all the women in the room stood immediately and gave him a rousing ovation, clapping, some of them cheering, and more slowly, about half of the men rose, and joined in. As he sat down, Reza leaned over to him and whispered: "I think you're on a winner. Some speakers will try and negate what you've said, but I think you've already won the day. Congratulations. We're going to have lots of work to do, but I think we'll eventually get there."

*

Two months later Dina was waiting at McMahon's Point to catch the ferry to Circular Quay, having walked down from Blues Point Road where she'd enjoyed a lunch with her friends Farida, Fauziah and Norani. The wedding day was looming up, and they were all full of excitement. But much of the chatter was also about how much had happened since the terrorists' reign of terror had been stopped. The police had rounded up more extreme-right groups, and the violence from that quarter had ceased. The government had mounted a massive media campaign urging peace and harmony between all the different groups in society, and it seemed that the general population, sickened by all the violence that had occurred, with both Muslims and non-Muslims at fault, was responding very positively to the Government's exhortations – harassment of Muslims had virtually ceased. The idea of implementing education about all major religions and some accompanying history to the curricula of *all* schools, from primary right through secondary, had been universally accepted and was being rolled out in the next school term. The ideas that Fariq had put forward at the 'An Islam for Australia' meeting were being debated at the mosques that the four ladies attended. Wahhabism had already been banned from the curricula of all Islamic schools, as was any funding from Saudi Arabia to any organisation. These two steps were initiated by the Muslim institutions and ratified by the government. And most heartening, there was a rush of volunteers from all sorts of backgrounds to teach new immigrants, not just Muslims, English.

Things have certainly changed, Dina thought, and in such a short time. It amazed her how much impact such horrific violence could have on a society, like a massive wake-up call. And on individuals, like her. Thinking David could be killed at the school, and then what happened at Fariq's meeting, hit home to her how precious their relationship was. And it rubbed off on David's family. When they announced their new engagement David's sister had a big party for the extended family and friends, and it was made very clear to her how much they welcomed her into their lives. And David was in a very good place. He seemed to have a purpose that was a little lacking before, when his persona was more one of a talented and charming but slightly frivolous man floating effortlessly through life. In addition to his usual day job, he had done as the PM had requested, taking on the campaign of acting as a bridge between Muslim community organisations and the government, and throwing himself into it with enormous enthusiasm. She thought about how he used to be very lukewarm about Muslims fitting into Australian society, but now he was championing them – what a turn-around. She was proud of him, and happy that she was going to share his life.

Her musings were interrupted by the sight of the ferry pulling up to the wharf, tying up, and the gangplank being hauled out so the waiting passengers could make their way aboard. Among the throng was a group of four young men in their early twenties, having a good time, and being quite loud and unruly about it. Also making her way towards the gangplank with considerable difficulty was a young woman in a veil, pushing a pram while two toddlers clutched at her dress. Seeing her predicament, the four young men moved forward, forged a path for her through the crowd, helped her with the pram and saw to it that she had a seat, joking with her as they did so. She gave them a grateful smile, and thanked them, and they moved off, continuing their loud interchanges as they moved through the ferry to take their own seats. Dina watched the little incident unfold with considerable interest, and some surprise, thinking how only three months ago the same men could well have been abusing the lady rather than helping her. "I think we're all going to be OK" she thought to herself, and it was a good feeling.

She gazed around. It was an early winter day, but as is so often the case in Australia the sky was blue, with not a cloud to be seen. A slight breeze rippled the surface of Sydney harbour, and the wake of crisscrossing ferries left dancing trails of frothy white. As they passed under the majestic Harbour Bridge and headed to Circular

Quay with its backdrop of skyscrapers, her reaction, as always, was – how lucky I am to live in this magnificent city, in this wonderful country. The sight of the still-stricken Opera House on her left couldn't dampen her spirits. Soon it'll be repaired, she thought, and we'll all rise above what happened, like an Australian Phoenix. But we won't forget how it happened, and we'll never let it happen again.

ABOUT THE AUTHOR

Bob Olivier has a business background - 24 years with an international management consultancy, then 25 years as founder/owner of a high-level executive search firm based in Muslim-majority Malaysia, where he lived for thirty years. He recently obtained a PhD in Political Science, specialising in Political Islam, from the University of Western Australia, and thus brings practical experience and theoretical knowledge to a complex and controversial topic.

His academic text: "Islamic Revivalism and Politics in Malaysia: Problems in Nation Building", was published in 2019 by Palgrave Macmillan.

ACKNOWLEDGEMENTS

There are, of course, many people who in one way or another helped me write this novel. First, the 100 Malaysians who allowed me to interview them as part of my PhD research and provided many personal anecdotes that allowed me to gain at least a little understanding of how Islam is practiced. Also, the many hundreds of Malaysians with whom I interacted in the thirty years in which I lived in their country. And then the three professors who guided me throughout the eight years my part-time PhD entailed, and who helped me obtain a solid grounding in the history of the development of the Islamic civilization, and in particular the politics that has accompanied that development.

I visited the very impressive Edmund Rice Centre in Perth, which gave me authentic background for the description of the visit by David Scott and Rachel Johnson to the refugee centre in Sydney. The stories told by the two people at that centre were inspired by the first-hand experiences related by Rosemary Sayer in her book "More to the Story". I obtained an understanding of the myriad of Muslim associations and community organisations in Australia by the examination of a number of excellent doctoral theses available on academic websites, and from similar sources for a description of extreme right organisations in Australia. Before commencing writing I bounced the broad concept off a friend from the Australian Federal Police who reassured me that the terrorism scenarios I was painting were, at least, feasible.

My heartfelt thanks to my wife, children, and a number of friends who took the time to read my early drafts of the novel, and who gave me excellent and largely sensitive, constructive criticism.

And finally, my publishing consultant who helped shape the final product, and guided me through the complex process of getting it to the general public.